OVER STEER

First Edition.

ISBN: 978-9-0832501-8-2

Cover Design: © The Pretty Little Design Co.

Editor & Proofread: Nice Girl, Naughty Edits

Formatting: NRA Publishing

OVER STEER

B. LUSTIG

NRA Publishing

OVERSTEER

[noun: **oh**-ver-steer; verb: oh-ver-**steer**]

the tendency of a vehicle to turn more
<u>sharply</u> than intended.

To all the girls whose hearts flutter
from roaring engines.
Me too, girl.

1

TRISTAN

"Yeah, we fancy like Applebee's on a date night..." I sing as the rhythm of the Walker Hayes song rolls through my mind. My hips sway as I dance my way forward, shuffling my feet over the metal ramp.

I spin myself around, facing the portable Callahan Motors motorhome, with a grin infectious enough to bubble up Axel's full laugh. All I need is a cowboy hat and I'd fit right into a honky-tonk, but I don't care. I'm the kind of person who starts dancing when I'm cheery.

And I have every reason to be cheery.

Finally, my car feels great. The first rounds of free practice went better than expected today, making me believe this is going to be a good weekend, and I needed some good news.

For this first half of the season, luck hasn't been on my side. I've had a rough start this year, having a hard time getting the car to do what I want on the track. But today is the start of a new phase. I can feel it tingling in my bones. I'm going to make it work and show the world I deserve another championship.

That I'm not some fluke.

"You really are a bit kooky, aren't you?" Axel's gaze aligns with mine from under his glasses, a dark eyebrow popping above the rim. My mouth crinkles with a smile as I hold my agent's eyes. We're nothing alike; he's the yin to my yang. The Patrick to my SpongeBob. Can't tell him that, though, because he'd probably fight me on it, arguing that he's not the pink thing with the pointy head. But he's also been my best friend since the fourth grade, the one who's been there for as long as I can remember. And for the last few years, the man who makes sure my career stays right on track.

"Come on, X-man." I glance up at the clear blue sky, the pine-scented breeze ruffling my already messy hair. "The sun is out. We're in Spa-Francorchamps. Free practice went *splendid*. It's gonna be a great weekend!"

Francorchamps is only a small village in the Belgium Ardennes, but the track is fun, and this circuit is known for its rainy days. The fact that the sun is out should be considered a blessing from the racing gods.

"*Splendid*? Really?"

We walk into the motorhome, taking the stairs to the executive office on the top floor. These portable constructions are the size of full, two-story buildings, and Callahan's is known for the fully windowed front with a huge logo on top. It still amazes me every season how a line of massive motorhomes creates an equivalent to the main street of a small town. It's a long way removed from the simplicity of the kart tracks, where I started my career once upon a time.

"Not good? Is *swell* better?" I goof.

"Definitely not." The wrinkle in his forehead is holding small drops of sweat, and he rolls up the sleeves of his gray dress shirt to let the AC cool his skin.

He's, without a doubt, the more pragmatic one of the two of us, always keeping my ass out of trouble and looking the part of my advisor in every way. But I can't help trying to poke him out of business mode every now and then, just because I know he's got a fun side to him. The side that turns him into a dauntless Steve Irwin when he's had a few drinks.

'*Oh! Look at that beauty!*' He will go to the first bee or ladybug he can spot, finding amazement or humor in everything around him. I always laugh my ass off. But on a race weekend, he rarely shows that side of him.

Always the professional.

"Outstanding?"

"No."

"Excellent?"

"You sound British."

"How about adequate?"

"How about you just shut up and look pretty?"

We enter the executive office, where Will Packers, CEO of Callahan Motors, and Lennon Brown, my team chief, are already waiting for us from across the table. The room is surrounded by big windows and the glass is fitted with a foil that allows us to look through, but prevents anyone outside in the paddock from peeking in. The real fans who find themselves lucky enough to have paddock passes, the celebrities who Instagram post their way around the track, holding up their phones, countless team members. Everyone is on their way to something, dying to get a glimpse of the drivers.

"Ah, you think I'm pretty?" I bat my lashes and hold my hands under my chin before Axel knocks the air out of my lungs, slapping me on the back with more force than necessary.

Dickhead.

"Shut up, *princess.*"

With a chuckle, we both sit down in the white leather seats.

"Will. Lennon. How are you guys today?" I fix my attention on the men who are technically my bosses, both sporting white Callahan polos, but only Lennon hides his full head of gray hair underneath a white and orange Callahan cap.

They exchange a look that makes my smile dissolve a little bit as I move my gaze back and forth between the two, feeling how the energy in the room shifts to something resembling a cloudy day. They look both tense and bored, their expressions flat. Both of them haven't been particularly chatty with me in the last few months, but still, the lack of movement has me swallowing away the dryness forming in my throat.

"Good, good, Tristan. Thank you for asking. There is something we need to discuss," Will replies.

Straight to the point, okay...

I don't miss how he doesn't return the pleasantry, and I hear Axel shift in his chair. But then again, Will is not the most amicable person I know. I've known him for a few years now and he's blunter than a butter knife with a vocabulary close to that of a caveman. Meaning, he doesn't give a shit about anything and isn't afraid to voice it. I'm used to it now, but the indifference both men are showing in their old and wrinkly features sets my internal system into defense mode while I wait for them to disclose the purpose of this meeting. I thought it was just to discuss the upcoming race, maybe discuss some strategy after the times I've set in the first and second free practice today, but the longer I sit in this uncomfortable chair, the more I feel dread washing over me.

"I'm sorry, but we have to let you go," Will says, and right away, something pulls me under. I can't pinpoint it, but my muscles turn into lead, challenging me to keep my back straight. Gone is my cheery mood, completely replaced by a cold shower that stings my every nerve.

There is an ease in the way he's delivering this news that's most unsettling.

I blink. I *just* blink because, surely, he didn't just tell me they were letting me go? My brain freezes, in serious need of a reboot. *Alt-control-delete.* That's what we use for computers, right? Is there something like that for the human body? Twist head, spin arm, wiggle leg, or something? Because I need my brain to start pulsing with electrodes again. Preferably toward my ability to speak.

My brain might not be able to fully catch up with the wording, but my eyes register the look on Will Packers's smug face just fine. His bald head shines under the fluorescent lights, fake tan sticking out against that row of perfectly white teeth. He tries to keep his flat lips pressed together, but fails when I find the tiniest lift of his arrogant cheeks. I can't describe it, but it looks something like, *'Ha! Got ya now, sucker!'*

"You're *what*?" I shake my head, ignoring the slow and torturous drum of my heart that pounds in my ears. *Ba-boom. Ba-boom.* "You can't do that. I signed for three years. I still have one year left."

"We will pay you double to cut you loose."

They will pay me double to *not* race?

I don't yell. I never yell. But I'm close to yelling now.

"Hold on—" Axel tries to cut in, but I snap my mouth open before he can.

"I don't want your money! I want to race!" Racing is who I am. It has been since I found my cousin's quad in the barn when I was five. I still remember the day in vivid detail. It was dusty and rusty, tucked all the way in the back of the barn, but it was the best Sunday of my little self's life. I raced up and down the wobbly field next to the barn, smiling from ear to ear. After that day, I begged my dad to take me karting the next weekend. And the next weekend after that. And the next. And now I'm sitting here, twenty-two years later. Being... *fucking hell*—being sacked?

"And we want you to win," Will spits back. There is venom in his tone, enough for me to suspect this is personal. Because I know it is.

"Come on, he has been on the podium a few times. It's not all bad," Axel argues on my behalf.

My back quickly changes to steel, unbending and hard as rock.

"It's also not good enough," Lennon shoots back.

Okay, so this isn't my best season. I can admit that. I've made a few mistakes. I haven't completely figured out the car, but I'm still a world champion. I've got fucking talent. That hasn't disappeared overnight. I just need time to get the car to work for me.

Like I fucking did today.

"I've been improving."

"Not enough," Will argues.

"I'm just not feeling the car yet. It will come."

There is a clear annoyance in the exhale that escapes his throat, tapping into my slow-boiling frustration, because it's no secret he wants me gone. He didn't want me on the team in the first place. His first choice was Franco Garcia, but Franco was smart enough to sign with SRT, one of the three best teams on the grid. I would've done the same if I was him; except, I already left them two years before.

"Look, we had high hopes, but Finley is doing better than you and he's less experienced," Lennon adds.

I resist the urge to scoff, because I have no grudge against Finley. He's doing better than expected this season, and I think he has the potential to set records one day. But he hasn't won a single race in his Formula One career and I'm a world champion. I think that earns me some credit, right? I think that buys me some time, for fuck's sake.

"I don't care," I fire back in a flat tone.

"We do." I snap my eyes back to Will. "This is a hard business, Tristan. You know that. You're not performing the way we hoped."

I snort. Of course I fucking know this. As an F1 driver, you have to perform every single race. There are only twenty seats in this sport, and if you fail, there will be countless new boys dying to take your place. But they gave me a three-year contract because I'd calculated that I needed to get to know the car first. Every F1 car might look the same to most people, but the truth is, each team engineers and manufactures the car by their own design. Becoming part of a new team means starting over. There are new engineers, new people to get to know, and also a brand-new car that you need to figure out how to maneuver to the best place on the grid: in the front. Not to mention how they like to change the rules almost every fucking year, and this season, I got a completely different car then last year.

"It's a new car this year."

"We expected more from you last year," Will argues.

"You're such an ass." It slips from my mouth, no longer willing to play polite with the man who wants to see me fail, and I sense Axel's gaze come my way with a scold, but I don't care.

My world is slipping from my fingers and I'm not having it.

"And your days on the grid are done."

"Excuse me?" My exterior grows, but on the inside, it feels like my organs turn into stone while my skin fires up with the anxious need to fight back. Fucking feverish and always killing me.

Axel huffs beside me, taking as much offense as I do. "That's unnecessary, Will."

"Just face it, Tristan. You're just not good enough to play with the big boys."

He did not just say that. "I'm a fucking world champion."

"Just because you got lucky one season doesn't mean you got the talent to do it again. Clearly, you can't do it in our car."

"That's because your car is mediocre as *fuck*."

"Tristan." Axel tries to dim me down, but knowing the guy for eighteen years makes it easy to detect the anger in his tone that matches my own.

"Your seat is taken by the end of the season."

Will says at the same time the timing of this conversation hits me.

That son of a bitch.

"You're doing this on a race weekend? Fuck with my head like that? You really want me to fail, don't you?" I snicker, feeling cynical.

"That's not true. But we want to give you enough time to find a new team before the end of the season." Lennon tries to smoothen out the situation, and if Will wasn't looking at me like he just hit the jackpot on a slot machine, I might have believed them. I might have been able to agree on the fact that we don't match as a team. That we tried, but we turned out to be a shitty fit. But the truth is, I'm done pretending it's all rainbows and unicorns like I have for the last eighteen months, when in reality, they never gave me a fair shot. They treated me as a second driver, but told me I'd be first when I signed the ten-million-dollar deal.

"You're making a mistake." I shake my head, expecting the ground to swallow me whole any second, and to avoid something dramatic like that, I get to my feet.

"You promised me big things," Will explains. "Big wins and lots of points. You're tenth on the championship list and we're fourth in the Constructors' Championship. You didn't deliver, hot shot. Don't blame me for your failure." He doesn't even bother to hide his contempt any longer.

"You never wanted me to succeed anyway, did you?" I point my finger at him, waiting for his denial. But I know there won't be any the second my gaze collides with his. "You're not even going to deny it, asshole?"

His silence is loud and clear. "The seat is yours until the end of the season. After that, it will be taken by Caleb Braz."

My heart does a backflip and not in a good way, before my voice fills with bucketloads of disbelief. Caleb Braz? Caleb Braz hasn't even won an F2 or F3 race. How does he earn a seat on the team when he has got nothing to show for? This is fucked up in so many ways.

"A *rookie*? You're replacing me with a rookie?" I run a hand through my hair, then waver my finger at both men as I ignore the heat flushing my skin while getting up. "You're going to regret it. Mark my words."

I don't know what I expect or what I want them to say. But whatever it is, it wasn't the disrespectful look Will Packers gives me when he says, "Close the door on your way out."

2

TRISTAN

"Tristan, your time with Callahan is up after this season. Do you think their decision to terminate your contract is fair?"

My jaw tenses, my lids low, as I throw him a glare that only reflects a fraction of how I feel inside. For the last two weeks, my blood has been boiling through my veins, my features set in a permanent scowl, and I've been avoiding talking to anyone but Axel and my trainer, Calvin, as much as I could for this exact reason.

I keep staring at the reporter in front of me, knowing it's not a wise thing to piss off someone from the biggest British broadcaster on the grid. But I haven't been able to control my anger in the last few weeks, snapping at everything and everyone.

"Do you have any more stupid questions for me up your sleeve?"

Today is no exception.

"It's a valid question," the reporter argues, a little thrown by my unusual aggression.

"And I've already answered it about twenty times this weekend. I'm over it. Let me know if you're done with your ridiculous questions and ready to start talking about the race and we can finish this conversation."

"Tristan." My Callahan PR girl gasps as she gives me shocked, wide eyes, her voice recorder still in front of my chest. Her freckled cheeks turn as red as a strawberry when she mutters an '*I'm sorry*' to the man in front of me, and I roll my eyes. Spinning on my heels, I bolt out of the area without looking back, then head back toward the garage with heavy feet. The salty air gushes around my head, the sun high in the sky on this hot September weekend in the Netherlands.

I love coming to Zandvoort. It's a small town along the Dutch coast, and I always appreciate the laid-back attitude of the locals, but unfortunately, it does nothing to change my foul mood.

I'm known as the driver that's always smiling, friendly, a professional no matter what the outcome of the race is. But I've been getting the same questions for the last two days, ever since Callahan announced my departure last week, and I'm sick of giving the scripted answer they want me to. It's bad enough to keep up a good front for my parents. I'm done selling this bullshit to the reporters strolling around the paddock as if they don't know any better. We didn't mutually decide to part ways. We didn't both come to the conclusion this isn't working. And they sure as fuck didn't wish me good luck in the future when they, quite literally, shoved me out the door after they told me I'm being replaced by Caleb *fucking* Braz.

I've been trying to keep my professional hat on for the last forty-eight hours, but I can't handle it anymore. I haven't had a good night's sleep in days, and all I long for is trashing myself to forget this hell of a weekend. My blood has turned into hot lava, burning me up from the inside out, and by the time I reach the garage with my name, I glance up with a cynical chuckle.

Nine races.

That's how long my name will still be up there before I'm no longer necessary in the pit lane. It's gutting me inside, and even though my neck is as strong as a fucking bull, Calvin hasn't been able to get rid of the stiffness in my muscles from my stress.

"Tristan, what the fuck happened?" I drop my gaze as Axel walks toward me from the engineering station, tugging his phone back into his pocket, probably having just spoken to my PR rep.

"Jack was asking me stupid questions. That's what happened." I walk into the garage to avoid my best friend's scowl.

"Look, I know you're mad–"

"I'm not mad, X!" I snap, twisting to face him, his pulled-together attitude pissing me off even more as he gives me an expression of pity. His white shirt brings out his steel eyes, looking way too fucking composed for my chaotic mind. "I'm frustrated!"

I'm fucking livid, that's what I am.

Axel tries to sympathize with me, wanting to tell me he knows how I feel, but he can't. He's not competing for the best seat in the world every single season. He loves racing, but he doesn't live and breathe it, not like I do. If I fire him as my agent, he can find a new athlete to work for by the end of tomorrow. Driving in Formula One is not the same.

Twenty seats. That's all there is. And the way it's looking right now? One of those twenty won't be mine come next season. Will Packers ripped my reason to get up in the morning away in one meeting and the son of a bitch is still smiling as he walks around the paddock.

"I know you are," he agrees. "And Dunham is a fucking asshole. But you can't go and talk to reporters like that. It will slim your chances of finding another seat."

I snort. "Get stuffed, Axel."

Finding another seat.

Every seat on the top teams is taken for multiple years and none of their drivers are having a bad enough season for them to switch up drivers. Forgive me if I'm not holding my breath for that to happen. I haven't exactly shown the world my full capacity in the last few months, and a big part of that is my fault.

"Shut the fuck up, you dickhead. Who died and made you the Grinch? You don't stop fighting. *Ever.* Why the fuck are you now?"

I hold his gaze, debating which answer I should give him.

Because I'm not so sure I'm still good enough?

Because I'm not so sure I can win another championship?

Because I wonder if maybe Callahan is right for letting me go?

I'm saved from answering as my phone starts to vibrate in my back pocket. Throwing my best friend a fake smile, I ignore him, then strut away to the gearbox area to separate myself.

"Yeah?"

"Tristan? It's James." James Button's deep voice slides into my ear and a small cordial smile curls my lips as I imagine the CEO of Baronial Pop sitting behind his desk.

Baronial Pop is the leading energy drink in the world, and even though I'm not a soda kinda guy, I've learned to appreciate the brand because they are the first company in the world to donate half of their profits to sustainable energy and farming, something that's held dearly in my family. It's why I've done everything I could to get a sponsorship with Baronial since the first day I started driving Formula One, knowing it would make my dad proud as hell.

"James, how are you?"

"I'm good, I'm good. How are you holding up, son? I'm sorry to hear you lost your seat."

My smile falters. "I'm alright. It is what it is, but I'm positive about the future. I'm sure it will all work out." *Fuck, I'm so full of shit.* A big knot sits in my stomach, and I hear my dad's voice reprimanding me for the bullshit that's spewing from my mouth.

"I hope so, boy. You are a great driver, and you deserve a seat."

"Thank you, sir. That means a lot."

"But..." I can hear the change in his tone, and I'm shot back into that conference room with Will and Lennon, seeing his next words suddenly coming my way like a bucket of bricks. "I'm sorry to have to tell you this..."

No, no, no.

I drop my gaze to the floor.

"It's the reason why we have to discuss the future."

"What do you mean?" I'm doing everything to keep a steady voice, but I can't fully prevent it from turning groggy due to the bowling ball sized lump that's now feeling like a rock in the back of my throat.

"We sponsor you and endorse you because you are on the grid. Twenty-one weekends in the year, your face is on that grid as one of the twenty Formula One drivers in the world. You are a great advertisement because you are there every racing weekend, doing your thing."

I hold my breath, excessively doing my best to swallow away the dryness in my mouth.

"But if you're not driving..." *Don't say it.* "We can't endorse you."

My knees wobble, and I squat down to prevent my body from collapsing while my brain tries to wrap around what's happening. I feel like the rug is being pulled from under me. For the last two weeks, my sponsorship with Baronial was the only thing that kept me moving forward. The only thing that gave me the confidence to pick up the phone every single time my dad checked in on me, knowing that at least I still had that. At least that was something that would still bring my dad pride after I got fired from the team.

"I see," I croak out.

"I'm sorry, son. I like you. I really do. But the board voted to pick another driver if you're not getting a seat next year. It's just business." I detect the genuinity in his voice, but it doesn't stop my chest from heaving. I rub a hand over my face, sucking in as much air as I can to pull myself together.

"I understand," I tell James, even though I really don't want to.

How is this happening? Three years ago, I had it all. I was a Formula One World Champion. I was endorsed by the biggest companies in the world. I made my parents proud and every Formula One team was dying to have me. And now, I'm staring at the cement floor in the garage, wondering how I all lost it in two weeks.

I don't know what to say. I don't know what to do. I don't know how to relax the hard muscles in my neck while I rub the emotion from my eyes.

"Is this final? Are you replacing me?" I finally manage to ask.

"The board wants you gone, yes. But I promise you, if you can get a seat for next year, I'll make sure Baronial Pop is still yours. I will fight for your position within our company, but you have to fight for me first. Can you do that?"

My heart says no. But Axel is right about one thing, and I won't ever admit defeat. Not to anyone else but myself, anyway.

"Yes, sir."

"Good. I hope you have a great race tomorrow. Sixth is not a bad place to start."

"It's not great either."

"No, but you didn't become a world champion for no reason."

The silence that follows is pregnant. I don't even know what to say to that.

"You can do this, Tristan. We'll talk soon, okay?" His confident voice strokes my ego, but only a little, because my mind keeps spiraling back to the one question I've been asking myself for days now: *Can I still do this?*

I thank him for calling, then hang up the phone as I keep my body low to the ground with my eyes shut.

I'm going to lose my sponsorship.

What the fuck will I tell my dad?

I shake my head, knowing I need to fix this, but I have no clue how. The more times I'm getting in that car, the more my insecurities are fueled. My race pace is nothing compared to that of Finley. He drives in the front of the field, showing the world Callahan is best of the rest, when I keep floating between eighth and twelfth place.

"Are you okay?" I glance up at Axel standing in the doorway. His eyebrows are knitted together in a deep frown that's laced with worry.

"No, X."

"What's wrong?" He carefully enters the room.

"Baronial is cutting me loose if I can't get a seat for next year."

Axel's face falls, but it's only briefly, because before I can blink, his frown turns into a smug expression. "Well, then it's a good thing you'll have a seat next year."

"You don't fucking know that!" I shout.

"I do!"

I shoot him a glare that's meant to kill, shaking my head. "You fucking don't!"

I get that he means well, but he has no clue about the pressure it brings to every fucking race. Ever since my champion winning season, I'm called The Outback Devil. But I haven't felt like that in a very long time. After winning the championship, it's like I fell down a black hole. When the three-day party and ultimate high ended, I had no clue what was next.

I forgot what I'm racing for, and I've been trying to get it back, but I can't find it. Something is missing and all I want is to take a two-month long vacation to figure out what it is. But that's not an option when you have hundreds of people depending on you. I'm merely on top of the pyramid that's a racing team.

"You're having one bad season. It's not the end of the world!" he yells back.

"Except in Formula One, it is!" *It's the end of my world.* "You have a bad race, you get scolded. You have a bad season, you get replaced by the next eager eighteen-year-old jumping to take your seat! That's how this world works!"

"You will get another team. Just let me do my job and you do yours."

"If I'd done my job, I wouldn't be without a team right now, would I?" I chuckle without humor, brushing past him and heading back into the garage. He's lucky I'm not a violent person because it's tempting to wipe the glare from his face.

"Tris, wait," Axel calls to my back.

"Where are you going?" Calvin walks into the garage, fully aware of my thunderous mood as I stomp down the coated floor.

"To get fucked," I growl.

"No, you're not."

"Tris, get back here," Axel bellows.

"Tristan, you have a race tomorrow. You need to be in bed in a few hours," Calvin adds.

But I'm done listening. My gut is telling me to walk away from the lion's den and take a fucking break. And right now, for the first time in a long time, I'm going to fucking listen to it.

"You two can either join me or fuck the hell off. I'm going for a drink." I twist my body, piercing a finger in Calvin's face, then swing it back to Axel's.

"Lennon will have your head if he finds out," Calvin argues.

"What is he going to do? Fire me?"

"Be the bigger person, Tris," Axel chimes in, his arms folded in front of his chest. "I've been the fucking bigger person for two weeks now. I'm done doing what everyone expects me to do and feeling more like shit every day."

"You can't drive 280 miles per hour if you went out the night before." Calvin's look is stern, and his argument is completely valid, but to hell with them all.

"You can't tell me what I can or cannot do. I'm going for a drink," I tell both of them, then take off to find myself a cab.

"You'll ruin your career!" Axel barks.

"Then it's a good thing it's already fucked anyway."

3

NIKKIE

I NEVER CARED FOR the color red.

It only reminds me of all the things I hate in my life.

Christmas, chili peppers, apples, *blood*.

And apparently, it's also the color they print on your mail when they want your attention.

I sigh, staring at the envelope in my hands, red letters stamped above my address with a font size big enough to make it readable for Mrs. Sanders from across the street. It's not the first one I've gotten, but this one has even bigger letters, screaming at me to take action.

"What's that?" Tess lifts her gaze from her laptop, sitting on the small dining room table. My heart stutters at the sudden voice, and I shove it between the other mail on the counter of our small apartment. The living room holds nothing more than a two-seater and a TV, while the all-white kitchen covers the wall across from the front door. It's tiny as fuck, but we both have our own bedroom, and it's ours, which makes it close to perfect.

"Nothing, just junk. Again." I turn, looking straight into her judgy blue eyes. Pity swirls in the deep pools of her gaze, her left eyebrow rising slowly like she trains her frown on a daily basis. It's a talent because I can't even fucking wink.

I'm not even joking; I have no clue how to do that and she can tell a story with just her eyebrows. Right now, they are telling me she looks straight through my bullshit, but I'm determined to brush it under the rug as quickly as I can. I charm a smile on my cheeks, hoping my best friend will let it slide.

"You know I'm not stupid, right?" She crosses her arms in front of her chest, her pink lips pursed in challenge.

"I know, but I can pretend you are." I pick up the two scented candles I just picked up at my favorite candle store, then take the three strides to reach my room, fully intending to hide, but as relentless as she is, the plastic chair slides over the hardwood floor and her bare feet follow behind me.

"You can't keep doing this, Nik."

I keep my back to her as I dive into my closet to avoid the disappointed look I know she's lasering at my spine. We've had this conversation more than once. It's not like me to not pay my bills and create a trail of debt and financial mess behind me, but the last year has changed everything. Life isn't as easy and carefree as it used to be, and I need to take responsibility. There is not much else I can do.

"I know. I will fix it, okay?"

"Don't mind fixing it. You just need to stop. You can't keep taking care of everyone else when you can barely keep your head above the water."

"I'm fine, Tess. Really."

Her silence makes me carefully twist my neck, her scowl hitting me like a bullet to the chest, and I rear my head back, taking off my sweater. Tess has been my best friend since third grade. We got paired up by coincidence on the first day of school and were best friends from that moment on. Tess says it was meant to be.

Destined to happen.

A few years ago, I'd agreed with her, but now? Agreeing with destiny is hard when that same destiny took everything away from me. In my book, destiny is a bitch and right now, we're not really seeing eye to eye.

"You're not fine."

"You didn't have to look for a new roommate, right? I'm still paying rent, so don't worry about it. I'll fix it." I always fix it. Sometimes I surprise myself, not even knowing how I do it, but it always works out.

"How?"

I shrug. "I'll organize some theme nights at the bar. Maybe ask my dad if he still has outstanding favors from some artists."

"Your dad really has his finger in every piece of the pie, doesn't he?"

"Pretty much, yeah." I grab a clean work tank top from the shelf, then throw it over my chest.

"You should tell your dad."

I fire a glare her way. "We are *not* involving my dad!"

The last thing I need is my dad making this an even bigger mess than it already is. I should've kept Wes far away from my dad's vision of solving things. It's bad enough I'm considering asking him to find me some Dutch celebrity to make an appearance at the bar just to bump up my sales.

Tess's brown hair sways around her cheeks as she shakes her head.

"You're working yourself to death for no fucking reason."

Deep down, I know she's right, but it doesn't outweigh the guilt I'm feeling. This is all I can do to somewhat make up for my mistake. It's all part of owning my life. I've learned from that horrid night, I truly have—the nightmares being proof of that—but I still have to pay my dues.

Even if they feel like an elephant is taking up permanent residence on my chest.

"I can't just stop, Tess. You know that."

"Yeah, you can."

"Look, I hear you, okay?" I sigh. "But what is going to happen if I stop? He's gone, Tess. We *all* have to live with that."

Her scolding dissolves, eyes softening in a way that grips my heart. I don't want her pity. I'm responsible for the situation I'm in. It's on me to fix it. To make it all better, even when I know I can never fully make amends.

Taking on his responsibilities is the least I can do.

"How many times do I have to tell you? It's not your fault."

"Except it is!" It's bizarre how swiftly those words ignite something deep within me I can't ignore, and I promptly tuck my emotions back into my chest.

I'm a tough girl. I'm not easily impressed. Throw in my Dutch heritage and I'm as cool as the national weather forecast nine months of the year, no matter how much you try to piss me off. But talking about what happened lights a fire under my ass that's hard to tame. It changed me more than I want to admit. There's a Nikkie before that night and after. I liked the Nikkie from before. Fearless and riding whatever wave life threw at her with a smile. But that girl died when Wes did. Now there's only the Nikkie from after. The one who's left with half smiles and more gloom than I know what to do with. We don't like her; we tolerate her, but it's what we gotta work with because I don't see the old Nik coming back any time soon.

"Sorry," I offer her an apologetic look. "It's going to be fine, okay? Trust me. I'll make it work." My hand reaches out to the denim jacket on my bed. "Will I see you at the bar tonight?" I smile, hoping she'll take my peace offering as a clear hint that I don't want to fight her. I know she means well, but this is my life. Maybe one day, I'll find a way to make everyone happy, but right now, it's not about me. Right now, it's about keeping Wes's legacy alive. Plus, she's a star of making sure I don't bite anyone's head off while I have to endure lame pick-up lines and throwing shots over my shoulders from guys that can't read my body language screaming *just buy your drink and fuck the hell off.*

"Can't. Need to prepare some stuff for school." She narrows her eyes one final time, before she gives up. *Thank fuck.*

"Did you watch the qualification?" she asks.

We walk back into the living room as I start gathering my stuff. "I did. Watched downstairs with Emir."

Tess rolls her eyes with a smile on her lips. "Let me guess. You told him you'd watch qualification with him, and he gave you a free lunch in return?"

"You're damn right he did." I chuckle with my chin high in the air.

It's what I do when Tess can't watch the race with me. I take the three stairs down to the shawarma place below our apartment, and watch with Emir. For some miracle reason, also known as me batting my lashes at him, he always ends up feeding me, but I'm not complaining. I would still come if he didn't, simply because it's not as fun watching alone, but him providing me with free meals is a welcoming turn of events every time it happens.

"Not a surprise Jackson Banks is in pole position again. The guy is a fucking legend in the making." Tess smiles, her eyes all dreamy about her F1 crush.

"I know. It's just a shame he drives for the wrong team." Arzano Centazari has never been my favorite team. I blame my dad, who always pushed me to root for the Schmidt Racing Team instead. I guess it stuck.

"I don't care what team he drives for." She shrugs.

"You're just saying that because you have the hots for him."

"I don't have the hots for him!"

"You totally do!"

The indignance on her face washes away. "You're right, I do. Never mind Jackson for a minute, though. Have you heard the breaking news?"

My mouth flies open, gasping, knowing exactly what she's talking about.

"The Tristan Reinhart thing?"

"Right! Apparently, he was a fucking dick to some reporter. Did *not* see that one coming."

"I know. I feel bad for the guy. I knew there was a chance he wouldn't continue his final year at Callahan, but I'm guessing he isn't taking it all that well, considering no one thought he could stop smiling, like, *ever*. Especially because he doesn't have a new contract yet," I add.

"Yeah, that's pretty shitty. That must fuck with his head."

"But I'm sure he will get his focus back. It's what they do." It's what I respect most about F1 drivers. It's not just the fact that they drive a car at 280 miles per hour like they are driving Ms. Daisy, but the amount of determination each and every one of them has. It's a lethal sport, but they still get into that car every weekend without any doubts.

It takes balls.

"True," she muses, as she falls back in her seat at the table. "Are we watching it together tomorrow?"

"Yeah, just don't wake me up before the race starts, okay?" There is a big chance I won't roll into bed before six a.m. since it's a Saturday night.

"You got it. I'll arrange snacks."

"Great. I'm leaving. Gonna grab a quick bite on my way there."

"Work that ass for some tips, girlfriend!"

It takes me thirty minutes to walk from our Amsterdam apartment to the bar in the center of the city. It's the one moment of my days that I don't have to put on a fake smile and can just be, as I stroll down the pavement in peace.

I'm walking toward Leidseplein with a strawberry slush in hand, my eyes scanning the people as we all make our way along the canals our city is famous for. It's almost ten in the evening, the moon shining brightly on the September night while the last rays of sunshine are disappearing behind the old brick buildings. The crowd on the sidewalk is a mix of the people whose nights are just starting and the people about to call it a night.

With my lips wrapped around my straw, I feel the corners of my mouth rise to my ears, listening to all the different languages around me. Amsterdam is not New York or Los Angeles, but I love the no-nonsense mentality of my city, knowing everyone is always welcome. Twenty years ago, any foreign language you heard on the street was most likely a tourist, but nowadays, so many people have traded their own country for the free spirit of Amsterdam.

It's why I chose this city to continue my academic career after high school, instead of picking a new area in the country to settle in. A little melting pot of different cultures and personalities, greeting my senses when I glance at everyone's faces and choice of clothing as I continue my steps down the cobblestone. The ringing of a tram passing by has me scanning my surroundings to make sure I don't get run over by anything else, knowing anyone on a bike can pop up out of nowhere like a fucking surprise party.

I catch three guys out of the corner of my eye, two of them laughing about something while one of them is sitting on the ledge of the old bank building on the square. My attention stays fixed on the three men, something compelling me to lower my pace and study their physiques.

They seem like tourists, their behavior telling me they don't live here. I don't know how to explain it, but after a while, it becomes easier to see if someone is heading down the street like they would every day or because they are here to have some fun. All three men have broad shoulders, their clothes showing they take care of themselves as I glance down at their clean sneakers and crisp shirts.

But it's the deep frown on the guy's face, who's sitting on the small edge of the building as he's nursing a can of beer, that curiously draws me in as I move closer. The difference in his stance compared to his friends has my eyes fixating on him a little while longer and I realize there is something familiar about him. His brown hair sits messily on his head like he didn't feel the need to bother when he darted out of the house this morning, and his golden honey skin sticks out against his light gray shirt, bringing out his green eyes. They are vibrant, luring me in, but filled with annoyance, framed by thick black lashes that make them appear even lighter underneath the streetlights.

I blink a few times as I slow my pace, wondering where I've seen his face before, then freeze when I figure it out. My pulse fastens, a rush of something jolting my heart as it starts beating a little louder.

That's Tristan Reinhart.

World Champion. Australian. *The Outback Devil.* Driver of Callahan Motors.

It's not uncommon to find the drivers strolling around the city on race weekend. Last year, Nicholas Jones drove by on a bicycle with his girlfriend, and two years ago, one of the drivers had drinks at Lie's before the weekend started.

I wouldn't know because I wasn't working that day, but Lieke jumped up and down like a frog on crack.

I could just wave and wish him a good night, but the bold streak I still have tucked somewhere inside of me stops me from doing that. I'm surprised to not see him with a huge grin like you always see him on TV, but then I remember his encounter with that reporter. He clearly isn't in the best mood since they terminated his contract, and I don't blame him. Knowing there are only twenty seats in Formula One, I'd probably be angry about that as well. Still, seeing him here sulking feels a bit out of character for him.

Don't do it, Nik, a little voice whispers in my ear.

A voice that apparently isn't loud enough for me to acknowledge because, high-spirited as I once was, I surprise myself as I take the final steps, until I'm standing right in their circle, establishing myself between his friends as if I have any place to be there.

I don't, *obviously,* but figuring this is the only shot I'll ever get to actually talk to an F1 driver, I shove away whatever resolve I have as words fall from my tongue before I can stop them.

"Is this Tristan Reinhart?" I cock my head, my vision sliding up and down his length.

"He is." One of the men beside me confirms, and Tristan's eyes snap up.

"Shouldn't you be in bed, considering your spot on the grid tomorrow?" Again, I'm a little stunned by my own brazenness. But I bury it by casually stirring my straw through the leftover slush in my cup, then take another sip.

What are you doing, Nikkie?

Inwardly, I roll my eyes at myself and my big mouth.

Tristan's chin lifts, a mix of confusion and annoyance etched on his features. His expression darkens a bit, a look he doesn't show on TV, and I square my shoulders, knowing that *if* he decides to bite my head off, I'm the only one to blame.

After all, if you poke the bear, you'll probably get bitten.

"Are you talking to me?" The tone in his voice translates to something like *how dare you talk to me.* My nerves rush with a warning of *mayday mayday mayday*, but for the life of me, I can't tear my gaze away. I've seen the man on TV, I know he's handsome. But having him in my line of sight within less than two yards, his eyes burning through my skin as he sizes me up, it kinda fucks with my head.

Good job making friends, Nik.

However, old me or not, I'm still too stubborn to show them the awkwardness that's creeping up my body, deciding it's too late to back down now.

"Do you see anyone else out here who's on the grid tomorrow?" I cross one arm in front of my chest as I take another loud sip, feeling fucking uncomfortable now that all three men have fixed their attention on me. This is the part where every sane person would say, *"sorry for bothering you, I'll be on my way now!"*

He cocks his head at me with a dark expression that jolts my senses alive and out of the numb state I have been for months.

"Excuse me?" I swear I detect a bit of awe in Tristan's voice, but it's overshadowed by the level of irritation I have evoked. *Poking bear: successful.*

I shrug, faking an innocence from Hell. "You're placing sixth tomorrow and you currently have a bunch of sharks coming for your ass, hungry for the seat you lost. Just thought you might need a good night's rest."

"I've had a shitty day," he scoffs.

"So? You're an F1 driver, right? Didn't really expect you to be a quitter."

Really, Nik? You couldn't just say, *"Hi! You're a great driver! Sorry they dumped your ass. Have a great race tomorrow? Maybe ask for a selfie?"* No, you let your big mouth scold one of the best F1 drivers in the world like he's your next-door neighbor.

"I'm not a quitter." Fire lights up his olive-green eyes.

"Really? Because it sure as fuck looks like it."

His friends snicker next to me, only motivating my chatterbox to keep pushing. There is an excitement showering me that keeps me from walking away, my brain seeing the dare in his eyes. Like he's both amazed and appalled at the way I'm talking to him, and for some twisted reason, I find it amusing.

"Are you trying to piss me off?"

"No, I'm genuinely wondering." It's not a full lie, because now that he's entertaining the option to answer me, I'm curious what his reply will be. These drivers are trained to never lose focus, not even when someone dies on the track, yet here is Tristan Reinhart, trying to drink his misery away with a shitty beer. He could've been sulking in his motorhome, getting wasted without the public eye, but instead he risks getting recognized, knowing his team boss will find out, possibly jeopardizing his seat for the rest of the season.

"You don't think I can win?" A challenging sparkle widens his eyes.

I pop a hip, showing him an unimpressed smile, even though I catalog how every sense of my body burning up the longer he keeps his attention solely on me.

"You can win."

I mean that. I think with his skills and the car he's driving, he can definitely win. His teammate has landed on the podium more than once, so it's possible. *Especially for a world champion.* "It's probably gonna be tight, but you can win. Just not when you're tired as fuck because you went strolling around Amsterdam when you should be in bed."

"You know there's a bigger chance of Jordan, Jackson, or Sam hitting the podium, right?"

"And also, a bigger chance two of those three will crash into a wall while fighting each other at some point in the race," I rebuke, catching the ghost of a smile that appears in the corner of his full lips as quickly as it disappears.

His gaze pins me down, my mouth drying up as the seconds tick by. There is a loud pound in my ears that's fueling the feeling you have when you're on a rollercoaster. Thrilling, yet daunting. The perfect combination to make you feel alive. He keeps staring at me while I wonder what his next move will be, almost expecting him to tell me to literally fuck off.

Instead, his features soften just a bit, dismissing me with a wave of his hand.

"Don't worry about my performance. I'll be fine."

I don't believe him, but I still nod, taking the vibrating of my phone in the back of my jeans as my cue to continue toward my destination.

"Alright, Ace. Good luck out there tomorrow. Have a nice night." I lock eyes with him one final time, offering him a tiny smile, before I slog off, putting my phone against my ear. "I'm almost there. Two minutes."

4

TRISTAN

I FIX MY GAZE on my trainer, Calvin, who tries to hide that he enjoyed the last two minutes way too much by diving into his phone. His tiny snorts are making him fail, like an elephant hiding behind a tree, as I flip my attention to my two friends.

"What the fuck," I mutter to myself.

Trust me, I know it was an act of rebellion when I told Axel and Calvin that I was going out. It was impulsive, stupid, and something Sam would do. He's the playboy of the grid, after all. Not me. But my fuck-it mood lasted exactly thirty minutes, ending right about the time the cab driver dropped us on a corner a block from here, and I disappeared into the nearest night shop to score some beers. The first lukewarm sip tasted great as I took off towards Leidseplein, known as the place to be on a Saturday night. The second sip made my legs feel like they were made out of steel, heavy and unbending, and by the third and fourth sips, I just was pissed at myself for being here in the first place, no longer fooling myself every drop wasn't tasting like piss.

I should be in bed right now, trying to get some sleep before the race, still giving it my all tomorrow. But my mind needs a change of scenery. After qualifying and the press release today, the paddock closed in on me like I was being trampled by a hundred bulls. I never felt so betrayed in my life. They couldn't wait another day before they announced their newest prodigy. Not to mention, the phone call I got from James that ripped my heart out. All hell broke loose on my already not-so-sunny day. Everyone wanted something from me. Either a statement, to give me their best wishes, or just to shoot me a sympathetic look. I've been getting shoulder pats and gentle smiles, people coming up to me and telling me how sorry they are for me but, *"don't worry about it, I'm sure you'll get a seat for next year."*

The thing is, they don't know that. Normally, I handle these setbacks pretty well, but the longer the day progressed, the more I was suffocating.

I needed a break from it all.

I expected it to come in the form of a few drinks, a few laughs, and maybe a little wiggle of the hips. What I didn't expect, though, was to be lectured by a cheeky blonde in a denim jacket.

Her light brown eyes kept me planted in my seat, hanging on her lips as she kept looking at me like I was disappointing her. There was no pity. No sympathy. Just a clear judgment that silently said, *"You're better than this."* And damn her if it didn't spark me alive more than anything else has since the last race.

It wasn't the expression I wanted to see tonight, but it sure as hell beats what I had to deal with at the paddock today.

"Did that just really happen?" I ask, a little baffled.

"Yup."

"She's hilarious," Axel chimes in, bringing his beer can to his lips. He was firmly against my plan to tell everyone to fuck off and drink away my sorrows, but like the good bro-bestie that he is, he came to act like my bodyguard. I'll probably thank him for it at some point, but right now, he's irritatating the shit out of me.

"Shut up."

Unsurprisingly, Axel doesn't. "She's right, you know."

"Shut up." I get up, throwing the half full beer can into the nearest bin while flipping my best friend off. Of course, I know she's right. I'm annoyed with life.

With my career. Myself. And I'm even fucking annoyed with her, but I'm not fucking stupid. A blind man can see she's right, but that's not the point, is it?

Calvin is still snickering, shooting me a knowing look.

"Thanks for the pep talk, dickheads."

"Where are you going?" Calvin questions.

I don't bother looking over my shoulder while I let my gaze follow the denim jacket around her shoulders as I put in my pursuit.

"To buy her a drink."

My eyes stay focused on her blonde head while she prances down the sidewalk.

She pissed me off, but the intrigue she ignited grows with every step she takes as she creates more distance between us. My heart beats faster, and not because of the boiling lava that has been settling in my soul for days now. There is a need to look into those piercing eyes again that's spreading throughout my chest like wildfire. My shitty mood is gradually being pushed away when I think of that sassy look she just gave me, smirking at just the thought of it.

She casually trots toward one of the bars with a clear goal, her hand in the air as she waves to the bouncer in front of it while tossing her empty cup in the bin at the entrance. The bald version of the hulk smiles her way, and I quickly jog the last steps until I can reach for her elbow, preventing her from going inside. Her neck snaps my way with a fiery glare that has the potential to be lethal when she detects my fingers wrapping around her upper arm, clearly not afraid to show her teeth if she needs to.

"Hey." I offer her a genuine smile, then direct it to the bouncer, who protectively takes a step forward, ready to kick my ass. "I come in peace." I move my free hand up.

Her face radiates confusion, her silence giving me the perfect opportunity to look at her up close. Her eyebrows are an ashy blonde, her slightly sun-kissed skin sprinkled with freckles over her nose and flushed cheeks. Brown eyes in a mesmerizing sienna look back at me, accentuated with gold rays like the sun molded her retinas herself. Without thought, I lower my gaze to her soft pink lips, which are plump and full, cushions that look like they are created for a lipstick commercial. My smile dissolves for a second as I swallow before her lips quirk, and I raise my chin up again to find her gaze.

"Are you following me?" she tries to scold, but the amusement slips through when she glances at my hand still clasped around her upper arm.

"Maybe?" I let go of her. "Is that a bad thing?"

"I thought I offended you."

You made me feel like you were yanking a pitchfork into my chest, babe, but I didn't mind it enough to let you walk. "You annoyed me a little." I nod. "But you *are* right."

For a few beats, she's silent, assessing the situation with slightly narrowed eyes, as if she's wondering why I'm agreeing with her.

To figure out what my angle is.

The truth is, I don't even know what my angle is.

"So..." She cocks her head, dragging out the word. "If I'm right, why are you here? Why are you not safe and sound in your bed at the motorhome?"

Her specific question lifts my eyebrows.

"How do you know I'm not staying at a hotel in the city?" Your average Formula One fan, who watches the races every weekend, doesn't know where we sleep. They assume we sleep in fancy hotel penthouses with an entire entourage. But in reality, we sleep in our own motorhome near the track while traveling in Europe. "I used to live near the track. I know the place where they park the caravans."

"You can hardly call my luxury motorhome a caravan," I scoff. The thing can house a small family, with a full bed and bathroom.

"Really?" she mocks, jerking her head back a little with a challenging expression. "You don't look like the kind of man that cares what I call your *motorhome.*"

I search her eyes. "What do I look like?"

"Like a frustrated racer."

The flirty smirk that had slowly crawled up my face freezes, because she's spot on. I've been frustrated for months, even though I try to hide it as I cheer my way through life. The truth is, I've been feeling the cloud build above my head for a while now, fueled by my lack of results in my Callahan car. Something inside of me is off, and I can't pinpoint it. I've been working with this team for eighteen months, really putting in my best efforts, but I can't get the car to work for me, nor do I feel like the team is listening to my concerns. It's like they are communicating on a different frequency than I am, and I don't know how to fix it. But I guess at this point there is no fixing it in the first place.

The sigh that deflates my chest is long and loud.

"Want to talk about it?" She gives me a look that has me balling my fists to prevent me from wrapping her in my arms at her question. It's sweet, but it lacks the melancholy everyone has been showing me today, and she doesn't even know how much I need that. For someone to not look at me like I'm some kicked dog with my tail between my legs.

A pang hits my chest, and I swallow, peering into her eyes. "I'm not allowed."

I'd love to talk to someone about it, just to get my frustrations out, but my contract prevents me from discussing anything regarding Callahan with anyone who isn't part of the team. Even though that's the same team that disregards anything I say. I haven't even gone into detail about it with Axel, not wanting to give them a reason to terminate my contract prematurely. Last week was the first time I told him about my struggles with the team, since I'm already sacked anyway. But talking to anyone else would mean risking a fine that's around half a million.

"It must suck. To not be able to talk to whoever you want. Vent when you need to."

"It's both a blessing and a curse." I smile, keeping my gaze trained on her brown eyes. They stare back at me like a light at the end of the tunnel, and I wonder if they cause the flutter in my stomach.

This is a first. I'm a flirt. And being a racecar driver means I have plenty of opportunities to flirt, but never has my body made these weird leaps that tingle along my skin. It's an entirely new feeling.

"Are you going to the race tomorrow?"

"No." She firmly shakes her head.

"No tickets?"

"No. That's not it." She chuckles, clearly amused by my obvious assumption. "I just want to watch the race."

"You can't from the stands?"

She gives me a flat look. "No, I can only watch y'all drive by a corner of a lap. I want to see the race."

My grin only expands, surprised by her explanation. I'm used to people wanting things from me. A selfie. A signed cap. Tickets. Time. In most cities, we are met by hordes of fans who want at least *something* from us. But this girl took the time to scold me on the street for being out way past my bedtime, showing her commitment to the sport, but isn't interested in asking me for anything else.

"What's your favorite team?"

Her lashes flutter with sass. "Not Callahan."

"Me neither." My amusement for this girl grows. "How come you're not all star-struck, asking for an autograph?"

"Are you gonna marry me?" I frown at her question, something swirling in my stomach.

"What? No?" I ignore the image flashing through my mind of seeing this girl in a white princess dress. Her blonde hair up. A tiara. Some sneakers underneath.

Fuck, it's already taking my breath away just thinking about it.

"Then why would I need your autograph?" she asks in a matter-of-fact-tone that instantly bubbles a laugh from my chest. There is something so uncomplicated, so grounding about her reply, that makes me appreciate her even more.

"I now remember why I like Amsterdam."

"Enlighten me." Her gaze twinkles as she waits for my laugh to die down.

"People just let you be. I'm pretty certain a bunch of people recognized me earlier tonight, but no one trailed behind me for a selfie or an autograph. *You* only took the time to tell me it was wiser to go to bed than ask for a selfie."

"Shit! So, it's too late to ask for a signed cap? Maybe a few t-shirts?" Her palm flies to her heart, enticing a chuckle from me again. "We dutchies tend to be a very down-to-earth species," she continues. "You're only human, after all, aren't you? Like the rest of us?"

Her explanation calms my head, settling the hinder that has been swirling through my mind all day. My eyes are trained on hers, unable to break the connection as I lower my face only an inch from hers. A whiff of something that reminds me of orange blossom slides into my nose, trickling pebbles down my arms even though it's a warm summer night. I'm tempted to dip my nose into her neck, breathing her in like she's my favorite blanket when I was a kid, but instead I suck in a short breath to keep it together.

"No," I whisper. "But don't tell anyone, or my alien siblings will demand to kidnap you and use you as an experiment."

"What kind of experiment would that be?" Her features stay flat, keeping up a good act of being unaffected, but the change in her voice convinces me I'm not imagining our mutual chemistry.

"A fun one." I wink.

"You're silly." She shoves my chest playfully, causing me to balance on my heels.

"You're beautiful."

Her attention flies up, something happening behind her eyes as she knits her eyebrows together. "Are you flirting with me?"

"Is it working?"

She presses her tongue inside her cheek. "A little?"

Her chest slowly moves up and down as I take a step forward, our eyes glued together. The gaze she aims my way intimidates me as much as it excites me, drawing me in like a firefly. There is something about her that captivates me, feeling the desire to tell her my life story while her back is pressed against my chest. The perfect girl to binge watch a new series with on a rainy day. My senses are overwhelmed, and I already feel addicted when I take in another breath of her citrus scent. I want to make a move, but I don't want to break the magic that pulls us into this perfect bubble.

"Nik! I already counted!" A woman's head pops out of the door of the bar, breaking our moment before my infatuation takes a step back.

"Thanks, Lie! I'm coming," she shouts back, keeping her eyes on mine, then smiles. It's wide, taking my breath away. "Gotta go! Have a good race tomorrow."

Quicker than my brain can register, she turns on her white Converse, disappearing through the door of the bar. For a moment, I'm blinking at the door glass as her blonde hair quickly fades out the farther she moves away from the entrance.

"Wait, where are you going?" I bellow to her back as I burst through the door. "Let me buy you a drink."

My feet bounce onto the worn-out wooden floor, a mixture of alcohol and cleaning supplies hitting me in the face. The place is empty, other than the girl behind the bar, humming along with the latest Ed Sheeran song playing in the background and a guy setting out candles on the standing tables down the walls.

"I'm honored, Ace. But I can't." She smiles over her shoulder, then lifts a panel in the bar to get behind it. She drops her stuff in the cabinet on the back wall, shrugging off her denim jacket and hanging it on the rack close to the side of the bar. I swallow when the swell of her breasts is now completely clear underneath her white t-shirt, covered by the logo of the bar. It's tucked into her high-waist jeans, bringing out the curves of her hips. The cream skin on her arms has the same tanned shade as her cheeks, a healthy glow that makes me roll my lips as I imagine how she would taste like a warm spring day on my tongue.

"You work here." I rest my elbows on the bar.

Her smile is wide, a little mischief in her gaze. "Can I get you anything?"

"I reckon you don't have some white wine?" The lukewarm beer I just poured down my throat wasn't really what I was after tonight. If I was going to drown my sorrows, might as well be in a good Chardonnay or something.

Her eyebrows meet in the middle, then she bends over and pulls a box from the cooler behind the bar with a tube sticking out.

"Only if you're into Vino de la Box?" Her mocking tone is amusing, and I resist the urge to shudder at the thought alone. Being raised on a winery ranch makes it practically illegal to drink wine from a box. My dad would have a heart attack if he ever found out.

"Two shots and a Jack and Coke."

"Two shots. What do you want?" She grabs a long drink from the workstation, filling it with ice before spinning a bottle of Jack Daniels upside down to pour the liquid into the glass.

"You pick."

She pulls her lips between her teeth, preventing her cheeks from fully rising while she's looking at me like she just won the lottery. Mentally, I take a picture of the glimmer in her eyes, knowing it will be something to remember when I'm in bed later.

"You sure?"

"I trust you."

She chortles, devilish enough to heat my groin, twitching my lower abdomen alive.

What is it with this girl?

She grabs a shot glass from the bar, then fills it up with water before placing it in front of me with a big smirk.

"You really shouldn't." She winks.

Amused, I size her up. Her grin is infectious, making it impossible to fully hide the smile that wants to crack through. "Are you serious?"

"Should've gone to bed instead, Ace." She shakes her head with a laugh, then tosses the glass in the sink before she collects my order.

My shoulders square a little more by her new nickname, telling me more about her opinion of me. I watch how she places the Jack and Coke in front of me, then pulls two shot glasses from the rack, along with a bottle of some kind of red stuff. A fire hydrant is displayed on the bottle from top to bottom, a flame in the middle.

With that same playful expression, she fills up the glasses, then gives me a nudge of her chin as she screws up the cap again.

I lift both glasses, then hold one up for her.

"Nah-ah." She shakes her head, lifting her hands to her hair to put it up in a ponytail. "I still have to work all night."

She's hot when her hair is down, her blonde locks dancing around her hypnotizing smile, but with her hair up, the soft skin of her neck is exposed, begging to be touched.

"Come on, you're a bartender," I press, tilting my head. "Isn't there a rule that you can't say no to shots that are offered?"

I know I'm right when a slight scowl knits her eyebrows together, creating a cute frown on her forehead. A strand of her blonde hair escapes the grip of her scrunchie, falling beside her eye. She looks sexy as hell, trying to scold me when, really, I can see her resolve fading quickly as I don't move a muscle, the shot still firmly up in front of her face.

"Come on, babe."

She groans, grabbing the tiny glass from my grasp. Our fingers touch only briefly, but it's long enough for me to feel her silky skin and speculate about what they would feel like against the rest of my body. Heat flashes my neck, and to tone down the desire that builds with the speed of lightning, I clink my shot against hers, then rapidly bring it to my lips.

My forehead wrinkles as my tongue is assaulted by the aroma of eucalyptus on my tastebuds. The red liquid surges down my throat with a boiling aftertaste of something like licorice. It's like a minty fireball exploded in my mouth, leaving me confused, while the sweetness of the anise I detect pleases in a soothing way.

"What the hell is this?" I wipe my mouth with the back of my hand, tossing the glass back on the bar.

She's looking at me with mischief as she licks her lips to get rid of the leftover residue, clearly a pro, not even slightly fazed.

"It's called Firemen. It's a Dutch liquor. Do you like it?"

"I'm not sure, but I feel like I'm about to turn into a dragon," I reply with a wrinkly nose.

"Seems fitting for the *Outback Devil*."

I shake my head, dazed at her smirk. My gullet tries to recover from that attack, when something clatters beside her and a woman with goldish-blonde hair stares at me with her jaw ready to hit the floor.

"Are you Tristan Reinhart?"

NIKKIE

I roll my lips, savoring the minty taste of the shot, while throwing him a playful look. Most foreigners need to get familiar with the distinct taste of eucalyptus combined with licorice, topped off with a shit-ton of burn down your throat. Especially if it's your first time. I always love to see the scrunched-up faces when flirty men tell me to pick their poison as they stand before me with a cocky smirk. Tristan Reinhart is no exception.

"I'm not sure, but I feel like I'm about to turn into a dragon," Tristan says with a wrinkly nose.

"Seems fitting for the *Outback Devil*," I tell him before my head jerks toward the crate that's clashing to the floor next to my feet. I jerk my foot away at the sudden noise, then I flip my irises up to Lieke. She gawks at him with bulged eyes, her thick lashes moving up and down with a speed that makes me believe she'll take off like a Boeing 747 any second now.

"Are you Tristan Reinhart?"

I rear my head back just in time to catch the irresistible grin he's famous for, causing my stomach to do a backflip when I see the sincerity in his expression. It's the one you see on TV that convinces you that he's truly grateful for his fans at any time of day and not just playing the act when the cameras are around. I already liked the man from the glimpses I see on the big screen, but the sweet look he's giving my friend ignites a growing urge to cuddle up beside him when I'm having a bad day. Like his smile is magical, capable of fixing all problems.

Wait, what?

My own thoughts surprise me, considering I haven't noticed, like, *really* noticed, anyone of the opposite gender since... well, since Wes.

"I am," he says with a little pride in his voice.

"*The* Tristan Reinhart? F1 World Champion? The Outback Devil?"

"That's me." A full smirk slides onto his cheeks.

"Oh my god, Tristan Reinhart is sitting on our bar." Lieke shuffles until her shoulder hits mine, then hisses from the corner of her red painted lips, "Nik, you're talking to Tristan Reinhart."

"I know," I mumble back, still fixated on the handsome man. He's nothing like the type of guy who normally catches my attention. He doesn't look like your typical bad boy or the men who walk the fine line of the law like I grew up around. He doesn't wear a leather jacket, or hide his full hair under a beanie. He doesn't smoke, or I assume he doesn't, nor does he seem like he's the type who's got anything to hide from the authorities other than the time he might have stolen a few extra jelly beans from the candy store when he was six. But something about his energy draws me in like a moth to a flame.

The F1 World Champion with a smile that has the ability to captivate you with only a glace your way, his lively expression becoming even more vibrant when standing right in front of you. I always enjoyed every interview he ever gave, his playful personality making it impossible not to. But I would've never guessed that in his presence, my heart would start pounding with heavy thuds, as if a tribe is preparing for a sacrificial ritual. His greens continue to stare at me like I'm one of the world's wonders, unlocking a door in my head that's been dead-bolted for a while now. *Sixteen months, to be exact.*

A wave of fear seeps through my body, but it's not as big as the pull I have toward this man.

"What the hell?" Lieke mumbles.

"I know," I agree when my attention is drawn to the door of the bar opening.

His friends enter with a confidence that can't be fabricated and come to stand beside him. They both snap their heads back and forth between the two of us, a curiosity in their gazes.

I now recognize the one on his right as his agent, Axel, the glasses on his nose being a dead giveaway. But I have no clue who the other guy is, as I quickly glance at his white Callahan polo. His freshly shaved jaw is set in an amused smile, his brown eyes fixed on his friend whose interest stays completely focused on yours truly.

"What's your name?" Tristan doesn't acknowledge his buddies as I swing my eyes back up when I realize he's talking to me. There is something slightly intimidating about getting the full attention of someone who you've seen hundreds of times on worldwide TV, but the kind look he's giving me also makes it feel so familiar. Like I've known him for years.

"Nikkie, and this is Lieke." I point my thumb at the girl still gawking like she's in the desert and he's the oasis. Lieke is witty, and right now, you wouldn't know it. She's also gorgeous, with flowing platinum blonde hair, a curvaceous ass that should be worshiped, and a mouth that's as dirty as a sailor. And she isn't impressed easily.

But she sure as fuck is impressed now.

I silently pat myself on the back for keeping my cool, though I can't completely deny he has no effect on me if I have to go by my flushed neck.

"Tristan." He offers me his hand, and I take it with a smile that vanishes as quickly as it came when my skin produces pebbles at his touch. The heat of his palm burns into mine, purring places in my body alive that aren't supposed to purr and bringing heat in more places that have been long forgotten about. A little startled, I quickly let go again, but the hunger that travels his gaze tells me the damage is already done. I swallow to shove my racing heart back down my throat.

"And these are my buddies, Axel and Calvin." He nudges both his friends.

"You're his trainer." Lieke points at Calvin, then Axel. "And you're his childhood friend slash agent."

Their smiles expand, the three men looking at Lieke with a little amusement while I'm grateful the attention has shifted to her, so I have a moment to breathe again.

"She saw the Callahan documentary," I disclose, tucking my elbow into her side to jolt her out of her fan girl mode. She mutters something like an *ouch*, then squares her shoulders while we both show them bright smiles like two doofuses.

"So I see." Tristan chuckles, then fixates on me again.

The expression he's giving me is kind and friendly, but I can't deny there's more sparkling in there. It makes me think he can see straight through my soul, wondering how he can make everything better with just his smile. *Or something else.*

My mind rolls straight into the gutter, my mouth turning dry as I wonder how chiseled he is under his shirt. If I could do my laundry on his six-pack, and if he has a happy trail that I can follow with my finger down his jeans. When my eyes move back up, his are narrowed with a wickedness that makes it clear he knows where my head is. *Oops.* Part of me wants to break the connection.

But I can't.

For a moment, the air fills with a level of awkwardness that would normally make me cringe, as I see everyone moving their chins back and forth between Tristan and I, but I can't be willed to look away. An invisible cord connects my eyes with his, a silent conversation spoken, though I have no clue what's being said other than confirming a chemistry that packs more intensity than my regular Saturday night flirts.

"He's looking at you with longing," Lieke whispers, loud enough for everyone in a three-yard radius to hear.

"He's not."

"Oh, I am." Tristan's quick reply has my heart now trying to jump out of my chest with force.

"He really is," Axel chimes in with a flat expression, then looks at Lieke. "Can I get a drink, love?"

She blinks at him as if he spoke French, before she snaps out of her hypnotic state. "Of course, what do you want?" Lieke's blonde locks bounce as she nudges her head at him, and she heads to her side of the workstation as both Axel and Calvin place their orders.

"What time do you get off?" Tristan asks.

"Way past your bedtime, Ace." I start pulling the clean glasses from the small dishwasher below the bar to keep myself busy.

"Can't you take the night off?"

"Sorry, hotshot, but I'm not in the position to miss a night of work. Got bills to pay."

That, among other stuff.

"I'll double whatever you earn tonight." My motions stop, my hand hanging mid-air with my fingers around a warm and clean long drink.

"You're joking," I blurt, though the determination that settles in his eyes tells me he's doing anything *but* that.

"I'm as serious as a penguin male sitting on his children."

A frown brings my eyebrows together as I prevent my laughter from escaping. "That's weird."

"Nikkie, right?" I reluctantly nod. "Can you find me your manager, please?"

"I am the manager." I slowly turn my head to Lieke's excited voice, a slight scowl on my face when I catch her impish expression.

"What are you doing?" I murmur with clenched teeth.

"Oh, great!" Tristan's green eyes travel to Lieke's. "Let's make a deal."

"I'm listening." With wide eyes, I stare at the smirk that Lieke is giving him, a mischievous twinkle in her eyes.

"I'll pay you a grand to run a little harder tonight so Nikkie here can take the night off."

"What?" My head rears back at the same time his eyes find mine.

He can't be serious, right?

"Then I'll pay *you* a grand to compensate for your hours."

I huff, a little shocked. "You think I earn a grand at night? Who do you think I serve? The prince of Abu Dhabi?"

I earn about one tenth of that a night. Double if I'm lucky and tips are good that day. Not that I've gotten a salary in the last few months.

Amusement travels his face, a taunt on his lips. "I feel like that's a trick question, but I know the prince of Abu Dhabi, so I have to say no." *Of course, he does.* "And to top it off, I will give you another grand to compensate for any losses you make by running this place with one person less." He directs his attention toward Lieke again, completely ignoring my indignance. She has a smug grin raising her cheeks to her ears like she is enjoying this way too much. She's totally going to sell me out; I can see it in her eyes.

Traitor.

"You realize it's a Saturday night?" Her hip pops as she crosses her arms in front of her chest. "This place will be packed within an hour. Without Nik behind the bar, we could easily lose 7 to 8k."

I stifle a laugh at her exaggeration.

"Please, Lieke, is it?" The way he pronounces her name with his Australian accent is hilarious, but the absurdity of the situation keeps me from uttering another syllable.

"It's Lee-kuh," she corrects. "Not, Lee-kee. I'm not some failing water pipe."

"Lee-kuh, this is my only night here," he says, referring to the common knowledge that he travels the world for a living.

"Lie, don't," I scold, even though I can feel her cheeky attitude coming at me in waves.

She shrugs. "He has a point."

"Lieke!"

Her reply is a hefty eyeroll before she tucks my wrist. "Will you excuse us for just a sec?" She offers the three men an apologetic glance while she drags me to the other side of the bar as I stomp my feet.

"I'm not going." I huff.

"You'll never have this opportunity again," she hisses in Dutch.

"We need the money!"

"Newsflash, sweety? I just named the number we will be making in one night with the three of us and he didn't even bat an eye. Besides, we could really use the money." *Don't I fucking know it.* "And to be honest? You and I are a fucking blast together, but I'd dump your ass for his the second I'd get the chance." Her blonde brows slide up in a reprimanding look as she continues. "He's not asking for me, though. He's asking for *you.*"

I release the air from my lungs.

Is this really happening?

"We need the money," she reminds me once more. I briefly find his swooning smile still aimed at my back when I quickly glance over my shoulder, making my stomach flutter.

"This is insane, Lieke." How is Tristan Reinhart standing in front of me, offering to give me a thousand euros just to spend the night with me? That sounds really, really bad when I think of it and a wrinkle creases my forehead.

"What?" Lieke asks.

"He's offering me money to spend time with me."

"Yeah, we already established that."

"It's like I'm a fucking prostitute!"

"More like a high-end escort, but that's not the point. Look at the man." Her eyes fly behind me, but I'm too much of a chicken to look that way again. "That face screams, *I want to marry this girl*, not treat her like whore. He could treat me like a whore, though," she mumbles.

"Lie!"

"Oh, come on, Nik! You know it's not like that. He clearly wants to get to know you. Just go! Have fun! Hit a bar with him! And if by the end of the night, you do feel like a little somethin' somethin', you just go for it." She bends her knees and puts in the action of her words.

"Oh my god, you're the worst."

"You haven't had some 'action,'"—her fingers lift with air quotes—"since the accident. You deserve to get that kitten of yours dusted off, girl."

My head falls back, my eyes shooting to the ceiling. "Thank you for reminding me! You and your dirty mouth."

"All I'm saying is that you deserve a break. *Especially* if that break comes in the shape of a very hot F1 driver with his tongue between your legs."

"Jesus fuck, Lieke!" My eyes roll to the back of my head, incredulous. "I'm not going to sleep with him, and I sure as hell won't find his tongue between my legs!"

"I wouldn't be so sure about that," she sing-songs.

"I don't even like the guy!" She cocks her head with a flat expression at my obvious lie. "Okay, maybe a little." Still a lie, but we're ignoring that. A minute ago, my mind was in the gutter, thinking of all the ways I would drag my tongue over his body.

"Just go."

"You sure?" I can't even believe I'm doing this, but I know she's right. My mind is curious as fuck, desperate to find out what the man is like behind the famous smile. He's only in Amsterdam once a year and the chance I'll see him again is pretty much zero point zero. "It's a Saturday night."

"We'll be fine. Go, Nik."

"Okay." I nod at the same time Lieke squeals in victory. "But I won't take his money."

"That's fine. I'll take it for you. Stop stalling. I want all the dirty details tomorrow!" She spins me, then pushes me forward, where my gaze collides with Tristan's boyish grin, raising the brittle hairs on my neck. It's then that I know I'm in some serious trouble.

"Oh, boy."

5

TRISTAN

AFTER A TWO-MINUTE-LONG ARGUMENT where the gorgeous yet stubborn as hell woman refused to let me hit the ATM and make good on my word, I ordered Axel to sort it with her friend. Lieke's dollar-sign gaze collided with mine in delight before she rapidly throws Nikkie's denim jacket in the air. Her eyeroll reflects in one of the mirrors behind the bar as she catches it, conjuring in a lopsided grin as I usher her out of the bar in victory.

The realization that she doesn't need an incentive to spend time with me only builds the cheery feeling in my stomach, but really, I would've paid double if that's what it took.

I carefully size her up when she pushes the door open, following her through it before the noises on the street reach my ears. A bicycle bell jerks my head up, having me quickly assessing the people on the sidewalk. Earlier, I was scowling at everyone, pissed at all those happy faces passing by, when I felt like I was being eaten from the inside. But now? I fit right in, and I blame the girl in front of me.

Something forced my legs to get my grumbling ass off that bench and follow her wherever she was going, but the longer I talk to her, the more I have to know. Like one of those gifts that has a box within a box and then another and another.

I've barely opened the first box, but the little boy inside of me is dying to get to the core of the gift, unwrapping it with a velocity like it's Christmas morning.

"So where do you wanna go?" Her blonde hair sways as she turns around, her amber brown eyes hitting me in the chest with an excitement that makes my heart stutter.

"You tell me. You're from around here." I put my hands in my pockets to prevent myself from doing something stupid, like taking her hand in mine. "What are the good spots? The places no one will know me." The last thing I need right now is someone taking away the little time I get with her.

"Basically everywhere."

"Ouch." I grip my heart, chuckling.

Her lips raise with a devilish gleam while she shrugs. "What can I say? We're more of a football country," she jokes.

"You mean *soccer*?" I taunt as we start walking toward the square, shoulder to shoulder. My fascination has a hard time taking my eyes off her, finding myself tempted to rear my head with every word she says. The air is soft and nurturing because of the humidity during the day, though my skin feels like it's a hundred degrees outside.

"Don't even go there, seriously."

"What? It's soccer."

She glances up at me with a scold, though her playful eyes give her lack of annoyance away. "It's *foot*ball. You know because you can only use your foot to get the ball in the goal." She puts her words to action, pretending to kick a ball.

"It's soccer," I deadpan, causing her eyes to roll.

"Oh, you're so from a different continent." My foul mood is completely erased, her sass acting like a potion to forget about all the shit happening in my life. All I'm focused on is the blonde beauty quickly crawling her way under my skin.

"Sorry." I laugh. "I guess it isn't really alive in Australia. We're not good at soccer. We're better at *foot*ball." I emphasize the words, dipping my chin close enough to suck in another breath of her citrusy essence. I expect her to maybe show some kind of discomfort by suddenly showing up in her personal space, but instead I just get another flashing smile as she gleefully shoves my shoulder.

"Ha, funny. It's the same thing." We continue our path, me following her regardless of where she wants to go. She could guide me down a snake pit right now and I'd still follow her, too eager to see another smile on her lips. "Are you hungry?"

Her question makes me aware I haven't eaten since this afternoon, my stomach roaring in protest since qualifying, but my throat too constricted to swallow anything since the press statement Callahan released. "I can eat."

"Cool, come on." Her hand wraps around the bare skin of my wrist and she tugs me forward. My brain registers the feverish touch that comes from her palm, shaking my groin alive more than I want to show while walking down the street. Luckily, it's only about a dozen steps before she lets go of me and we stop in front of a small food joint.

There is a small counter where you can order, but half of the snack bar is made out of an automated wall with food that I keep my eyes focused on to try to settle down the bulge in my jeans. The only thing I understand is "burger," as the rest of the words look like a bunch of jumbled letters.

Kaassoufflé, frikandel, speciaaltje.

Nikkie reaches into the pocket of her jeans, throwing a few coins in the slot that says *kroket.*

She pulls two of them out of the wall, handing me one with a napkin around it.

"What's this?" I look at the thing in my hand. It has the shape of a roll, the skin covered in breadcrumbs that have turned a deep brown shade after being deep fried in oil.

"Are you kidding me? Only the best snack ever." She takes a bite, holding her lips a bit open to let the hot air leave her mouth.

"It looks like dung," I tease.

Her face freezes, her eyes darkening. "Are you trying to get on my shitlist?"

"No, but *that* clearly is."

"Shut up, Ace." She cocks her head, then looks at the *kroket* in my hand to urge me to take a bite. Giving her a skeptical look, I carefully sink my teeth into the crunchy surface until it reaches a soft substance. The inside is filled with a meat ragout that's hot as hell, but tastes freaking amazing. The flavor of salty meat and herbs makes my eyes bulge as I let the mix of flavors sit on my tongue.

"It's—damn this is good," I mumble with my mouth still full.

"Told ya!"

"How have I never had one of these?"

"Because you clearly haven't been hanging out with the right crowd." She winks, and it makes the air leave my lungs.

"Clearly." We finish the rest of it, her eyes joyfully finding mine as she notices I'm devouring the thing like I haven't eaten in weeks. When we're both finished, I get us another one as she nudges her head for me to follow her. We eat the rest of it in silence, walking down the canals.

"So, you wanna tell me why you are strolling around the center of Amsterdam when you should be in bed?" She brushes her hands together to get rid of the breadcrumbs sticking to her fingers. "I bet your team principal will have a field day when he finds out you're going rogue." Lifting her brow at me, she wipes her lips with a napkin while I do the same.

"I think you just made it worth it."

"Maybe." She's quick with her reply, but her blush still shows the effect I have on her. "Or maybe he'll be on a rampage when he finds out."

"Ah, yeah, maybe. I'm sure it will work out." I give her a comforting expression, but she sees right through my bullshit.

"He's gonna wanna kill you."

"He'll want to, yeah. But what's he gonna do? Fire me again?" I try to hide any cynical tone that might've etched through as I look into the night. The streetlights reflect onto the water in the canal, twinkling as we keep walking along the cobblestones. There's a calmness forming with each step, as smooth as the lack of ripples in the water. I sense her examining me carefully, as if she's trying to wriggle her way into the depths of my soul. The longer her eyes rove the length of my face, the faster my heart beats.

"I gather you didn't see it coming?" she finally asks.

"No." I shake my head, then sigh.

Fuck, who am I kidding? I saw it coming from a mile away. "Or maybe I did," I confess. "You watched this season, right? I'm not really in a good place."

"How come?" I feel her gaze turn up to me again, but I keep mine fixed on the sidewalk. Too chicken to look her in the eye and find the pity that everyone has given me. Laced with sadness, as if my time in Formula One is over.

It's not. I refuse to believe that.

But her question doesn't spark my rage alive like every other person before her. No, with her, I actually want to share what's bothering me.

"I don't know." I shrug. "It's like I'm not feeling the car. Like she doesn't connect to me."

"What's different from before you went to Callahan?"

Other than it all feeling wrong, like a dozen voices screaming in my head that this isn't where I'm supposed to be? That I made a stupid decision leaving SRT when I did and I've been punished for it ever since?

"Everything. Nothing. My state of mind."

"Are you unhappy?"

I blink, contemplating her question.

I don't know. I'm a glass half full kind of man, always trying to look at the bright side, trusting that everything I face is something I can handle. Sure, I've been frustrated about the car and my lack of control with it, but I never thought I couldn't do it, and that thought alone kept me smiling as I walked through the paddock every weekend. But I can't deny that something has been off this year. Not just the season, but life in general.

"No." I firmly shake my head. "But I do feel like something is missing."

A chill trails down my upper arms when I think of the true feelings I've experienced these past two weeks. I was pissed, frustrated, and worried. All the emotions you'd expect when you get sacked. But I also felt lighter, like a weight lifted off my shoulders. I don't know why, because I don't think I can live a life without racing. It's what's been hurting me the most. That pull from the black hole that would show up if I don't get to race next season.

I don't think I can do it.

I'm not ready to quit yet.

But if I'm being honest with myself, I know something hasn't been right for a long time.

It's like there is this big ball of contradiction settling in my stomach, not knowing how to continue my career or in what direction. That sense of feeling that I have no idea what I'm doing it for.

"When they told me they were letting me go last week? It was a relief, in a way," I confide. "Like they gave me an out to quit fighting every *fucking* thing. Giving me a breather. But at the same time, I'm fucking fuming I won't have a seat next year."

"You'll have a seat next year." I can't deny the self-evident tone in her voice, and I twist my head to look at her. She's giving me a scrunched-up face, as if my worries are completely unwarranted and it does something inside me. I know it's easy to take kind words from a stranger, but her opinion somehow feels more significant than anyone else's right now.

"I don't know that." I stop for a moment, a deep sigh falling from my chest.

She cocks her head, huffing. "You are one of the best drivers out there. Besides, you're not even thirty yet. You still have many racing years inside of you."

Her level of confidence in me expands my heart to proportions I can barely control, the organ beating like a madman with a sledgehammer. The gold in her eyes glints brightly underneath the light of the moon, acting like a beacon that radiates comfort.

"What?" she questions as I keep staring at her.

Her pink lips are slightly curled, an expression of anticipation coming my way, and for what feels like the longest moment, I wonder what those plump lips would feel like against mine. If she tastes as sweet as she smells and if touching her would feel as good as just being around her. My chest slowly moves up and down while the atmosphere changes. It's as if a translucent curtain separates us from the world around us while I lock onto her parted lips taking heavy breaths. Our eyes stay connected, my body fucking with my mind as I try to convince myself to take the thing that I have silently decided is mine. *To kiss her.*

"You know what you need?" She breaks the magic with mischief in her eyes. Part of me is displeased when the moment is over, but my lungs welcome the fresh air as I exhale the pent-up breath before I fill them with air again.

"What's that?" I reply with a lazy grin.

"A little fun."

6

NIKKIE

H<small>E'S LOOKING AT ME</small> with anticipation, as if I'm a magician and I'm about to pop a bunny from my head as I smile at him while taking two steps backwards. It's a diversion, but I saw the hole he was sucking me into. One that's tempting me to wrap my arms around his body, not just connecting my skin with his, but the part where he can say and do all the right things to make me create sentiments for him, easily and quickly. I know because, for a second there, a contentedness slipped back into my body that reminds me of Wes.

"What are you doing?" He frowns when my feet get closer to the front door of one of the many manor houses along the canal.

"Having a little fun."

His attention darts up to the lights coming through the window. "You know these people?"

"No." My smile is devious, but for the first time in who knows how long, I'm enjoying myself. Enthusiasm bubbles up my throat as I remember how much fun this was when I was a kid.

"What do you mean, no?" The thrown look he's giving me combined with the alarm washing his face has me giggling like a schoolgirl.

"I mean, I don't know them."

The moment it clicks in his head, my grin expands. I turn around, pressing the doorbell with force, keeping it under my thumb as I count to five. The sound is loud and shrill, feeling like a fucking minute long instead of five seconds, igniting a thrill in my veins as if I have three steps to dodge a freight train from hitting me in the face.

"Stop! What are you doing? You can't do that! It's eleven o'clock!" His scolding is there, but he can't hold back the laugh that's coming through.

"It's never too late to have fun, Tristan. Don't they teach you that in your fancy ass race world?" I tease, pressing my tongue against my teeth before I take off. Then I'm running, squeals of laughter coming from my chest, and my adrenaline quickly kicks in, but when I realize there are no footsteps following behind me, I turn around.

Tristan is still standing in front of the house, a puzzled look on his face as he flips his eyes between me and the front door of the manor with a slight panic. It makes me laugh even harder.

"Come on! You never played *belletje lel*?"

"What the fuck is *belletje lel*?" I cackle at his pronunciation.

"Wattle bell," I explain, but his frown stays in place. "It's when you ring the doorbell for no fucking reason and then you run off. You never played that when you were a kid?"

"I grew up on a ranch."

"Right." I chuckle at the same time another set of lights turns on in the house.

"Shit," he hisses. "Now what?"

"Now, you run!"

Finally, it hits him, and side by side, we sprint to the corner of the street, shrieking from hysteria. My heart is racing, my body temperature quickly rising with each step we take and, for a second, I feel like I'm ten all over again. My laughter is genuine, and I try not to focus on how good it feels, pushing away the little reminder that it won't last when the sun comes up again.

"This way!" I can feel him right behind me, and I grab his arm to tuck him behind me before we hide around the brick wall of a street porch.

We press our backs against the cold stone, our chests heaving as we both look up to the sky, a shared smile splitting our faces before I break out into a full laugh.

"You are crazy, girl," Tristan puffs, catching his breath. His eyes illuminate in the dark alley, a level of shock in his expression.

I glance around the corner to see if anyone opened the door.

"Hello? Anyone there?" a male voice calls out, and we both freeze, doing a shit job of holding back the laugh still sitting on our lips. I glance at Tristan, his green eyes wide, his hand covering his mouth until we hear the sound of a door closing and the hilarity is unstoppable. For a minute, we just laugh while we try to fill our lungs with oxygen, but the whole combination makes it really damn hard to breathe.

I didn't expect pride to hit me in the chest when I take a mental note of his laugh full of life, but it does. There is something mesmerizing about being able to make this man laugh after the interview he gave this afternoon. It makes me feel like I have superpowers, and they are more than welcome.

"I'd totally blame you if I end up on the news because I played *whatever bell* on the streets of Amsterdam."

"*Belletjelel*," I tell him in Dutch, still laughing. "It's fun."

He holds my gaze, and my laughter stops. "*You* are fun."

Like a vortex, I'm sucked into his energy again, but this time, I'm not sure I want to find an escape.

"You played this as a kid?" Tristan asks, as we've calmed down a little.

"All the time. Sometimes people get mad and chase you down the street. We'd be laughing, all sprinting another way, hoping we wouldn't get caught."

"You're a little thrill seeker, aren't you?"

I hold his gaze, searching his features. My entire life, I've been told I'm too wild. That I need to think more before I act. I'm the girl who'd pick the books about pirates when it was reading time. The girl who climbs the highest tree as a dare and the girl who never backs out of a challenge. Anything to make me feel alive, and people would always judge me for it. But I've been trying to do better. To stop being reckless and act like a responsible adult, and I feel busted for letting my wild side slip through.

Naturally, I expect him to judge me for my longing to get adrenaline pumping through my veins. But if anything, he looks down at me with an expression I can't really describe. It's a balance between awe and amusement with a little sparkle of reprimand. But his sharp jaw is free from judgment.

"Maybe a little." I smirk, feeling better about myself than I have in a long time.

I push off from the wall and reach out my hand. I don't even know why I do it, but it feels normal, and he links his fingers with mine, a boyish grin coming my way. My stomach tingles, my skin sparking while he holds our hands intertwined, then throws his arm around my shoulder.

"I don't believe you. I bet you have a ton of stories to tell me."

Our connected palms hang over my shoulder and I circle my free arm around his back, settling in the crook of his arm as we move down the street again, our hips bringing our feet forward at the same time. His woody scent fogs my mind, wanting to wallow in it like a happy puppy in new sheets. *Safe.* It feels safe. *He* feels safe. A feeling I barely remember.

"Maybe."

"Wanna share them with me someday?" There is genuine interest in his voice.

"Maybe." I let out a deep breath through my smile, wondering if I should tell him all the details of my rebel childhood as I try to keep myself from being an open book. I barely know this guy, other than the fact that he's a racecar driver, yet here I am, roaming down the street like we've been doing it forever. My reason tells me to keep my distance, but it's the feeling in my gut that has the upper hand and makes me say shit like:

"Wanna walk me home?"

"So what do you do? Besides bartending," he asks when he clearly doesn't want to talk about his Formula One career any longer.

We're getting closer to my house, and I'm getting more nervous with every step. He has been holding my hand for the last thirty minutes, and I'm completely guilty of taking the longer route home for two simple reasons. One, walking down the street with him, just talking, feels more normal than I've felt in a long time, and I want to stretch this moment for as long as I can. And two, the closer we get to my street, the more indecisiveness forms in my racing thoughts.

Is my front door symbolic of the end of this night? Or do I invite him in, knowing there's a big chance it ends in my bedroom? A voice in my head screams no, to convince me I'm not ready to get physical with anyone yet, and I'm equally tempted to listen to it as I am to ignore it and take my chances for this one night. To listen to my body that wants to drop to my knees, beg him to touch me in all the right places and make me feel alive again.

"That's it," I disclose.

"That's it?"

"Is that weird?"

"No." His chin falls to the side so he can briefly connect our gazes, his messy hair bouncing toward me. "But for some reason, I have the feeling this isn't what you wanna do for the rest of your life."

Closing my eyes for a second, I quickly debate how much I'm willing to share with him. But the way he keeps looking at me like I'm the most magnificent creature in the world compels me to tell him anything he wants to know. I'd expect that to freak me out, but instead it feels eerily comforting.

"I studied physical therapy," I confess.

"Really?" There is excitement in his tone, with maybe something that can be mistaken as a hint of pride, but I hope it is. I know I was proud when I finally got my degree, but it all slid down the drain at some point. It's hard to have a day job when you're standing behind the bar at night.

"Yeah. I graduated last year. College was fun, but it was also hard. Especially last year." A lump swells in my throat. "I was in a car accident." I keep my gaze locked with the ground as we keep strutting forward. "With my best friend. He didn't make it."

Sharing that part of my past with him feels like I'm showing him the depths of my soul, but then again, it also feels like it's something I need to do. Like it's the only way forward, confessing my grief to someone who doesn't know me. "I need time to just *be* for a while, you know?"

I quickly decide to move down this route, not fully ready to share everything, too scared to break the magic of the way he looks at me. He builds my confidence, making me believe I'm not as much to blame as other people might think, even though the truth lingers around me like a parasite.

"I'm so sorry that happened to you." When I look at him from the corner of my eye, I find admiration in his expression. "I can't even imagine what that's like. I graduated high school and then went straight to the SRT Junior Academy in Germany."

"You never went to college?"

"I reckon driving around a track doesn't count?"

I chortle, shaking my head. "Though impressive, no."

"Then no." He chuckles lightly. "I think at this point, I don't even know how to hold a pen anymore unless it's to sign an autograph."

"It's like riding a bike; you never forget how to do it." I wave his worries away before we both break out into laughter.

This feels good.

Being around him feels good.

"So, what's the dream?" he asks when our giggles subside.

"The dream?" I swallow, my lashes briefly lowering for just a moment when I think about how I haven't dared to dream lately. How the future was crushed, and the present has been nothing more than a hollow shell for months.

"You gotta have dreams and goals. Otherwise, you got nothing to live for."

I sigh, because he makes it sound so easy, but the answer feels so difficult for me to say out loud. "The dream was always to travel. Offer free services for board and see where the world brings us."

"Your best friend?"

I smile at him with my lips still pressed together. "His name was Wes. He's the one that got me hooked on F1." I try to change the subject and Tristan lets me, pushing away the curiosity that's washing his face.

"Really? How come?"

I exhale through my nose. "We lived in the town next to the track. And every year when we were kids, we'd go to the dunes on race day and listen to the cars passing by. I fell in love with that sound. The roaring of an engine makes my heart thunder with excitement. It gets me all giddy and gushing. Then as we got older, we'd just go for free practice and qualifying and watch the races at home." The second I hear a heavy engine slide into my ears, butterflies fly through my stomach, and my eyes anxiously look for the object of the sound. Doesn't matter where I am.

"Your heart thunders with excitement..." he trails off, then beams, "I love that."

"It probably sounds lame to you." I lower my eyes, suddenly realizing I'm talking to the man who drives these cars for a living. "But that's what it feels like."

"Oh no, it's the same for me. That's why I'm a little worried about next year."

I turn my head quick enough to catch the frown that wrinkles his forehead as he runs a hand through his chestnut hair. It's the same look I've been seeing on TV today, filled with worry and frustration. But it's the insecurity showering his handsome face that lassos around my heart.

"Oh, please." I roll my eyes at him, and he amusingly tilts his head to lock his gaze with mine.

"What?"

I shake my head as we round the corner of my street. "Don't be. I know that's easy for me to say, but you have an insane talent. That was clear when you still drove for SRT."

He grunts, running his palm over his face. "Don't say that. That decision still haunts me."

I can imagine, because SRT was doing better every season, and it made me wonder why he would leave that for a team that was doing less on the grid. It seemed like a money-driven decision at the time and having the opportunity to get to know him a bit better in the last few hours, it seems out of character for him to leave a team for a better financial deal.

"So you have made some bad decisions. Doesn't mean you're not still talented. Callahan just failed to bring out that talent. But you will be fine. A better team will offer you a contract before the end of the season."

"You really think so?" I stop in front of my house, and he twists his body to face me.

"I know so." And I mean it. I think he's one of the best drivers on the track. In fact, I think that if he gets a better car, he'd win the championship for a second time.

He searches my expression for a moment, his green irises moving back and forth over my face, as if he's looking for the bullshit in my remark.

"Thank you." He finally smiles, and I awkwardly look up at him.

"This is me." I fish my keys from my jacket, my fingers wiggling the metal. A shiver runs down my neck, but I blame the soft breeze that makes my hair dance at the same time, before I decide to kick my doubts away and tell my mind to shut the fuck up.

"You wanna come up?"

7

TRISTAN

"**Y**OU WANNA COME UP?"

Honey-brown eyes find mine, with thick lashes framing the anticipation in her gaze.

Her question constricts my throat, my heart beating loudly in my ears as my pulse speeds up.

I think the answer to that question is clear in the way I keep looking at her, the longing glances I've been giving her all night. She heightens every nerve in my body just by being in the same energy space as I am, and the longer I don't get to touch her, the more excruciating it feels. I didn't expect anything from her just strolling around the streets of Amsterdam, but I can't deny I don't want this night to end.

"Yeah," I manage to croak out.

Her head bobs a little as she swallows, then turns around to open the front door. A blonde strand of her hair swishes under my nose, the fruity notes now cutting off the willpower to not touch her in a way that I've desperately been holding off for the entire night.

When the massive wooden door pops open with a long squeak, narrow stairs appear, and she starts climbing up. I follow behind her while I keep my eyes trained on her jeans.

Her tight, curve-hugging jeans.

Keep it together, Tristan.

I try to focus on the stuffy smell of the stairwell, the paint chips on the wall, and the stains on the carpet that have probably been there since before the second world war. Anything to settle down my shaft from pushing uncomfortably against my jeans. But nothing fucking helps. The higher we climb, the more aware I am of the fact that I'll be walking into her home, a private space where I have the possibility of getting her completely to myself.

The way she's swaying her hips from left to right with each step is freaking torture, and when we finally hit her floor, my hands are twitching to put them on her body and push her against a wall.

Any fucking wall.

I hear her suck in a deep breath when we reach a white door that leads to her apartment. She fumbles with her keys, trying to find the lock way longer than she should, considering she lives here. Her rigid stance tells me she's nervous like I am while she keeps her attention fixed in front of her.

She finally puts the key in the hole, but then she freezes, and I hold my breath.

I ache to place my hands beside her head and cage her in.

Her neck cocks to the side, exposing a bit more skin, and I take a step forward. My chest is only an inch from her spine, our bodies fusing together by chemistry alone, even though we're not fully connected just yet. Like magnets waiting for that final pull.

"I need you to know," she starts with a groggy voice. "I don't—"

I cut her off by pulling her blonde hair completely from her shoulder, revealing her delicate skin as my fingers brush along the frail hairs on the top of it. She's flushed, her pulse throbbing in the vein that's sitting in the crook where her collarbone starts.

The walls feel like they are closing in around me, my eyes unable to look away from her as I dip my mouth toward her bare skin. My breath graces the area below her ear, and I know that whatever resolve I still had, whatever reason I gave myself to not cross that line with this girl, it's gone when a trail of pebbles rises along her nape in response.

"I don't normally do this," she says, her voice gruff like she has a hard time forming words.

"I'm going to kiss you," I announce.

She swallows, then nods before I softly press my lips against her skin. Her gasp is loud, but her moan is louder when I do it again. A sense of victory washes over me, spurred on by the sounds coming from her throat. I keep repeating the move, desperate to find out how many different noises she will make for me.

Her skin tastes sweet, the softness addictive for my every nerve. It's a feeling that makes me high, lifting my mind like it's light as a feather. All I can think of is how I want it to last forever and she's not even naked yet.

"Tristan?"

I hum, continuing to place open-mouthed kisses on the skin that's not covered by her denim jacket.

"One night, right? That's all this is."

There is an insecurity in her voice, like she's still debating if this is the right choice. I don't know. Probably not. But now I need to find out how she would feel when my body is pressed against hers. I need to know how it feels to be inside of her, and dammit, if tonight is all I'm getting, I'll take it with both hands if she lets me.

"I want you, babe," I murmur against her skin. "*Really, really bad.*"

She stays still, and I wonder if I should stop kissing her, but for the life of me, I can't find the will to stop. I can't find the motivation to give her a breather and look into her eyes to see if she really wants this, but I know I have to. I release the air from my lungs, as I square my shoulders with my eyes closed.

"I want you," I repeat, "and if tonight is all we have, then let's make sure we won't forget." I grab her waist and spin her slowly to look at her. Her gaze is peering at my chest, her lips parted. I place a finger under her chin, lifting her eyes to mine, and I hide a satisfied curl of my lips when I see the lazy look in her eyes. Her dark lashes are hooded, and even though I can see she's still nervous, I also see she wants this just as much as I do.

But I need to hear it.

"Tell me you don't want this and I'll go right now. I'll thank you for the best night I've had in a long time, walk down those stairs, and smile tomorrow when I think of you while driving around the track." Her chuckle sounds like music to my ears, and I move my hand to spread my fingers over her freckled cheek, my thumb resting in the corner of her mouth. "But if you do, and you want me to stay. You have to tell me."

Our faces are close enough to feel shallow breaths falling from her parted lips. Her eyes keep searching mine and I wait, hoping, wishing, and fucking praying she won't shut me down.

"I want you." It's barely a whisper, causing my breath to stop.

"What's that?"

"I want you, Tristan Reinhart." She speaks loud and clear this time as a smile plays along the edges of her full lips. "I want you to stay. *Stay.*"

"Thank fuck." I lower my mouth until it's touching hers, and she replies by tucking me closer while she grabs my shirt. The silky touch of her lips has me growling as my hand dives into her hair. I grab the silky strands with enough force to tilt her head, deepening the kiss. My lips open, teasing hers until she gives in. I can feel her tongue slide along mine while my other hand locks around her spine, and we both share a moan at the feeling. At first, our kiss is sweet and searching, thoughtful as we explore each other, each brush of her lips sending shivers of desire rushing through my core, but soon, it turns hungry when her palms slide underneath my shirt, her fingers digging into my back. A mewl vibrates against my throat right before she reaches for my neck, then jumps up to wrap her legs around my hips.

"Goddamn, woman," I groan, just in time to catch her before I slam her back against the door. Her mouth smothers me with a demanding mastery that only raises the urgency inside my jeans.

"My roommate," she huffs, never disconnecting her hungry kisses from mine. Her hands are everywhere. My hair, my neck, my shoulders, my face. Every time she finds a spot, it's there for only a split second, like she can't decide where to settle but, nonetheless, it makes my skin burn from her searing touch.

"She's home." She rolls her hips, and I groan. "We need to be quiet."

"We'll see about that. Open the door." I bite her lip, diving into her neck, then lower my lips to the skin below her ear before I trail them back to her jaw. Her head is resting against the wood, giving me full access to her slender throat while she tries to twist the key.

"Open the door, babe."

"You make it hard to concentrate."

I lift my head, peering into her toffee eyes. With one hand, I hold her up, and the other wraps around her hand on the key, before I push the thing until the door falls open behind her. For a second, I need to rebalance myself, but when I do, I step inside with big strides, my hands cupping the plump cheeks of her ass. She reaches behind me with her lips finding mine again, and two seconds later, I hear the door fall into the lock again.

"Room?"

"Right behind you."

I glance over my shoulder, finding an open door I assume is hers, then stroll us both inside. My eyes roll to the back of my head when I feel her tongue swipe over the crook of my neck, knocking the oxygen from my lungs as I lower her onto the marine-blue duvet. Shielding her body with mine, I grind the bulge she's responsible for against her core, and she replies by lifting her lower body for more.

Her kisses sing through my veins as I continue to rub my groin between her legs. Each time, her small whimpers grow louder and louder until she's gasping for air. My hands trace a path up to her breasts until the lace of her bra touches the tips of my fingers, and I eagerly push them underneath the fabric to find her hard nipples. The hard-as-rock nubs make me disconnect our lips as I reach for the hem of her shirt, then pull it from over her head and throw it through the room before doing the same with my own. The ferocious hunger in her eyes keeps me fixated while she arches her back to undo her bra, letting it fall beside her.

I gasp when I admire her breasts, speaking to me like they should be worshiped with kisses and sensitive touches. They are divine, but taste like sin, when I lower my mouth and swirl my tongue around them. Her head falls back, her eyes closed when I take the nub in my mouth, roughly sucking it before I do the same with the other one. My free hands massage the soft flesh that sits perfectly in my palm as she curls against my body.

The sweet skin I keep tasting on my tongue has me wanting more, and I crawl down her body until my feet reach the ground. With our eyes connected by an invisible chord, she lies spread out on the bed, awaiting my next move.

I feel like I've been waiting for this my whole life without knowing I needed it. She's everything I didn't expect to find this weekend, but fuck me, she's all I want.

She's perfect.

I stay fixated on her, taking off my shoes, then my socks, before my toes hit the soft fabric of her bedroom floor. Her chest slowly moves up and down, a lustful expression on her face that I know will forever be imprinted in my brain. A sight I'd want to photograph and frame in case I'll never see her again after tonight, but the thought alone makes me quickly decide that's not going to happen. I can already feel in every bone keeping me on my feet that one night with her is not enough. I need more than just a few hours.

I lift one of her legs, taking off her white Converse sneaker before it falls to the floor with a thud, then do the same with the other. Slowly, I pull her socks from her feet, pressing a soft kiss to each heel, then I lower my chest again. My face lands between her legs with a mischievous grin as I lick my lips while reaching for the hem of her jeans. The fabric is taunting me, being the barrier between us, and it takes all my patience to not tear them apart.

With ease, I roll them down her body, until they reach her ankles, dropping them to the floor after one tug. My palm encloses her ankle, widening her eyes as she bites her lip. A shriek echoes through the room when I yank her core toward the edge of the bed, her legs falling to the floor.

I spread my fingers on each knee, then drag them up, placing kisses when I reach the inside of her thighs. She huffs in the air, fueling my desire. My nose brushes against the sky-blue lace that's covering her sweet pussy, and I suck in a deep breath.

The sultry scent shuts my eyes for a second.

"You smell so good," I whine, then trail a finger along the ridges of her thong before I rub it over the core of the fabric. The dampness hits the tip of my finger, and I silently slam my own chest at the effect I seem to have on her. "You're wet for me, aren't you?"

She dips her chin to her chest, getting up on her elbows. The expression she's shooting me is taunting and so goddamn sexy, it's not even funny. She brings a hand to her thong, lowering the fabric from her hips until it reaches her knees and she can push the rest of it down with her toes.

"How about you find out?" She licks her lips and, for a moment, I feel like the world around me freezes. Everything stops. Nothing else matters but the girl in front of me. She's like an enigma I didn't know I was looking to unravel. A desire I didn't know I felt, and I'm not sure I can ever go without. The perfect combination between a porn star and the girl you bring home to your parents.

"Where the fuck have you been all my life?"

I pull my lip between my teeth, glancing at her glistening cunt that's waiting for me as she spreads her legs even wider. Without another word, I lower to my knees, then push my palms underneath her ass while I gaze down at her. The flesh of her folds is tempting me to feast, like the snake tempting Eve with the apple. It will probably get me in trouble, already knowing I'm going to want more after tonight, but I'm more than willing to take the risk.

But as much as I'm dying to tear her apart in the most sensual way, I also want to savor this moment. To treat her like the goddess she is.

I close my eyes, connecting my lips to her core, then softly push my tongue against her flesh. Tiny moans come from her throat as I kiss every inch with affection, my mouth opening more with each touch before I start licking my way through her slit.

Letting a grunt escape, I suck up the sultry taste with more desperation the more of her moisture coats my tongue. She really does taste like a summer night, warm and comfortable, like coming home after a long day. Her whimpers and moans become more desperate as I swirl my tongue around her clit, nibbling the soft nub with a level of care that's firm but gentle, wanting to build her up. I want the rise to her release to be something she'll never forget, erasing every fuckwit who has been lucky enough to find himself in the same position as I am right now. I eat her up like she's a Sunday dinner, lashing at her sensitive center in no hurry whatsoever.

"Oh, shit," she puffs, writhing underneath my face.

I keep her flush with my mouth, my palms on her ass keeping her locked in place.

"Hmm, I could do this all night." I smile, my breath causing her to shudder with her hips.

"I ain't stopping you, Ace." Her tone is laced with that craving I've been feeling for her since we met, and my pride gets a boost when I lift my gaze and find her smiling at the ceiling. Her pretty brown eyes are closed, but every feature in her expression is relaxed and filled with content.

"You couldn't stop me, babe."

"You don't know—"

I push a finger inside of her, leaving her lost for words, and I chuckle against her sweet, *sweet* pussy, knowing I'm soooo fucking screwed already. Her gasp pushes me to keep going, my lips caressing her clit as I start fucking her with my finger.

"Oh, that feels amazing."

"Yeah? What about this?" I slide another finger inside of her, pumping them both with a steady pace. Her reply is nothing more than a release of air from her lungs and when she lifts her hips to give me better access, I take that as my answer.

"Keep going," she cries. "Please, keep going."

I keep my motions constant, working my way around the sensitive nub before I feel her jerks become more forced. She tries to wiggle herself out of my grip, the sensation almost becoming too much when I look at the frown on her dampened forehead.

"Oh, fuck. It's too much."

"Let go for me, baby. Let me suck you dry."

As if on cue, her quads shake, a high-pitched wail reverberating through the room. There is no way in hell her roommate didn't wake up from that banshee cry, only expanding my grin to my ears.

"Godverdomme," she huffs when her lower body relaxes in my palms, and I get up, looking down at her.

"What's that?" I smile at whatever Dutch just fell from her lips. She blinks at me, as if she's trying to get back to earth, her cheeks painted with a sex afterglow that makes her even more beautiful.

"Nothing." A frantic look forms in her deep brown eyes before she lifts her chest and then wraps her arms around my waist. She gently places a kiss on my throbbing cock, her tongue swirling around its head. My head falls forward at the sudden sensitivity while I grind my teeth together. It's the most gorgeous thing I've ever seen, her Bambi eyes looking up at me while she's French kissing my cock like it's the best thing she's ever tasted. But it's not what I want.

"Lay down, baby."

My cock jumps from her lips with a pop, and I drag her lip down with my thumb to get rid of the pout she's shooting my way.

"I'm on the verge of coming just looking at you. The first time we are doing this, I want to be inside of you."

"The first time?"

A smirk paints my lips. "You and I are far from done after this."

Pushing her to the bed, she crawls up until her head hits the pillow. I slither on top of her, my heat merged against hers when our skin connects, and my lips find hers again.

"Have you ever tasted yourself?" My tongue pushes inside of her while I drag the tip of my cock through her folds.

"Maybe." She winks, then her eyes roll to the back of her head when my tip presses against her clit. Our tongues work together like they are the driving engine for what's happening between our legs. Her nails dig into my biceps every time I circle my cock around her entrance until she breaks her lips loose. Her delicate fingers reach for the drawer of her nightstand, and she quickly pulls a condom out. A possessive part of me hates the conclusion that she probably had guys before me in this bed, but I push my inner caveman back to its crate when she holds it in front of my face.

"I need you inside of me. *Please*."

"Begging." I kiss roughly. "I like it."

I take the condom from her hand before I tear the wrapper with my teeth. She grabs the rubber as soon as it's open and slowly pushes it down my shaft while her eyes meet mine again.

"Fuck me."

Smiling against her mouth, I slide inside of her with ease, her wetness coating my cock like a warm bath after a winter day.

"Oh, damn." My forehead falls against hers, our breaths mixing while I cup her cheek, then start pumping inside of her. My hips thrust forward, our bodies integrated as one and, for a minute, it feels like my soul is leaving my body while I stare into her eyes. The world around me vanishes, and all I see are her amber eyes shining at me as if they own me. The gold specks that dance around her irises hypnotize me more with each move I make, wondering how she finds nerves in my body I never knew existed. Like she's spelled me, causing my entire nervous system to run on overtime, but it's my heart that's getting me confused as fuck.

My pulse is high from the exertion of each pump, but I'm hyper aware of the electric jolt that surges through my bones as I keep going while a flutter takes control of my entire stomach. My mind floods, unable to make sense of it all.

I'm hooked, terrified of the consequences, but addicted from the first taste.

"You feel amazing," I confess, my lashes squinting. "You feel like you're made for me."

No other woman has felt this good underneath me, and part of me wants to know if it's the same for her. If her mind is blown like mine is, reaching for the stars right now.

She arches her back, curling even deeper into me, and I can feel how her abdomen grinds against mine.

"Oh, fuck. I think you're right." Her eyes widen, telling me I've found the perfect angle, and I keep sinking in and out of her tight pussy. "That's it. Don't stop. I'm close. *Soo close.*" The last two words come out with a shriek, and I pick up speed, chasing my own surrender while making sure I never change the angle I have her in.

Her walls gradually tighten around me, milking my cock like a pro.

"I need you to come, baby."

"Almost," she cries. "I'm almost there."

I pump three more times and she shatters in my hands, her body shuddering underneath me while her pussy clenches around my cock. She screams a *"fuck"* that's loud enough to wake up the neighbors, and if there was any doubt her roommate heard us, there sure as hell isn't any now.

I grab her hips when her legs fall to the side as she rides out her orgasm, then I use the lazy look on her face to hunt down my own liberation. I focus on her pretty features, her eyes willing me to take advantage of her. With a few more thrusts, my ejaculation floods through me. A tsunami of pleasure drags me under in a way I've never experienced before, and every feature of my face tenses as I continue until the last drop is shot inside the condom.

Panting, I look down at the rare gorgeousness below me. She bites her lip, her eyes glazed like she's high on something as strong as I am. I lick my lips, enjoying the after-rush that still fogs my mind, ready to admit that I'm high on her. She's like a drug I never knew I needed, and I'm already anxious about my next fix.

"What?" I smirk when she keeps staring at me. I reach for a tissue on the nightstand to dispose of the condom, and then slide out of her, dropping my body on top of hers as I rest my head on her shoulder. Her chest is heaving as much as mine as we try to catch our breath.

"I think—"

"Nikkie!" A loud bonk hits the wall above the headboard and her eyebrows shoot up while her hand covers her mouth with a glint in her gaze.

"Ja?" she replies, carefully.

"Shut the fuck up!"

"Sorry!" she yells back, before we both snort, our shoulders shaking from laughter.

"I guess your roommate is up."

"It's all your fault!" she scolds.

"My fault? You're the one screaming like a peacock in heat."

She pulls a face. "How do you know what a peacock in heat sounds like?"

"We have peacocks on the ranch I grew up on."

"And I sound like a peacock?" she asks, unimpressed. My finger trails up and down her hip, enjoying the warmth she radiates against me.

"Hmm, a really pretty one, though."

Her eyes narrow, sporting a dirty look that doesn't quite hold up.

"You need to be punished."

"For what?" I chuckle. "Calling you a peacock?"

"Fuck yeah!" Her hand is pushed against my groin, and I hiss, shutting my eyes, my palm still stroking every swell of her body. "And for waking up my roommate."

"That was all you, baby."

"Still your fault." The playfulness is audible in her voice as I enjoy her soft touch on my balls as she easily stirs my cock back to a firmness. Ready to go like a well-behaved soldier.

"You'll piss her off even more if you keep going."

I sense her mouth moving closer to mine before she wraps a leg around my waist and I tuck her against my chest. Circling my arm around her spine, I open my eyes.

Her golden browns are flushed with desire. "I guess you just have to silence me with something."

My dark brows move to my hairline at that, but I barely get any time to process before she crawls down as she licks her lips.

"What are you doing?"

She settles her face between my legs, glancing at my cock like it's a five-course meal, then lifts her lashes to me. "Making *you* scream like a peacock."

That's it.

I'm fucked.

8

NIKKIE

E VERY INCH OF MY body feels like it's glowing in eternal bliss, my inner
self purring like a kitten in a big box filled with fluffy feathers. I think if
I'd have to describe heaven, it would be feeling like this all the fucking time.

I've drifted off after the second round, waking up with my head resting on
his shoulder, his arm around my waist, keeping my ass and back firmly pressed
against the side of his body. My hands are curled around his bicep, as if it's my
goddamn teddy bear.

Fucking hell, that was amazing.

The sharp tension in the air was loaded like a bazooka when we walked up the
stairs, but the moment he flicked my blonde hair away to find my neck, I knew
I was done for.

He quickly found his way around my body, like he does with a racetrack,
hitting every corner in the right spots and with a steady pace.

I gave myself the silent peptalk that I shouldn't sleep with him, that I would
probably just be another name for him to add to the list. That he'd walk out
of my front door before the sun was high in the sky, doing the walk of shame
without any shame at all, for that matter.

But the second his lips touched the back of my neck, I couldn't give a flying fuck. If he wants to use me? He can use me in all the shades of fucked up he wants. If I never see him after today, I can live on this memory forever, giving me an infinity of butterflies just by thinking about it. He was everything I didn't expect him to be, the perfect amount of affection and fucking me hard and rough. His touch settled a hunger I didn't know I possessed.

I spin in his arms, tilting my head to search his face. His breath has evened out, chest steadily moving up and down.

I glance at the nightstand, checking the time.

03.30.

A hum slips into my ear as he announces his awareness, tucking me closer against his torso, and I catch his satisfied smile.

"Tristan, you fell asleep," I whisper.

He squints an eye open at me. "What time is it?"

"Way past your bedtime, Ace," I joke, repeating my words from earlier.

"It was worth it." The beating organ in my chest swells, and I try my best to ignore it by shoving it away.

"You might think differently while you're speeding around that track later today."

His pleased smile deflates, his head falling my way. The worry in his eyes grips my soul harder than it should, considering I've known him for five hours, but I can't help but feel sad that his light is dimmed. That something fucked with his head so badly, he now has forgotten about the level of talent and commitment that got him into Formula One in the first place.

He rubs his hand over his face, and I know it's not my place, not to mention there's probably zero chance he'll believe me, but I can't watch this in silence.

"Hey. Look at me." I sit up and take his face in my hands. "You got this." His frown pisses me off, but it roars my anger alive as well. "Don't give me that look. You are one of the best drivers out there. You've done amazing with a mediocre car." Callahan is a good team, but it's not the best there is. There is a reason it's best of the rest and from what they've shared in the media in the last few years, they brought Tristan to change that. To help them compete for the world championship. They wanted his experience and expertise to help them develop the car further and further until they were right there at the top, like they were thirty years ago. They might have chosen a different path now, but they can't deny his talent, since that's the same thing they signed him for in the first place.

"You can win this," I add. "All you have to do is believe in the possibilities." Thinking back on how I've been living my life for the past year, I sound like a hypocrite, but my ostrich syndrome is well developed.

He holds my gaze for a few beats, then conjures a tiny smile. "Just like that, huh?"

I sink my lips against his, trying to tell him by showing him. The faith I have in him isn't a lie, and I want him to feel it. His arms snake around my back, locking my body tight against his as he curls into me.

"If you don't believe in yourself," I whisper onto his lips while I rub the tips of my fingers through the stubble on his jaw, "believe *me*. You can win this. I know you can."

"You really believe that?"

"It's a given, Tristan. Who cares if they don't believe in you? All that matters is that *you* believe. You can win this." I'm sure he didn't become a world champion because everyone believed in him and carried him to this point in his career. I'm sure there have been plenty of people who wanted to see him fail and crash to the ground. But he kept going. He might not be on top now, but he's been there once. He knows the road to get there. He can do it again.

"I can win this." He nods, and I smile at the self-assured sparkle in his gaze.

"Yeah. You really can."

He replies by crushing my mouth in a bruising kiss, and an overwhelming emotion that I can't place almost pulls me under, causing goosebumps to trail up my neck. *What the fuck?*

"I just really don't want to leave," he huffs against my lips while I try to catch my breath.

I want him to stay, desperately. I long to wake in his arms when the sun comes up, and I want to drink coffee with him when our hair is still messy and our eyes still sleepy. But I don't want to set any expectations, convinced I'll probably come out disappointed.

"You can stay, but I don't think your boss will be amused if he finds out you weren't safe and sound in your motorhome last night."

"I know." He chuckles, giving me another expression that makes my toes curl. He keeps staring at me like I mean the world to him, and he reminds me of better times. It makes me long to keep him close and hope he will keep looking at me like I matter, wishing I meant something to him. Or anybody again, like I used to.

His grin expands as he brushes his palm up and down my upper arms. "I should go."

"Yeah, probably."

I get another peck before he gets up from the bed and starts collecting his clothes.

"Nice room." He glances around, and I follow his gaze.

My walls are navy blue, with white cheap-ass Ikea furniture and some soft pink accessories, like candles and pots with plants. My closet is nothing more than a rack with hangers sitting on the left side of the bed, most of it filled with different types of denim jackets and tops. Below is a row of sneakers, *my classics,* I call them. There's Converse, Adidas Superstar, Nikes. All white, other than the occasional accent in color or print. It's small and crowded, but it's mine.

"Thank you." I push a lock of hair behind my ear, suddenly feeling really exposed as he puts on his boxers and jeans.

"Don't get shy on me now, babe." He smiles.

I get out of the bed, and pull an oversized white hoodie from the rack, then drag it over my head. "I'm not."

When my head pops out, he covers his perfectly chiseled chest with his t-shirt and takes a few steps to get into my space.

"You did. But it's cute." His hand holds my chin before he lifts it to find my lips. The moment they are linked with his, my toes curl, fueling the craving that's growing all over again at the unnecessary move. When we disconnect, he cocks his head and winces a little.

"Do you have neck pain?"

He hums, rubbing his nape with his eyes closed before they fly back to me with a sheepish grin. "I strained it a bit when I got out of the cab with the energy of a raging bull."

"Come here, let me." I motion him to turn around, then knead his muscle between my fingers. "This one?"

"Fuck," he hisses, trying his best to stay still. "Damn, woman. You've got fingers of steel."

"Told you, physical therapy. My fingers are trained."

"No shit."

He relaxes under my touch, taking deep breaths as I continue to massage the tissue with my hands. His neck arches more with every movement until I detect a smirk lifting his lips.

"Is it working?" I ask.

"Oh, it's working. But if you're hellbent on getting me in that car with at least a little bit of sleep, you might want to stop before I haul you back to your bed."

I snicker. "Come on, I'm sure you have some restraint." But my hands drop when he twists his green eyes to mine, swirling with an intensity that sucks the air from my lungs.

"Not when it comes to you." Lost for words, I'm glad he takes away my discomfort at finding a reply by giving me a soft kiss. "Walk me out?"

I hum in agreement, then he takes my hand and leads me out of the room. The moonlight is shining through the dark living room as we walk out my bedroom door, creating a path that illuminates the front door.

"Morning." I jump in the air, my heart almost dropping to the floor at the sudden voice, before the light in the kitchen flips on.

"Gee, Tess." I hold my heart with one hand while the other is still woven with Tristan's. "Why are you up at four in the morning?"

Her narrowed eyes lose the fake relaxation that was sitting on her face, her brown hair up, bringing out her sharp cheekbones and fire now evident in her glare. She takes a sip of the water in her hand. "Excuse me? What am I doing up? Well, I don't know, *bestie*. Maybe my roommate decided to take a guy home and fuck him until I couldn't escape her pleas anymore. You are on my shitlist, missy"—she points an accusing finger at me, then swings it to Tristan—"and so are you." She stands still, her finger hanging in the air. "What the fuck?" Her jaw drops to the floor, and I fold my lips between my teeth to stop my grin from slipping out.

"You're Tristan Reinhart."

"Hey." He waves at her, flashing her his teeth.

"Nikkie, why is there an F1 driver standing in our kitchen?"

"He's leaving."

"He's leaving?" She wags her head, as if this is no big deal, then shrugs sarcastically. "Oh, okay. Cool."

I push Tristan toward the front door, ignoring the awkwardness that fills the room. Tessa's eyes are burning through my back, and I don't have to look behind me to know she's got her eyebrow cocked, all expressive and annoying as always. When I open the door, Tristan rapidly spins, taking me into his arms like I belong there, and I swear my heart melts as I'm caught in his embrace.

"You're amazing." I hear Tessa gasp as he smiles against my lips.

"You're not so bad yourself, Ace." The kiss that follows settles deep into my bones, all my senses making a mental memory when I think of the possibility that I will never see him again. That I've simply been his fun time in Amsterdam. The chance of it being anything else is pretty much zero, and even though I accepted that before I invited him up, there is still a big part of me that is far from done with this man and it has nothing to do with the public figure that he is. My heart wants to find the man behind the smile and is fascinated by the way he dances through life, wondering if maybe that could be me. A life that doesn't feel so dark and cloudy all the time. "Go score some points."

"I will. For you." I get another longing touch of his lips, before he breaks our connection, taking a step back. "But just so you know? *This*"—he waves his finger between the two of us—"is far from over, babe." A boyish grin travels his face, followed by a wink that makes my sore pussy silently beg him to get back inside, but my ability to speak has left the building.

I just stand there, gaping, trying to not take his words as seriously as I want to.

"I'll see you."

"Bye, Ace." With my teeth in my lip and my cheek pressed against the edge of the door, I watch him walk down the stairs, then slowly close it until it falls into the lock.

I suck in a lungful of air, bracing myself for what's coming.

"I don't have any words," Tessa muses before I have fully twisted my body to her.

"Neither do I." I chuckle at the shocked expression of my best friend.

"What the motherfucking hell, Nik? You slept with Tristan Reinhart?"

"I thought you had no words?"

"Oh, I got words now!" She takes a step forward, her hands up in her hair. "How?! And how?! And how about, what the motherfucking *how*?"

"I don't know, okay!" My grin is wide, but the weirdness of the situation is clear as Tessa tries to wrap around it.

"He's the one who made you scream like you were fucked straight into heaven."

"Yup." I tuck a strand of my hair behind my ear. "You still mad?"

She waves her hand, moving to the fridge and taking out a bottle of wine. "Oh no, girlfriend, all is forgiven."

"What are you doing?"

"Pouring us some wine." She points to the couch. "You, sit."

"Tess, it's late," I argue. "We should go to bed." In reality, I don't know what to make of this and how I feel about it other than I'm sore as hell. I hope to convince myself that this night means something, at least until I wake up tomorrow morning and Tess will probably knock me off my cloud real quick. But the look in her eyes tells me she won't let me off the hook.

"What you *should* be doing right now"—she pulls a face—"is working, but unless you got a sugar daddy in the form of an F1 driver all of a sudden, you clearly are not doing *that*. So, sit down." She takes the two glasses of wine from the counter, and I clear my throat at the accuracy of her words. "You're going to tell me *everything*."

9

TRISTAN

MY FOOT BOUNCES AGAINST the concrete of the track as I sit before the garage with my dark blue headphones on. I smiled when I put them on ten minutes ago, reminding me of the walls in Nikkie's bedroom. My ass is plastered on the ground, my arms resting on my knees, my head resting against the wall of the building. Chris Stapleton's "Starting Over" blasts through my ear louder than is probably good for me, but I couldn't give a damn as I'm drifting off in a peaceful state. The sun is warming my cheeks, that are becoming sore from the grin that hasn't left my face since I woke up this morning.

I barely slept for three hours before my PA was knocking on the motorhome, telling me to wake the hell up, because I was late for the briefing, but nothing can knock me off cloud nine. Not even Will's resentful glare this morning, nor the questions at the press conference an hour ago, that was more about my replacement than my chances of winning the race today. *Again.*

I don't care, because the front of my mind is fully consumed by the face of a pretty Dutch girl, her smile infectious. Within just one night, she managed to get rid of my boiling anger, replacing it with the feeling of flying. I'm the one driving a racecar for a living, but she has quickly become a superstar in my eyes.

My head bobs with the melody as I let my mind float back to last night, trying to get into a comfortable state before it's time to get to work and meet for some final briefings with my engineers. Her room reminded me of an oasis, bringing me more peace of mind than my own bedroom has lately. There were blue and pink candles all over her room matching the dark blue walls, and even though they weren't lit, I could see myself lying there all day if she'd let me.

I never expected the night to end the way it did, although I would be lying if I told you I wasn't hoping for it. But the biggest mind-fuck was the feelings she evokes in me. It's like she found a whole new bucket of emotions, messing with my mind in the best way. The memory of her body glued to mine, my cock sliding in and out of her as I looked into her eyes reminding me of a pot of liquid gold, is more than enough to keep my cheery mood unbreakable. And now, ten hours later, I'm even starting to get addicted to the flutter that keeps surging through my stomach, over and over again, even without her near me.

And her laugh...it's the most incredible sound I've ever heard.

She did something to me. I know myself well enough to admit that, and I'm not planning to let that go any time soon.

Fuck the logistics, but this isn't a story that begins and ends on the same night.

I refuse to let it be.

"What the fuck are you so happy about?" My headphones get knocked off my head, falling to my neck before someone blocks my rays of sunshine.

I squint my eyes, finding Sam's blue-green gaze staring back at me, wearing a blue and orange SRT polo. His blond hair sits sloppily on his head, the strands glistening in the sun as he shows me a wide grin.

"The sun is shining. It's race day. What's not to be happy about?"

He lowers his body to come to sit beside me, his gaze searching me with suspicion.

"You and sunshine," he mutters. "What did you do?"

"Nothing."

"Don't bullshit me."

"I'm just positive. I'm always positive."

He grunts. "I know that. It's damn annoying. But considering you were strolling around the paddock looking like Growly Pete all week, this"—his finger circles my face—"is scary. Even for you."

"I wasn't Growly Pete," I sputter.

"Excuse me? I actually told Benjamin to follow you around everywhere before you were going to bite anyone's head off with that grimace you plastered on your face. And you know I don't talk to Benji if I don't have to."

"I got sacked, Sam." I'm happy because the words don't evoke the set of negative emotions like they did yesterday.

"I know!" His head flinches back an inch. "That's why I'm not sure why you're smiling like you woke up to a new job offer. *Holy shit!*" He slaps my shoulder with wide eyes. "Did you get an offer already?"

"No." I chuckle, and he disappointingly settles his back against the garage again.

"Then what?"

I roll my lips with mischief. "I snuck out yesterday."

His face falls flat. "Shut up."

I nod.

"Without me?" The indignance is clear on his pretty boy face, and I laugh.

"Sorry, mate. It was a heat of the moment kind of thing."

"You, dick. So, where did you go?"

"I dragged Axel and Calvin to the city with me."

"You chose them as your babysitters?"

"Oh, totally."

"Fuck," he argues. "I would've been an amazing babysitter, T. Why would you exclude me on that?"

"You'd be a shit babysitter because you'd get us wasted as fuck and you draw way too much attention with your pretty boy face."

"True, true. Not on a race weekend, though."

He impatiently wags his head to support his comment, and I stay quiet for a moment.

"I met a girl."

"You met—you dirty dog! You didn't bring me to this unplanned night out *and* you hooked up?"

"It wasn't like that. She was cool. She actually scolded me for not being in bed when I should've been."

"What?" He jerks his head back in shock. "She didn't."

"She totally did."

"Sounds like trouble—and fun," Sam says, a little impressed. "I'm guessing the night went well?"

My PA, Benjamin, walks out of the garage, looking down at both of us with a little contempt, but I'm used to it after two years. He's a grumpy son of a bitch when he's stressed, but he's a damn good assistant, so I've learned to live with it.

"Oh, look, it's *Growly Ben*." Sam isn't a fan. Never has been and probably never will be. He keeps telling me to find a nice girl, one who doesn't look like she's got a stick up her ass the entire time, but Benjamin does his job, so I've been sticking with him for the last two years.

"Tristan, we need you for a meet and greet."

"Yeah, okay." I get up, brushing a bit of sand from my ass, then glance down at my friend. "I'll tell you the rest tonight. I can fly with you, yeah?"

"Sure thing."

I mock salute him, then follow behind Ben with a never-faltering grin.

"Wait, T." When I turn around to the sound of his voice, he gets up and gives me a smirk with a nudge of his chin. "How good?"

I think about it for a heartbeat, looking for the right words, but I soon realize there is only one way to describe it. "Best fucking night of my life, mate."

10

NIKKIE

AFTER LIGHTING MY TRAY of ocean breeze scented candles, I suck in a deep breath, the fresh sultry notes calming my senses before I flop onto the couch.

"I got some cheese, sausage, and some bread with different kinds of spreads.'" Tessa unpacks the groceries as she basically lists a Dutch plate of antipasti that she bought for the race. "Any updates?"

"Nothing much, just Andrea Rossi talking about the cars. Jackson Banks is starting at the back. Arzano got him a new engine."

"Oh, that would give Callahan a better chance."

"Definitely," I mutter when my phone starts to hum with a private number. I stare at the device, slowly vibrating its way down the table while I feel my pulse quickening with every second that passes.

I haven't had a call in two weeks, and I knew this day was coming like it has been for a year. Every few weeks, she's stalking me until I answer that phone and give her what she wants. The first time it happened, I told myself it would pass. But it didn't. Then a few months ago, I told myself I should tell her to stop. But I didn't. I expected by now, the guilt would've simmered down to something bearable, and I would feel brave enough to stand up for myself. But my bravery never came, swallowed whole by the bucket load of guilt I'm carrying with me like a parasite. And here I am once more. Peering at my phone like it can explode any second if I don't answer it.

Tessa gives me a side glance. "You're not going to get that?"

I swallow, trying to get rid of the lump in my throat. "Uh, yeah."

With a tingle in my fingers, I swipe the thing off the table, then suck in a deep breath as I answer.

"Hello?"

"Hey." I frown at the unfamiliar voice.

"Who is this?"

"You already forgot about me?" The panic that crept up on me is quickly replaced with a long exhale. *Thank fuck,* it's not who I thought it was. But then my eyebrows squish together when I link the voice with the face I spent my night with and a crate of butterflies is released inside my stomach.

"Tristan?"

"Oh, so you *do* remember me," he snickers.

I couldn't forget if I wanted to, because I'm sure every single thing about Tristan Reinhart's chiseled body in my bedroom will be a memory that's tattooed on my brain forever... and possibly a little piece of my heart as well.

"How did you get my number?"

"Put my number into your phone when you were asleep. Then I called myself."

I tilt my head at the easy confession, running my tongue along my teeth. "How did you unlock it?"

"Face ID."

A shriek erupts from my chest. "That's creepy. Should I be worried?"

"Nah, you're safe, babe." *Babe.* It's probably a nickname he uses for plenty of women, but I swear every time he calls me babe, it makes me giddy like a little schoolgirl, wanting him to pull my pigtails and play a game of *miss tease, kiss please.*

"Soo," I drawl when the line goes silent.

"Soo..."

"Why are you calling?" My insecurity is trying to convince me he forgot something important last night. Or that he wants me to sign something practical like an NDA. Anything to not convince myself he meant what he said when he said we weren't over just yet.

Because that would be ridiculous, right?

"You sound disappointed."

"I'm not!" I clarify with a high-pitched voice. "Definitely not. Surprised, that's all. Didn't expect you to call me."

"I told you this wasn't over."

"I know you did, Ace. Doesn't mean I believe you."

His chuckle seems genuine, as if he can't blame me for not expecting anything from him.

"I get that, babe. But I'm not Sam. I don't fuck and duck."

"Shut up, asshole," I hear someone I'm assuming is Sam call out in the background.

"Sam? As in Sam Devereaux? SRT's first driver? Future world champion?"

"Oh, damn. You're not going all star-struck on my friend now, are you?"

"Nah, I'm pretty hung up on this Australian guy at the moment."

"At the moment?" he huffs.

"Don't worry." I laugh at his jealous tone. "I don't have a thing for Sam Devereaux."

"Good to know." I smile into the air, the butterflies creating little shudders down my back. "Are you sure you don't want to come to the race? I can have someone pick you up."

I prevent my jaw from falling to the floor at his offer, not sure what to do with it. My heart is jumping for joy at the assumption that must mean that he really wants to see me again, but my mind quickly knocks her down with the obvious defense. He will be flying to another country tonight. Whatever he claims, this was just for one night, right?

"Missing me already, Ace?" I joke.

"Actually, I do." I can hear a smile in his voice, but there is no teasing in his tone like in mine, and the air is sucked from my lungs when I understand he's serious. It's extremely cute, as much as it terrifies the shit out of me.

"Thank you, but I promised to watch the race with Tessa."

He sighs, and I'm expecting him to push a little more, assuming he's used to getting his way.

"Is she still mad at me?"

I glance at Tessa, her narrowed gaze lasering through me since the moment she realized who was talking on the other line. Her lips are pursed, adding to her smug expression while her arms are crossed in front of her body. "Nah, she forgave you."

"So you'll definitely be watching?" he asks, carefully.

"What kind of question is that?"

"I don't know, maybe you are too tired to watch. We've been up all night, after all." My lips curl at the mischief in his voice.

"And miss you win? Not a chance," I counter. I've never missed a race in my life, and I'm not going to start now. Especially not after the night I had.

"You still think I can win?"

I think about his question, not wanting to lie to him, but there's a gut feeling in my bones that tells me I don't have to. "Yeah, I do."

"Shit, I gotta go." Murmuring sounds in the background. "I'll talk to you later, okay?"

"Wait, Tris?"

"Yeah?"

I gather my nerves and find the words I have a feeling he can use. Part of me thinks I'm silly for thinking whatever I say will have any significance, but I'm still compelled to speak them out loud anyway. To build his confidence. If it can only give him one percent of an extra boost, it's already worth it.

"You got this."

He's quiet, as if he's letting it sink in. "Thanks, babe." There's a relief in his tone that warms my chest before he ends the call.

I hold my phone clenched in my hand, still staring at the screen. A picture of Wes and I stares back at me, and for a moment, the air evaporates from my lungs. The lighthearted feeling and butterflies are flipped by a lump in my throat and the weight of an elephant on my chest. His amber brown eyes stare back at me with a comfort that now feels like a lie, even though they've been keeping me up and going for the last year. We're both smiling, as he holds me up in the air with my legs around his bare waist. His black hair is still wet from our swim, a blush pink bikini bringing out my sun-kissed skin.

We had it all figured out.

Until we didn't.

With a frown to keep my eyes from releasing my tears, I suck in a deep breath. I need to stop torturing myself. The smell of my scented candles suddenly suffocates me, wrapping me into a dark blanket that feels heavier than normal. Without thinking twice, I lean forward, blowing out the entire tray, then settle back into the couch as I watch the smoke drizzle into the air.

I ignore Tessa's voice in the background and completely merge into my bubble. I head to the settings of my phone, then swap the picture for one of Tessa and me. It hurts, guilt trying to tighten the balloon around me, but the lightness that it brings is sharper this time, and when I exhale, I burst it the moment my eyes find Tessa's.

"Are you okay?"

I nod. "Yeah, I'm good."

I mean it. For the first time in forever. I'm not lying to myself when I tell everyone else *I'm okay.*

"That was him, wasn't it?"

"It was, yeah."

She places the wooden plank with snacks on the table, then curls up on the other side of the couch before popping a cube of cheese in her mouth.

"I can't believe you're hooking up with Tristan *fucking* Reinhart."

"We're not *hooking* up. We *hooked* up. Once. It will probably be a funny story I tell my grandchildren one day."

"You mean his grandchildren?"

We both laugh, and I shove her shoulder. "Shut up."

She holds my gaze with a playful smile, her lips pressed together as she assesses me with her arm resting over the back of the couch.

"What?"

"Nothing. I just haven't seen you smile since–well, since that day."

"What are you talking about?" I scoff. "I've smiled. We laugh all the time."

"We do, yeah. But this is the first time you smile with your eyes." I swallow as she keeps her eyes locked with mine. "He did that."

"He didn't do that," I mutter, averting my attention to the TV at the same time Tristan is shown walking to his car with his teeth flashed at the camera, and out of my control, I feel myself smiling.

"See!" She slaps my leg. "He's totally doing that!"

With a guilty expression, I roll my eyes, then reluctantly admit what she's accusing me of.

"Okay, maybe he does." My voice quickly rises again. "But that doesn't mean a thing! We hooked up, yes, and it was amazing. But I'm pretty sure he's too busy for anything more than what this was. *A hookup.*"

She licks her soft pink lips with a cocky look. "He just called you, didn't he?"

I hum.

"And he said last night you two weren't done yet."

"Yeah, so?"

"So, I wouldn't be so sure, Nik. If you were a one-time thing, why would he still call you? He surprised you by following you into the bar in the first place. He might surprise you again."

I rear my head back to the TV, just in time to catch Tristan's eyes before they disappear into his helmet. One single glance of his green eyes is enough for me to feel my thighs clench, remembering how good it felt when his mouth was between my legs.

My mind is trying to keep myself from getting sidetracked by the truth, but I have to admit, I really, really hope she's right. But doing the sensible thing, I shove the feeling away as we follow the preview of the race until all drivers get into their cars and the track is cleared to start the race.

I'm on the edge of the couch when the formation lap has passed, and each driver takes their position on the grid. Red lights indicate the start of the race when the marshal waves the green flag behind the lined-up cars until the final light turns off and they are on their way. My fingers tingle more than usual, and my pulse fluctuates in the crook of my neck as I hold my breath with tense shoulders, feeling more invested than ever before.

Both drivers of Barrington and SRT are quickly in a battle for first and second place in the front, but my eyes are set on the white car behind them. Tristan passes the Baker & Baker driver Raul Morena, starting from fifth position, before the first corner, and sparks fly over the track when Nicholas Jones and Franco Garcia end up in a collision.

I grip my heart, hoping Tristan can avoid the two cars as one of them spins on the track, while rubber is sprayed through the air until the other one is driving on nothing more than its rim. Smoke showers the cars that follow, but I release my pent-up breath when Tristan maneuvers past it with an ease that has my heart trotting with pride. He quickly follows the two leading men, Sam Devereaux and Jordan Hastings, as they are in a heated battle for first. Both of them don't want to give up their place, speeding through every corner with urgency and velocity, but also an aggression that's becoming known for these two drivers. The rookie versus the veteran. It's something that has been building more and more with every race and, normally, I'd enjoy these fights in the front of the field, but this time, my eyes stay fixated on the white car behind them, following with finesse.

Tristan looks completely in control, driving the car through each corner like he's waiting for the right time to make his move, and the more the race progresses, the more I feel a hopeful current in my body I don't dare to speak out loud. Fifty-nine laps of seventy-two are done, and Tristan is on a set of fresh tires of the softer compound, starting his last stint of the race. He quickly claims back his track position, driving a faster compound than the drivers he has to overtake after his three second pitstop, until he's only two seconds away from sitting on Jordan's tail. Sam is only half a second quicker than his direct opponent, not giving him any space to attack, even though Jordan is desperately trying to.

"I can't take this," Tessa yelps, biting her nails.

"I know." My eyes stay fixed on the screen, my knee bouncing like a tap dancer. The two men leading the race head into the straight, and Jordan has the pace to put his car next to Sam's as they drive toward the next chicane. The crowd goes nuts as the excitement is audible in the commentator's voice at this twist everyone was waiting for. They both take the turn, wheel to wheel, and for a second, it's like Sam is coming out of it first, but then they make contact and Sam's car spins in the opposite direction.

Our gasps are loud as our eyes widen, but it's the shocked shriek that echoes through the room that has my jaw dropping to the floor. In the action of the two cars colliding, and Sam's losing control over his vehicle, the rear hits Jordan's car with enough force to drive both cars off the track, leaving them wheel-spinning in the gravel.

My heart stops for what feels like forever while I try to process what this means, but when I see Tristan's white car glide past the two on the side of the track, it jolts back to life, and I jump up.

"He's taking the lead! He's taking the lead!" I hop on my toes, clapping like I won the fucking Powerball jackpot.

"AAH!" Tessa follows my move and we both jerk up and down like damn bunnies as our eyes never deviate from the TV. The crowd goes completely crazy and even the commentator is laughing his ass off. Tristan's track position is confirmed over the team radio and the "let's do this!" he buzzes back has me smiling from ear to ear.

"He's going to win this, isn't he?" Tessa asks when there's only two laps left.

I don't want to jinx it, but the hopeful feeling has grown as big as a skippy ball with each lap that passes by. I can't stop the nodding of my head. "Yeah. He is."

"Holy shit, Nik."

"I know."

A mist forms in my eyes, the happiness I feel for him indescribable. You don't have to have spent the night with him, like I did, to know this win is significant for him. It's the confidence boost that he needs after his team kicked him to the curb so brutally, and I'm pretty sure every Formula One fan is rooting for him right now, no matter what team you support.

"He's gonna win," I chant to myself, over and over again.

Goosebumps trail up all the brittle hairs on my skin as I feel the adrenaline build when the final lap is announced. Brief shots of Jordan and Sam pissed at each other interrupt Tristan's perfect driving skills, but when he hits the second last corner, the commentator's tone is building the anticipation more and more with every word. I hold my breath, my arms up in the air, knowing this victory is in the bag. I see the final shot, the finish line in sight, a checkered flag in the corner of the screen as he drives up to the end of this round, and the commentator declares what we've all been waiting for.

"Callahan decided to terminate his contract, but Tristan Reinhart shows them what they are letting go. Tristan Reinhart wins the Dutch Grand Prix!"

And then I scream. We scream. We jump. We bounce. We dance. We're standing on the table. Pride keeps my teeth flashing, while moisture pools at the corners of my eyes.

He won.

He fucking won.

With butterflies moving rapidly through my stomach, I've been following the entire after show of the race, hoping to find a glimpse of Tristan while Tessa left to have dinner with some study mates. My pulse pounded in my ears when he placed himself in front of the camera to do his rounds of press with that captivating grin tightly on his full lips. I suck in a deep breath as I remember how they felt on my body, my neck instantly glowing with heat by the thought alone. He's gracious as ever, not addressing the issues he's been having with his team, but instead, he professionally rears every reporter back to the more important matter of today: *he won the fucking race.*

I think it's insane to have feelings for someone after one night, but the longer I look at him, especially through the anonymity of the TV, there is no denying that he does more to me than I expected. I wonder if it's because he's a public figure, maybe causing me to feel more intimidated by him, but every time I travel back to that answer, there's a voice in my head that's telling me it's *bullshit.*

I've been a Formula One fan since I was eight, so Tristan's career has been easy to follow, like every other guy on the grid right now. And I've seen his infectious smile more than once. Never did he cause me to feel a flutter before that flash of teeth was aimed directly at me in the middle of the street. Never did I have a fascination with the F1 driver until he gave me a glimpse of the man behind the driver, and not once did I look at him thinking I'd use my hall pass on him until his mesmerizing gaze was peering through my body and making my heart stop.

But last night changed the way I look at him, and now I've been staring at my phone for the last two hours, contemplating if I should send him a text. I filled my hunger with the leftover snacks, not feeling in the mood to eat a proper meal as I try to keep my anxiety in check. I don't want to think about the possibility that I might never see him after tonight, but my fear keeps me from reaching out.

Numerous times I've typed out the words, only for me to delete that as soon as my insecurity kicked in, telling me it was too desperate, too lame, and too obvious if I'd push send.

Come on, Nik. What's the harm in sending him a text?

Other than the absolute humiliation if he doesn't reply? *Nothing.*

But then I'm reminded of the fact that he called me before the race, and I ask myself how many girls he does that with.

Probably a dozen, Nik.

I really wish I could shut my mind up and tell it to go fuck itself because my heart is just whispering all the reasons in my ear that convince me to just do it.

I blow out a frustrated hot breath when the doorbell rings and I frown when I look at the time.

It's nine o'clock.

On a Sunday evening.

Please don't let it be her.

A little reluctantly, I get up and look through the peephole. My heart jumps from my ribcage with a tiny gasp when I recognize his honey-brown hair. His arm is resting against the post, his head hanging, but I know it's him, and I yank the door open.

I stare at him, and his chin lifts, that boyish grin plastered over his face like it's sculpted there in a permanent position as he looks at me with his hooded eyes.

"Hey," he says, his voice gravelly, yet smooth. I can smell his woody cologne and it's taking everything I have to not drag him into my house and kiss him senseless.

"Hey."

"I won."

"I saw."

"It's because of you."

I resist the urge to snort at his ridiculous assumption, but my spine straightens a tad.

"I didn't do anything."

"You believed in me." There's a gratitude in his deep green eyes that quickly floods my brown eyes that I'm trying my hardest to keep at bay. I haven't seen anyone look at me like that for a long time now, and it's spreading confidence quicker than I've gotten used to after the accident. It's completely unfounded, but I'm taking it right now.

"You believed in yourself."

He shakes his head. "Not for a long time now."

His eyes are glittering against the dim light of the hallway, cutting through me, his gaze intimidating as much as it's exhilarating.

I feel completely clueless about what to do with this situation, not exactly knowing what he's doing here right now, even though deep down, I do. If he just wanted to talk, he could've called. He has my number now. But instead, he's standing here at my front door, four hours after he won the race.

"Shouldn't you be on your way to the next city?" I ask.

"Sam is staying in Amsterdam tonight. I can fly with him tomorrow," he explains, then straightens his body as his gaze turns darker, and I swallow.

"Why?"

He replies by pushing me into the house with the tips of his fingers planted on my stomach, crowding my space as I move backwards until he slams the door shut with his foot. My heart pounds in my throat, parting my lips on a gasp. I let my eyes roam his white t-shirt with a small orange Callahan logo over his heart, standing out against his tanned arms. They look chiseled and broad when he wraps one of his palms around the front of my neck, then pulls me flush with his body as the other lands on my back.

"Because you and I aren't over."

I don't get the chance to reply, because his lips crash against mine, and I eagerly welcome his tongue. The warmth of his mouth heats every inch of my body, spreading throughout every limb. My muscles relax, and I curl my body into him, giving in to my heart that's desperate to connect with his.

I register how his hands trail underneath my shirt, brushing softly over my spine, and I push away my common sense. It's the safe way to make sure we're on the same page, that we both expect the same thing as we did yesterday: a fun night. But I don't want to play it safe with this man. I want to go all in, consequences be damned. My heart is already broken, so what's the worst thing that can happen?

Turning my body, I take him with me while our lips stay linked, slowly backing up to my bedroom. "Will you stay tonight?" I huff, pushing his shirt up his chest so he can take it off.

His smirk appears from underneath the fabric before he tosses it on the floor.

"Was hoping I could," he says, before slamming my bedroom door behind him, his gaze darkening with a need that ignites the fire in my heart. It's this look, this expression, that makes my mind want to run for the hills. But at the same time, this is also the look that is hooking my heart and telling me I'm fucked, and I'm not going to fight it.

Tonight, I'm going to live like I don't have a care in the world.

11

TRISTAN

"Yo, dickhead. I'm out front," Sam's voice blasts into my ear, and I chuckle.

"Alright, I'll be down in two minutes." I hang up the phone, and then turn to Nikkie, nursing a cup of tea as she leans against the counter. Her cheeks are still rosy from the warmth of her bed, and her messy hair frames her beautiful face, her appearance begging me to drag her back to her room. "My ride's here."

She glances up at me over the rim of her mug. "Duty calls."

"I'm tempted to tell them to go fuck themselves." I place my hands beside her on the cold surface, caging her in.

"Fair, however... that will not be a good impression for the new team you'll be racing for."

"What new team?" I cock an eyebrow.

"The one who will sign you—*duh*."

"Duh?" I smile at her childish tone, letting my nostrils flare as I suck in the flowery notes of her shampoo. "You really have a lot of faith in me."

"Why are you surprised? You're an amazing driver. You know that. You will find a new team. I know you will." The tone in her voice is so pure and filled with confidence that it almost knocks me off my feet. It's hard to catch my breath, but I imagine Cupid striking me in the chest because it feels like an infusion of something is creeping all over my body. She's like my light at the end of a dark tunnel, and all I crave to do is pick her up and take her with me everywhere I go.

My lips press against the soft cushions of hers. I can taste the cinnamon of her tea on my tongue when I softly press it against her tip, a tingle stirring alive low in my abdomen. With a groan, her touch sparks every nerve in my body alive, and I curl her into my torso.

The sensible part of me is telling me I should take things slow and get to know her before I put all my attention on a girl I barely met. But every bone in my body is in very loud protest with that option. My hands want to touch her every chance I get. My mind wants to be fueled by her voice as much as I can, thinking about the excruciating truth of not seeing her or talking to her since I'm heading for another country today...

She makes me want to be reckless and take her as fast as my driving skills on the track.

In every fucking way possible.

"Thank you." I break the kiss, resting my forehead against hers as I let my hand fall to the side of her neck. Her pulse bounces against my palm, and I look into her golden eyes. They are glittering in the morning light, the level of appreciation delighting me as much as it's confusing me. Like it's the first time anyone makes her feel worthy. Of value for anyone else but herself.

"You do know *you're* amazing, right?" I tilt her head so her gaze is set with mine, and it's unable to ignore the glassiness taking over her beautiful eyes.

When we met Saturday night, she looked like the epitome of self-confidence, scolding me like I was a little schoolboy. It's what drew me in, wanting to know the girl behind the strong front. But in the last twenty-four hours, small hints make me believe she doesn't feel it as much as she's acting it. There's a hint of self-contempt that confuses the hell out of me, making me wonder what's on her mind.

"I'm really not." She averts her eyes, swallowing away the tears that gloss over her sight. My instinct is to ask her who hurt her, so I can fix it for her. But I don't want to scare her away by acting like she's mine. So instead, I settle with patience, focused on giving her a reason to trust me as whatever it is we have progresses.

Because whatever happens, there's not a chance in hell I'm letting her go that easily.

"Hey, look at me." I take her face in my hands, forcing her to keep her vision focused on mine. "You are. I mean it. You are amazing, babe."

The tiniest smile breaks through her stern lips as she presses them into a flat line.

"Thank you." An expression of relief washes her face, and I take that as a win as I give her another peck.

"I have to go. But I meant what I said last night. This ain't over."

I shoot her a wink before I open the front door, then glance over my shoulder to take in the image of Nikkie in her light blue pajama shorts and tank top, the swells of her perfect breasts shown through the sheer fabric. She looks relaxed, and I silently pray it won't be the last time I'll see her like this, but just in case, I etch the scene in my membrane. "I'll call you."

She gives me another curt nod, and I leave before breaking the Guinness Book of Records to try to kiss all her insecurities away.

My grin stays wide when I trot down the narrow stairs until my feet reach the sidewalk and my sight falls on the red McLaren 720. Sam is sitting behind the wheel, looking like a proper douchebag, as he lets his sunglasses fall to the tip of his nose to shoot me a glare. His blond hair is perfectly styled, his crest casually falling to the right side, even though I know it takes him at least ten minutes to get it as smooth as it looks right now.

"It's about time, asshole," he calls out through the open window.

"Where the hell did you get this pretty baby?" I take a moment to let my eyes trail every curve of the car before I lower my head and find Sam petting the wheel.

"It was the prettiest thing I could rent. She's gorgeous, ain't she? I called her Red Angel."

"Red Angel? Sounds like a stripper."

"Sssssh, you'll hurt her feelings. Though, she purrs like a stripper. Listen to this." He hits the throttle with a glint in his teal eyes, the roaring of the engine catching more attention than it already was.

"Is that Tristan Reinhart?" I awkwardly smile and wave when someone recognizes me on the street, then take it as my cue to jump into the car.

"Stop!" I yell over the loud sound of the engine. "We're getting recognized." I point my thumb at the rear window, and Sam glances into the side-view mirrors, noticing a few people approaching the car.

"Oh, shit. Buckle up, buttercup." His smirk is infectious, already adding to my cheery mood. He hits the throttle as I put my seatbelt on while he drives the car over the small streets along the canals before we hit the freeway that leads to the private airstrip next to the airport.

The sun is shining just as bright as it has the last few days, the heat penetrating the car even with the AC blowing at high capacity.

"So…" Sam starts. "You wanna tell me what the deal is with this girl?"

"What do you mean?" I snap my head toward his smug face.

"Oh, please, T. Don't bullshit me."

I shrug. "I told you. She's cool."

"She's cool?" I don't have to find his eyes to know he's shooting me a dull look, calling me out on my simple explanation. "Cool enough to miss *your* flight, beg me to change *my* flight plan, and hit her up for another booty call to celebrate your win?"

"She's not a booty call," I argue. "It wasn't like that."

"Yeah, I know, genius." I drop my head to the side, meeting Sam's taunting expression.

"I'm not like you, Sam. I don't fuck a new girl every night."

"One, that's a lie, because I recall two or three weekends that you were indeed just like me." The pride that fuels his smile makes me chortle in reply. "However, this is the first time you changed your entire schedule for a girl just to fuck her again."

I keep my gaze fixed on the road as I register the sign that leads to the airstrip while I try to come up with an explanation that makes sense. None of it does, though. I met her only forty-eight hours ago, but I feel like I've known her my entire life. A sense of possessiveness is planted deep inside of me, anchored into concrete when I think of not seeing her again. The thought of her being with another man tightens my throat, and even though I have no right to claim her, everything inside of me tells me it's already too late for that.

She's mine.

"I don't know, man." I rub a hand over my face when he parks the car in front of the jet that's waiting for us.

"Oh, shit." Sam's head dramatically falls to his seat after he swirls it on his neck. "Oh, shit. Oh, shit. *Oh, shit!*"

"What?"

"You're falling for her."

"I'm not falling for her."

"Think about it." Sam cuts the engine, and then twists his body towards me. "You follow her into a bar like a freaking puppy."

"And there goes my masculinity," I mutter, as he continuously keeps talking, unbothered.

"You take her out of the bar to get to know her, then spend the night with her, even though you could've just fucked her and been on your way again. Then the next day, you can't fucking stop smiling, win a goddamn race, that *I* should've won, might I add," he jokes, and I laugh at his faux bitter tone. "And then you decide to celebrate by ambushing her at her house *again*, when really, you and I could've hit the clubs. You missed your flight for this girl, and you begged me to stay another night in this country so you could fly with me instead. Not to mention, you practically forced me to pick you up at nine a.m. on a Monday morning because you didn't want to tell *Benji* what you were up to. You have feelings for this girl."

"I didn't beg you to stay. You were thinking about staying anyway because you, and I quote, '*wanted to see if you could pick up a pretty Dutchie like me.*'"

His face falls flat. "You begged me to stay."

"I didn't."

"I believe the words were '*please, Sam, please.*'"

"Yeah, okay, maybe I did." I shake my head with a smile, then blow out a breath. I feel exposed by one of my best friends, but I can't deny it. Not to him. Axel and Calvin are my friends, and I trust them just as much as Sam, but Sam is living the same life I am. He knows what it's like to be on the grid every single weekend. The pressure of getting that car over the finish line in one piece, scoring points, keeping up appearances for the press, and making shit work. Sam knows every feeling that comes with the job and when it hit me that the only person I wanted to celebrate my win with was the girl I met the night before, I knew he was the only one who wouldn't judge me for it. He understands that sometimes we just want to escape it all. To take a beat and not think about what we should do, but do what we want to do.

"You like her, don't you?" he asks after a few moments of quiet.

"I do. I know it makes no sense, but she's—different." Her face keeps flashing through my mind every few seconds, her smile responsible for the constant tremble in my stomach.

When my eyes collide with Sam's again, a wide smile splits his face.

"What are you laughing at?"

"Nothing." His chin moves from side to side. "I'm just thinking I'm going to have a lot of fun with this."

"With what?"

He snorts. "Watching you fall in love with a girl that lives 900 miles away from you."

I want to deny it, but when my wide eyes find his smug expression, the words sitting on the tip of my tongue feel like a lie, and I know he's right.

I'm not just falling. I'm falling down the deep end.

Sitting down in the motorhome buffet area, I pick around in my salad while my eyes keep flicking to my phone beside me on the metal table.

Taking a bite, I shake my head at my own obsession.

I wasn't surprised by how easily I talk to her every night on the phone. But what did surprise me was how quickly it felt like a habit I didn't want to break. For the last three days, she's been the first thing I think of when I wake up, and every night I feel this deep need to tell her how my day went. To ask about hers.

Since I left her house on Monday, we've been talking for hours, falling into comfortable conversation like we've known each other for years.

I confessed how shit I've been feeling while driving for Callahan, knowing in my gut they weren't happy with me anymore. She reassured me once again that something better would come along. When I told her how that was something my mother would've said, I could see her smile flashing in front of my eyes as she replied, *"she must be a wise woman."*

She shared some stories about drunk patrons at the bar that made me bark out a set of full laughs, and I asked her if she ever wanted to become a physical therapist again. She was hesitant in her answer, followed by a doubtful *"yes, someday,"* but last night when I hung up the phone, a thought bounced in my head and it hasn't left since.

I'm crazy.

That's the only explanation I have. I must have picked up a sun fever in Zandvoort.

But regardless, I pluck my phone from the table in the restaurant, my fingers moving over the screen before I can stop myself.

Tristan: I got a job offer for you.

It doesn't take long before the three dots appear, and I'm quickly add a wink emoji to take out the serious tone, hiding behind me playing around.

Nikkie: If you're about to say something that feeds into your sugar daddy tendencies, the answer is no.

Tristan: Sugar daddy? Really? I wouldn't mind being your sugar daddy. *wink emoji*

Nikkie: Don't even think about it.

Tristan: Boohoo.

Tristan: Not what I was going to say though.

Nikkie: Fine, let me hear it.

I keep myself from telling her I can get her a physical therapy job with any team in the paddock, but instead take the more casual route.

Tristan: Travel buddy.

Nikkie: For who?

Tristan: For me, duh.

Nikkie: Does this involve sex?

I snort with a chuckle, pleased her mind is just as much in the gutter as mine is.

Tristan: I sure as fuck hope so.

Nikkie: Then no.

Tristan: What? I didn't hear you say no the other night.

Nikkie: I'm not a whore.

My heart stutters with the same flutter as my eyes blink.

Wait, what?

I press the dial button as fast as I can, then wait for her to answer with a ticking jaw. It's not more than five seconds before her sweet voice slides into my ear, but they feel like utter torture.

"Hey."

"Let me make one thing perfectly clear," I groan. "I'm in no way saying you are a whore, nor do I want to pay you to sleep with me." It kills me to think that's what's going through her mind. I get that my job, working for the most elite traveling circus on the fucking planet, isn't something that works in my favor to convince her she's not just another pussy in a different town, but it's rubbing me the wrong way that she might think she nothing more than a booty call. I lift my Callahan hat from my head to let my damp hair breathe as I wait for her to say something. Anything. But the line stays silent for way too long than my heart can appreciate until a laugh bellows through the phone.

"Did I hit a nerve, Ace?"

What? Yes. Yes, she fucking did. "As long as we're on the same page."

"What page is that?" Her voice is sultry, easily turning my frown into a smile.

"The one where I want you to travel around the world with me."

"Are you asking me out on a date?"

A date. I should've asked her out on a date, but my mind completely missed that step.

"Would you say yes?"

"Maybe. What kind of date would that be?"

I lift my eyes to the Italian sky, the light blue looking spotless and calming as I think about everything I know about her already. "Something fun."

"Something fun?"

I hum in agreement. "Something fun like a theme park so we can get slushies."

"I love slushies." I figured as much with the way she sucked her straw the first time we met.

"And fries," I add.

"Love fries."

"Somewhere I can make you come in public before I bring you home and take you nice and slow, surrounded by two dozen candles, then fall asleep with you in my arms."

"It's insane how you can switch from a romcom to a cheap porn movie within one breath." She chuckles, though the excitement is audible.

"I'm a man of many talents."

"And I have to get to work. It's inventory day."

"Alright, baby. Talk tonight?"

"Sure." My skin warms with her agreement, and I pull my lip when I think about how much I sense the desire to kiss her lips right now. "Bye."

"Bye, babe," I say, then hang up, quickly diving into my phone again to text her.

Tristan: I'm serious about that date.

Nikkie: You're in Monza and I'm in Amsterdam.

Tristan: If I'll make it work, will you say yes?

Nikkie: Yes.

That's all I needed to hear, and I push my phone back into my pocket with a smile splitting my face before I dive back into my salad. I have to check with Benjamin to see what my schedule is like this weekend.

"You're smiling like the Cheshire Cat." The sounds of metal screeching over the floor flips up my gaze as Axel takes the seat next to me.

I swallow my bite, then rest my back against the chair. "It's better than Growly Pete, right?"

"Who the fuck is Growly Pete?"

"Never mind."

He rolls his eyes. "You wanna tell me what's on your mind?"

"What do you mean?"

"I mean, the shit-eating grin that's been on your face ever since we left Amsterdam and the fact that you have become one with your phone." Mischief fills my eyes, and I feel my cheeks expand. "See, that's the grin I'm talking about. I appreciate your good mood, but do you mind sharing what's causing it?"

I twist my neck to face him, locking with his gray eyes. I can lie to him and feed him a bullshit story. He will not believe me, because he knows me too well, but he'd take the hint and shut up for a little while longer. But I want to see her again, so I know there is no use lying about it anyway.

"It's Nikkie," I confess.

A long sigh deflates Axel's chest, concerned brows arched above his eyes. "Fuck, T. You've only met her four days ago."

"I know."

He holds my gaze with a slight narrow, his lips pressed into a flat line as he studies me for a few beats. "You like her, don't you? Like, really like her?"

"I do." I know it's fucking premature, but I know it's different with her. Like jumping from a bridge and hoping your lifeline is securely attached, but you won't find out until you're crashed against the ground. I hope she catches me because I'm free falling and there's nothing I can do to stop it.

"So what's the plan?"

"With the race?" I question, rubbing my chin as I find his gaze, then stab into my salad.

"No, dickhead. With *Nikkie*."

My fork stays still in mid-air before it drops to my plate with a big clink. "I'm sorry. I'm looking for my best friend. Have you seen him? He has stupid glasses on. His hair is thinning out, a bit on top." I rake my fingers over my scalp. "He can be really annoying, telling me what to do and all that shit?"

He shoves me in my chair, laughing. "Don't be a fucking dick."

"What? I just expected you to tell me I should keep my focus on anything but the girl I slept with last weekend." Like he always does. He sees it as his job to keep me on the right track mentally. *Which only makes me appreciate him more.*

"I thought about it. But you've been really gloomy ever since word broke out about you and Callahan breaking up. It wasn't you. It was... scary." His tentative look cuts through my bones. "Even though it's only been a few days, she seemed genuine, and she makes you smile. And as much as I hate your cheery ass ninety percent of the time, I think you need to smile to get your head in the game again."

"What?" I shriek. "Ninety? More like fucking fifty."

"Nah, I'm pretty sure it's ninety."

"You fucking liar."

"Shut up," he mutters, his smile slipping through. "So, what are you going to do about it?"

"I don't know," I admit, truthfully. "Ask her out on a date, I guess."

"A date?" he pauses, a little ridicule in his features. "With your busy schedule? How the hell do you wanna do that?"

A smirk slips free, and I tilt my head with a bit of arrogance.

"She's into racing. Has been watching F1 her entire life."

"Right..." he drawls.

"If only I knew an F1 driver who could take her to the track and let her watch a race from the garage." I tap my chin with mischief, looking up at the ceiling, then rear back to Axel.

"You're going to fly her out here?"

"You're damn right I will."

12

NIKKIE

I BLOW OUT A breath up my face, a shitty attempt to fan cheeks from the blistering heat. The hot days are unusual for this country, but nonetheless, they have been tormenting me for two weeks now. I love the sun. I love the heat. Just not when I have to work at the bar that is already hot as hell on a cold winter night, let alone an Indian summer. My white t-shirt feels damp against my skin, making my shower before I jogged out the door completely useless, and I lift my hands to put my blonde hair in a quick ponytail.

I'm in a mood.

I don't know why I'm in a mood, but I know I'm in one and it's not even noon yet.

The entire morning, it has been feeling like a storm is about to break out above my head, putting a dark cloud over my blissful smile. Tessa has been teasing me with it every single day, but it has been useless to deny. Every time Tristan texts me, I'm grinning from ear to ear.

I had zero expectations when he left my house Monday morning, thinking I'd be lucky if he calls me again next year, but the man surprised me and is making a full effort to keep my attention, completely pretending like he's oblivious to my apprehension. Probably because he can hear me giggle through the phone every time he sends me a message. My common sense tells me to protect myself and not pretend this is anything more than it is, but the heightened nerves in my body—don't even start about the shit load of butterflies I'm ignoring—they tell my mind to shut up every time he lights up my phone again.

When he makes jokes about me traveling around the world with him, it doesn't make it any easier to keep my cherry mood in check. There's no way I'm going to be swooped into some fairytale by the prince charming of the racing world, but just the thought alone made me giddy for the rest of the night.

I prance down the street with a steady pace, using the memory of my now favorite race driver as a tool to get rid of my foul mood, and when I see the bar appear in front of me, I realize I'm smiling again. Tristan Reinhart has the ability to cure my mood and make me smile, without him even being present. The man is a fucking superhero.

"Hey, Nik."

And there's the thunderstorm I sensed.

I freeze in my tracks, close my eyes for a second, then suck in a deep breath before I twist to follow the voice I've come to dread. I let my eyes run down the length of her body, her legs balancing her torso on her rusty bike. When I look at what's covering her skinny hips, I stop. She's wearing a denim skirt that flares out, with a washed-out shade. A skirt I loved from the moment I bought it three years ago, but haven't seen in more than two years after she borrowed it. I've been asking it back since Wes was still alive, but after the accident, I never got the nerve. Her white t-shirt shows more cleavage than should be allowed and her black hair looks like it hasn't been brushed in weeks.

"Hey, Nina." I swallow, locking my eyes with the sacks underneath hers. "How have you been?"

I regret the question the moment it leaves my lips, knowing I just gave her the perfect opening to drag me through the dirt.

"It's hard, Nik. Real hard." The friendly smile she was sporting disappears in the blink of an eye and I brace myself for what's coming, knowing I deserve it. "I'm all alone, you know." *I know, Nina. So am I.* "I can't get a job. The house is empty. I got nothing left." You'd expect her to push out a few tears, but all I'm getting is contempt. It's all I've been getting since the funeral. It's my fault he's gone, and she doesn't waste a day to remind me.

"I know, Nina." The sad little body fires an expression my way that reminds me of Wes, but never did he aim it at me. He'd let hell freeze over before he'd let anyone look at me like that.

"No, you don't know, *Nikkie*," Nina snaps. "You don't know anything, because he wasn't your son! You don't know what it feels like to bury a child." I know what it feels like to bury my boyfriend, but I guess son triumphs over boyfriend every time. "You don't know what it's like to struggle. You still got the bar. I got nothing." Which is where I'm headed really quickly if I don't start paying my suppliers sooner than later, but I keep my mouth shut.

"I need money," she informs me, and I don't know why my shoulders slug like I wasn't expecting this. She always finds me when she needs money. And she never has enough. For a split second it makes me regret I didn't take the money Tristan offered, but I quickly remind myself how it would only make her come back for more, faster than a snap of my fingers.

"I don't have any, Nina. I'm broke. I'm behind on my bills. The bar is in debt." *Because you keep asking me for money*, I want to add. But I don't.

"You're broke?" She pushes her bike onto the sidewalk, trying to get closer. "At least you still have the bar. I am broke! I have no one left to take care of me and I can't work. You know that! Wes took care of me and, because of you, I got *nothing!*"

"I know," I agree, my voice small and thick.

"I need money! I haven't even eaten today. Do you know what that feels like? Feeling hungry every single day?"

"No, I don't, Nina."

"You're right! You don't! You're protected by your *daddy*," she emphasizes the word with a mocking tone, like my dad is some money tree. The truth is, I'd never go to my dad for money, and if I started asking him for money now, he'd know something was up. "I need money. You can get more from your dad."

I slide my purse from my shoulder, looking past the sandalwood candle I just picked up because it reminded me of Tristan, then rummage inside, knowing I saw a twenty-euro bill before I left. "Here"—I hand her the blue note—"this is all I've got right now. I swear. Just take this."

Throwing another glance into my bag, I now feel guilty that I spend ten euros on a fucking candle, but it's the only thing I've kept doing for myself over the years. The one thing I can't let anyone take away from me, even if I can only afford to buy myself one every few weeks.

"I got rent to pay, Nikkie." She gives me an incredulous look, her nose scrunched up as if I'm offering her a handful of shit. I fill my lungs with the humid air, shaking my head as I do my best to keep my tears at bay. I long for the moments I only had to worry about my own rent. The moments when life was simple.

The moments Wes was still here.

"I will help you with rent, okay?" I concede. I always concede because the guilt eats me up inside. Wes loved his mother, and he'd been taking care of her since the day he turned sixteen and could get a decent job. He was a mama's boy, and I loved him for it. I loved his mom too. She was the mom I never had, and deep down, I still love her. Despite all the shit she throws at me, that hurts like hell, and despite the grave she's slowly digging for me. I made life a living hell for her, so the least I can do is honor Wes's life by taking care of her as much as I can. "I will help you with rent. But I don't have it right now. I will save up my tips and stop by before the weekend to give you some money, yeah?"

She snatches the euros from my grasp with a look that gives me chills, then gets back on her bicycle without giving me a second glance.

"Before the weekend, Nikkie!" She cycles off, leaving me standing there, statue-still, on the sidewalk with tears watering my brown eyes. I yearn to scream as much as I want to break down and cry my eyes out, but instead, I suck in a deep breath, then breathe out and repeat as I count to twenty.

I don't have time to feel sorry for myself. *Literally.*

My only option is to make the bar more profitable so there will be some money to spare.

When most of my tears are pushed back, I continue my path, plastering a smile on my face as I reach Marvin, setting up at the front door. Thursday isn't as packed as a Friday night, but with the sun out like a hot day in Spain, we can expect people coming by for drinks almost the entire afternoon. These shifts are always long, but they feel like hanging out with friends until the real party crowd turns up around ten tonight.

"You good?" He skeptically cocks his head at me, but I brush past him.

"Yeah, I'm fine."

"Hey, gorgeous," Lieke greets me as I enter and get behind the bar. "Any news from your superstar boyfriend?"

I laugh tightly, trying to lighten my own mood. "He's not a superstar."

"Oh, wait? So he *is* your boyfriend?"

"That's not what I meant!' I fling my gaze to hers, her blue eyes almost falling from her sockets.

"You didn't deny it either."

"He's not my boyfriend, okay?"

She gives me a teasing look that says *bullshit* before her attention flies to the door and a frown forms on her forehead. "You got a visitor."

My heart flutters, thinking Nina is back for more, but when I look up, I find my dad approaching the bar. A mixed feeling of relief and annoyance raises my pulse. Relief it's not who I thought it was, annoyance that it's yet another person I really don't want to see today.

His silver-gray hair is smoothly styled, the dress shirt he's wearing above his black jeans, making him look like one of those silver foxes you read about in smutty books and he knows it. His deep brown eyes radiate a charm that has the ladies falling to his knees, no matter what age they are. I had more than one friend swoon over my father's appearance. Add in the common knowledge that the entire city knows he's one of the men dancing on the fine line of the law, and you have yourself a middle-aged bad boy who gets more attention than is good for his heart.

Or mine.

"Hey, kid."

"Hey, Dad." I reach for the bottle of Jack Daniels that I know he's going to ask me for in two seconds. "I swear I saw Nina just riding by on her bike. Did she come by to visit you?" I can see a hint of suspicion in his eyes, but I'm just going to pretend I didn't.

"Oh, really? I didn't see her."

His narrowing eyes tell me he doesn't buy my lie, but I distract him by pouring a tumbler of his favorite whiskey.

"So, you were in the neighborhood?" I ask.

"Yeah, had a meeting at the Hard Rock Hotel."

"Before noon? Must be important then."

"Please tell me your buddies aren't joining you?" Lieke throws him a glare.

"Don't worry, blondie. I won't bring my business into my daughter's workplace."

"Good, because we sure as fuck don't want the trouble you come with, Johnnie." Lieke takes the moment to roll her eyes at him with derision, then takes off to the stockroom.

"She really needs to get over it." My dad brings his glass to his lips, and I can't help smirking.

"You slept with her, never called, and then started a fight in the bar while she was working, dad."

"I wasn't the one who started it."

"Your *friend*s were."

"Oh, come on, Nik. It was Robbie. You know how he gets when he drinks."

"You mean a righteous asshole?" I smirk, knowing Robbie as my dad's blunt best friend since before I was born. Looking just as sly as my dad, they are like the dynamic bad boy duo, throwing around money when they decide to go out and have some fun. It was pretty convenient when I was still in school, knowing no one would mess with me just because of association. But it became a bit of an inconvenience when I discovered boys. I was lucky they liked Wes, otherwise I'd probably be wearing a chastity belt right now.

"Pretty much, yeah."

"You weren't supposed to be here."

"I was keeping an eye on you," he argues.

"You mean, you were checking out your prize from the other night," I counter, referring to Lieke. "Why don't you just admit that you like her?"

"Obviously, I like her, or I wouldn't have fucked her."

"Geez, Dad. That's my friend."

He shoots me the dull look he's famous for. He's known on the streets just as much as his name is infamous amongst the cops in town. But the people in the city love him for his laid-back attitude, not giving a shit about pretty much anything other than... well, me.

"You already know I fucked her."

"You don't have to be so blunt about it."

"Whatever. What's up with you? You good?"

I squint my eyes at his attempt to change the subject, ignoring the skeptical look that's coming my way. "I'm fine."

"You look stressed." Yeah, Dad, probably because my dead boyfriend's mother keeps asking me for money I don't have, and I have balls of guilt the size of Utrecht eating me from the inside out. Don't even get me started on trying to keep the bar afloat.

"I'm fine." I can't tell my dad the truth, because there is a big chance he will be standing on Nina's doorstep within the hour. He would never tolerate the way she's talking to me, no matter if I'm guilty of my sins or not. But I can't ruin the woman's life any more than I already did.

His deep brown eyes narrow, the gold becoming smaller, yet still slashing through me with that parental supervision I don't need. Or want. I take after my father. I have his blond hair, his expressive brown eyes, his big mouth, and a great talent for calling people out on their bullshit without actually calling them out on their bullshit. I see it when I question Tessa about her latest conquest or how easily Lieke shared all the dirty details about her night with my dad. Even the bits I really didn't want to hear. Over the years, I've learned to resist my father's piercing gaze, pissing him off more than he cares to admit, but even though I have enough attitude to keep my mouth shut when I'm not ready to share my secrets with him, his eyes still pierce through me like a laser cutter.

"You're full of shit," he calls me out. "Is it a boy?"

"I'm not discussing my love life with you, Dad." I start washing the beer glasses on my workstation, giving him a flat expression.

"So there is a love life?"

"Please stop talking."

"What? If you're hanging out with someone, I should know."

"No, you shouldn't."

"It's my duty to keep you safe." With the stern look he's giving me, you'd expect him to be some kind of soldier, always living to keep everyone safe. I can tell you, he's not. He's a selfish motherfucker who would leave any of his friends behind in a heartbeat if it meant not having to spend the next few years behind bars. Henk's loyalty stops the second his own luck is on the line, and even though he's not a shitty dad, he isn't exactly nominated for Dad of the Year either.

"Oh, please. You let me do whatever I wanted since I was sixteen."

"Not the point." He runs a hand through his silver hair, then takes a sip of his drink with a smirk. He knows he's not the best dad, but at least he owns it.

"Lie, do you know what's on my kid's mind?" he asks, when Lieke walks back behind the bar.

"Even if I did, I wouldn't tell you."

"Ouch."

"You got burned, Dad." I chuckle when I feel my phone vibrate in my back pocket. I glance at the screen when he mutters something that's probably not worth repeating and the blood rushes to my face at the same time. My heart rate quickly picks up as I try to keep my features straight.

"I'll be right back." I ignore Lieke's frown, making my way to the stockroom before I answer the phone.

"Hey."

"Hey, babe." Fuck, goosebumps trail my back just by those smooth two words, like he's been saying them to me forever.

"How are you?" I ask, a little hesitant to not make it awkward.

"Come to Italy."

"What?" My eyebrows quickly knit together, thinking I didn't hear him correctly.

"Come to Italy."

"Now?" My incredulous tone shows my confusion, not sure what to make of this as my mind immediately goes into overdrive. I quickly flutter back to our conversation last night. *Shit, he wasn't joking.*

"Fuck yeah."

"Tristan," I croak out, not sure how to reply.

"Baby, please."

I don't know what to make out of this and I don't even know what to say. Spending more time with him sounds like a fucking dream, but I know dreams are nothing but nice thoughts that vanish into thin air. Not obtainable. But it's slammed back like a tennis ball, because why the fuck do you make it so serious, Nik? Why can't you just say yes and have some fun. He's not asking for your fucking hand.

"You're working," I quibble. "In fact, doesn't free practice start in like an hour?"

"I'll make time for you." His tone is so resolute that I can't stop my heart from swelling as I swallow away the emotion that comes with it.

"Why?"

His sigh is deep and the pause that follows is pregnant, as if he's carefully picking his words as I wait in anticipation.

"Because I keep thinking about you and this is the last race in Europe. I have a feeling this will be the only shot I've got to have you fly over for a weekend until the season is done." That answer makes my knees weak because I can't find any bullshit in it. I'm trying my hardest to not make this any bigger than it is, but he's making it really hard.

"I don't know," I admit, showing my insecurity as I stare at the bottles of liquor on the shelf in front of me.

"You're overthinking this."

"What is *this*?" I've kept every bit of male attention as far away from me as possible, not ready to let anyone at an arm's length to protect myself. And I don't know if I'm ready now, even though Tristan has a pull on me that I can't deny. But for some unknown reason, I can't muster the thought of shutting him down either.

"Fuck if I know, Nikkie. *One weekend*. Give me that. I just know I want to see you. Please come." His voice has a hint of desperation that is bringing me closer to the edge.

I want to. I really, really want to. I want to feel safe in his arms, like the memory I've been cherishing from the morning he left. I want to feel his body heat dampening my skin as he brings my mind into a high that's equivalent to drugs. *One weekend*. One weekend to end this mind-blowing adventure before he takes off to the other side of the world. I deserve that, right?

"Will I be staying with you or get my own room?"

"Are you shitting me?" I imagine the stern frown he's been sporting after he found out Callahan was letting him go.

"Look, I'm not your girlfriend. You've known me for less than a week, but here you are, asking me to come fly out to you?" I pause, filling my lungs with the stuffy air of the stockroom to gather my nerves as I try to be at least a little bit more responsible about this.

"And here I thought you knew me better than that after one night." His sarcasm is undeniable.

"You know what I mean."

"No, I don't know, Nikkie." His disappointment hurts a little. "We had fun. I had fun. So, make out of it what you want. But if I fly you out to Italy, there is only one bed you're sleeping in and it's mine." The tone in his voice changes to a possessiveness that makes my pussy roar.

I did not see that one coming, but damn, it makes my thighs clench. There is no way I'll be able to tell him no after I detect the gruffness in his voice.

Lieke steps into the stockroom, giving me a suspicious look.

"What are you doing?" Her eyes move up and down my body as if she's wondering if I'm taking shots in here by myself before she glances at the phone to my ear.

"Tristan," I mouth, and her eyes shoot open before she wiggles her eyebrows.

"How does this even work?" I finally ask, thinking about the option I have to not leave the bar understaffed tomorrow.

"You're coming?" I don't miss his excitement.

"I don't know. What do you suggest?"

"There's a car waiting for you outside."

"Outside? Outside where?" I huff.

"Outside the bar. You're at work, right?"

I blink, holding Lieke's gaze. "It's scary how you're becoming my stalker and I don't even care."

He chuckles. "You ain't seen nothing yet, babe."

"You're crazy."

"Maybe. The car outside will bring you home so you can pack, then it will bring you to the private airstrip next to the airport."

"Wait, wait, wait," I shush him. "I have to work. As in today. *Tonight.* I might be able to fix something for tomorrow, but I can't leave tonight."

"Is Lieke there?" I'm tempted to say no, but I'm also a bit swooned by his efforts.

"Yeah."

"Put me on speaker." I do as he says, and Lieke's grin widens when she gets included in the conversation.

"Hey, superstar," Lieke sing-songs.

"Hey, Lie! How are you?" He sounds charming as ever, and I imagine him being the ideal son-in-law.

"I'm good, but I have a feeling you're going to ruin my mood." Her voice is stern, but her expression is anything but.

"I want to take our girl to Italy for the race. Can you miss her for the weekend? I'll compensate you." Her eyebrows curl up at his words, and I shake my head.

"Can you hold on for one sec?" I press the mute button, then direct my gaze back to Lieke.

"Why is he asking me for permission?" Lieke asks before I can say anything.

"Well, you're the *manager*, right?"

"And last time I checked, it's *your* bar." Her blue eyes are big.

"Yeah, let's keep that to ourselves for a little while longer."

"Why?"

"Because this man is loaded, and he's talking about flying me out to Italy. The bar is the only thing that's giving me some leverage to somewhat keep my distance."

"But why do you want to keep your distance?"

I think about it, a small voice in my head asking the exact same question. But if I ever take off the locks around my heart, it will not be for someone who travels the world for a living and is bound to break it. I'm not that stupid.

"Just one more weekend, Lie. That's it."

She snorts. "You're kidding yourself, Nik."

"Please, Lie."

"Fine." Rolling her eyes, she rips the phone from my hand and unmutes it.

"How much compensation are we talking about?" she questions.

"I'll double whatever you make without her."

My eyes bulge, wanting to blurt that's too much, but her hand falls over my mouth.

"Deal."

"Really?" The excitement in his voice is undeniable.

I keep my gaze on Lieke, incredulous, and she keeps her eyes locked with mine for a moment, then lets them drop the phone I'm holding up between the two of us.

"We'll manage without her. Just make sure she's taken care of, okay?"

She lowers her hand away from my lips.

"Are you sure? Because I got a car waiting for her right now."

Her jaw drops and I stifle a laugh at the weirdness of the situation.

"You don't half-ass anything, do you, Reinhart?"

"I just recognize a gem when I see one."

"Aah," Lieke coos. "That's so cute."

"You both realize I'm right here, right?"

"Yeah, why are you, babe?" I can hear Tristan's smirk through the phone. "You got a plane to catch."

"You heard him! Why are you still standing here? You got a plane to catch."

"Lie, my dad is right outside."

She scoffs. "I'll deal with him. You go!"

"You're coming, baby," Tristan snickers smugly over the line. "You know you're coming."

My eyes lock with Lieke's, a glint in her blues that slowly curls my cheeks.

This is absolutely freaking crazy. I have no clue what I'm doing, but I can't say anything other than: "Yeah, I'm coming."

We say our goodbyes, then hang up before I give Lieke a slight scowl.

"Double is a little excessive, ain't it?"

She throws me an innocent look. "We need the money and you know it. You get a great weekend in Italy with the hot racecar driver, which will never ever happen again, *and* the bar is making more money this weekend than it ever could. It's a win-win, Nik."

"You're a cold, hard businesswoman." I chuckle.

She pushes me out of the stockroom. "And you got a plane waiting for you."

Fuck, I got a plane waiting for me.

13

NIKKIE

I T'S SURREAL.

I've never been picked up by a car with a chauffeur. I've never flown on a private jet. I've never been to Italy. And I sure as hell have never entered a racetrack through the staff entrance.

My brown eyes have been wide since the moment I stepped into the car waiting for me. The hot sun burns on my scalp, yet it feels completely different from the sun back in Amsterdam, and my white Converse heat on the hot concrete as I show the steward the VIP pass my chauffeur just handed me.

I can't believe my own words as they run through my mind, but I'm here.

I'm at the Autodromo Nazionale Monza, walking into the paddock like I belong here. Everywhere I look, people are walking swiftly in every which direction, wearing merch from different teams. I saunter past the motorhomes of all the teams, each looking more imposing than the other, until I reach the glass building of Callahan Motors.

A man holding a tablet in hand stands on the ramp in front of the entrance. A white Callahan polo matches the white cap covering his black hair that peeks out from underneath.

Tentatively, I approach, and his head swings my way with a half glare, but then he shows me his pearly-white teeth.

"You must be Nikkie."

"I am."

"Nice to meet you. I'm Ben, Tristan's Assistant." He extends his hand, and I take it while I try to form an opinion about him.

"You too."

"Tristan is still at debrief. He will be with you in a few minutes. Let me show you to his room."

He throws me another smile, then nudges his head, telling me to follow him. With his iPad tucked under his arm, he leads me into the motorhome and starts a tour that moves through the facilities the portable construction holds. A buffet area, a bar, a marketing office, facility room, industrial kitchen, several meeting rooms we are not allowed to enter, and on the top floor, the drivers' rooms with an outdoor area in the middle. It's insane to think about the fact that this building will be packed up and transported to the next track as soon as the checkered flag has waved on Sunday.

"This is Tristan's room." Ben holds the door open for me as I walk past him.

It's nothing fancy, just a small room with a couch, desk, closet, a TV on the wall, and some cabinets. The simplicity surprises me. Above the desk is a Transformers movie poster that makes me chuckle as I take it all in before I turn back around.

"You want me to wait here?"

"Yes, Tristan will be here after he's done."

"I'm done!" Tristan's cheery voice is loud as he strolls into the hallway with his eyes set on me. His race suit is still hanging on his hips, the sleeves dancing around his legs. The tan on his cheeks brings out his shiny teeth as he takes each step with an energy that's infectious. But it's the pink slushie in his hand that makes my panties damp and butterflies fly freely in my stomach.

"Thank you, Benjamin," he says, never dropping his eyes from mine before he moves past him and reaches for my neck.

"Hi," I manage to tell him before his palms bring my lips to his and a warm, affectionate kiss curls my toes. I didn't realize how much I missed him until I breathe him in while he gently laps his tongue against mine. My hands loop around his spine, and I pull him flush against my body. The lightness in my head is addictive. It feels like I'm dreaming.

"Hi," he whispers against my lips.

"Is that for me?" I glance at his hand.

"Yes. I had to sprint to the other side of the track because it's the only food truck that sells them."

My heart is trying to jump out of my throat at his confession. When did my life switch genres from horror to full-blown fairytale?

My gratitude is shown in the long, heated kiss I push against his lips, balancing on my toes to bury myself against him.

"I'm so happy you're here," he says when I break loose.

"You didn't give me much of a choice, did you?"

A smirk raises the corner of his mouth. "No, and I have no regrets."

"Sir, do you need anything else?" I tilt my head to look past Tristan. Benjamin is giving him a look that's showing a hint of disdain, but a smile is conjured like before when he sees my eyes coming his way.

"Yes, close the door, please." His hands still hold my face, the heat feverishly burning through my skin.

"We need you back in the garage in forty."

"I know, Ben. Just close the door, please."

A sigh from Benjamin follows before the door falls into the latch and Tristan turns to flip the lock.

"You have no idea how much I missed you," he says when he faces me again.

He licks his lips, a hunger cutting his expression that I'm dying for, and the rebel inside of me takes over after being cooped up in her box for too long.

"How about you just show me?"

"I'm so happy you're here." Tristan needs to stop looking at me like I'm some kind of rock star or I will hand him my heart with some whipped cream and a fucking cherry on top. We've been hanging out in his driver room for the last thirty minutes, which is the equivalent of the 0.5 version of Netflix and chill. We've chatted, we've made jokes, but mostly, I've been enjoying his hands underneath my army green shirt and his scorching kisses down my neck.

"*I* can't believe I'm here."

"I know, this is the best break I ever had." He takes my half-finished slushie from my hand, removing the straw tucked between my lips so he can nibble my lower lip. "I need to get back to the garage, but tonight, I want your hands on my body again."

I arch a brow with a smirk. "Is this your subtle way to get into my pants?"

"No." He smiles against my lips. "This is me telling you that whatever you did with my neck last weekend, please do that again." He's looking at me with gooey eyes, his lashes fluttering up and down.

"What's in it for me?"

His tongue darts out, licking the seam of my lips. "A massage with my tongue right after?"

Heat spreads up my neck while I feel my thighs clench.

"I think that's a good deal," I rasp.

"I think so too. But now I have to get back to work." He drops a peck on my mouth.

"Do you want me to wait here?"

"What? No. Come on." He gets up from the couch, fully putting his suit back on before pulling me up with his hand linked with mine. "Leave your stuff."

"Where are we going?"

"To the garage." Holding my hand, he leads me down the stairs, and I reluctantly let him drag me behind. It's hard not to notice the surprised glances from the corner of my eye as we pass numerous people and, suddenly, I feel exposed.

The itchy insecurity that I don't belong here feels like a big mark printed on my forehead, clear for everyone to see and I chill runs down the length of my arm.

"Tris, am I even allowed there?"

"Of course you are. You're with me." He makes it sound so easy, but my mind fiercely disagrees with his argument. I'm not his girlfriend. I'm not family. I'm his friend, at most, and right now, I don't even know if that's what we are. It feels weird for him to hold my hand through the motorhome like it's the most normal thing in the world.

When we reach the ground floor, he takes me to the back of the motorhome and opens a door that leads outside before we walk into the back of the garage. My eyes scan the area as my feet move forward on autopilot, slipping back into awe. The back of the garage is divided by screens, creating a path between the rooms. An open door reveals a room with computer screens, before we take a left, and I register the dozens of headphones I've seen everyone wear on TV.

"Tim, can you give my girl here headphones so she can follow FP2?" Tim throws me a curious expression, his black hair standing out against his white Callahan shirt.

"Sure, Tris." He hands me a set of headphones, then pushes a few buttons before Tristan tucks me against him again.

"Tris, where are we–" My words are swallowed when the shiny floor of the front of the garage blinds me, and I feel like I've walked into the TV. The garage is divided into two areas, one for each car driver on the team, and in both are mechanics working on the cars while engineers are staring at the screens in front of them at the station that splits the garage.

Oh my fucking god.

Then my eyes fall to the literal engine of the sport: the cars. They look even more impressive in real life. I become fully excited finally looking at the fastest vehicle in the world, realizing it's a dream come true after watching hundreds of races on TV.

"Are you okay?" Tristan turns around to flip me a smile.

"Yeah, I'm okay." I'm great. Like waking up in a fairytale after a long and dreadful slumber.

"This is my head engineer, Massimo." Tristan introduces me to an older looking man. His hairline is non-existent, and even though his cheeks have that older men puffiness, his physique makes him look fit and handsome. He takes his eyes from the screen and offers me a wide smile, though I don't miss the watchful eye he aims at Tristan when he reaches out his hand. "Massimo, this is Nikkie."

Massimo takes my hand. "And Nikkie is..."

"She's mine." Tristan's voice is firm, snapping my head up to catch his smirk. "I just haven't told her yet. I don't want to scare her away." He winks.

Puddle. Me. *Right now.*

"Well, nice to meet you, Nikkie." I swing my attention back to Massimo.

"Err, yeah... Nice to meet you too."

"Nikkie will be watching free practice from the Pod, okay?"

"*Si, esta bien.*" Massimo waves his hand through the air, indicating for me to go, and Tristan leads me to the bar behind his car.

"We call this the Pod. It's basically a place where you're close to the action and follow what's happening on the track, but can't get in the way or get hurt." He walks me inside, then lets go to show me around, even though it's not much bigger than a small jacuzzi. There are two monitors on the wall, showing the data from the car and the worldwide broadcast on the other. Inside the bar is a couch that rounds the entire "Pod" with a table in the middle. "In here"—he flips a switch on the side of the table and a small fridge pops up. The cold air escapes with a fog and my eyes widen—"are some beverages. Feel free to take whatever you want. That cabinet holds some snacks, and if you need anything else, just ask Axel here who will be joining you."

Axel walks into the Pod, smiling when he catches my expression. "It's a lot, isn't it?"

"It's insane."

Tristan pulls me against his chest, then kisses my forehead.

"Axel will take good care of you." The loss of his body warmth feels like a cold shower when he steps out of the Pod and I'm left with his best friend.

Axel puts his headphones on, and I follow his action while we observe how Tristan gets geared up. He sends me another wink as he puts on his helmet, then lowers into the car. A handful of men work on his car doing God knows what, and a few minutes later, he drives out of the garage with the engine roaring my heart alive. The vibrations are unreal, and I shiver at the feeling, giddy when I twist toward the monitors in the Pod.

"Having fun?" Axel asks. He takes two bottles of water from the mini fridge and hands one to me.

"This is like a dream come true," I beam.

"You've been a lifelong fan?"

"Since I was a child, yeah. My b–" I swallow my sentence, recovering. "My best friend and I have been watching Formula One since we were eight," I recover, throwing him a small smile. "We always talked about going to the races together, but it never happened." I pause. "He–he died." Axel's eyebrows shoot up with sympathy. "Car accident. Last year."

"I'm sorry to hear that."

"Thank you."

A tightness makes it hard to breathe, caused by the overwhelming feeling of anguish that builds inside of me. Suddenly, it's like Wes is sitting next to me, scowling with judgment for my betrayal of giving my attention to another man. I'm fully reminded of how this was always *our* dream and not just mine. It all feels wrong. Wes would've loved this. He would be so pumped up if he could be sitting where I'm sitting right now.

The beating organ in my ribcage has been beating with delight the entire day, but now it's like the cracks that have been there since the accident are expanding with every breath I'm taking. We both should've been here. We should've been able to share this experience like we always vowed we would, but instead, I'm sitting here by myself with one of the best F1 drivers demanding me to stay.

She's mine, he'd said. It felt good to hear him say that, but now it feels like I'm cheating. Wes, Tristan, *myself.* In my head, my heart still belongs to someone else. But now I wonder if that's a lie, holding on to the feelings Tristan evokes in me while at the same time something screams that I still belong to Wes.

"Are you okay?" I snap my head to Axel, who's looking at me with a worried expression. "You look a bit pale."

I smile with my lips pressed together, popping my head back to reality.

"Yeah. I'm okay," I tell him.

But in reality? I'm balancing on a fine line of flying and crashing.

14

TRISTAN

THIS WEEKEND HAS BEEN amazing.

And the blonde in my bed is responsible for it.

I stare up at the ceiling of my luxury motorhome, my body still recovering from the hour of exercise I got when I dragged Nikkie in here. She's normally not allowed to be in here, but I paid off the overseer of the campsite for a few extra hours before we have to leave the track. I gave her a quick tour in the RV, but then stripped her from her clothes as fast as I could, wanting to claim her as my prize.

I brush her arm while her cheek is resting on my chest, her knee tucked between my legs. She radiates a calmness for me I haven't sensed in years. She's like a kid's favorite blankie. Soft, comforting, and the one thing you can't sleep without.

"You're my lucky charm."

She rests her chin on my heart. "Lucky charm?"

"Hmm." My fingers trail up and down her spine. "I've been on the podium since I met you."

I ended up in third place today, and even though it wasn't first, it felt just as great, knowing I've got another podium on my belt after the horrendous first half of the season. My urge to bite people's heads off has been non-existent, and I know it's because it's replaced by the urge to kiss the blonde in my arms instead.

"You only had two races since you met me."

"It's two more podiums than I've had the entire season. I'm telling you, you're my lucky charm."

"I highly doubt that." She rests her head back on my chest.

"No, I mean it." I see the hint of disbelief in her golden gaze. She doesn't think as highly of herself as I do. But my gut is telling me I'm right. I was lonely before her. I have it all. A great family, great friends, a career that will be registered in history. But I didn't know how empty it all felt until I met her. I want to make memories with her. I want to explore the world, and I want a fucking stupid ritual that will provide me good luck before every race.

I want that.

And I don't just want it with anyone. I want it with her. I want it *since* her. She makes me want to call up my mother and gush all about her.

"Baby." I run my hand through her blonde hair. "I'm serious about you." She moves a bit up, settling her head in the crook of my shoulder so she can look up at me fully. Her eyes make flutters swim down my stomach, the gold specks dancing around her irises like stars. I don't think she realizes she speaks through her eyes, but she's an open book. I know something is tormenting her, but I have to gain her trust before I pry her about the pain she's carrying. Let's focus on walking first, before we start running. On the track, I aim to be the fastest there is, but off the track, I'm willing to wait for the things that matter the most.

"We've known each other for eight days, Ace."

"I know and you haven't left my mind once in all of those days." I slide out from under her, resting on my side so I can look at her. "*I know* this seems crazy, and I'm not going to promise you anything." Even though I'd promise her the world if it meant she'd stay with me. "But I'm not going anywhere. I want you. *Exclusively.*"

"Why?" It's only one word, one syllable, but it cuts through my heart like a knife, hearing the doubt in her tone. Like she can't figure out why I have set my eyes on her and am refusing to let go.

I bring my palm up to cup her cheek. "Because you're amazing. *And you're mine*."

15

NIKKIE

*T*HE BLOOD. *I LIFT my hands in front of my eyes. It's everywhere. I can still feel my heart pounding in my ears, the only indication I'm still alive, but something makes it hard to breathe as my chest moves up and down. The muscles in my neck are hard as rocks and I try to rear my head to the side, looking at Wes behind the wheel.*

"Wes? Baby, are you okay?" His eyes are closed, the skin on his face lacking the blood that I have on my hands, and I glance down, seeing the glass in my lap. In a lightheaded daze, I look for any blood gushing out of my body, but switch my attention back to Wes when I can't find any.

"Wes, wake up," I say, trying to stir him awake. "Wake up, baby. Wake up. Wes? Wes, wake up. Wes!" My voice becomes more frantic with every word leaving my lips until I'm screaming his name, panic threatening to drag me under the surface. "No, no, no, no. Please, no. Baby, wake up. Wake up. Don't fucking leave me! Don't you fucking dare leave me!" I hit his shoulder, clenching my jaw as I growl with each move. I register the small whimpers coming from my lips, freezing in despair, my voice growing smaller. "Wes, please. Please, don't do this to me." But I know he's gone. I can feel it in my bones. In the atmosphere in the trashed car and how the area grows smaller with every second.

"Wes!" I snap a final time, before his eyes spread wide, causing my heart to jump from my chest in shock as I gasp for air.

My body jolts forward as I painfully suck air into my lungs. Heaving, I throw off my blue covers, trying to get rid of the heat dampening my skin, then let my eyes frantically scan the room to check my surroundings. Panicked, I slowly register the navy walls, then focus on my breath to calm myself down before I rub my hands over my face.

I inhale slowly, then exhale as long as I can, until I feel how my heart settles, even though I can't completely get rid of the dread I'm feeling. I never can. Whenever a nightmare hits me, it will linger around me for at least half a day before I can let it go. They haven't been there as frequently as before, now only tormenting me about once every two weeks instead of days, but they still take a lot of my energy.

Sighing with every muscle in my body, I get out of bed and put on a sweat suit, then walk into the living room, glancing at the clock. *2 a.m.* Within the warmth of my clothes, I make myself a cup of tea before lighting a scented candle. Then I dive into the administration for the bar, knowing I won't be able to sleep for hours anyway. It's supposed to clear my mind. Make me tired, so in an hour or so, I can go back to sleep.

But the longer I'm working, the more I'm woken up by the worry it brings. The bar was in debt when Wes died, but the more time flies by, I'm wondering what he was spending all our profits on. We should've had at least some of a buffer saved up, but instead, the bar has been breaking even since we bought it two years ago, even though our weekends are swamped. Which would've been fine, if Nina wouldn't be asking me for money every week, causing me to postpone payment on my suppliers.

What mess did you leave me in, Wes?

"Can't sleep?" I look up to Tessa, strolling out of her room.

"Nightmare."

"You actually had one, or you're talking about the pile of papers in front of you?" She cocks an eyebrow, taking a cup from the cabinet to pour herself a glass of water, then drops down into the chair across the table.

I push out a hot breath, stretching my neck. "Both."

She hangs her head a little above the scented candle, then scrunches her nose a bit.

"Sandalwood?"

I don't look up, knowing my face will look guilty at that single question. Ocean breeze has always been my favorite scent. The one that reminded me of my childhood. My summers at the beach. The sultry air when we went to the track near the beach. *Of Wes.* But the last few days, it only reminds me of the dread and the pain. Of everything I no longer have.

I shrug. "It's time for a change." I don't share how one sniff of this candle reminded me of Tristan, realizing how it will make me look like a naïve schoolgirl with a celebrity crush.

"I like it." I feel how her gaze silently drills into me, long enough to make me look up with a sigh. "You have to tell her you can't help her anymore."

I shake my head. "I can't do that, Tess. You know that.

"Yeah, you can. She's not *your* mother."

"Wes would've wanted me to take care of her."

"Not at your own cost." I stare back at her, not even knowing what Wes would want anymore. He was my best friend, and I thought I knew him better than anyone. But after he died, I slowly found out that he was keeping more secrets from me than just selling drugs to pay off the debt of the bar.

"She needs to eat." I shrug.

Tessa lets out an incredulous huff. "Right, because *that's* what she's doing with the money you give her."

My features turn hard as concrete, shaking my head. "Don't even go there."

"She's an addict, Nik. And she's blowing away your hard-earned money. *Literally.* If you don't give a shit, that's fine. But it's not just your money anymore. It's your supplier's. It's me when you can barely make rent." There is no accusation in her voice, but it still cuts me deeply because I know she's right. We're not at the point where I barely give myself any money to live from. We're at the point where I can't pay for everything to keep the balance. My suppliers are threatening me if I don't pay. My personal bills are stacking up, and rent has been fronted by Tess more than once. *Everything is falling apart.*

"Why don't you just sell the bar?"

I gasp at her, a chill running down my spine as if Wes himself is making an appearance.

She stares back at my brown wide eyes with a look that shows she doesn't know why it's such a big of a deal. "You never thought about it? You never wanted that bar in the first place. You always wanted to be a physical therapist."

I swallow away the lump that's quickly expanding my tongue to proportions that makes it impossible to speak as tears try to break through the surface. Of course, I have. The bar was Wes's dream. Not mine. We did it together, because we wanted a future together. But I was never supposed to run the bar. That was his job. And now that he's gone... it's the last piece of him that I have. I feel obligated to keep his dream alive, even if it means pushing away mine.

When I bring my gaze back up to Tessa's blue eyes, her face softens. "You don't *have* to do this, Nik. He wouldn't want you to live in the past. Just think about it."

She strolls back to her bedroom, softly closing the door behind her, while I let her words sink in.

You don't have to do this, Nik.

Could that be true?

"Ugh, when are you going to teach me how to do this?" Lieke is petting my side braid hanging over my shoulder while I rub a dishcloth over the already shiny bar.

I twist my neck to give her a flat expression. "Can you please stop touching my hair?"

"I'm sorry! But you won't teach me." She pouts, taking a step back.

"That's because we're always working when you ask me. You want me to teach you while pouring shots?" I roll my eyes, but a smile breaches through. She doesn't really want me to teach her, she just wants me to do her hair for her. Preferably before every shift.

"It's not that busy tonight." Lieke shrugs with a diabolical smile, glancing around the handful of people that are scattered through the bar.

Nine out of ten times, I do it for her, but over the last week, I've been getting in later than normal because I'm too caught up with Tristan. I flew home the day after the race because he needed to get back to the factory to work as soon as everything was packed up and to fly back to England. The European races are done for the season, which means I will not see him for a while. He's been at the factory, having a lot of team meetings, time in the simulator to practice his skills for the next race, and I know Calvin is working him to the bone to prepare him for the heat in Asia.

But my heart still flutters like a happy bumblebee because he's spoiling me with attention, turning me into a Tristan Reinhart junkie. I'm getting used to his *good morning* texts that wake me up at noon after a long night at the bar, and I'm loving the fact that he always calls before I get to work when he goes to bed. I like knowing I'm on his mind, because he sure as fuck is on mine.

You are mine.

He said it. It was loud and clear, and even though I'm trying not to focus on it... it's useless.

"It's almost one," Lieke mentions. "You wanna go for another hour and call it a night?" I throw the dishcloth in the sink, then wipe my moist hands dry on my jeans.

Mischief mars her face, and I cock an eyebrow at her. She's up to something. Something that will probably give me a lack of memory and a hangover in the morning.

"Sounds like a plan…" she trails off.

"But?"

"Let's make a deal."

I pop a hip and fold my arms in front of my chest because this probably means she wants me to do something I don't want to. "What is it?"

"You dust the upper shelf and start re-stocking the beers while I close up my register."

"That's a shitty deal." I'd much rather be counting money than dusting shelves.

"I'll bring down a bottle of cherry schnapps?" Her lashes flutter like an innocent little schoolgirl, silently asking me permission for a private afterparty. "Just for you and me?"

I do love cherry schnapps.

"Fine." I don't mind getting my nerves numb after all the Tristan excitement. It's something we've been doing every now and then to unwind. After closing, we hang out, listen to loud music, and dance the rest of the night away until the sun tells us it's time to go home. *I love those nights.* Especially after the accident, those are the ones that help me relax when I feel like the world is closing in on me and the stress is becoming too much.

She jumps up cheering, then bolts for her register.

"We better be dancing on the bar!" I add before she throws a "sure" over her shoulder and heads upstairs with her cash drawer in hand.

I take the order of a guy at the bar, then get started with the upper shelves, and a few minutes later, I walk to the stockroom to get two crates of beer. Now, I'd rather get this over with as quickly as possible so I can pour myself a drink and relax. When I get back, a few more people are leaving, and I start restocking the mini fridge underneath the bar. By the time both crates are unloaded, my knees hurt from sitting on the floor, and I get up with a big grunt.

Automatically, I scan my surroundings to see how many patrons are left before I move my eyes forward and the empty crates clatter to the floor along with my jaw.

I blink a few times, thinking my eyes are betraying me, but when Tristan's coy smile is replaced by a shit-eating grin that splits his face, I know I'm not imagining shit.

I shake my head, confused. "What are you doing here?"

My gaze flips from Tristan to the guy standing next to him. His blond hair sits perfectly styled on his head, and he's letting his eyes run down the length of my body with a smirk. It's Formula One's very own playboy and prodigy, Sam Deveraux. The biggest rival of the current champion, Jordan Hastings. And he's standing at my bar like it's the most normal thing in the world.

"Yeah, funny story!" Tristan beams. He's looking hot as fuck with a denim shirt, his sleeves rolled up, bringing out his toned arms. "We were bored and decided to go for drinks."

"In Amsterdam?"

"Yeah."

"You live in Monaco." I know these two probably have the entire world at their feet, but even they must realize how ridiculous that sounds.

"It's only a ninety-minute flight," Sam chimes in.

"Is that Sam Devereaux?" I swing my head to Lieke, who's strolling back behind the bar, a bottle of cherry schnapps in her hand. Her blue eyes almost fall from her sockets, but really, who can blame her? One F1 driver at the bar was weird enough as it is. Now there's two.

"It is," I confirm while Sam gives us both a smoldering short wave.

"What the hell? When did you become an F1 magnet?" Lieke mutters.

"I didn't."

"Sure looks like that." She gives me a knowing look, and I roll my eyes as she pulls her phone from her pants with a smirk. "Can I put you two on the bar's IG? Would be great for business."

"Lie!" My friend is getting way too comfortable with this entire situation, and it's slightly getting on my nerves, because I can't really get used to it.

"Wat? Ik kan het vragen, toch?" *I can ask, right?* she replies in Dutch.

My mind flicks between confused as fuck, to not knowing how to act because I don't know what's allowed. Is it weird that my friend wants a selfie? Is it weird that I keep fixating on his lips? Or that I want to mess up his neatly styled hair with my hands. We talk like we're more than just a booty call, because it seems natural, but does this mean I can jump up over that bar and kiss him like he's mine to kiss?

"Come on, let's take a selfie. Just promise to post it when we leave." Tristan gestures for her to round the bar, and she smugly shows her teeth.

"Deal."

She wants to dart out, but I pull her back, bringing my lips close to her ear. "You know he's only buttering you up."

She turns around. "Have you looked at them? I *want* to be buttered up. In fact, I want extra butter. Buckets of it."

"I'm pretty sure he's here for me," I deadpan.

"Don't ruin my fun. Besides, it's good exposure and we need that." She moves over to the guys, placing herself between them as they start a little mini shoot with her phone in front of their faces. I sigh, unable to stop a handful of eyerolls while I refuse to admit she's right. Having two F1 drivers pop up in my bar, when it's not even a race weekend, will bring in a lot of people who hope to be lucky enough to run into them. And we need every extra penny we can get. I shrug, then ask both guys what they want to drink.

"You're not going to ask me to take the night off again, are you?" I place their orders in front of them.

"Would you say yes if I asked?" Tristan counters. Hope crosses his mesmerizing green eyes.

"Nope."

"Then no."

Lieke's eyes find mine, but I quickly divert my gaze, not willing to keep looking at her wiggling eyebrows. She's having way too much fun with this.

"Where are you two staying?" Tristan and Sam exchange a look, but their lips stay firmly pressed together. "Are you kidding me? You don't even have a hotel?"

"I'm sure we can find something." Tristan takes a sip from his drink with a boyish grin that has the ability to melt my panties. What does it mean when a man visits you out of the blue, completely unprepared? I'm sure there is some kind of precedent that should warn me that I'm dealing with a stalker and I should run.

Tristan winks.

But he's so fucking hot.

"Where is your stuff?" I ask when Lieke moves herself to her side of the bar to start counting the bottles in the fridge.

"What stuff?" Sam chuckles. A diabolical streak alights in his sea-green eyes, a look that's most definitely up to no good. "Got a credit card and my phone, don't need much more."

"You are crazy." It must be nice to not have to worry about anything and just being able to bring a fucking credit card, knowing you will always have a backup on that little piece of plastic.

Sam points his thumb at Tristan. "It was his idea. I'm just along for the ride."

"What time are you off, babe?"

"Closing time."

"What time is that?"

"Until 2."

Tristan nods, then glances at Sam. "You want some shots?"

My eyebrows fold together, and I rest my palms on my sides. "You two are seriously going to sit here until I'm done?" It's like I've walked into an alternative world, and this is the result. F1 drivers are stalking me. It could be worse.

"What?" Sam scoffs. "No. He is. I'm sitting here until I find someone to suck my cock after I take her to a hotel room." He twists his neck, looking around the half empty bar before he rears back to me.

My eyes shoot open at that revelation before I press them shut with a small whine. "Please don't talk about your cock in front of me."

Sam Devereaux lives up to his reputation.

"Why? Getting jealous?" Sam snickers.

"Nauseous."

Tristan stomps his shoulder, scolding. "Shut up, dickhead. Don't listen to him. He thinks with his dick."

"It must be small, then." I smile sweetly.

"Ha!" Sam brings his drink to his lips, his eyes dancing over the rim. "I like this one."

"Me too." My eyes fly to Tristan, his expression feeling like it's cutting through my soul. The desire is clear, only increasing the heat between my thighs as I clench them together. Swallowing the nerves away, I let out my pent-up breath, hoping it will release the tension in my spine. *Newsflash,* it doesn't.

"This is so weird." I continue organizing the bar, avoiding Tristan's burning gaze on my skin.

"Nik?" I look up at his friendly green eyes. They radiate a level of care that I haven't seen in so long that it keeps throwing me off, wondering if I still deserve those kinds of expressions coming my way.

"Are you okay with us being here?" *No.*

"Do you want us to leave?" *Fuck no.*

I shake my head, my heart already roaring in protest at the thought of them leaving without me getting my kiss. "I just didn't expect it. For you two to be sitting at my bar on a Tuesday night."

"Oh, but that's me, you know. I'm like an onion, layered and all."

Sam snorts. "Yeah, no. You're really more of a potato." His chortle is infectious, and I can't hold back a chuckle. "Like a couch potato."

"Shut the fuck up." Then Tristan's eyes land on mine again. "You think that's funny?"

"A little."

His white teeth are accompanied by squinting eyes, only adding more to my amusement.

"I got a few things in mind that I think are way funnier than my best friend trying to outshine me." He playfully shoves Sam, never diverting his eyes.

Instantly, my cheeks flush while my hands itch to touch him.

"Oh, yeah? Want to share with the class?" Sam jokes.

"Please don't!" I blurt.

It's bad enough that I have to deal with him sitting at my bar. I don't need him to rile me up even more. But Tristan's eyes stay locked with mine.

"I was thinking about dragging her to the bathroom for a few minutes."

I close my eyes in despair.

"Yeah, you only last a few minutes?" Sam frowns.

"I hate you."

"You're the one pointing it out."

My smile is huge. *These two.*

"I can go on for hours," Tristan scoffs. "Just ask her."

You've got to be kidding me.

Sam snaps his gaze my way in anticipation, meeting my glare.

"I don't think she's willing to share, T."

I grunt. "Can you please go somewhere else until I'm done?"

"Why would I do that?" Tristan looks a little lost.

"Because I can't concentrate with you around."

Tristan gives me a look that basically says *not my problem* before he says, "I have about sixteen hours before Sam's plane is flying us to Russia. I'm not wasting a minute."

Stalker. He's a stalker. I'm being stalked by Tristan Reinhart.

They promised to leave me alone for thirty minutes while I clean up, preparing everything for closing while I kept getting secret glances. Tristan's eyes are looking at me with an intent that liquifies my insides. Sam's fuckboy grin makes me roll my eyes every time, even though a smile slips through after I turn my head. Lieke makes indecent gestures when neither of the boys are looking, and I want to strangle her as much as she makes me laugh. I'm trying to not think about what happens next and just enjoy the attention Tristan has for me, but it's hard to not let my mind roam to all the shit it could bring. A small voice in my head is telling me that he doesn't really know me. That he deserves better than me. That whatever we have is just for fun.

I walk into the ladies' room with a few rolls of paper towels underneath my arm, and while I'm fumbling to get a new roll into the dispenser, the door flies open, and I shriek.

With a little force, I panic when I'm pushed farther into the small space before I straighten my spine and look up into Tristan's dark gaze. One hand is on my hip with a firm grip. His woody cologne hits my nose and parts my lips as we stand chest to chest. He locks the stall with one hand, then lifts it to cup the side of my neck.

"What are you doing?" I huff.

"What I've wanted to do since the moment I got on that plane tonight."

His reply literally takes my breath away before his mouth is on mine. The rest of the rolls fall to the floor when I bring up my arms, holding on to his shoulders. His hands are exploring every inch of skin they can find while our tongues meet at a slow and torturous pace. Each stroke, each push, and each swipe are more deliberate than the last and the wetness between my legs is dampening my panties more and more by the second. This man kisses like he's possessed, but with a delicacy that can only be described as divine. It's like he invented the power of the kiss, igniting every nerve with a domino effect. My hands trail down his toned arms with a slight pressure, wanting to feel his skin underneath my palms before I snake them underneath his shirt. He groans against my throat when my fingertips run down the bare skin of his spine. Forgotten is the fact that we're standing in a bathroom stall; all that's important right now is feeling him close to me.

He breaks loose, bringing his lips flush to my ear. His breath trails a shiver up my arms, my eyes rolling to the back of my head.

"I've jerked off to your image every day this week." His confession takes my breath away. "You ruined all women for me." The warmth of his hands feels feverish on the small of my back, while the heat in my jeans is almost unbearable.

"Jesus, Ace."

"It's true, Nik. I want you, every minute of every fucking day," he pants in my ear while I feel his erection pushing against me. The friction it brings to my clit weakens my knees, and he keeps me up while I fall against his body. He grips my face in his hands, tilting my head so I'm forced to look at him.

"Can I come home with you tonight?" Is that even a question? I physically don't have a fucking choice. Tristan Reinhart has me under his spell at this point.

I nod, my eyes hooded, desperate for him to settle the ache between my legs.

"You are mine, baby." His eyes narrow, his palm fisting my hair with a little pull. "Tell me you're mine."

There it is again. Those three words that frighten my heart, while also making it beat faster in excitement. I don't know the true meaning of it. I don't know if it will last, but damn me, it feels so good to hear it.

"I'm yours."

"You're damn right you are." Before I can say anything else, he pushes two fingers into my mouth, then flicks the button of my jeans open. "Lick."

Eagerly, I do as I'm told as I feel the humid air enter my opened zipper, and he pulls his fingers from my mouth. They push behind the fabric of my thong, easily sliding down my folds and erupting a moan from my throat. "Oh, fuck."

My head falls back against the wall, my body completely limp and giving in to his touch while my toes keep my body somewhat straight.

"I love the sight of you like this," he whispers against my mouth while his fingers form a V, slipping up and down my clit. "Completely surrendered." The friction and release build me quicker than I anticipated, lifting my mind to the fucking sky. My eyes roll to the back of my head, my parted lips turning dry at my heaving, my heart trying to pound out of my chest while I hold on to his shoulders as I ride into internal bliss.

"Na-ah." He slows his pace, and I give him a heated but incredulous look. His green eyes glitter back at me with a bad boy look that's new, but oh-so sexy. "I want to enjoy this view a little while longer."

I match the mischief on his face, lifting the corner of my blistering lips. "If you're going to keep torturing me, I might scream."

But then he wraps his other hand over my lips, smirking. "No, you won't."

He continues his torturous movements, my mouth glued shut by his fingers, and I just close my eyes as I sink into this scorching level of desire, because I know he's right. *I won't.*

I'll stay perfectly quiet in this shitty bathroom stall forever, if it means I'll never have to leave this state of mind.

16

TRISTAN

"N ICE ONE, T. KEEP this up and you'll be getting a new seat in no time. You really upped your game. What changed, Aussie boy?" Sam hands me a beer from the minibar while I sit on the sofa in his suit.

I got another podium today, placing third in the Russian Grand Prix, right behind Sam in second place and Jordan Hastings taking first.

"I don't fucking know." It's a straight up lie because I do fucking know, but I feel like I can't tell anyone without them thinking I'm crazy. Maybe I am. Maybe Nikkie took away my sanity, but I don't give a shit. My eyes have been covered with pink glasses because of her and it's working to my advantage. I can't stop smiling. I can't be bothered to worry about anything, and no one seems to be able to piss me off.

I sense Sam's eyes settling on me for too long, and I drop my head to the side. "What?"

"I know." His lip curls in a cocky grin, taking a sip from his drink as he props his feet on the table. "It's that blonde Dutchie." I snort defensively, bringing the bottle to my lips. "Admit it. That girl got you grinning from ear to ear like a maniac and it's why, suddenly, your mind is in the right headspace, and it's shown on the track."

"It makes no sense." Yeah, I'm feeling better every day and I know Nikkie is the biggest part of that. I love talking to her and even if Will finds another way to piss me off, her smile melts whatever annoyance I feel like one of her slushies on a hot summer day.

"Mindset is everything, man. She's making you smile, and it shows when you drive the car."

"And suddenly I get podiums? I only scored two points in the first half of the season."

"And now you've scored fifty-five in three races. The first one being Zandvoort." He pulls a face. "In the Netherlands. You know? The one where you snuck out *without* me? *And met a certain Dutch hottie?*"

Three weeks. It's nothing more than that. But I can't deny that my good mood was triggered the night I met Nikkie, and it hasn't left since.

"You seriously think that's it?"

"I *know* that's it."

A sigh leaves my lungs while I run a hand through my hair. "I feel like she's my lucky charm," I admit.

"I don't think she is." He shakes his head. "You're a fucking good driver. Not as good as me, but you are an amazing driver—"

"Do you forget the part where I'm already a world champion? Where's your trophy?"

"Not the point. I'm going to be a World Champion more than once."

"Only if you and Jordan don't kill each other first."

"Pfft, show pony got nothing on me." Sam scoffs. "The only reason he's winning right now is because his car is better. I'd beat his ass if we were in the same car, but fortunately for him, I'm not. *Yet.* But *anyway...*" he continues. "You're a great driver. That's not something you have to work harder on. But last year, you've been off. That girl switched you on, yes. But she isn't responsible for your talent. Your skills. She's the one who made you realize something was missing."

"Meaning what?"

"I don't know!" Sam throws his hand up before it falls on his lap with a thud. "A new challenge?"

"She's more than a challenge," I quickly counter.

Nikkie is not some pit pussy. Every time I'm with her, I learn more about her, and every time I leave, I want to stay and beg for more. More kisses. More late-night cuddles. More stories about her life. I crave to study every molecule in her body and soul, and I'd still not be bored.

"I'm not saying she is. But for someone who got the world at his feet, you've been bored as fuck. Until she came around."

I let his words settle in my brain. Sam isn't the type that will settle down and have kids any time soon. He loves his bachelor life and the many options this traveling production offers. But he knows it's in my plans someday, and he would tell me if he thought I should end this.

"You really think I'll get a new seat?" I lift an eyebrow at him to catch him on any bullshit, but he doesn't even flinch.

"Without a fucking doubt."

My smile spreads from ear to ear while I look at the cheering crowd below. The Star-Spangled banner dampens the encouraging sounds, but the combination is exhilarating. Not as powerful as when the Australian National Anthem is blasting through those speakers, but getting a podium in the Singapore Grand Prix is still one hell of a boost.

I let my eyes roam the mass of people, locking eyes with all the mechanics on my team, Axel, and some of the guys on Sam's team who we hang out with while on the road. They are all there, even Will fucking Dunham is there, even though I can look right through the fake smile he's flashing up at me. All except one.

I suck in a deep breath, letting my lungs fill with the humid air before the thought of Nikkie makes me blow out in content.

If only she could be here. I know she's following the race from home, but I'd give everything to see her smiling up at me right now. When the final musical note of the American National Anthem is played, Sam and I lock eyes, standing from the other side of the podium before the Formula One official calls out my name and hands me over my third-place trophy. I thank him with a huge grin, then take the prize from him to lift it up in the air, followed by the audience clapping.

It's nothing compared to the huge sterling cup Jackson Banks will be presented with for his win, but I appreciate the heaviness of the cold metal in my hands. It will be shipped to the factory after this, for every employee to witness in real life and show what they are a part of, but it's not the trophy for me. It's what it represents. It shows how I'm still capable.

With pride, I stick through the ceremony, until Jackson has his huge-ass cup in his hands, holds it up in the air, and the crowd goes nuts. Each one of us picks up the bottle of champagne beside us and sprays it over whatever body is close enough.

Within seconds, I'm soaked with champagne and put the massive bottle to my lips to let the sweet-sour substance stroke my tongue. I take a few gulps, figuring I deserved it, then wave one final time at the crowd before I follow Sam and Jackson off the stage.

"Congratulations, Jackson. You deserve this win." I slap him on the shoulder as we both take the towel that's handed to us, along with a bottle of water.

"Thanks, man." Jackson's pale blue eyes fall to mine, his kind smile expanding. "I heard some rumors about you walking through the paddock, Reinhart. Got any comments on that?"

"I have no idea what you're talking about." I chuckle innocently, though we can speak more freely now that the cameras aren't in front of our faces anymore. But his question does swell my chest with pride, even when I can't confirm anything yet. The fact that a team is interested sparks my hope like a match in gasoline. *Bright and furious.*

He takes a huge gulp from his bottle of water while still wiping off the rest of the champagne from his hair as Sam comes to stand beside him, matching his taunting smile.

"Really, T? No idea?" Sam pushes.

"Come on." Jackson cocks his head. "Is it true? Are you talking with my boss?"

I shake my head. "I'm not." Then I add with a conspiring tone, "Axel might be, though."

I have a good feeling, finally believing Nikkie's words that I'll get signed with another team. *A better team.* But don't mistake my always cheerful mood for someone who's down to earth and sober about shit like that. I'm superstitious as fuck, and I don't want the jinx shit. Reverse manifesting and all that crap.

"Congratulations, *papi*! You'll be champion next year! I can feel it!" Raul walks into the room, taking his best friend into a tight hug.

"That's still a long time ahead," Jackson mutters humbly, but the sparkle in his eyes is undeniable. He's on a streak and he fucking knows it. He might not have enough points to beat Jordan or Sam this year, but if he keeps this up, next year those boys will have another competitor up their tail.

"*Lo que sea.*" Raul brushes his modest reply away, swinging his arm around his neck, then rubbing his knuckles in his already messy blond hair. "Stop being such a nice dick and just own your talent like this one." Raul's chin flicks to Sam, who shrugs with a smile.

"He's not wrong."

"Anyway. Let's have drinks tonight. Who's up for it?" Raul suggests. Sam and Jackson raise up their hands before all three of them swing their attention on me.

My reply is nothing more than a loud exhale as Ben walks over and holds my phone up in the air.

"It keeps ringing."

I take the phone from his hands, sending the boys an apologetic look. "Wait for me when you guys leave. I have to take this."

"You act like that's a girl calling," Jackson snickers.

"What? No," I huff.

"Pretty sure it is. Bet is that blonde *mamacita* he flew out to Monza." Raul's accent makes me roll my eyes, especially when he starts to wiggle his hips.

"You flew a girl out to Monza?" Jackson's eyebrows shoot up.

"He did," Sam confirms like the fucktwat that he is. "I'm telling you, boys. We're losing him. Before you know it, he's got a thumb right in the middle of his head. She got him whipped." He puts action into his words, pressing his thumb on top of his head with puppy eyes.

"I need to go," I deflect, laughing.

"Will you ever introduce us, asshole?" Jackson continues.

"Probably not." I walk away, feeling busted as fuck, but also not giving a damn.

I am whipped. I'm more than whipped. I want my lucky charm *with* me.

A happy feeling bubbles up my throat, heavy enough to warm my insides with a deep flutter. "Hey, gorgeous. Did you get any sleep?" I ask, knowing she worked at the bar last night.

"Sleep is overrated." I can hear the tiredness in every syllable, but it's the smile creeping through that pushes my worry about her lack of rest away. "You know what isn't, though?" I hum in response. "Trophies. They are most definitely not overrated. Congratulations, Ace. You got another podium."

"I bet I would take first place if you were here."

"You give me too much credit."

"I miss you." I lower my voice, glancing around to make sure there isn't another set of ears listening before locking eyes with Ben. He's ticking his watch to tell me it's time to talk to the reporters waiting for me.

"I miss you too."

"What are my chances that you will just quit your job and become my personal physical therapist?"

Her laugh is loud, causing a ripple effect of flutters shuddering through my body. "I can't do that, Tristan."

"But why not?" My voice is light and whiney, still easily mistaken as a joke, but really, I'm dead serious if she is. I want her and making her part of this damn speed circus is the only option I have if I don't want to wait until I retire from F1. "You want to be a physical therapist, right?"

"You're serious?" I don't miss the hint of panic in her voice.

"No. *Yes.* I mean, only if you are," I quickly backtrack. "Forget about it. I just wish I knew when I was going to see you again."

"Well, Ace. I'm not going anywhere." She sounds sad, as if that's something she's said out of habit, and not because she's happy her life is in Amsterdam. Or happy at all. I can see the way her coffee brown eyes are haunted when I peer up at them. Just like I can see sparks popping through every now and then that tell me she's not as composed as she pretends to be. Like that first night when she pushed that doorbell. My gut tells me *that* was the real Nikkie. A girl who grabs life by the balls and makes it her bitch if she wants to. A girl who lives for spontaneous shit. I know I saw that side of her, but her pain has muted that version of her. All I want is to get to know her better, so she'll feel comfortable enough to let me have every bit of her. I just want her to know I love her for who she is, no matter how dark her past might be.

Fuck, really?

"I know," I sigh with a tight smile as I blink at my own thoughts. But I know they are true. "And the second I will find an opening to come sit at your bar... I will." *Because I'm falling in love with you.*

My chest is roaring to let those words out, but I don't. She deserves to hear them at the perfect moment. A moment when she'll actually believe me because I've shown her I'm all in. I want her and I'm not letting anything stop me from convincing her.

I hear the smile in her tone, her reply only fueling the hope that maybe she feels the same. "Can't wait, Ace."

17

NIKKIE

I TROT DOWN THE street in the rain, my hoodie covering my head and my phone pressed against my ear. My boots are splashing up water with every step while I squint my eyes to see where I'm going.

"It's pouring." I hate rain. I'm a summer girl, always have been. I prefer a margarita in the sun over hot cocoa every fucking day, and the unpredictability of fall doesn't do much for my mood. But this time, fall hits differently. This time, I'm still smiling through the thick clouds, roaming the streets unbothered on a Thursday morning while I turn more into a drowned kitten by the minute.

"I'll buy you a car?" Tristan jokes. Or I'm assuming he's joking, because the entire world knows he has enough money to buy me a car without even blinking twice. He flew me to Italy in a jet, for crying out loud.

"Don't you dare," I bark.

"Why not? I don't like that you'll be walking through rain and cold for the rest of the winter."

Yup, definitely serious.

"Tristan, you can't go around buying people cars."

"Not people. Just *you.*"

I snort. "You can't buy me a car."

"Why not?" He makes my reply sound silly, as if I'm denying his offer to fix my light in the kitchen.

"Because—" I huff, opening the door to the stairwell of my apartment. "That's what you do when you're married for five years."

"Fine, marry me." He dares with a chuckle while I wonder what he'd do if I said yes. Would he be arrogant enough to call my bluff? Or would he laugh even harder.

"Shut up, Ace." I climb the steps, feeling my quads tense with each move, even though I do this every day.

"Too soon?" I don't know how to reply to that, to fixate on the image of myself in a wedding dress flashing in front of my eyes. I wanted to marry Wes. We talked about going to city hall on a Monday morning, when it's free, and tying the knot. Be bound as one forever. But my vision never grew further than walking down the aisle with jeans and boots.

Until now.

Luckily, he saves me from answering when he says, "I have to go. I'm going to dinner with Axel."

"How do you cope with jetlag?" I ask theoretically, knowing it's almost eight o'clock at night in Japan.

I know each driver is on a tight schedule and their trainers help them be as fit as possible for each race with melatonin, even telling them exactly when to take a nap. Tristan told me his trainer orders him to wear sunglasses at certain times to block out sunlight too. But it must be annoying to change time zones every single week, if not for the simple reason that you can't speak to your family and friends when you want.

My day is starting, and his day is ending.

"Easy. I think of you and my happiness will help me fall asleep."

A laugh bubbles up my chest. "What about staying awake?"

"Same deal. I think of you and my happiness will keep my mind up and pumped."

"Hmm, just me, huh?"

"I told you, babe. You're my lucky charm."

I gasp, my feet glued to the last step while I stare at who's standing in front of my door. My heart jumps from my chest, and I blink.

"Nik? Are you okay?" Tristan's worry snaps me out of my dread.

"Yeah," I croak out, "just a spider on the wall."

His full laugh slips into my ear. "I'd better not leave your side when I bring you to Australia, then."

"Right." I chuckle with my teeth still grinding together. Nina's gray eyes are glaring at me like a cobra, ready to lash out.

"I'll call you in the morning, yeah?" I hum in agreement, too focused on Nina to be giddy about him still keeping his streak to call me every single morning when he wakes.

He mumbles a bye, and I do the same before the line goes dead, and I'm left with an unsettling feeling like I got an audience with the devil.

Honestly, at this point, I'd prefer the devil.

"Nina." I offer her a tight smile as she bounces off my front door to let me open it. "Wat doe je hier?" *"What are you doing here?"* I ask in Dutch.

"I came to see you." She smells like liquor and cigarettes, a scent that will be forever haunting me like the bad memories they are connected with. "Are you alright?"

"Yeah, sure. You?" It's the polite thing to do, but I really don't want the answer. I know it will be the same answer as she's been giving me every time I've seen her since Wes died. But today, she doesn't elaborate on her wellbeing.

"I heard a rumor on the street," she says. She follows me into the apartment, evaporating half of the oxygen in the air when she does. I move myself behind the tiny island to create a barrier between us.

"What kind of rumor?"

Her tacky burgundy red lips lift into a smile that is meant to comfort me and look sweet for anyone who doesn't know her well enough. But I do, and it doesn't match her narrowed eyes. "The one where Tristan Reinhart was spotted at the bar last month. *Twice*. He seems to have a thing for one of the girls behind the bar. Do you know anything about that?"

"What do you want, Nina?"

"What I want is my son back," she snaps.

Here we go.

"That's not fair." Living with this travel-sized backpack of guilt is worse enough. I don't need her to remind me every time I see her. I miss Wes just as much as she does.

"Not fair? What's not fair is that my son is dead because of a mistake you made!" She slams the wooden surface of the island hard enough to hear her keys rattle in her faux leather jacket.

"That's not true."

"Not true? Not true?" she snarls, waving her hand through the air. "Do you see him sitting anywhere? Does he still warm your bed?" My lips are pressed tightly together while her silver-gray eyes feel like bullets hitting my chest. Wes had her eyes, and it's like they are staring back at me, living out his anger for my mistake through his mother.

"It's true, isn't it?" Nina continues, cynical. "You've forgotten all about my boy, and you taint his memory by sleeping with one of the drivers he looked up to. He loved racing!"

"So do I!" I retort, shouting. She can't take that away from me just because I can't share it with Wes anymore. "He wouldn't want me to stop loving that."

"What about sleeping with Tristan Reinhart? Would he be okay with that? It's like you kicked him into the grave and started dancing on the fresh soil."

"It's not like that." I shake my head, my heart suffering another beating.

Half the time, I don't even know how it happened.

"Do you feel disgusting when you fuck Tristan Reinhart in the same bed you slept in with my son?"

"I'm not with him!" At least not officially.

"But you do know him."

My lungs deflate as I briefly close my eyes. "Yes."

She snorts, the contempt cutting her wrinkled face. "And what else does a girl like you have to offer a guy like him? Your pussy, right? I always knew you were a filthy little whore."

"I loved Wes." The words come out as a whisper while I try to keep my welled-up eyes under control.

"Not enough to stop him," she says.

"I'm sorry." The first tear rolls down my cheek and many follow.

But my former pseudo mother-in-law didn't stop by for sympathy. She never does. "Shut the fuck up. I want cash, Nikkie. And soon." She only wants me to fill the void Wes left with cash. "Otherwise, I'll make sure your shiny little boyfriend will find out what really happened. Who's *really* responsible?"

"It was an accident!"

"Maybe." She shrugs. "But he would've never done that job if you didn't force him to move out with the bar being in debt. *Your* greed basically killed him." Deep down, I know it's not fair. Deep down, I know that's not what happened. But every time she opens her venom-spitting mouth, I freeze. Partially, because I don't want to fight with her, but also because I'm too tired too. "I bet the tabloids will give me a big bucket of money when I tell him Tristan Reinhart has fallen for a murderous whore? Or what about I tell them all the shit your dad does?"

"No!" I vigorously wipe away my tears, shoving my finger in her face. "You leave him out if it."

The thought alone snaps my throat into a chokehold. He's been doing better the last few races. I will not have his chances slim for getting on a new team because the media finds out he's hanging with a criminal's daughter. It will kill his career.

"I need a grand."

"A grand?!" I bellow indignantly. "Nina, I don't have that kind of money! The bar isn't making any profit, and I haven't been able to give myself a salary. I can barely give Tess enough for rent every month!" If I give her a grand, it means

I can't pay my own bills this month, and I'm already behind on half of them. This woman is working me into bankruptcy.

"Then it's a good thing you have a rich boyfriend."

"I'm not going to ask him for money, Nina." I might be filled to the neck with guilt, but I'm not a gold digger. Never was and never will be.

"I don't care what you do. Rob a bank, for all I care. But I need that money before the end of the month, or I will go to the press and tell them everything you don't want them to know." I swear, the smug grin she's giving me must be taught by a demon. I wonder how Wes was related to this cruel woman, but at the same time, I know that's what grief does. It destroys you from the inside out.

"Fine," I give in. I don't know what else to do. I couldn't protect Wes from my selfishness, but I can protect Tristan. "I will make it work."

"Great." Without a second glance, Nina turns on her heel, not even acknowledging me any further as she walks through the door before it shuts with a loud thud. The sound jolts my shoulders, my eyes slamming shut. When I open them again, I turn my head over my empty apartment as water pools my eyes before the tension buckles my knees and I fall to the floor.

How will I ever get myself out of this mess?

18

TRISTAN

I'M TIRED AS FUCK, the only sleep I got being the nap on the plane, but nothing can kill my mood. I'm sitting in a red leather chair, suppressing the expansion of my cheeks as I look for the dotted line. My eyes travel over my name while a giddy feeling settles in my stomach. For the first time in weeks, it's not caused by a pretty blonde, but my own effort and abilities. I've put in the hard work during every single race, fueled by the motivation that I was never going to lose my sponsorship, and ended up with more points than I gained last season.

And it fucking paid off.

With a sense of content, I put the pen to the paper and sign the contract.

"Congratulations." I look into Eli's hand, then take it as my smile breaks free. "Welcome to the Arzano-Centazari family."

A sheepish chuckle comes from my throat as we shake hands before I offer my hand to Eli Arzano himself. "Thank you so much for the opportunity."

"We will accomplish great things together. I can feel it." The middle-aged man offers me a kind expression, and I feel like I'm being personally blessed by God with a thick Italian accent before I offer my hand to his right-hand man, Nico Ricci.

Eli Arzano of the Racing Gods.

Arzano has been the longest active racing team in the world, their history going back as far as the 1920s. They are a traditional team, and their expertise has made them part of the top three in more than one decade. It's literally a dream come true, so when they showed interest in giving me a contract for next year, it was very hard to listen to Axel and let him do the negotiations. I was willing to drive for them anyway, but Axel did a killer job and got me an even better contract than the one I have with Callahan.

I rear my head to Axel and just nod my head before he mimics the move, no need for words.

We're both extremely happy about this turn of events and a weight has lifted from my shoulders.

Eli and Nico get up as an assistant takes the papers with them.

"Good luck with the rest of the season," Eli says.

"Si, good luck, and I look forward to getting to work in January." Nico throws me another grin before they both walk out the door, and Axel and I sit there in silence for a few seconds.

"X?"

"Yeah?" I can hear the excitement in his voice.

"I signed with Arzano."

"I know." Excitement turns into awe.

"*I signed with Arzano.*" I can't believe it. I can't wait to tell my family.

"You fucking did, mate!" Axel slams me on the shoulder, jerking my torso forward.

"Yes!" I shout, jumping onto my feet. "Give me a beat."

Axel's jovial smile dissolves as he wags his head. "No."

"Give me a beat!"

"No!"

"Give me a beat before I make one, X."

"Oh, goddamn." He pulls his phone from his pocket with a dull expression as she starts to look for a song.

"Come on, X. I can feel it. I need music!"

A few seconds later, a beat kicks in, and I wait for the song to register in my brain.

"Yes!" I shout when I recognize Joel Corry's "Head & Heart." I jump up to the chair as I point my fingers in the air, wiggling my hips as I bite my lower lip.

"Tristan! Get fucking down from there!"

"Fuck no! You get up!"

"No!" Like the stubborn ass he is, he shakes his head.

"X! We signed with Arzano!"

"Yeah, and I'm sure they won't appreciate you standing on their expensive chairs!" he scolds, though a smile slips through.

"Come on, *bestie*! Dance with me!"

He shuts his eyes, his shoulders lowering as he releases the air from his lungs, and I know I got him.

With even more joy, I step down, and I continue my happy dance on the floor before he gets to his feet and joins in.

"I signed with Arzano!" I shout at him.

"You signed with Arzano!"

Then we howl like wolves in victory.

Tristan Reinhart is fucking back.

"I can't believe I let you talk me into this," Sam mutters as he raises the zipper of his green padded jacket, flopping a blond strand in front of his forehead. We saunter through the cold weather in Amsterdam, both our hands tucked into the pockets of our winter coats.

"Shut up. You love spontaneous shit like this."

His smirk is wide. "Yeah, you're right. I do. Not sure if your girl can appreciate it, though."

"I think she will. Let's just ease her into the plan first, okay?" I missed her like crazy, and when I suddenly flew back to Italy to sign with Arzano, I figured it was the perfect time to break the three-week streak of not being able to kiss my girl.

"Sure. You gonna tell her you signed with Arzano?"

I move my neck from left to right. "Not yet. I'll tell her when she comes to Dallas. I want to wait for the right time."

"You mean, you want to fuck her five ways into Sunday first?"

I jam my elbow into his side. "Shut up, dick."

"Ouch! What? Am I wrong?"

"No," I snicker. "But you don't have to be so blunt about it."

"I hate you, man." Sam pouts, rubbing his side before we walk into the bar. It's only eight in the evening, and I know the bar doesn't open for another hour, but that's exactly what I want. My eyes fall to the mahogany bar, and right away, I spot Nikkie putting a few new bottles on the shelves behind her. We slowly stroll inside until we're standing in front of the bar top, the sound of our arrival making her turn.

"Hi! Us again." Sam waves.

Her eyes widen just like last time, but this time the whites in her gaze are bloodshot and sandbags are decorating her expression. I frown, a little worried, but it's quickly replaced by a satisfied grin when she squeals, then climbs on top of the bar, jumping into my arms. I catch her, and Sam takes a step to the side, right before his face is met by her arm.

"Fucking hell. I think she's happy to see you, T."

"I think so too." I hold her tightly against my puffy jacket, burying my nose into her ear as I breathe her in, relaxing when her orangy scent flares my nostrils.

"You're here," she whispers against my neck. The warmth of her breath makes my skin flush and my jacket unnecessary, but I'm enjoying this too much to let her go just yet.

"I'm here."

"I missed you." She pronounces the words with care as if she's scared to speak them out loud.

"I missed you too."

She breaks loose, peering up at me. Her expression is tired as hell.

"Are you okay?" I place my palm on her cheek, and she settles her head in my touch.

"I am now."

Our lips connect, and I stifle a moan, the feverish feeling of desire settling in my bones.

Fuck, I missed kissing her.

I part my lips, melting them with hers, wanting to drink her in. How I have managed without her all these weeks is beyond me.

"Yeah, okay. That's enough. You two can suck face for the rest of the week." Sam literally breaks us up, then demands a hug from Nikkie with his arms wide.

I laugh when she moves herself into his chest.

"Hi, Sam."

"Hey, witch."

"Witch?" She looks up at him, bewildered.

"Oh yeah. You've put a spell on my homeboy over here. It's ridiculous. You must be a witch."

Her cheeks blush before she brushes his comment away with a short wave before planting her fists in her sides.

"How is it that you two travel the entire world, yet end up at this bar every month?" she jokes.

"We are here for the Heineken," Sam replies.

"You have Heineken in every country that allows alcohol."

"You make a mean Moscow Mule?" I offer.

Her lashes lower as she purses her pretty plump lips. They are the epitome of perfection, soft, sweet, and all fucking mine.

"You two are up to something."

"Maybe." I shrug.

"Most definitely." Sam nods.

"What is it?"

"We're kidnapping you to the states." Nikkie snaps her head at Sam before flicking it back to me.

"You're what?" Her blonde hair bounces around her glare and I launch one at Sam.

"I thought we were going to ease her into this?"

"Sorry, man, figured I'd rip off the band aid." I'm tempted to smack the smug smile off his face, but instead I roll my eyes.

"Tristan," she scolds.

"I want you to come to Dallas with me this weekend," I confess.

"I have obligations, Ace."

My initial response is to blurt out *'like what?'* because I know for a fact that Lieke won't mind. I've been secretly texting her already to make sure she was off work, and I even offered to find someone to cover Nikkie's shift for her. Am I being presumptuous? Yes. Am I acting like a spoiled little brat, throwing money at things in order to get what I want? Also, yes. But what else am I making millions a year for if I can't enjoy it. I have a house. I have three cars. I have more money than I can spend in the days I actually have time to spend it, and I'd rather spend it to buy some time with my girl if that's what it takes.

"Actually..." Sam drawls, causing Nikkie's glare to intensify.

"What?" she barks.

"He's been calling your boss." He points at me like a little kid snitching on his friend. I swear he enjoys seeing me struggle.

"My boss?" Her eyebrows curve with confusion.

"Yeah, Lee-kuh? T told me she's your boss."

A hum accompanies her wide eyes before her features turn a bit dark. "Right, my boss. And what exactly have you been discussing with *my* boss?"

"Baby—"

"Oh yeah," Sam cuts me off. "You basically don't have to work until next week, but really, I wouldn't worry about it, little witch. Homeboy can make sure you don't have to work another day in your life." He throws his arm over my shoulder, and I pinch the bridge of my nose when I see the blood drain from Nikkie's freckled cheeks.

"I'm not a gold digger."

"Oh, no! I'm not saying you are!" Sam quickly retorts, realizing his screw up. "I'm just saying..."

"*What* are you saying, Sam?"

"Yeah, *what* are you saying, Sam?" I chime in.

"I'm just saying that he can afford to cover your costs. Any costs. He can pay you for—" He swallows his words. "I'm gonna stop talking now. Is Lieke around?" He shows his teeth with a sweet smile, then backs up toward the stairs, pointing at the stockroom door. "Is she up there? In there? Don't worry about it. I'll find her."

"Idiot," I mutter when he climbs up the stairs before I take a seat on the barstool, pulling Nikkie between my legs. "I'm sorry about him."

Her expression softens when she feels my hands slip under her shirt, exploring the heat of her skin.

"So," she starts, her features still a little stern. "You want me to come to Dallas with you?"

I press my forehead against hers, enticed by her fresh smell. "It's only fair. I haven't seen you in three weeks. I don't think I can handle suffering much longer."

"Suffering?"

"Complete torture." My lips brush against her smile.

"You're overreacting."

"I'm addicted to you."

"You can't keep intervening with my work," she changes the subject.

"Hmm, yeah I can."

"Ace."

"Baby, I make a shit ton of money every single year. I have access to a lot of resources that get me what I want. And *I want you.*"

"I can't keep letting Lieke take double shifts to cover for me."

"Then quit." It really is as simple as that. I get that she doesn't want to depend on me; I knew it the second I laid my eyes on her. She wants to be independent, and it only makes me appreciate her character more. She's strong, spirited. She can take on the world with a fucking sword and still come out on top. But if that means I need to bribe her boss to let me take her with me after three weeks of absence, I will do it.

Her gaze averts as she bites her lip. "It's not that simple."

"It could be."

"You sound like a brat."

"I'll own up to it if it means you'll come with me." I tuck her deeper into my body, arching her back. "But let me make something really clear."

"What's that?"

I dive into her neck, trailing kisses down her sensitive skin and making her giggle. It's the sweetest sound, though complete agony for my dick.

"I'm not leaving here without you."

She tilts her head, giving me better access. Her lack of a reply motivates me to keep going while I make each kiss more sensual than the other. With an open mouth, I caress the skin underneath her ear, letting my tongue stroke her unexpectedly between kisses. I feel her body relax under my touch, until she's resting all her muscles against my chest, and I smile in victory.

"Hmm, fine."

"What's that?" I whisper, igniting a shiver to shake through her body.

"Fine." Her voice is thick and calling to my shaft pushing against my jeans. "I'll come."

"I know." I smirk at the same time Sam and Lieke make the descent down the stairs.

"Oh, my god. You two are so cute!" Lieke squeals in delight at the same time Sam says, "You two are disgusting."

Nikkie swings her head toward Lieke with a stern expression. "You and I need to talk."

Lieke winks, a big smile splitting her bubbly face. "Be mad all you want, but that man"-her finger points at me-"is offering us 10k to steal you away for the weekend. I'm not gonna reject that kind of money. As the *manager*, I need to act in the best interest of the company," she continues with an innocent look while Nikkie's narrowed eyes stay trained at her. "Which means I'll happily send you away for the weekend if we can make even more profit. Besides, you need a bit more action in your life, sweetheart."

"You hear that?" I dip my chin. "You need a bit more action in your life."

"And I'm guessing it's coming in the form of a Formula One driver?"

"Not just '*a*' Formula One driver. A world champion."

"You mean, she's gonna move on to me when she's sick of you?" Sam cheers.

"You're not a world champion." I cock an eyebrow.

"*Yet.*"

"You won't be anything if I chop off your hands if you even think about touching her." I smile jokingly. Even though it's hardly a joke. "This one is mine. Get your own blondie." I wrap my arms tightly around her shoulders as Sam lifts his hands in surrender.

"Geez, okay, don't touch the Dutch girl. Got it."

"How did you get so perfect?" Lieke gives me dopey eyes. "I need a guy like you."

"If it's perfection you want, I'm your guy." Sam pulls her into his side, dipping his chin with a boyish grin, but Lieke is not impressed.

"I bet you've used that line at least a dozen times."

"Works every time."

"Yeah," she trails off, condescendingly tapping his stomach, "not today, stud. *Not today.*" Then she flips her attention to Nikkie. "You have fun, girl. You deserve a break." I don't miss the sympathy in her eyes and a bang hits my chest when I remember Nikkie's bloodshot eyes.

I try to follow the silent conversation going on between them, but I can't read Nikkie's face when she mutters a "thanks" while pressing her cheeks deeper against my shoulder. My cheery mood is a little tainted now, sparked by an ominous feeling trickling down on me. The feeling that something is on her mind. Something that's bringing her to tears and causing a lack of sleep. "Are you sure you're okay?"

I take her cheeks in my hands again, peering into her brown eyes.

Her sigh fans my face, but then she nods. "Yeah, but I have a confession to make."

I let my hands fall to her lips, bracing myself a little at her guilty expression. "Okay."

"Lieke is the manager of the bar." My eyebrows curl a little, since that's not new information for me. "*But*–I'm the owner."

I cock my head in surprise as my lips part and a pent-up breath is pushed out.

"What?" I chuckle. "This is *your* bar?"

"Yeah," she muses with a tiny smile, before it dissolves again as she holds my gaze. "Well, it used to be mine and Wes's. We bought it together, and he was supposed to run it. I would only work here on the weekends so I could start my physical therapy job during the week. But then–"

"Then he died and now it's yours?" I finish for her when I see she's having a hard time talking about it.

She nods. "Wes wasn't just my best friend…"

"No, he was your boyfriend."

Her big brown eyes grow wide at my assumption before she frowns. "You knew?"

The expression I send her way is dull. "Of course I knew."

"How?"

"I saw your phone background that first night."

I can see the relief hitting her before she barks out a full laugh. "God, I'm so stupid."

"You're not," I tell her, then dive into her neck, pressing my lips against her warm skin. "But why didn't you just tell me?"

"I don't know. I didn't think you'd stick around after that first weekend."

My instinct is to scold her for that, but I can see why she'd think that. I live in a different country. My life takes me all over the world, while her foundation is firm and settled into the city of Amsterdam. But to be honest, I don't really care about it anyway. Wes is part of her past. But I intend to be part of her future.

"I'm sticking around for as long as you'll let me, babe."

19

NIKKIE

COUNTRY MUSIC FLIES FROM the speakers around the track, and everywhere I look, I see people wearing cowboy hats. *Including Tristan.*

With our hands linked, he makes it no secret that I belong with him as we make our way to the garage for the start of the race.

I glance up with another faint smile, enjoying every ounce of his silliness.

"What?" he asks when he feels my eyes on him.

"Nothing." I shrug, then say, "I like you, Tristan Reinhart."

He stops in his tracks, twisting my body toward him when I take another step. His eyes are wide and filled with happiness.

"What?"

"That's pretty straightforward for you."

His hopeful expression almost wants me to tell him everything that's on my mind. My grief. My pain. My fears. But right now, I don't want him to worry about me. I just want him to know that I meant it. I like this guy more than anything in the world.

"It's true." I shrug, holding his gaze with intent.

For a few heartbeats, I think he's shell-shocked or something. He just stands there, not moving a muscle with a straight face and bright eyes. But then he takes my face into his hands, claiming a bruising kiss from my lips.

"Thank you for telling me." He pushes his forehead against mine.

"You sound like you were ready to give up on me," I joke.

"Not a chance, baby. It told you, you're mine." Before I can reply, his lips connect with mine again, sinking deep into my soul. I swear it's like he's jolting me back to life piece by piece, my resolve getting chipped away with each kiss. "Come on." He tugs me behind him, directing me to the trucks parked behind the garages.

"Tristan, where are we going?"

The sun is burning my head, the breeze killed by the trucks we walk in between. We move past them all, until we reach the fence of the track and he shoves me behind a little maintenance cabin, far away from the crowd. Behind the steel is nothing other than dry land. His gaze searches through the small window, looking for any of the staff members, but when he's sure there's no one there, he dives his mouth into my neck.

"What are you doing?" I ask, but either way, my neck arches, giving him better access.

"Naughty shit." He trails kisses up and down my neck, each more tortuous than the last.

"Tristan, someone could see us."

"Not if you're quiet and we're lucky."

"I don't think luck is on my side." With my eyes closed, I rest my head against the wood, sinking my teeth into my lip while I feel my hips tense in desire. My pussy is screaming yes to whatever he's doing, while my mind is telling me we're basically in public.

"Are you kidding me? You're my lucky charm."

I laugh at his reply, but the abrupt pull of his lips off my skin quickly muffles that when I see his stern look. "You're serious."

"Will you ever tell me why you feel like you don't matter?"

I barely hold in my gasp at the question hitting me like thunder, then fold my lips together to prevent my eyes from welling up. It's like he hit my heart with a cupid's arrow, but it hurts just as much as it feels like euphoria. I pray he doesn't pull it out, knowing it will ignite the floodgates of my emotions.

He holds my chin, seeing my pain, and comforting me. "Shhh, it's okay, baby. You don't have to tell me now. Just someday, okay?"

With a smile, I silently agree before our lips melt together. My hands go on an exploring mission as he lifts my hips so he can wrap my legs around his waist. Immediately, I'm met by the bulge in his jeans, pressing against my core with an urgency that has me moaning into his mouth.

"I didn't know you were such an exhibitionist, Ace." My tongue breaks our connection and I suck his earlobe into my mouth, causing a shiver to run down his shoulders.

"I'm not," he puffs. "But you do weird things to me. Do that again."

"What? This?" I roll his earlobe between my teeth, and his shudder almost drops me to the floor.

"Fuck, Nik." He lowers my feet to the ground, lifting my arms above my head. "Keep them there."

Before I can protest, he drops to the ground, peering up at me with a smirk. Softly, he moves his palm between my legs, rubbing my pussy through my jeans.

"How wet are you for me, babe?"

"Not wet enough," I dare, licking my lips. My pussy is dying to push herself into his face, not giving a shit at who might see us. All I want is for him to stop the throbbing ache he's causing.

"Is that right?" He unzips my jeans, then drags the fabric down while he pushes his nose against my lace thong. "I smell lies."

I gasp, feeling equally turned on by the sight of him looking with hunger at my pussy as him not doing anything more than teasing me with his nose. I feel like his drug, enjoying every second of giving him his fix as he traces the lines of my underwear, then takes the lace in his mouth. The lack of cover feels cold against my skin, both blistering and feverish. Pushing the fabric down, he then rubs his full hand over my slick folds.

"You're such a little liar." He holds up his hand, glistening from my juices.

"I know. *Punish* me."

His index finger slips through my core, then thrusts into my body with a force that has me glued against the wall of the cabin. And it isn't until he torturously slowly slips it back out that my body jerks forward, heightening every nerve inside my walls. This man doesn't just know where to find all the buttons of his Formula One car. He also finds his way around my body like he's read the manual from cover to cover. *Twice.*

"Oh, you're wet for me already." Tristan chuckles. "Now, let's see if we can get you even wetter." I let my hooded eyes drop to his, my lips curling when he takes my pussy in his mouth. He starts by tilting his head so he can twirl my inner lips around his tongue, and I suck in a breath. *Godverdomme.* He kisses them with intent, like he needs to kiss everything better, and part of me wishes he could kiss the pain in my heart away. Then he dives inside my walls, slowly lapping away all the juices from my entrance.

If it isn't his tongue that slowly drives my mind up in the air, it's definitely the sight of him in front of me, on his knees in the dry dirt, while the Texan sun sparks in his mischievous eyes.

"Hmm, you taste so good." His voice vibrates against my skin.

"Hmm, you lick so good."

"You like this, baby?"

I hum, running my nails over his scalp.

"What about this?" He takes my clit in his mouth, slowly pulling with his lips, and a ripple of pleasure moves through me.

"Oh, yes. Love that." His finger slips back inside of me, as he continues working my clit. I vaguely register the muffled sounds of the crowd in the distance, but it's drowned out by the way he's caressing my core. My breathing speeds up, alternating with little gasps every time he switches up his movements. Gradually, I feel the tension build in my core.

"Ace," I huff.

"I love it when you call me Ace."

I don't even want to say his name anymore, because in my head he's Ace. He's one of the best racecar drivers. *Ace.* He makes me laugh when rarely anyone can. *Ace.* He makes me come multiple times in thirty minutes. *Fucking Ace.* But even though it's something I have a hard time admitting, I can't deny he's also curing some of the ache in my soul. *Motherfucking Ace.*

"I'm close."

"Na-ah." His breath tickles my core before he moves up, pressing his sultry lips against mine. I can taste myself on his tongue and it makes me moan. "I want to feel you come on my dick, baby." He unbuckles his jeans while his mouth travels up and down my neck. I hear his belt clink before he cups my ass to wrap my legs around him again. I let out a squeal, feeling his hot tip press into my body as I hold on to his shoulders, but not before he opens a foil wrapper with his teeth, then fumbles to roll it onto his shaft as he holds me up with one arm. My palms feel the tight veins on his biceps, biting my lip as he keeps me up with a strength that makes me even more desperate for him to fill me up. Finally, he slowly slides inside, but my desire makes me flick my hips, fully bringing him deeper as fast as I can.

"Fuck, baby." His muscles flex under my hands, holding me up, then he thrusts inside of me. There's an urgency in each move, yet he's also slow and torturous. My walls are stretched wide while his pumps bring me into that whimsical state I was hoping for.

My consciousness withers away, completely consumed by the fog that is Tristan Reinhart.

The sunshine continues to burn my cheeks, but it's nothing compared to the heat Tristan is responsible for. Tristan makes my body feel things I don't think I can live without ever again. And it terrifies the shit out of me most of the time, but right now that's overshadowed by the friction on my clit and the tensity of my muscles.

"Ace, I can't hold it."

"A little longer, baby." He picks up his pace, each pump boxing into my pussy, making my senses vibrate.

"Baby, please," I cry.

"I'm close."

"Yes!" I shout, loud enough for Tristan to cover my mouth.

"Shh, we don't want your bare ass on the news tonight, baby." The smirk on his face tells me he would actually enjoy that, but I'm too preoccupied to reply with something witty. Only one more thrust and I feel a tidal wave rush through my core, rippling every muscle below my belly. I shriek beneath his palm as he grunts like a bear in my ear to find his own release. I hold on to his neck while he rides it out, then presses his forehead against mine, heaving, while I'm still enjoying the aftermath of my internal bliss.

Pressing him closer against my body, I ignore the breeze chilling our asses, just to memorize this moment. To cherish this feeling. The sense of safety he's giving me.

He chuckles against my shoulder, keeping his arms around my back.

"What?" I ask.

"You're like a little koala."

Initially, I want to let go at his remark, but he keeps me firmly against his torso. "No, I like it. Don't let go. I'll be your tree." He kisses my cheek. "Firm." He kisses my other cheek. "Strong." He kisses my mouth. "Solid."

I think my heart is growing out of my chest.

"Will you let me?" His green eyes represent every color of the tree he's talking about, vibrant green, comforting brown, and specks of both dancing in the wind.

I nod, smiling up at him, wondering what he sees in me. He slips out of me, leaving a hollow in my body before we both pull up our pants again.

When we're fully clothed again, he gives me a dreamy look, and then slides his palms to the small of my back. "I have to tell you something."

Relieved he's changing the subject, I swallow away my glassy gaze.

"I got signed."

"What do you mean?"

"I got a seat for next year. I signed with Arzano."

"You signed with Arzano?"

"Yeah!" His white teeth split his face and I jump up and down. "For three years!"

"Oh my god! That's amazing, Ace!"

"I know, right!"

"Yes!" I jump into his arms, and he spins me around.

"It's because of you," he says when he puts me down again.

"Because of me?"

"You've changed the game, babe."

"You're crazy." I shake my head.

"I mean it." The truth in his eyes cuts deep, even though I thought he couldn't go any deeper. "Without you, my mind would still be in the gutter. You helped me get back on track, baby."

"No, I'm not taking credit for that. That was all you. You worked hard for this." I poke my finger into his chest.

"True. But before I met you, my mind was nowhere to be found. Take this, baby. Let me be your tree, but accept that you're my soil."

Something grips me, sucking me closer to his body.

How do I say no to this man?

So, I just nod.

"Come on, Tess. Pick up, pick up," I mumble into the phone as I glance down at the paddock standing on the hospitality VIP section of the track.

"Howdie, cowgirl!" Tess finally cheers.

"Damn, it took you long enough."

It stays quiet for a brief moment. "I'm sorry. Who pissed in your boot?"

"He calls me his lucky charm!" I exclaim, gripping my hair.

"Who does? Tristan?"

I hum, glancing around the balcony to make sure no one is listening in on my conversation.

"Nikkie! That's sooo cute!"

"It's not cute, Tessa!"

"Oh..." She sounds confused. "Okay, it's not cute. Why is it not cute?"

"Because he's put me high onto this pedestal and I'm bound to hurt him." Today he might think I'm his lucky charm, but the very next, I'm probably breaking his heart.

"Why are you bound to hurt him?" The mocking tone in her voice is undeniable, and I roll my eyes.

"Because—" There is not one answer I fully am committed to, but more all these little things that make me insecure about what Tristan and I have. "He's a Formula One driver. He travels the world the entire year. He actually has a career. I can't ruin that."

"How exactly would you ruin that?"

"Well, I don't know? Maybe because of the fact that I basically killed my boyfriend." When I hiss out the words, my heart clenches.

The grunt that comes through the line tells me a full fucking novel of her disapproval. "How many fucking times do I have to tell you it was a fucking accident?"

"I pulled the wheel, Tess! If it wasn't for my stupidity, we wouldn't have crashed against a goddamn tree." I've only spoken those words out loud just once before. It was when I told Tessa the truth, needing to share what I did with someone. Other than that, I've never told a soul, and even though it hurts to hear with my own ears what has been internally ruining me inside, there's also a hint of relief when they roll from my tongue.

"Yeah, and if it wasn't for *his* stupidity, you wouldn't even have been in the car with him."

I sigh with my entire body, carefully glancing at all the people passing by me through the paddock.

"He's the one who thought doing a drug run would be a good idea to fix the mess *he* created," she continues, with a bit of contempt in her tone. "I loved Wes, Nik. I really did. And I'm sorry he's gone. Neither of you deserved what happened. But you are not to fucking blame for wanting to protect him from the mess he was getting in deeper and deeper. Stop torturing yourself."

I can't. Tears flood my eyes.

"And since when do you fucking suck at relationships? What you and Wes had was great. I was fucking jealous of the two of you."

"Yeah, and then he died," I bark, a little harsh. Maybe it's not that I think I suck at relationships. It's more than I don't think I can give my heart away again. I'm not recovered from the last time I did that, and frankly, I don't think I ever will.

"Yes, Nikkie." Tessa's exhale sounds like a gust of wind. "Look, you loved Wes, but he's not coming back. And he's not Tristan. But they have one thing in common." I keep quiet, scared to ask what she means. "They both adored you. I know it's scary. Losing Wes broke you."

I feel my cheeks growing wetter by the second. "It really did."

"I know. But do you really want to let that control the rest of your life? Whatever you're freaking out about... it has nothing to do with Tristan. You're only twenty-three, Nik. You deserve to be happy. Why are you so scared of being happy with Tristan?"

It's a question I've silently asked myself numerous times in the last couple of weeks.

And every time I come to the same conclusion. "What if he dies?"

"You know we all die at some point, right?"

"He's a racecar driver, Tess. He can get into an accident every other weekend and fucking die." The memory of our crash hits me like a freight train, without mercy. I've been able to tuck it away for so long, pretending I'm okay. But it's like my body can't store any more emotions, making room for whatever I feel for Tristan by pushing out the grief that comes with it.

The silence is crackling. Long. Painful.

"Tess, say something!"

"He's not Wes, Nik."

Pain washes my entire body, turning my heart into stone. I know he's not Wes. But what is scaring the shit out of me is that I feel just as much as I did for Wes. I've known Wes half my life. I have known Tristan for two months. What happens if we're together a year from now? Two years from now? And he decides I'm not enough?

"I'm scared, Tess."

"Of course, you are."

"He lives in a different country. He's from Australia, for crying out loud. He travels around the world for a living, risking his life for a podium. What if, at some point, he thinks I'm not as important anymore?"

"Why do I have the feeling you're not talking about Tristan right now?"

I press my fingers onto my eyes, gathering my thoughts and finding the words to explain.

"He picked her over me," I explain. "Wes. He always picked his mother over me, and that night, I forced him to choose. I begged him to choose me. I just wanted him to break loose. For us to start over, *together*. Away from his... his..."

"His bitch of a mother?" Tessa finishes my sentence.

"Yes," I sniff. I still see the disappointment on his face when I told him it was me or her. The utter betrayal that was the last expression he'd ever give me. "It's all my fault, Tess."

"I can't believe this," Tessa mutters harshly through the phone. "You wipe your tears right now, Nikkie Peters." She pauses. "I mean *right now*. Do it."

I swallow, not saying a word, just staring up at the sky.

"Do it," she repeats.

Blowing out a breath, I wipe my tears with the back of my hand, then inhale and exhale slowly with my eyes closed.

"Did you wipe your tears?"

"Yes."

"Good, now listen to me really fucking closely. Did you push Wes to rob the grocery store when he was fourteen?"

I frown, pursing my lips at the memory of him getting pulled out of class in high school. "No."

"Did you push him to start selling coke at the club?"

"No."

"Did you push him to steal Michael Bakker's car because he was pissed he stole his pack of smokes?"

"No."

"Did you push Wes to start working for your dad?"

"No."

"Exactly!" she exclaims. "Stop acting like a fucking martyr! Wes knew exactly what he was doing and why. He bought half of that fucking bar with dirty money, for crying out loud! It wasn't your fault, Nikkie. It was an *accident*."

I let what she's saying marinate in my brain, slowly seeing some truth in her words.

"You know I'm right," she adds.

Maybe she is right. Maybe I'm not the only one responsible for what happened, but just the only one who survived. Maybe being the one who has to keep living without him is punishment enough.

"Now, I know you," Tessa continues when I still stay silent. "You don't want to admit it to yourself, because you're scared. I understand. I would be too. But you are falling in love with Tristan Reinhart."

I want to blurt out a no, but I can't. I don't know if I'm ready to say it out loud, but I'm not willing to lie about it either.

"You are falling in love with Tristan Reinhart, and I'm pretty damn sure he's already in love with you."

"You really think so?"

"Are you kidding me? It's either that or he's stalking you. Either way, he's head over heels. Now, are you really going to let a guy like *Tristan Reinhart* slip out of your hands? I'm pretty sure half a million girls would want to be in your shoes."

I stare into the clear blue sky, blinking, not knowing what to fucking do or feel.

"What if it turns out to be nothing and we break up?"

"What if it turns out to be the love of your life?"

"Tess."

"I'm serious," she huffs, though I can hear the smile on her face. "Either way, you won't find out until you try."

Like the universe is telling me something, I glance down to see Tristan making his way through the paddock. He looks so fucking hot with his sunglasses covering his eyes. The fresh memory of him between my legs in broad daylight only a hundred yards from where I'm standing right now has my frown turning into a tiny smile, and as if he can feel my eyes on him, he looks up. His grin expands as he stops in his tracks, giving me a thumbs up in question.

"So, the question is... are you going to try?" I hear Tessa question, and when I'm staring back at this man, I know there is only one option.

I nod to Tristan with a smile. "Yeah, I'm gonna try."

20

TRISTAN

FEELING THE COLD HARDWOOD floor underneath my feet, I walk to the kitchen, sleep drunk, and running a hand through my messy hair. There's a whiff of apple cinnamon still hanging in the air from the scented candles that are placed all over the small living room, and my lip curls. Living in Monaco since I was eighteen, I can't remember when I last experienced fall. I always thought I was lucky. I get to spend most of my days off in summer, warming my skin by the sun of the Cote D'azur, other than the occasional bad weather that we deal with when we travel from one track to another.

When I met Nikkie, she was a hot summer night. Hot, fun, and sassy.

But now, I think she is autumn. Cozy, warm, and filled with kindness. I know when I walk outside, the streets of Amsterdam are cold with a blistering wind, but it's not the outside part of fall that I now appreciate more than anything. It's the part where you go back inside after a crisp day. It's the part where you cuddle up on the couch, light the fireplace, and watch a movie with a blanket and some tea. I sound like a fucking grandmother, but I've been looking forward to these moments more than anything.

Every free couple of days I have, and they are rare, I've been stealing Sam's jet, desperate to curl up in Nikkie's bed and wake up with my nose in her hair.

Our schedules don't match for shit, me working mostly during the day and her working at night. But the moments we do get together are getting me through the rest of the days.

I take a glass from the cupboard, pouring myself some water before I let the cold liquid surge through my chest with big gulps. The action pops my eyes a little more open and I turn around, leaning my back against the counter. It's a small apartment. Nothing fancy. In fact, my room at my parents' ranch is bigger than the entire square footage of the home. But every single time I step over that threshold, I feel all my muscles relax. Like this is my little escape from the stressful life that I can have.

My eyes fall to the pile of administration that she took home from the bar on the counter next to me, thick red letters standing out against the white of the envelope. Curiosity lets my fingers trail between the paper before I fish it out of the stack. I sense my eyebrows knitting together when I read three words that give me a bad taste in my mouth: *last notice.* She's having money troubles? Did I drag her out of work too much, causing her to now get behind on payments?

I know it's not my business, but I go through the rest of the stack, finding four more letters with payments that are long overdue. The letters are all opened, and I check for the details in each one of them, suppliers waiting for back payment, all of them threatening to send out debt collectors if she doesn't pay quickly. Without thinking twice, I tiptoe back to the bedroom, checking if she's still asleep as I hover above her.

She doesn't stir when I push my knee into the mattress, before pressing a kiss to her cheek, then grab my phone from the nightstand. I get back to the counter, taking pictures of each letter.

"What are you doing?" A little busted, I spin on my heels, locking eyes with Tessa's scold. Her blue eyes stand out against the moonlight, making her look a lot scarier than I know she is.

"Did you know she's in trouble?" I hold up a letter, and Tessa's expression softens. She lets out the air from her lungs, then saunters to the sink.

"Of course, I know."

"Well, doesn't this worry you? They will come after the bar if she doesn't pay."

Tessa takes a glass from the cupboard and fills it with water before mimicking my stance as she rests her hip against the counter. "I know," she whispers, spurring me on to lower my voice as well. "She keeps telling me she'll handle it."

"How?"

Her sigh is deep. "Truth be told? I don't know."

A tight grip takes hold of my heart. "Is this because of me? Does she have money problems because of me?"

She smiles. "You really are a good guy, aren't you? Not just an arrogant F1 driver."

"I do my best, yes." I'm a cocky son of a bitch when it comes to my driving, but my parents raised me to be good and true to any person, no matter what rank, status, or level of wealth. I don't care about your profession or what number is on your paycheck every month. I care about the person that you are, and Nikkie is pure gold. I know that as much.

"It's not because of you." I don't know why that's both a relief and something that worries me. "And it's also not because of the times you whisked her off her feet and took her to a foreign country like Prince fucking Charming. The bar was already in debt before that."

"Then what is it?" If she's in trouble, I need to know.

"You do realize I can't really tell you, right?" She takes a sip.

"Tess, please."

But she shakes her head. "I'd be breaking best friend rules and all that crap. But I'll tell you this, it's Wes. Sorta."

"Sorta?" I skeptically lift an eyebrow, not liking that the name of her dead ex-boyfriend is now lingering in the air like a thundercloud.

"I'll tell you if she's really in shit, okay? Pinky swear." She brings her pinky up, and I give her a dull look.

"Pinky swear, really?"

"Isn't that what you Americans do?"

"I'm Australian."

"Potato, potato."

"That's not how that goes."

"You're missing the point."

"Fine." I roll my eyes, grabbing her pinky with mine for a second, before my feet guide me back toward the bedroom.

"Tristan?" I turn around. "You're gonna fix that for her?" Tessa nudges her chin at my phone, talking about the pictures I took.

"Don't tell her."

"I won't. She won't be happy with it, though."

I nod, figuring that much, but also not really caring. I have more money than I can spend. I'm not going to let her lose her bar if it's so easily fixed.

"You have to promise me one thing," Tessa continues.

"What's that?"

"Whatever happens, you don't break her heart. She won't be able to handle it."

There is a deeper meaning in her words, accompanied by a sadness in her eyes. I'm tempted to ask her why, but I've learned something about these girls rather quickly: they don't tell you shit until they are ready. If Tessa wanted to tell the full story that I know is there, she would've already done it.

But luckily, I have no issues making this promise.

"I promise," I tell her, then close the bedroom door behind me.

I quickly send Ben a message with the photos I just took, then slide back into bed, tucking her back against my chest as I slip my hands over her stomach. A soft moan follows when my lips land on her neck before she settles her ass against my groin. The little spoon to my big spoon. A position that has become my favorite over the last few weeks.

The position that I aim to be waking up in every single day for the rest of my life, knowing she's mine. Making that promise wasn't hard at all. I know I'll never break her heart.

But deep down, I wonder if there is a part of her that will truly let me have her heart at all.

"I'm surprised you still have our phone number." It is meant as a scold, but the lightness in my mother's tone does nothing more than comfort me. My parents showed me what it was to work hard for what you want, building up their own wine empire. But at the same time, they made sure we had enough family time, creating memories that still make me smile.

It's a stupid cliche, but I love my mother more than anything.

Damn mama's boy.

"It's not been that long, Mum."

"The last time we spoke, I spotted you with a pretty blonde in Texas. I'm guessing she's getting all your time now?"

I snicker, walking into my Monaco apartment as a yawn escapes my throat. "Maybe."

"Maybe? Is that why you're tired in the middle of the day?" She sounds more amused than I expected her to be, making this the perfect time to tell her what has been on my mind.

"Maybe." I smile from ear to ear, throwing my keys on the counter before jumping over the couch and planting my ass in it to get comfortable. "Did you ask what Zoe wants for Christmas?"

"You coming home is fine. You are coming home, right?"

"Of course, Mum. I can't wait."

"One more race and the season is already over." She pauses, her thoughts lingering in the air. "I'm proud of you, you know?"

"I know."

"Do you? Because your father mentioned how you were worried about your sponsorship with Baronial."

I sigh, followed by a hum.

"Why?"

"I don't know. I know how proud Dad was when I landed that deal. It's his favorite company."

"And you're his favorite son."

"I'm his only son."

"Exactly. Do you think he cares about a sponsorship deal? I'm sorry you've been struggling in the last two years, but I hope it's not because you feel like we've put too much pressure on you."

"No, no, Mum." I shake my head, hating that she came to that conclusion. "You're nothing but great." Baronial has always been a measurement for me. If I can get them, I can get anything. When they told me that I might lose it, I felt like everything I'd built was crumbling around me. I saw walls crashing down, and I was disappointing my parents with every brick falling. "But I didn't want to disappoint you either."

"You can never disappoint us." Her answer makes me smile while I look out over the Cote D'azur. "We just want you to be happy. And you haven't been happy in a while."

I'd contradict it if she was wrong, and a few months ago, that would've been the truth. But since Nikkie, I know the difference. I know what happiness feels like.

"I know. I'm happy now. And I'm excited to start with Arzano after winter break."

"Yes, they are a good team."

"They are. I hope to win another championship with them."

"Well, no matter what you do, we are proud of you."

"Thank you, Mum."

"How was Amsterdam?" It's like my mother can see right through me, but when I think about that one time I stole some candy from Woolworths and she could see it written on my face. I suppose she can. She has that sixth sense that all mothers claim to have.

"Wet. Cold. *Fun*." I smirk.

She stays quiet for a few seconds. "When will I meet her?"

"I want to say winter break."

My mother can hear the doubt in my voice. "But?"

"*But* I don't want to scare her away."

"You're serious with her, aren't you?"

The easiest part would be to throw the whole situation in the we're-having-fun box and keep my mother in the dark a little while longer. But it feels wrong to lie to her, and anything less than confessing the truth swirling in my chest, would be exactly that.

A full lie.

"I am, Mum. She's amazing," I gush. "She's sweet, sassy, high-spirited, and funny."

"She sounds like a treat."

She is a treat. She's like one of those candies you can't help but keep eating. I expect to get nauseous any day now, but I'm still hungry for more.

"But?" I question when I hear the reluctance in my mother's tone.

"But is she on the same page?"

"I think so." I hope so. But the truth is, I don't know. I want her. When I look at my future, I see her standing by my side, but I can't shake the feeling that she isn't completely on board just yet. I know she cares about me. I even feel confident enough to say she has feelings for me. But every time I try to get closer, I also see her retreating just a bit.

"You think so?"

"I know so. But she's had a tough year. She—she lost a... friend." I don't know if she'll bite my head off for mentioning this, but I want my mother to like her. Even though they haven't met yet. "I think she's still hurt from that."

"I'm so sorry to hear that."

"Yeah, I think she's still having a hard time with it. Plus, my occupation doesn't help."

"She doesn't like racing?"

"Actually, she loves racing." It's another thing that makes her absolutely perfect. "It's more the traveling part. I'm away a lot. I can't take her with me all the time, even if I want to."

"She doesn't want to?"

"She owns a bar, and she doesn't want to rely on me."

My mother huffs in delight, like I thought she would. "I like independent women."

"That makes two of us." I laugh.

"Well, as long as she's not in it for your money, just give her time. And bring her home. I want to meet this girl."

"She's not in it for the money." If she was, she would've asked me for help with her bills, and she has done nothing but hide it from me. She made it clear that she values her own money, and nothing in her actions dictates otherwise.

"Maybe she can come spend Christmas with us?"

I bark out a laugh. "Really, Mother? I haven't even made it official yet because I'm scared she'll run off, and here you are inviting her for Christmas dinner with the entire family? That will definitely not help my case."

"Fine. But if you're still with her when the season starts again, you better bring her home."

That's four months. Four months for me to make it official and convince her I'm in it for the long haul. I can do that.

"Deal."

21

NIKKIE

I CLEAN UP THE dishes in the sink with my phone tucked between my shoulder and my ear. The hold music is playing Ed Sheeran's "Bad Habit," and my hips wiggle while I dry the plate in my hands, staring out of the window. Pedestrians walk the cobblestones, covered up in thick scarfs and beanies. Winter replaced fall quicker than expected this year and a thin layer of ice lays on top of the canals.

I did some extra shifts at the bar this week to collect more tips, and now I'm hanging on the phone with one of the suppliers dying to take my money, asking them for a payment reference so I can at least give them something. I can't find the old letters, and I don't want to risk transferring money if I don't know all the details.

"Miss Peters, thank you for waiting," the woman on the phone says in Dutch. "I'm a little confused because you don't have outstanding payments."

I purse my lips. "I think there must be a mistake because I got a final notice two weeks ago. Are you sure you have the right person? My name is Nicolien Peters. Born in 1999."

"Let me check again, please hold."

"Sure," I reply as I continue to tidy the kitchen.

A minute later, the hold music stops again. "Miss Peters?"

"Yes?"

"It seems like your outstanding payment was paid ten days ago."

"Ten days ago?" That can't be right, because I haven't paid anything. It's why I kept the bar open a little longer every night, hoping I would make some extra cash. "Can you see who paid them?"

"It's a foreign account number."

"A foreign account number?" I parrot as the wheels start to turn in my head.

"Yes, miss."

"Can you tell me the account number?"

"I'm afraid I'm not allowed to give you that information."

"But you're sure it's paid? I don't owe you any more money?"

"Nothing other than the upcoming month, which you will receive a notification for next week."

What the fuck.

"Can I do anything else for you, Miss Peters?"

I shake my head with wide eyes and surprise in my voice. "No, that's it. I guess."

"Alright, I hope you have a good day."

I return her wish with a mutter, then blink around the room before I start calling all the other organizations that I still owe money. Thirty minutes later, I'm stunned.

All my bills have been paid by a foreign account number, and after the fourth phone call, I have a good guess of who is responsible.

We haven't talked to him all day, knowing he's prepping for the last race of the season, but I'm not willing to wait until he calls me before I get to the bottom of this. I check the time, knowing it's only two hours earlier in Abu Dhabi and hoping he's not in some kind of team meeting, then set my phone back against my ear.

"Hey, baby." Tristan's smooth voice glides into my ear with the ease of melting butter, boiling my heart to the exact right temperature.

"Did you pay my bills?"

I already know he did when he's quiet for just a few seconds too long.

"What are you talking about?"

"Did you pay my bills, Ace?" I do my best to not sound reprimanding, but I can't fully help it.

Finally, he blows out a breath. "Yeah, I did."

He paid my bills. Moist burns behind my eyes, and I'm not sure if I want to get mad at him or cry, because that's the nicest thing anyone has ever done for me.

"Why would you do that?"

"Because..." he trails off, pausing for a moment. "I felt bad that I stole you away two weekends when, clearly, you're struggling to get by. I saw the letters. I couldn't help myself."

"I don't have to be saved," I say quietly, tears filling my eyes.

"I know you don't. Please don't make a big deal out of this."

"Tristan, that was almost eight grand worth of outstanding bills."

"Babe, listen to me. I know this is going to make me sound arrogant as fuck, but frankly, I don't care. Eight grand? I make that kind of money in half a day, and I don't blink or blush spending it on something that's worth it. *You're* worth it." His emphasis cuts deeply.

My heart is on fire. The kind that's unable to put out, no matter how many buckets of ice you throw on top of it. It's a feeling that's been growing inside of me at a steady pace, even though I've been trying to keep it out as much as possible.

"Thank you," I tell him. No one has ever done something like that for me. I understand it's not a lot of money for him, but even he must acknowledge that it's a pretty big deal to pay off someone's debt like that.

"Don't even mention it, baby. But also better prepare your pretty little head for stuff like this."

My deep frown settles, not sure how to feel about that. "What do you mean?"

"I want to spoil you. In fact, when the season is over... I want to come and stay with you for a while and spoil the hell out of you."

The thought of someone taking care of me, *spoiling me*, it's something I never longed for. I'm not the kind of girl that dreams of being swept off my feet and being pampered by a prince that wants to court me as we live happily ever after. I work for what I want. My independence means the world to me, and I'll be damned before I give that away to anyone.

But then why do his words give me the fuzziest feeling behind my chest?

"In Amsterdam?"

"Yeah, the season is almost over. It's winter break. I don't want to sit in Monaco knowing you're in Amsterdam. And I don't want to go to my family and spend winter break in my board shorts. I want to spend it with you. *If you let me,*" he adds.

Tristan Reinhart, all to myself for a few days? "Can't wait, Ace."

"Great. In that case, let me finish this race so I can come home to you."

Home. I shake my head with fucking heart eyes and a giddy feeling I want to hold on to like a life raft. He put *me* and *home* in one sentence. I expect to freak out about it, waiting for the wrecking ball to knock through my smile, but nothing happens. The quiet, the dread, it doesn't come.

"Go score some points, Ace," I tell him before we say goodbye and end the call.

Five minutes later, I'm still grinning on our shitty little couch when Tess strolls into the living room. "What are you so happy about?"

She lets her body fall into the cushions, then pulls up her legs.

"Tristan wants to stay here during winter break."

Tessa pops up an eyebrow as the corner of her mouth curls. "Stay? For how long?"

I shrug.

"Well, you got yourself an F1 boyfriend, Nik."

Out of habit, my mouth opens to deny it, wanting to brush it off like it's nothing, but then I quickly close it because I know that's bullshit. It's the fear that's still tucked deep inside of me, but I don't want to feel like that anymore. Tristan fired up my will to live again. He's the fucking sunshine that I was missing for so long and I'm sick of pushing him away.

I nod with the excitement of a little girl. "I think so too."

"Is he gonna stay here?"

"If you're okay with that?"

"Sure, I'll go to my parents more for a while."

"You don't have to do that!" The last thing I want to do is kick Tessa out of her own house.

"Don't be silly." Her hand lands on my knee, locking my eyes with her caring expression. "I'm just happy you're smiling again. I like him for you."

Her words do something to me. I know Tessa always has my back, but it means the world that she likes Tristan. "Thank you."

"I mean it, though." She pulls her hand away, running it through her chestnut hair. "Ever since you met him, you're happier again. Brighter. *More you*. I know you'll never be the same as before the accident, but I missed your sass. Now all I need is your streaking down the canals and I'll fully believe you're happy again."

We both start laughing while I try to push through a reprimanding look. "We promised to never talk about that night ever again. *Besides*, I was really, really drunk."

"What?" She cocks her head. "I can't tell Tristan about that night?"

"Don't you dare, woman!" I prick her in the side with my index finger, and she jerks away.

"Okay, okay! I won't. Just promise me one thing." Her smile dissolves, replaced by a serious look.

"What's that?"

"Promise you'll think about selling the bar." My sigh is loud, but she doesn't let it stop her. "Just think about it, Nik. You never really wanted that bar. It's giving you a shit ton of headaches. And if this thing between you and Tristan grows any further... it will stand between the two of you for no fucking reason." I swallow, holding her gaze. "I know you loved Wes. You probably always will.

But you don't have to force yourself to keep his dream when it's standing in the way of your own. It's okay to choose *you*."

A shiver lifts the hairs on the back of my neck, because I see the truth in her words. But I don't just see them. I *feel* them deep within my tainted soul. I'm falling for Tristan, but I can never fully commit if I'm trying to keep Wes alive by keeping the bar.

"You don't have to decide now. Just promise you'll think about it."

And though reluctantly, I nod. "I promise."

22

TRISTAN

"I CAN'T BELIEVE YOU brought me candles," she beams up at me, a little glitter in her eyes. "I love candles."

I snort, chuckling, then glance around the small living room, letting my gaze run past the various trays of scented candles. "I noticed, hence the big box of every scent they had in the store." I might have overdone it a little, but that look of wonder she's shooting me makes it all worth it.

"You really didn't have to," she whispers.

"I know. But I wanted to." My lips brush over her hair, holding her close to my body, as I look at the tray of candles she set up on a plate on the coffee table. "Do you like them?"

"I love them. You picked all the right ones."

My spine unwillingly straights a bit at the comment.

"Are you sure Tessa won't mind us kicking her out?" Her eyes are set on the Transformers movie I put on, with her hand resting on my stomach, her thumb absentmindedly moving up and down the fabric of my t-shirt in a scorching yet comforting pace.

"No, she was going out anyway. Besides, if I'm with you, it makes her worry less about me."

Her confession knits my eyebrows together, bringing that gut feeling of concern about her back to the surface. I hoped by now she would tell me what's haunting her deep brown eyes, but she hasn't. So I swallow, pushing out the question I've been wanting to ask for weeks. Slowly, I put my fingers underneath her chin, then direct her so she can look at me.

"You were in that car with Wes, weren't you?"

Her eyes widen just a tad, the sheer horror flashing through them for a brief second before she shuts them with force, taking in a deep breath.

When she finally opens them again, what feels like a minute later, her gold retinas are glossed over. It pains me to see her like this, and for a second, I decide we don't have to have this conversation. I'll just easily kiss her pain away.

But I'm in it for the long haul with this girl. I need to know she can trust me and that I'm here for her, no matter what.

I'm not going *any-fucking-where* and she's going to need to accept that.

"I was." A tear rolls down her cheek as she pushes out the words. "We crashed against a tree. I still have nightmares about it." I let go of her face, giving her the time she needs now that she's finally opening up, while at the same time I try to ignore the despair that's dropped over my shoulders when I think of her in pain. "There was blood. So much blood. I still have no idea where it came from because it was mine, but I came out with a few cuts and scratches. Wes... it was as if he was sleeping. He wouldn't wake up." She's now sobbing through her words, each syllable more frantic than the last. "He wouldn't *fucking* wake up. He should've woken up. Why didn't he wake up?" Her haunted eyes snap to mine, stopping my heart. I feel paralyzed, lost for words.

So I do the only thing I can do: I pull her to my chest with all I've got, holding her head close to my heart.

"Shh, I got you, baby. I'm here," I breathe against her hair. "You're not alone. I'm here for you." A big lump grows the size of a bowling ball in the back of my throat, my own eyes growing moist with every sob she pushes out as she buries her face in the safety of my body. And I just hold her.

I want to take it all away for her. The bad memories. The pain. The hurt. The *grief.* But I know this is all I can do. So, I hold her as tight as I can, grateful she's finally letting it out. From what I've picked up since the day I met her, she's been feeling alone since the night of the accident, and I don't want her to ever feel like that again. She's not alone. She's got me.

I'm here and there's not a goddamn hair on my head that's willing to let her go.

"I'm sorry," she sniffs as she brings her head back up, her intensely sad eyes restricting my throat.

"For what, babe?"

"I'm such a mess." Her gaze drifts down with a shame that only pisses me off, erupting a fiery emotion from my throat that comes out with a force even though I do my best to hold it in.

"We all are. Everyone is in their own way. Don't you dare apologize for who you are or what you're going through. *Ever.* Especially with me." It's gutting me to see her like this. Even more when she flips her attention to me with a clear question.

"Why me?" Her tone feels like a knife that's jammed straight through my heart, because deep down, she didn't always question her own self-worth. I know that. *I can feel that.* And I just hope that strong girl, the one I *know* is tucked deep inside of her, is still there. It's what I see when I look into her eyes, my vision roaming the deep depths of hers even when she tries to hide it behind the skyscraper-sized wall she has put up.

But I didn't become a world champion by giving up. And I will definitely not give up on her.

I take her face in my hands, brushing my nose against hers. "Because you can put up a mask to protect yourself, but I see you, Nik. *I see you*, the real you. You're the most beautiful woman I've ever met. And I'm falling in love with you."

The small curl that lifts her cheeks vanishes as quickly as it came, her eyebrows shooting up.

"What?" she mutters from her pent-up breath at the same time the doorbell rings. I let out a chuckle when she jumps up like the couch is on fire.

"Saved by the bell." I eye her moving toward the door with flushed cheeks, a small smile on my lips. I'm not even offended. In fact, it's a breath of fresh air, that for the first time in ages, I want something from someone else instead of someone wanting something from me.

She shoots me a puzzled look after looking through the peephole, wiping away the wetness from her cheeks. Her blonde hair swings over her shoulder from the jerk of her head. She has no clue. No clue that she makes my entire body sigh just by looking at her, taking in every inch of her.

"It's Sam."

"Sam?" I repeat while she opens the door.

Like he fucking owns the place, he strolls inside with messy hair before wrapping Nikkie in a side hug in greeting, then lifts his nose in the air. "Hey, Nik. It smells nice in here."

"What are you doing here?" I lock eyes with my friend, who's giving me a cocky smirk.

"I got bored." He shrugs his green puffy coat off his shoulders, then hangs it over one of the dining room chairs before flopping his ass beside me.

"So you decide to appear on my girlfriend's doorstep?" I don't miss the small gasp coming from Nikkie's lips when she hears the word "girlfriend," but I fix my gaze on Sam with a cocked eyebrow.

"Why is that weird?"

"Because you live in Monaco?" Nikkie opts. She moves past me to sit on the other side, but I quickly pull her wrist and tuck her onto my lap, holding her close enough to silently tell her that I got her. *In every way possible.*

"Yeah, Monaco is no fun without you." Then he rears his head with accusation to find Nik's gaze. "You stole my wingman. Tristan told me you're good with your hands. You owe me a massage."

My fist hits his stomach, and he hunches forward with a huff. "Okay, no massage."

"Isn't half of the grid living in Monaco?" she counters, chuckling.

"Everyone left for winter break, except for Hastings." He scrunches up his nose, as if the name alone might poison him.

"You could do some bonding with him? Who knows, maybe the two of you can make sure you don't drive each other off the track next year?" Nikkie gives him an amused glance.

"The only bonding I will do with Jordan motherfucking Hastings is showing him where he belongs when I beat the asshole next year."

"You really hate him, don't you?"

He shakes his head. "That asshole isn't worth my hate. The title would've been mine if he didn't run me off the track in Monza."

"I don't know. He had a pretty good season."

Sam snaps his dull look back to hers, then flicks his blue eyes to me. "Up until now, I really liked her."

"Oh, shut up. You still do." Nik waves his comments away, and I chuckle.

"I don't know, Dutchie. You're kinda ruining it here. Might consider switching you to my naughty list." He winks, mostly to get a rise out of me, and I narrow my eyes at him.

"Dutchie?"

"Yeah, you like?"

"Okay," I boom, then slap a firm hand on his knee before I squeeze it tightly enough to conjure a grimace on his arrogant face. "Thank you for stopping by. I'm sure you have a lot to do. I will see you back home."

"No, we're going out." He slaps my hand away.

"We are not."

"Come on, T. I'm all alone except for my fucking sister walking into my house whenever the fuck she wants."

"You really need to ask for that key back," I suggest.

"I know. Who knew my sister wasn't smart enough to figure that pulling a bottle of wine from my fridge doesn't count as an emergency. You'd think considering she's my manager, she has a set of brains." The roll of his eyes has

Nikkie chuckling in my arms. "But that's not the point. The point is that I'm bored and you are the one I go to when I'm bored."

His beaming smile is hard to ignore, the white of his teeth almost blinding me.

I breathe out, pinching the bridge of my nose, though I can't hold back my smile. "You are ridiculous."

"We've already established that. Now, let's just go." He slaps my knee, and I lock eyes with Nikkie. Picking between my best friend and my girlfriend. *Not a hard decision.*

"No," I answer, resolute.

"Fine." He crosses his arms in front of his chest, triumphantly placing his white sneakers on the coffee table as he settles himself deeper into the couch. "We'll stay in then. It's nice here anyway. Love the whole candle setup. All I need now is a blanket. Do you have another one?" He locks eyes with Nikkie. "Never mind, I'll just cuddle up against the two of you." He puts his words into action, rubbing his shoulder against mine.

"Get the fuck off me, fool."

"Well, then let's go out!" he exclaims.

I push my lips into Nikkie's neck, groaning because I really don't want to leave the comfort of her living room. "He's not gonna leave until we wear him out."

"I figured." Nikkie quickly finds my lips, then fixes her gaze on Sam again. "I'm not going clubbing. Standing in a bar five days a week is more than enough for me."

"Fine. You live here. You tell us what's fun to do around here. I heard they have a sex museum." We both reply with a silent frown. "Okay, no sex museum. I guess that rules out the Red Light District as well?"

"You don't need us if you wanna go there." Nikkie purses her lips with her eyes narrowed to slits. "I can easily tell you directions right now."

"Yeah? You've been there a lot?" I know he's only teasing, but it still makes my fist slam into his shoulder with force. "Ouch! Okay, crossed the line. Sorry."

He gives me an apologetic look, though I can still see the mischief in his eyes. "Come on, Dutchie. Help me out here."

The corner of her lips curl, her brown eyes sparkling. "I have an idea."

"Hit me with it!"

"Can you skate?"

Sam's blond lashes blink at her with a straight expression, as if she just asked him to eat shit. "No."

And Nikkie's grin expands to her ears. "Oh, this is gonna be fun."

23

NIKKIE

"**J**UST KEEP YOUR BACK straight and your arms wide." It's hard to keep in my chuckle as I yell at Sam across the ice. The air is crisp against my cheeks, and I glance at the Rijksmuseum behind the outdoor ice rink while keeping my eyes trained on Sam. He's got on a black *I Love Amsterdam* hat that I bought for him and Tristan to make them less recognizable, and the dim lights dance over it as he tries to stay on his feet and move forward over the ice.

"I'm fucking trying, Dutchie!" He wobbles a few yards farther, like he's fucking Bambi before he falls on his ass with his legs up in the air and I lose it.

I shudder as a thread of laughter wheezes out of my lungs, my body folding forward from the hilarity. I let it all out, not holding back. And it takes me a while before I catalog how good it feels. There's a lightheartedness that I haven't felt in ages, and it only expands the smile on my face when I straighten my back. My stomach hurts from laughing, but the muscles in my shoulders feel more relaxed than they have in months, and it makes me sigh in content. I'm still cackling as Sam's trying to get back on his feet, but failing miserably.

"You're fully enjoying this, aren't you?" Two strong arms slide over my stomach, and I let out a shriek when Tristan's chest jams into my back as his skates screech over the ice to a halt.

Automatically, I slide my hands over his, settling into his weight. "Probably more than I should."

"Nah, he can take it." We both keep our attention fixed on Sam squirming on the ice.

"Are any of you assholes ever gonna help me?" He glares, his body spread out like a starfish on the ice, ready to give up.

"Sorry, man. This is way too fun to watch."

"I hate you!" Sam barks, rippling another laugh from my throat before Tristan spins me in his arms, pulling up my chin to brush his lips against mine.

"I love hearing you laugh."

I peer up at him, my heart fully agreeing. The truth is, I laugh more when he's around. At first, I didn't want to admit it to anyone, let alone to myself. But earlier on the couch made it impossible to ignore. In the last year, whenever I would be overcome with a moment of grief, it would last days, maybe even weeks. But with Tristan, it's all different.

He made it so easy to confess the way I felt, to release the tears and let him break through my walls, at least for a little bit. And this time, just feeling him close made me push away the gloom that came with it within minutes. It evaporated from my body when Sam walked in, and by the time the three of us made our way toward Museumplein, it was completely replaced with a feeling of peace as I felt Tristan's fingers linked with mine.

"You make me laugh," I confess. My heart aches staring up at him. The light strings around the rink are dancing in his green eyes, causing a box of butterflies to fly viciously through my belly. I heard him when he said he was falling in love with me. I thought about that while he and Sam were discussing football while we made our way over here, and the entire time I was waiting for the fear to creep in. But it never happened. Not only did he comfort the grief that's deep inside of me, just by being with me, but he also made me feel giddy when I thought about the honesty he gifted me with.

Tristan Reinhart is in love with me.

As if he can read my mind, his expression turns serious, but I'm not tempted to run for the hills and duck for cover. This time, I hold his gaze, feeling safe in his arms regardless.

"I meant what I said earlier."

"I know." His surprised look makes me smile, but I don't want to guard myself any longer. Not from him.

"I'm *in* love with you," he emphasizes with a firm grip on my body, as if he's scared I will skate out of his grip when the words really hit me. And truth be told, a tiny voice inside of me is telling me to do exactly that. But it doesn't drown out the roaring of my heart that refuses to hide behind the perfect brick wall I've built.

"I know," I whisper.

He searches my eyes. "You're not running."

"No," I shake my head, smiling. "Because I'm in love with you too."

His handsome face glows up with a shocked smile. "What?"

"I'm in love with *you*." Speaking out loud what I've been feeling in my heart for weeks feels liberating. It's like the sun is finding its way through the clouds, pushing until it can warm my cheeks in a way that I've once known.

I startle, laughing, when he throws his neck back, letting out a full howl.

"Sam! She's in love with me!"

Sam rolls his eyes, lifting his back from the ice. "Tell me something I don't fucking know and help me up!"

"Can't! I'm busy!" Tristan spins us in a rapid move, too quick for me to keep my skates underneath my body. We both crash onto the ice, chuckling as he finds my face with his calloused hands. His breath warms my face while the cold surface freezes my butt at the same time, yet I've never felt more comfortable. "I love you."

"I love you." His grin splits his face before his lips press against mine with an urgency that rings all the way to my toes. My entire body comes alive under his touch, as if he's trying to ink his feelings into my heart, claiming his space until the end of time. Warm fingers find their way into my hair while he forces me to open up to meet my tongue. A moan vibrates against his throat, and his body pushes deeper against mine, registering the bulge that's forming in his jeans. The world around me disappears; the only sound I can fully register is the beating of my heart that's pounding in my ears.

I love him, and it elevates my heart in a way that I can only describe as utter fucking bliss.

"Thanks for the help, *friends*." We break loose, sheepishly looking up at Sam, who's peering down at us with an evil eye. "You two *really* are disgusting."

I twist my gaze between Tristan and a glaring Sam, wondering how all of a sudden I got so lucky.

"Can we please get some gluhwein or something? I fucking drive cars for a living. I'm not going to die because I broke my neck on an ice rink." Sam pulls Tristan off of me, almost dropping to the floor again when his skates start to wiggle, then Tristan offers me his hand to help me back on my feet.

"I'm disappointed. I really was expecting you to be an athlete that has multiple talents, Sam." I brush the snow of the rink off my jeans.

"You want to see multi–"

"Don't flirt with my girlfriend!" Tristan cuts him off with a scowl, and I suppress the smile that wants to crack through when Sam shuts up like a kid with his hand in the cookie jar.

"Fine," he grunts. "But you better buy me some fucking gluhwein."

"Nik?" My face falls, recognizing that voice from anywhere before we all turn around to where it's coming from.

"Oh, boy." I shoot my dad an awkward smile, wondering how much he has seen before I decide it doesn't really matter. I guess there's no better time than today.

"Who's that?" Tristan glances up and down at my father with a curious frown while my dad is gracing all of us with a slight scowl. He looks every bit the bad boy that he is, with his leather jacket and gray beanie covering his head of hair.

I sigh, then conjure a smile on my lips before I skate off to the edge of the rink with ease. "My dad."

"Your dad?" The shock in his voice is inevitable, and I swiftly turn mid-way, then shrug when we lock eyes again. Tristan's eyes are wide, blinking as if he's hoping he can blink the situation away.

"He won't bite," I snicker. "I think." I turn back around, closing the distance between my dad and I. "Hey, Dad."

24

TRISTAN

"Τ HAT'S HER DAD," I mutter to Sam, as I observe her skate to the man in the leather jacket with a finesse that shows she's been skating every winter since she was a kid.

"I heard, T." I don't have to twist my head to find out what look he's shooting at me. "Well, why are you standing here? Go meet the guy. Find out how much he hates you."

"What? No one hates me," I rebuke, snorting, though his words cause a little bit of worry to creep through my gut. I only had one girlfriend and I wasn't worried about the whole meet-the-parents thing because she was the daughter of my mother's best friend, so I already knew them. But this time, there's definitely a pressure of wanting to be liked and accepted.

"You're fucking his daughter. He's definitely going to hate you."

I drop my head at his crass comment, then bring it back up as I shake my head.

"Do you ever use a filter?"

"Nope." He pushes me forward, and I skate toward Nikkie while flipping him off before I place myself beside her with a smile. "Evening, sir."

"Tristan, this is my dad, Johnnie. Daddy, this is my boyfriend, Tristan." Nikkie gleams.

"Boyfriend?" Her dad snaps his watchful gaze back to his daughter. "Hoelang ken je deze gast al?"

My eyebrows shoot up with a little dread at the Dutch words I can't understand.

Yeah, he definitely hates me.

She awkwardly clears her throat before she scolds her dad. "I've known him since September, Dad. Don't be rude, *please*."

The man clearly has a lot of respect for his daughter, because he holds her gaze for a few seconds, showing his disapproval, before his coffee brown eyes somewhat soften a tad as he offers his hand. "Johnnie Peters."

"Tristan Reinhart, sir. It's a pleasure to meet you." His grip is firm, and I do my best not to wince until he lets go.

"I would've said the same if I knew of your existence in the first place."

"Hou je mond, Pa," she hisses through her smile, which translates in my head as something like 'please stop talking, Dad.'

"Hi, I'm Sam Devereaux." Sam wobbles his way over to us, giving Johnnie a short wave.

"You're the son of Jack Devereaux, aren't you? Third time F1 World Champion?"

"That would be me." Sam's grimace is undeniable, not having the best memories of his father in general.

"I heard you will be taking the title next season." There's a bit of awe there that has me clenching my teeth. If people like Sam more than me, the world has gone mad.

"That's the plan, sir," Sam replies.

"You have great talent. I'm sure you will." Johnnie briefly gives me a once-over, then his frown deepens on forehead as he fixes his attention to his daughter. "How come you never told me you hang out with Formula One drivers now?"

Nikkie rolls her eyes. "Maybe because you're busy with *business* all the time?"

Why do I have the feeling "business" is a synonym for something else?

Johnnie ignores the reprimanding look she's giving him, then flicks his gaze to Sam and me. "I need to talk to Nikkie for a minute, boys."

Nikkie's sigh vibrates through my entire body, and I look for her eyes. She softly gives me a nod in approval.

"Of course, we'll be at the bar getting some gluhwein." I point my thumb over my shoulder, while the other wraps around Sam's shoulder as I shoot her dad a smile. "I hope we can get to know each other a little better, sir. Come on, Sam."

Nikkie shoots me a grateful smile. "I'll be there in a minute."

"Take your time."

Sam and I turn around, me slowly helping him leave the rink with some dignity as I hold him up by his arm.

"Her dad looks like a badass," he says with a smirk that I want to wipe off his face. "You're gonna have a hard time getting on his good side."

"You're loving this, aren't you?"

"Someone is immune to your cheery attitude and annoying smile? Fuck yeah. But don't worry, I can put in a good word for you."

"Thanks, *mate*." I let go of him and roughly pat him on the back. "But I got this." He falls forward, landing his knees on the ice again, and I grab my phone to snap a picture.

"Delete that," he growls.

"Not a chance." I chuckle.

25

NIKKIE

"**Y**OU ARE DATING TRISTAN Reinhart?"

"Really? You had to be a dick and pretend you don't know who he is?" I throw my dad a scowl.

The asshole has been watching racing since before I was born. He probably knows every single driver on that grid from 1990 until now.

A low chuckle rumbles out of his chest like he's the class clown. "I gotta keep the guy on his toes, kid. Famous or not."

"No, you really don't." My dad is protective. But not in the *don't come near her* kinda way. He's the dad who just lets me do whatever I want, then comes to clean up the mess whenever shit hits the fan. And by cleaning up, I mean he makes a bigger mess. Like trashing the house of my first boyfriend because the prepubescent shithead decided it was fair game to have two girlfriends instead of one. I wouldn't be surprised if his balls are still traumatized after the golf club my dad launched between his legs. That's my dad. He comes after you fuck up. He doesn't warn you about it. Tristan shouldn't be any other way.

"What?" I roll my eyes while his stay fixed on me. I know that look. It always comes with some model dad comment that I don't need, like, *"be careful,"* and let's be honest, he doesn't really feel.

"You're really into this guy, aren't you?"

Okay, not what I was expecting.

My eyes widen a little before I huff his comment away. "Dad, please."

"Come on, Nik. I can see it in your eyes." He tilts his beanie covered head a little toward me, never dropping his gaze, as if he's trying to find the truth in my irises.

He won't, even though I do have a hard time really pushing my feelings away.

"See what?"

"Less darkness."

I swallow, wishing that comment didn't make me so gloomy, but I guess there's no denying it.

"He makes me smile," I confess with a shrug.

"Do you trust him?"

"Well, you clearly don't."

A dull look comes my way. One that basically says, *don't be a brat.*

"The boy flies all over the world year-round. Wouldn't be surprised if he has a different girl in each city."

I shut my eyes and take a breath, not appreciating the thought he's putting in my head, then open them again with a glare because there's not a bone in my body that believes that to be true. "I hate you."

"I just want you to be careful."

I can argue with him that it's bullshit because he hasn't told me to be careful since I was sixteen. And even then, being careful meant *whatever you do, just don't get caught.* But when I detect a hint of sincerity in his features that is rare, I decide to tell him the truth.

"I'm in love with him, Dad."

"What?" He jerks his head away.

"I don't know how it happened and I tried to stop it." *God, how I tried to stop it.* "But I'm in love with him. If that means you want to have the whole I'll-break-you-if-you-break-her-heart talk with him, go right ahead. But to answer your question, yes, I do trust him."

It feels like the elephant that took residence on my chest is lifting his ass a bit as I speak the words out loud. "I trust him more than I do myself. As fucked up as that might be. So, please. *For me.* Don't go all badass dad on him and *be nice.*"

He holds my gaze, searching my face to detect if I'm bullshitting him. But for once, I'm not. I'm in love with Tristan Reinhart and admitting it to my dad feels better than I expected.

"Okay, I will." He says the right words, but I still squint at him with daggers of suspicion. "I swear!" His hands fly up, placating.

I soften my evil eye. "Thank you. You wanna have a drink with us?"

"You want your old man to join?" His fake reluctance is rolling my eyes to the back of my head.

"Might as well get to know him, right?"

"And here I thought you'd be embarrassed by me."

"Oh, I am." There is no doubt about that. "But I can't hide him from you forever."

"Glad we agree on that. Here," he sticks his hand in his back pocket, then pulls a stack of notes from his dark jeans.

"Dad…" I drawl with a side eye as he pulls a twenty and holds it out to me. "No, I don't want it." I shake my head.

"Don't be such a brat and just take it."

"I'm a brat for *not* taking your money?" I laugh.

"It's not like I'm giving you a grand, Nik." He cocks an eyebrow, his hand not moving an inch with the blue piece of paper tucked between his fingers. "Just take it. Go buy yourself some candles or something."

I breathe out loudly, then press my lips together before they form a small appreciative smile as I take the money from him. "Thanks, Dad. I appreciate it."

"No worries, kid." He throws me a grateful grin.

"Alright, I'll meet you at the front." I turn around to skate back to the bar, giving my dad the chance to walk around the rink to join us.

"Just one more thing."

I twist on my heels, facing the frown on his head. "Lieke told me Nina has been stopping by the bar, asking for money."

I match the wrinkle in his forehead. "You and Lieke are talking now?

My dad lets his shoulders hang, before he cocks his head in a reprimanding way, totally seeing right through my deflection. I sigh with my entire body.

"Nik?" he presses.

"I'm just helping her out with groceries and stuff."

"Don't bullshit me." There's venom in his voice. The one that is ready to clean up the mess.

"I'm not," I screech, probably a bit too indignant for him to fully believe it.

"Half the time, you can sell me any lie you want, but not this time. Is she harassing you?"

"No." *Yes.* But who can blame her? The woman lost her son. Because of me.

"Nik," my dad grunts.

I lock eyes with the man who raised me, seeing the fire that I appreciate, even though my upbringing was anything but conventional. "She lost her son, Dad."

He shakes his head, but the way his gaze softens tells me he isn't going to push me for more right now, and I offer him a tiny, yet victorious smile.

"She's not your responsibility, kid."

"I know."

"Do you?" My mind is screaming yes, but I can't comprehend why my actions of the last year have been contradicting that in every way. His words settle deep in my brain while I feel them slowly seeping down to my weeping heart. I know my relationship with Nina is ten colors of fucked up. I shouldn't get into trouble helping someone else. But I don't know how to get rid of the need to make it right.

"You don't owe her shit," he adds, as if he can read my mind. Normally, I'd argue that I owe her a son. But lately, my mind has been wondering if Wes wanted me to be unhappy as I let his mother take advantage of me more and more.

"I know," I concede.

"Don't let her tell you otherwise, Nikkie. You take care of yourself. Let her deal with the messes she makes. Do you hear me?" A stern look comes my way.

"I do." I just need to find the strength to tell her.

26

NIKKIE

"**W**ELL, THAT NIGHT ESCALATED a bit quickly." We walk through the door of my apartment, both a little buzzed from the cups of gluhwein we poured down our throats. My dad kept his promise and has been behaving, even though he clearly declared Sam as his favorite of the night. "Sorry if that was awkward for you."

Tristan takes off his jacket, hanging it over the dining room chair before he settles himself on my tiny couch with a hand rubbing his tired expression. "It was fucking awkward. But I'm still glad it happened."

"You sure?" I lift my leg, straddling him, then bring my lips forward to find his.

His warm hands land on my back, moving up and down my spine. "Of course. I told you. I'm in this for the long haul. Your dad is part of that. Even if he hates me."

He pulls a face that has me chuckling against his lips. "He doesn't hate you." If my dad hated him, he'd probably have a black eye and Tristan wouldn't dare to set foot in the Netherlands for any other reason than a racing weekend.

"I'm sure the only reason he was nice was because you and Sam were there," Tristan argues. It's cute seeing him all insecure, and a little offended that someone doesn't appreciate his cheery attitude. It makes the superhero in my head more human.

"He doesn't hate you." I kiss him in reassurance. "I promise. He's just an asshole who wants to give you a hard time for the sake of it. See if you can take it."

His fingers move slowly underneath my shirt, the heat on my skin making me moan against his lips. "So he's a little sadist?"

"Oh, you have no idea."

His grin expands with a little squint of his illuminating green eyes. "I don't want to find out, either, do I?"

"No, you don't." Let's keep my father's questionable past buried deeply, where it belongs.

"Hmm, good thing I can take on anything when it comes to you." His tongue swipes over my lips and I eagerly open for him. His calloused hands move all over my body, sparking every inch of my skin on high alert while I enjoy the scorching feeling of his kisses. The sensuality of our mouths dancing as one quickly lifts me into a higher state that I've become addicted to, wanting to rip his clothes from his body, but also wanting to drag this out for as long as possible. My thighs rub against his groin, and I feel it rise by the second, pushing against my clit.

But when I drag myself down his chest to bring my face between his legs and feast on him, the doorbell has my head jerking to the front door.

"Are you expecting anyone?" he asks with a groggy voice that turns me on even more.

I shake my head, then get up to pull the intercom phone from the wall.

"Who is it? Hello?" I ask in Dutch.

"Open up, Nikkie." Nina's voice feels like a slap back to reality, but this time, it's not just dread that it's loaded with. It's annoyance. Irritation. And when I let out a sigh, I can also register a little bit of anger.

"This is not a good time."

"I don't care," Nina snarls.

Her aggravated tone would normally swing me right back into that pool of guilt, but my dad's words are still ringing in my ear. *She is not your responsibility.*

"I'll come down." I hang the device back on the wall with a glare, then flash Tristan a wide smile. "I'll be right back."

"Everything okay?" The worried glance he gives me only fuels my confidence to stand up for myself, and inwardly, I thank him for it.

"Yeah, I just need to handle something." I grab my keys from the kitchen counter and stomp down the narrow staircase until my feet land on the cobblestone as I reach the street. I find her sitting on the bench in front of the closed bakery, a cigarette set between her lips as she lifts her face with a glare.

"Hi, Nina. How are you?" I decide to try this the calm and collective way, though her features already tell me that will be useless. The December temperature makes me cross my arms in front of my chest, a lame attempt to protect myself from the cold.

"I need money," Nina cuts right to the point.

No surprise there.

"Are you okay?" I search her gray eyes, looking more iced and zoned out than usual. I remember that look. I haven't seen it in a while, but I wasn't under the illusion that she suddenly got clean and bettered her life. She's been asking me for money, after all. "Are you high?"

"That's none of your business," she snaps. "I need money."

Don't we all. "I know. So do I. But I don't have any."

"Fine, I'll go grab some from the bar." She quickly spins on her heel, but I catch her by her elbow, dragging her back.

"No, you won't." I will no longer tolerate her in my bar, harassing the staff to slip her a few bills from the register. I'm done with that bullshit.

I'm done with her.

"Don't touch me."

"You are no longer allowed in the bar," I announce as I let her go, witnessing her face turn as red as a tomato.

"That's my son's bar!"

"No, it *was* his bar," I rebuke, emphasizing the word *was*. "He left it to me. It's *my* bar now, and I'm no longer letting you drive it into bankruptcy. Or me."

"You took everything from me!"

"I'm sorry. I truly am. But it was an accident, Nina." She can't keep blaming me for the rest of her life. It wasn't just my fault. I'm just the only one who survived.

"You're pissing on Wes's legacy by doing this."

"No, Nina!" I yell with a vicious glare, as I step closer, no longer willing to take her shit as truth. "You are! You keep forcing me to give you money, slowly destroying the last thing that was his." She holds my gaze with her chin held high, but I see her uncertainty when she swallows. "No more. Do you hear me? I'm sorry you lost your son. I miss him too. I know I can never feel the pain you feel because he's not my son, but I miss him more than anything and I wish he was still here." Her jaw clenches as she averts her gaze, and I feel for her. I really do. I hope to never experience what it's like to lose a child. Losing my boyfriend was devastating enough. I don't think I would survive losing anyone else.

"But he's not," I continue in a softer tone. "And we have to live with that. All of us. If you ever need a meal or a place to stay, you're welcome anytime. But I will no longer give you money, Nina." I shake my head, waiting for her to say anything, but she just keeps staring at the cobblestone of the pavement. We stand there for a few seconds before a cold breeze knocks me back to the man waiting for me upstairs. "Have a good night, Nina."

I don't look back as I open the door that leads to the stairwell, and when I take the first few steps, I wait until I hear the door fall into the lock before I stop. I suck in a deep breath, letting the air fill up my lungs, then I exhale as long as I can. Swallowing away the emotions, I shut my eyes, letting my sense of pride swell in my chest. I hope Nina finds peace someday, but I'm not responsible for it.

I take the last few steps up the stairs with big leaps, then burst through the door, eager to find the man who I know is still waiting for me on the couch.

"Are you okay?" His brows shoot up, a grin sliding in place when he sees my smile.

"Actually, I'm great," I tell him before I dive on top of him.

27

NIKKIE

"HOLD THIS. IT'S ALMOST midnight." Sam pushes a topped champagne glass into my hands, almost spilling it on my cornflower silk top before I jump back to make sure it doesn't drizzle down on my black pants either.

I take the drink from his hands with a slight scowl, but before I can open my mouth, he's already gone, slogging back to a brunette who looks like a supermodel, with her voluminous hair and little black dress.

"Who's that?" I take a few sips to keep the champagne from escaping over the rim of the glass before Tristan takes it from my hands, repeating my move.

He winces when the liquid lands on his tongue. "My dad would be horrified by this dusty shit that they sell for a hundred a bottle."

"Not a fan of champagne?"

"Not a fan of *bad* champagne. It's the result of growing up on a winery. I'm pretty sure my dad taught me the difference between a Riesling grape and a Chardonnay probably around the same time I learned how to walk." He drops the glass on the table next to us while I glance around the room.

The penthouse party is hosted by some oil sheik from Abu Dhabi, causing me to have a mini freak out when Sam listed all the celebrities who would probably be attending while I was getting ready, but so far, the brunette clinging to his arm doesn't ring any bell of recognition.

"Who knows? Who cares?" Tristan's hands slip around my stomach from behind before I feel his lips connect with the skin below my ear. I arch my neck, giving him better access, covering one hand over his as I let my weight sink into his chest.

"I can't believe I'm in Monaco on New Year's Eve." I stare down the port of the city, the reflection of the lights dancing on the dark water where the yachts are docked. It's surreal to see the road paved around it, the same one that's conjured into a racetrack every year in May. The people around us are so much different from those I normally see at my bar, which is why I was hesitant to come at first, but Tristan hasn't left my side, being more occupied with touching me every chance he gets rather than mingling with all the famous people around us. He gives them his signature smile in greeting, introducing me to a few people within the racing community, but other than that, his full focus is on yours truly.

It makes me feel like I'm on top of the world.

"I hope you'll be here more often after tonight." Tristan's low voice vibrates against my cheek, humming every part of my being alive.

"Yeah?"

"I'd ask you to move in with me, but I still don't want to scare you off." He spins me until I face him, his fingers locked on the small of my back to keep me in place.

"Smooth, Reinhart." I rest my hands on his arms, peering up into his green eyes. They spark with mischief, a small smile dying to break out in a wide grin.

"I know."

"I can't leave the bar," I tell him, even though I hear Tessa calling *bullshit* in my mind.

Not now, girlfriend.

"Sell it."

I've been thinking about it. I really have. But my feelings are still conflicted. I feel like the bar has been the only thing that kept me going. That kept giving me a reason to get out of bed. Selling the bar would leave me wondering what I really want to do again, and I don't know if I'm ready for that. I don't know if I'm ready to not know.

"What would I do?"

"Work for me?"

I chuckle, seeing exactly how that would benefit him. "I'm pretty sure sex buddy isn't tax refundable."

"Excuse me," he huffs, playfully offended. "You're my sexy girlfriend slash *buddy*. But no, though that sounds fucking amazing, that wasn't what I meant. You could be a physical therapist. I can get your name out there." My lashes fly up. I've thought about looking for a job as a physical therapist, but the thought of going into a practice every single day, working from nine to five, just makes me break out in hives. I know once upon a time, it was what I wanted to do, but now I'm not so sure anymore. I'm not sure of anything, if I'm being honest. All I wanna do is soak up all the time I get with Tristan, not wanting to waste a minute.

"Just think about it, okay?" he continues. "You don't have to decide now. As long as you know you're not getting rid of me."

"What does that mean?" I bite back a grin.

He points to the wall. "It means that when that clock strikes midnight and fireworks explode in the sky, I'm making this official."

"Official how?"

His hands land on my neck, and I enjoy every second of his warm palms on my skin. He's looking at me like someone with intent, I don't think I will ever get sick of it. He makes me feel like I'm important. Makes me want to do better.

"You're mine, Nik," he says with a tone that leaves no argument. "And I'm yours. And I'm no longer going to hide you from the world. Are you ready for that? Are you ready for a new start? With me? It means the press will be haunting you for a while. And certainly around races." My heart is roaring YES, totally ready to beat up my mind if I try to sway to any other answer than that. But funny enough, the fear isn't as overwhelming as the desire to keep this man in my life. To let him brighten my days like only he can.

"As long as you hold my hand every step of the way."

"Oh, babe, I'll never let go," he says when the crowd around us starts the countdown.

Our eyes lock, his lip curling as I draw my own between my teeth. The intense stare that lands on me slowly sucks the air out of my lungs, captivating me as he pulls me into our own little bubble. The chanting sounds more muffled with every count, amplifying how I feel about him. Nothing else matters when I'm with him.

Nothing else but us.

And when the clock strikes midnight, our bubble expands when our lips connect with a kiss that I can feel in every sense of my body, jerking me through a barrier that kept my heart safely behind bars. It's finally completely crashing through, and I realize that this is what I want. I want a life with him.

"Happy new year," he whispers, warming my lips with his breath.

Happy fucking new year.

28

TRISTAN

"CAN YOU GET OFF your phone for two seconds?" A throw pillow hits me in the face before it bounces to the floor, and I whip my head to Sam's scowl. I'm planted on his gray velvet sofa, texting Nikkie while I should be focused on the movie he put on thirty minutes ago.

"Sorry." I laugh, then rub a hand over my face, dropping the phone to my side, even though I really don't want to.

This week it was time to go back to work, having several meetings at the factory to see exactly what they've been working on during the winter break.

I've been excited, especially now that I'm an Arzano driver. They welcomed me with so much enthusiasm that only heightened my gut feeling that I made the right choice. But as soon as my days are over, there is only one thing on my mind. My girl.

"Man, you got it so bad." Sam shakes his head, rolling his eyes.

"Shut up."

"No, really. It's like your brain has melted since you met her." I let my head fall to the back of the couch, shooting him an unimpressed look. "What?"

"I love her, Sam." I haven't felt this good in years. I'm relaxed. I'm focused. I'm ready for the new season, and I know it's because of her. I've been going back and forth between Monaco and Amsterdam, snatching up every free hour she can spare, but having her in my own home for a week around New Year's really changed the game. Watching her stroll around my penthouse, wearing nothing more than one of my hoodies, ignited the desire I feel to move her in with me. I want her on the road with me. My dream is to see her when I wake up in the morning, and I want her to be the last thing I see when I close my eyes at night.

"Really? I didn't realize through the thousands of messages you send her every day." Another eyeroll. "Or that whole fucking stunt you pulled on fucking Valentine's Day. You're setting the bar way too high for all of us, man."

"No, I mean, I *love* her." I'm not just talking about how I'm serious with her and how I wanna see where this is going. I know where this is going. "She's the real deal. I'm not talking, *this has potential*. She's the only one I want. I want to–"

"Don't say it," he interrupts with a scowl, the motion of his head dancing a blond strand in front of his forehead.

"I'm gonna say it."

"Don't say it." His tone intensifies, lifting a chuckle from my lungs.

"I want to marry her."

"Oh, fuck, he said it." He lets his body fall back with as much drama as a five-year-old, giving me a disappointed look, yet he can't hide the sparkle in his blue eyes. "Why did you do that, man? Now there's no way back."

"I don't want there to be a way back."

Sam closes his eyes and links his hands together, resting them in his lap. "We're gathered here to remember the soul and annoying smile of Tristan Reinhart."

I pluck a pillow from the couch, smashing it in his face. "Shut up, asshole."

He laughs, throwing it back, then fixes his gaze on me with a tentative expression. "You're serious, aren't you?"

I focus my eyes out of the floor-to-ceiling windows, looking out all over the city. I don't think I've ever been more serious about anything. I've got it all. I'm a world champion. I'm wealthy enough to live a good life until I die. But I'd still give it all up if it doesn't include the blonde that has carved a permanent place in my head. I know it hasn't been long, but it just feels right. I'm not saying I'm going to get down on my knees right this minute, but some day in the future? *Definitely.*

"I don't care what happens. As long as she's there with me."

Sam gags, and another pillow is launched his way. "I'm kidding," he snickers playfully. "I like her. She's good for you. Are you taking her to the gala in the desert?" he asks, talking about Saudi Arabia.

"I haven't asked yet, but I want her to."

"I'm just pissed." He shrugs. "This means I need a new wingman."

"Jordan still lives a block away," I suggest, mentioning his biggest rival on the grid right now. The glare that hits me is dark, quickly turning the blue in his eyes into ice, which only makes me laugh.

"Not funny."

"It's a little funny."

He looks like he's about to jump me, but we both freeze when we hear the front door, followed by a set of heels prancing over the gray tiles on the floor.

"I'm going to kill her," Sam mutters. He throws the pillow to the side, then sits up with a scowl hardening his face. "What the fuck did I tell you about using that key?" he barks when his sister sets her first designer heeled step into the living area.

"What? This is an emergency?" Ava Devereaux lifts her sunglasses into her hair. She has the same blonde hair and blue eyes, but where Sam acts like an asshole most of the time, Ava is an asshole to the deepest point of her soul. She's been Sam's manager and agent since his days in Formula Three and she's great at what she does. She negotiated deals with companies like Adidas and Coca Cola, setting Sam up with a fortune while he did what he does best behind the wheel. But man, she's a fucking bitch.

"Are you dying?" Sam scolds.

Her pink painted lips purse a little in amusement as she slips her hands in the pockets of her cream pantsuit. "No."

"Someone else dying?"

"No." Ava rolls her eyes.

"Then it's not a fucking emergency!" Sam snaps.

"Lighten up, Sam."

"What do you want, Ava?"

"I got some endorsement requests, so we need to go over them."

"And we couldn't do this over the phone?"

I know Sam and his sister used to be thick as thieves, especially after their dad died and nineteen-year-old Ava had to take care of her fourteen-year-old brother. But over the last few years, I've seen Sam's irritation building up, and it's audible in every syllable he speaks to her.

"No, because I want to make sure you're in the right headspace," she argues.

"Oh, this will be good," Sam murmurs as he gives me a knowing look.

"What? Last season was a shitshow."

"The fans loved it." Sam shrugs, unbothered.

"*Your* fans loved it," Ava rebukes. "But a lot of people think you're an arrogant asshole."

"He is an arrogant asshole," I chime in.

"What he said." A sarcastic smile lifts the corner of Sam's mouth.

"We need to take care of your reputation, Sam."

"What I need to do is win races."

"On the track, yes. Off the track, you need to behave and show the great sportsman that you pretend to be." There's a hint of disdain in her voice that lifts my eyebrows as I press my lips together, locking eyes with Sam's incredulous look.

"Geez, thanks, sis," Sam growls.

"Don't be dramatic." Ava blows out a breath of annoyance, then lands her cold eyes on me. "Help me out here, Tristan." I'm sure it's supposed to sound like a plea for support, but really it comes out like a bark, not making it tempting in any way to help her. Even if she has a point about his reputation.

"Nah-ah, leave me out of it." My hands shoot up in the air, before I flip my attention back to Sam.

"So what do you suggest?" he says.

Ava crosses her arms in front of her chest, popping her hip with a pleased expression. "I talked with Sadie," she says, referring to Sadie Salazar, right hand of the SRT Team Boss. "They're getting the team a PR Specialist."

"Ah, how cute, Sam." I chuckle. "You got a babysitter." Every team has a few members who are the head of PR. Setting up signings, sponsorship appearances, and keeping a positive presence in the media. But as soon as they get a PR *Specialist*, it means the drivers are misbehaving during press meetings and are being put on a leash.

"Shut up." I catch another pillow he chucks my way, laughing. "What does that mean?"

"It means you're not allowed to speak without her present, so she can prevent you from blurting out stupid shit."

"See, babysitter," I point out, just to piss him off.

Sam glares at me with daggers of ice hitting me in the face, before he snaps his eyes up to his smug looking sister. "I don't want a babysitter."

"You don't get a say in this. It was a team decision." Ava keeps a flat voice, but the evil brat can't hide the little glimmer of victory in her eyes that dissolves my smile.

I really don't like her.

"Right, and you have nothing to do with it?" Sam narrows his eyes in suspicion.

"Nope."

"You suck," he huffs.

"You don't think I suck when your bank account adds another zero, baby brother."

Sam's sigh is loud as he runs a hand through his hair. His fire is dimmed with a little fatigue, probably because he's getting tired of her. "Are you done?"

"We need to discuss those endorsements."

"Well, plan a meeting with my assistant," he opts with a matter-of-fact tone before he flashes her a taunting smile. "Oh, that's right. That's you."

She quickly flips him off, then puts her sunglasses back on her nose. "Tomorrow at nine. Breakfast at Cafe de Paris. Be there, or I'll be charging."

"Bye, Ava." Sam waves.

"Bye, asshole." I follow her strut back into the hallway, then wait for the front door to fall back into the lock before I twist my neck to Sam. His features are stern, his look vacant, as if he's wondering if he could get away with murder.

"You can't kill your sister."

He gives me an incredulous look, but not for the reason I'm thinking. "You didn't have to burst my bubble like that." I laugh. "She annoys the shit out of me, man. She does a great job handling my shit, but she has zero boundaries."

I nod. "She's definitely intense. But I will give her one thing, though."

"What's that?"

"If you want to become a world champion this year? You gotta get your head in the game. No distractions and no more letting Hastings get under your skin."

His cheeks puff up when he blows out a breath, then he nods in agreement. "I know."

A few hours later, I'm walking the single block home, my chin covered in my Arzano wind jacket while my phone is pressed against my ear.

"How was your night?" Nikkie asks.

"Good, been playing video games with Sam. I wish you were here, though." I sound like a needy asshole, but the thing is... I am when it comes to her. I hate that she's 900 miles away from me.

"Me too."

"I've been thinking. If I invest in the bar, would you be able to hire someone new?" I know I have to address this carefully. It's no secret the bar is struggling, and I know she won't accept me paying the outstanding invoices once more. The last thing I want to do is make her feel like she's incapable or that I'm making her dependable on me. But it's been toying in my mind for selfish reasons. "It's just, I want you to come to a few more races with me this season.

"I'd love that too." I can hear the *but* lingering on the horizon as I walk into my building, stepping into the elevator.

"But?"

"But I need to think about investing." She's not mad. That's good. All I can detect is hesitation. I can work with that.

"I understand."

The ding of the elevator is the only sound in the conversation, a pregnant silence lingering between us.

"It's not that I don't want to be with you, Tristan," she finally says, with a little bit of apology in her tone. "I want this. I want *you*. But this is my bar. My life."

She keeps telling herself that this is her life, but there's no denying her uncertainty. This *was* her life. And I have a feeling that she doesn't want the bar anymore. She just can't get rid of it yet.

But that's okay. I can wait. I will make this work until I'm ready.

"I know. Take your time. But the offer stands."

"Thank you. I appreciate it."

"Just promise me one thing." I get out of the elevator with a smile splitting my face to lighten the mood before I pull out my key and usher myself into my apartment. "Promise me you'll come to the gala with me in Saudi Arabia. It's the second race of the season, which means you'll have until March to find someone to cover you at the bar. *Please*." I glance around the apartment. My eyes roam over the big cream U-shaped sofa, before I slightly shake my head and avert my gaze to the city of Monaco at night, placing myself in front of the window. I used to love my house. My sanctuary. But now it just feels empty and too big without her in it.

"Am I allowed to come in jeans?"

I snort, scrunching my nose with a chuckle. "No, but I'll buy you whatever dress you want."

"You're spoiling me.'

"I know." Something she will have to get used to. "Will you come?"

I'm prepared to argue with her, blackmail her, or even kidnap her if she's going to object. But the same flutter I've been walking around with for weeks takes presence when she says:

"Yeah, I'll be there."

29

NIKKIE

I STARE BACK AT my reflection, my eyes moving up and down the yellow—I want to say dress, but considering I feel like some fucking debutant, I have to go with ball gown. My legs are covered from hip to toe in sunflower yellow tulle, the skirt so puffy, I'm pretty sure I can barely get through the door if I'd try.

"This is not me." I blow out a breath to get rid of a blonde strand that has been hanging in front of my eyes, trying to keep my boobs from falling out of the heart-shaped body.

When we strolled into the store, Tessa was a little more eager than me. The temperature was nice, and the sweet scent of fresh cotton and atmospheric feel instantly put me a bit more at ease. But now? I feel like I'm about to break out in sweat in a €600 ball gown, like I'm going to prom in a heatwave.

"I agree." Tess takes a sip of her complimentary glass of champagne before setting it on the white side table next to her. "Because you need a blue dress."

I just blink at her. Simply because my brain can't seem to fully register what's going on right now. It makes perfect sense that Tristan basically *ordered* me to go buy a dress for the gala, but I have a hard time accepting that we're in a store where the cheapest dress is €450. €450? Who spends that much money on a dress?

"What?" Tessa knots her brows in the middle. "Blue is your color. I'm pretty sure if they had a ball gown made of denim, you would buy it right now."

I nod, my lips pursing. *I would definitely want to try that on.*

"I probably can't afford it."

"You're dating an F1 driver. You can afford anything."

And that's my fucking issue. "That's not my money, Tess."

I have a hard time shopping for a dress, knowing I won't pay for it myself. It's not buying drinks, you know? It's spending enough money to have a very relaxed weekend at the spa.

"I know. I know," Tessa concedes, refraining herself from rolling her eyes, though I see the urge lingering under her frown. "But the guy wants to spoil you. Who are you to ruin his fun?" She switches her attention to the saleswoman. "Excuse me, can you grab every dress you have in blue?"

I sigh, then step down from the plateau to get out of this yellow tulle Easter egg.

"I'm nervous, Tess," I confess, when I pull back the curtain of the dressing room and start peeling the fabric from my skin as gently as possible to not tear anything.

"For what? You've been dating him for months now. It's clear the guy is crazy about you. If it was up to him, he'd be packing your bags and have you move in with him."

"No, it's not that. It's *this*. This whole thing. Dating him in private is great, but dating him in front of the rest of the world, that's a whole different thing."

I'm just a working-class girl from the Pijp. I have no business dealing with the rich and famous like I actually belong with them. I'm the girl who serves them.

"What do you mean?"

I pop my head out of the dressing room, standing in nothing more than my underwear. "What if I embarrass him?"

Her eyes narrow a tad, glittered with annoyance. "Since when are *you* the sensible one and I'm the one dying for some adventure? And by adventure, I mean you getting us into trouble again."

"I've had enough trouble for a lifetime."

"Can you please stop?" Tessa grates. "Ever since Wes died, you have become this shell of who you really are."

My stomach hardens and my instinct pushes me to lash out, but I know she's right. It's the version I vowed to be after the accident, showing my level of gratitude that I survived by doing better. By suppressing my wild side. The part of my DNA that I've inherited from my father that has this need for anarchy. To just do whatever the fuck I want without worrying about what other people will think of me. But it doesn't feel like me. Like I'm spending my days in a purgatory between the girl I used to be and the girl I desire to be.

"What if I don't know who I am anymore?" I frustratedly let go of the curtain, my shoulders hanging, not even bothered my half naked body is on full display. "What if I'll never be the same?

"You're right," Tessa agrees. "And you won't. You *have* changed. You don't have to get yourself mixed up in the gray area of the world anymore. I mean, getting arrested for public intoxication isn't nearly as funny now as when you're sixteen," she mutters before she continues. "But deep down, you're still that wild child who faces every adventure, every challenge with excitement. I know you don't want to live the rest of your life in fear."

"No." I don't know everything, but I know as much as that.

"Then don't." It rolls off her tongue so easily, like it's as simple as two plus two.

"Is it that easy?"

"It is if you want it to be." She shrugs, and I hold her gaze for a moment.

If it's that easy, why does it feel like such a huge mountain then?

The saleswoman holds up three gowns, hanging them in the dressing room for me before she gives me privacy by closing the curtain. I let my hands move through the different fabrics of the dresses, then pick the one that's completely made of midnight blue silk.

"Have you thought about selling the bar?" Tessa questions from the other side of the curtain.

"I have." It's been on my mind at least once every day.

"And?"

"And I haven't made a decision. *Yet*," I add as I pull the dress over my head, then let the soft and thick fabric fall over the rest of my body. It's snug around my hips, but loose enough to keep me comfortable. It feels luxurious, fitting me like a glove, and I can't deny that wearing this gown heightens my confidence.

"He asked me to become his physical therapist so I can travel with him," I confess, staring at my reflection.

"Excuse me?"

A smile creeps up at her response.

"He also offered to invest in the bar if that would help me free up more time."

"Are you serious?"

I hum. "A few months back."

"Nikkie! You love him. He loves you. He wants you to travel with him so badly he's offering you your dream job and wants to invest in your bar. One you didn't want in the first place, might I add." She cocks a daring eyebrow. "You're gonna do it, right? You're going to take the job?"

"I don't know," I whine. *I want to.* I shove the curtain to the side, then walk out with a big smile, stepping onto the plateau, pleased by Tessa's jaw dropping to the floor.

"This one," she gushes, wiggling her knees in excitement. "This is it, ma'am! We want this one!"

"Wait, what's the price?" I lock eyes with the saleswoman, looking at me through her glasses with her lips into a flat line, as if she just realized that I might not be as wealthy as Tessa made us appear when we got through the door.

She fixates on the register, typing something in, then twists her neck back to us. "€1200."

I suck in a sharp breath, then blow it out with disappointment as I shake my head.

"It's too expensive." I hold Tessa's gaze, but she just reaches into the pocket of my oversized denim jacket with a sassy expression. "What are you doing?"

She pulls out my phone, not uttering a word. Unlocking it, I curse myself for telling her my passcode, before she taps the screen and a dial tone is audible through the store.

"Tess!" I hiss, my molars grinding together.

"Hey, baby," Tristan's lively voice has me smiling and shutting my eyes with fatigue at the same time, because I know Tessa is effectively calling for backup.

Literally.

"Tristan, it's Tessa."

"Hey, Tess." Amusement is dripping from his tone.

"Congrats on your first podium of the season. I bet you and Jackson are very pleased you opened the season for Arzano with a bang, placing third and second and all."

"Thanks."

"Speaking of Jackson... how does he feel about blind dates?"

"I never dated him, so I wouldn't know."

I snort at Tristan's reply, covering my mouth with my hand.

"*Ha-ha*, you're such a funny man."

"I'm just curious. Is it still considered a blind date if you know what the man looks like?"

"Blind date for *him*, not for me!" Tessa huffs, and I release the chuckle that was trapped behind my palm. "I don't do blind dates, are you kidding me?"

Tristan laughs. "Did you call me to hook you up with Jackson?"

"No, but please feel free to send him my schedule whenever you have time," she mumbles, then cuts to the reason she's calling in the first place. "What is the budget for the whole dress thing?"

"There is no budget." I shake my head at Tessa when she gives me a smug look.

"Sooo," she drawls, "anything with four digits is good to go?"

"Anything less and you're not doing it right."

Oh, damn.

He's serious. He's never serious. But he's serious about this.

"Tess!" I hiss. "That's too much!"

But she just shakes her head, mischief marring her entire face.

"I knew I liked you for a reason." She chuckles into the phone. "Nikkie will call you back later."

"Wait, can I see?" he booms, undeniable excitement in his voice that gives me butterflies.

"No! It's bad luck," Tessa exclaims.

"Isn't that with weddings?"

"Potato, potato," she counters, saying the same words twice, triggering my cackling.

"You really need to start using that properly."

"Whatever. Bye." She hangs up before I can get a word in between, then throws my phone next to her on the couch. "See. It's this one. And I'm not just talking about the dress." She winks.

I rest my hands on my sides, biting away a smile while I hold her determined gaze. I know that whatever argument I will start, I won't win. Chances are, she'll be back within the hour, asking for Tristan's credit card details to pick up the dress for me behind my back. I know, because I would do the same if the situation was reversed.

I give myself one more glance in the mirror, twirling around, then take a deep breath as I conjure a giddy grin. "It's this one."

30

TRISTAN

"I F YOU KEEP STARING at her, she might sue you for sexual harassment. You look like a stalker," I say, following Sam's eyes to the new PR Specialist of SRT. Her blonde curly hair sits in a perfect knot on top of her head, a few loose strands dancing around her smile as she strolls around the ballroom with her pink dress.

"What? She's easy on the eyes." Sam doesn't even deny the fixation of his attention, just keeps gawking with his hands tucked into his tux.

"Oh, boy. You're gonna bang the new PR girl, aren't you?"

Now I got his attention, and a smirk breaks free. "If she'll let me."

"Don't bang the new PR girl." I tilt my head with a reprimanding expression.

"Why not?"

"She'll get fired."

"She works for me," he retorts.

"No, she works for SRT."

"Same thing." He pulls a face, then his jaw falls to the floor before he blows out a soft whistle, and I follow his line of attention.

"Bloody hell," I mutter when my heart stops ticking, along with my registration of time. Nikkie strolls in, her body covered by a silk blue dress that highlights every delicious curve. Her blonde hair sits in a neat ponytail on the back of her head, showing off her delicate neck. Sparkling brown eyes find mine, and the way she looks at me takes my breath away. Vibrant. Energized. Happy.

She looks fucking amazing.

"Stop staring at my girlfriend." I nudge Sam in the side, causing him to jerk forward a little. My eyes stay fixed on her long legs that peek out from beneath the slit of her dress as she makes her way over. "Go find your own."

"Sorry we couldn't come together," I tell her as she approaches, referring to the fact that Arzano wanted me and Jackson to arrive together to have a private drink with the sponsors.

I take her hands in mine, pulling them behind my back, before mirroring the action around her body, then find the warmth of her lips. "You look like a fucking dream."

"Thank you." Her skin turns a soft pink, her golden eyes looking up at me through her thick lashes. "You're so cute when you blush." She bites her lip, holding back her smile.

Bringing her close, I brush my lips over hers, waking up my groin more than is tolerable wearing black trousers.

"Baby, we're in public," she scolds, her eyes darting around her.

"I should care..." I lift my hand to grab her chin. "But I really don't."

"Dios Mio, get a room, Aussie." A thick Spanish accent has my neck twisting with a chuckle, pulling Nikkie against my chest before offering my free hand to one of the drivers of Baker & Baker.

"Have some sympathy, mate. You'd be touching her like this too if she was yours."

"Yours?" His black brows shoot up, then he aims his smile at Nikkie, taking her hand. "Ola, mamacita. Encantado. My name is Raul."

"Nikkie." Her lips curl in amusement.

"If you're ever done with this kangaroo"—he wiggles his eyebrows—"and want to have some real Spanish bull—"

"I'll be sure to stop by Franco Garcia's garage," she cuts him off with a taunting grin, referring to Sam's teammate. "He's from Spain, right?"

"Oh, burn." Jackson Banks comes to stand beside him, a beaming smile aimed at Raul.

"No, it's no burn," Raul rebukes. "Obviously, she doesn't watch a lot of Formula One. She doesn't know who is in front of the grid."

"I know it's not you," Nikkie counters with a sweet smile.

"She's been watching F1 her entire life," I chime in, snickering.

"Oh, double burn." Sam holds his fist in front of his mouth, hiding his grin.

"You shut up, nepo baby."

"Nepo or not, I've still won more races than you."

Raul glares at Sam, then rears his head to Jackson. "Why do we like this American?"

"Because I'm a good wingman, and I buy all your bottles in the club." Sam slaps him on the shoulder, slowly dragging him toward the bar.

"Si, this is true," Raul agrees as they walk away.

Jackson shakes his dark blond head of hair, then points his attention to Nikkie.

"I apologize for those two idiots." His eyes radiate the kindness he's known for, his southern drawl sounding charming as ever.

"It's okay," Nikkie titters. "I'm used to Sam by now. I can take one extra."

"Jackson Banks." He offers her his hand. "Sam's teammate."

"Jackson, this is my girlfriend, Nikkie." I tuck her closer into my side, pride swelling my chest. I don't think I will ever get tired of introducing her like that. Though, at some point, I want to change girlfriend to *wife*.

"Right, someone told me you're off the market. Nice to meet you, Nikkie."

"Pleasure is all mine. You're an amazing driver."

"Thank you." Jackson's grin is wide, yet he will never brag about his success. But she is right. He's one of the best. It's only his second year in Formula One, but he got signed with Arzano right after becoming world champion in Formula Three. Most drivers go from Three to Two then One if they are lucky enough.

But Jackson's driving skills are promising enough that Arzano decided he was good enough right off the bat. We all know he's going to break records one day.

"Hold up, how come you never told me I'm an amazing driver?" I frown, giving in to the small jealous streak flaring within me.

"Probably because she doesn't want your head to grow any bigger than it already is," Jackson pitches in, generating a glare from me.

"And it really is big." Nikkie looks up at me through her lashes, glowing with an unfounded innocence, and I can't help but join in when Jackson barks out a laugh.

31

NIKKIE

"**Y**OU GOT SASS, WOMAN." Jackson pushes out a chuckle, a little awe in his eyes.

"Bucketloads."

"I like her, Reinhart. She's as cheery as you are."

I feel how Tristan presses a kiss on top of my head. "That she is."

"Okay, who wants to do shots?" Raul comes back and points his finger around, his eyes both demanding and questioning, while Sam comes to stand beside him, taking a sip of his drink. I open my mouth to decline, but before I can, a brunette with a short bob slaps his hand out of the air. Her black dress fits right over her curves, her full lips covered in red lipstick. She's tiny, but her energy comes close to a hurricane. A force to be reckoned with.

"No, no," she admonishes with an Italian accent. "You need to smooch with the sponsors first. Hi! I'm Emilia, PR Assistant for Baker & Baker." The contrast of the friendly smile she's flashing me, before she aims her stern look back at Raul's, makes me cackle in amusement.

"More like a PR dictator," Raul mutters.

"As long as you're scared." Emilia shrugs. "Let's go."

"I don't want to." He pouts like a little puppy, giving her an expression like she asked him to eat bull testicals or something.

"I don't care. Let's go." Emilia pushes him forward, not bothered by the fact that he's twice her size.

"You're whipped, man," Jackson calls out at his back.

"Cállate tonto!" Raul barks over his shoulder, while Emilia wiggles her eyebrows in agreement, her hands still on Raul's back to keep his feet in motion.

"I don't speak Spanish," Jackson replies.

"I'm pretty sure that was universal anyway," Sam snickers, then his eyes trail off to something behind us. "I'll catch you later."

"Where is he going?" I frown at Tristan in question.

"Chasing the sun." He and Jackson share a look before their faces split into wide grins.

"Probably." I want to ask what the hell they are talking about, but Jackson's deep sigh keeps my lips in a flat line when he points at a man waving at him from the entrance of the venue. "I'm being summoned by the boss. Nice meeting you, Nikkie."

"Likewise." He slogs away from us until warm lips ignite a little moan from my throat.

"This is a very, very bad situation," Tristan hums against my neck. His arms are tight around my waist, hugging me from behind, and I can feel his touch all the way to my toes.

"What do you mean?" I reply, my voice soft and filled with contentment.

"You. Looking like that. And no one around me stops me from touching you."

"First off, we are literally surrounded by two hundred people. Two, looking like what, exactly?"

"Like a blue popsicle I need to lick." His breath tickles my ear, the blood rushing to my neck instantly. The flutter that bounces through my organs is deep, throbbing between my legs. I shut my eyes, my mind easily imagining his tongue swiping through my folds.

"Oh, fuck."

"Yeah, exactly. *Oh, fuck*." He nibbles my ear, the movement of his teeth and lips slow and torturous. The warmth of his tongue slips out every few seconds, causing shivers to run down my spine while he effectively sets my skin on fire.

"You're torturing me."

"It's my favorite activity," he says, diabolical as hell, only turning me on more. I've been trying to behave and act accordingly, meaning doing my best to fit in with this million-dollar crowd, but here he is, poking my wild side alive like nobody's business.

"I thought it was racing," I muse.

"I thought so too. Until I met you." He bites my neck, and I jerk my eyes open with a chuckle, just in time to see a man coming our way.

"Someone is coming."

"Who cares?" Tristan continues torching my skin with his kisses until I shove my elbow in his stomach when I register who it is.

"Hello," Will Packers says when he's standing before us, offering me a kind smile that doesn't match his eerie gray eyes, then he swings them up. "Tristan."

The energy shifts to something thick and tense, enough to make a rock get uncomfortable, but automatically, I put on my game face when Tristan freezes up beside me.

"Will."

"Who is your date?"

"This is my girlfriend, Nikkie Peters. Nikkie, this is Will Packers."

Another flashing smile hits me in the face, charming as expected. "Nice to meet you. I'm Will." He offers his hand, and I eye it before I take it with a grace that I don't feel inside of me.

"I know who you are." I smile. I've been watching F1 for as long as I can remember, and the CEO of Callahan Motors isn't someone you can miss when his bald head is featured in any post-race interviews.

"You're a fan?"

"Of F1, yes. Of you? No." I also remember how he treated my boyfriend like he was some kind of rookie last summer, and as much as I can put on a mask and be polite, I will never pretend I like you if you're on my shitlist. Will Packers is currently holding the number one position.

Tristan snickers into my neck, not even hiding it, but instead pressing a long kiss against my skin in encouragement.

"Don't believe everything you hear, Miss Peters," Will says calmly, though his smile has vanished from his greasy features.

"Oh, I don't, Mr. Packers. If that was the case, I'd still believe you're an upstanding and honest man." I wink.

His glare could be deadly, probably capable of intimidating people left and right. But I'm raised by a criminal. This entire party intimidates me, but wearing this dress also makes me more confident than I've felt in a long time. There's business and there's being an asshole, and Will clearly is the latter.

I hold his gaze, doing my best to not let my cocky grin break free as I ignore Tristan's soft yet relentless chuckles in my ear. I expect Will to retaliate, probably throwing out some shitty comment, but the man is wiser than I thought when he rears to Tristan instead.

"Tristan, George Callahan would like to have a word with you if you can find the time."

Tristan flips his attention up, tucking me into his side with amusement still radiating off his warm body. "Sure. I'll be there in a minute."

"Miss Peters." Will nods, and I give him the same courtesy, resisting the urge to flip him off.

"Will."

Regardless of the fact that F1 is a brutal sport, where anyone can take your seat on any given day, no matter how great the terms are of your contract, I still believe there's etiquette on how you should treat people. The way Will treated Tristan is anything but professional.

He strolls away with his shoulders squared, seemingly unbothered, but I can see how his big energy has shrunk just a little, swelling my chest with pride.

"Oh, you are a fucking trooper." Tristan kisses my cheek.

"I hate him."

"You and me both, babe."

"What do you think Callahan wants?"

He shrugs, his hand stroking the bare skin on my shoulder. "Probably just to wish me good luck. The old man is okay. I'll be right back." He slowly guides me a little backwards, until I hit one of the barstools, then gives me a quick peck. "Don't move."

I wave him off, taking a seat as I nurse the last of my drink. My head twists to the left when someone takes the stool beside me.

"You're the new PR girl for SRT, right?" I blurt, letting my eyes rake up and down her punk dress. Her curly hair is set on top of her head, a few strands casually framing her face.

"I am. Casey Boyd."

She smiles at me as I take her hand. "Nikkie Peters, nice to meet you."

She settles into the leather pillow of the stool, doing her best to cover up her legs with the soft fabric of her dress. She seems a little shy, but considering she works in F1, she's got at least a little badass in her. I'm pretty sure you wouldn't survive a day working in this male-dominated world otherwise.

"So what is it like working for these arrogant assholes?" I ask.

She chuckles, pushing out a deep breath at the same time as she tucks a strand behind her ear. "Exhausting. But also fun. I used to work for the Vancouver Canucks, and as much as I love hockey, it's nice to have a change of scenery."

"Still arrogant athletes, though, right?"

"Definitely." She rolls her eyes at the bar. "Are you European?"

"I'm from the Netherlands."

"Ah, windmills and tulips."

I laugh at her reply, a little surprised. "I was actually expecting drugs and whores, but yeah, that's us too."

"I'm more of a flower girl." Her beaming cheeks are peppered with freckles, nothing but sincerity coming at me in waves. Her beauty is au natural, and her oblivion about it makes me like her straight away.

"I can see that. You look like a cute flower girl."

"Thank you." She takes a sip from her tumbler, deviating her gaze.

"What is your poison tonight?" I ask, noticing the almost empty glass.

"Kentucky Mule."

"No way." My brown eyes grow wide, loving that I've talked to the girl for thirty seconds and we already have something in common. "Oh, you and I are gonna get along just fine."

32

TRISTAN

A FTER TWENTY MINUTES OF talking to the old Callahan, I excuse myself, ready to find my girlfriend and corrupt her like I've been desperate to do ever since I saw her walking in wearing that dress. She has been looking like an excruciating temptation all night, and all I want to do is bury myself inside of her.

I spot her at the bar where I left her, and smile when I see her chatting with Sam's new PR girl. At first, he was pissed SRT gave him a "babysitter," as he called it, but as soon as he found out what his newly appointed babysitter looked like, he's been more than eager to spend every free minute of his time with her.

"Hey, baby." I slide my hands around her waist, pressing my chest against her back, then drop my lips against her neck. She murmurs in delight, expanding my smile before I bring my gaze up to the blonde sitting next to her. "We haven't formally met. Tristan Reinhart," I say, offering my hand.

"Casey Boyd." She gives me a tentative smile, her silver-gray eyes sparkling, though she quickly lowers her lashes before taking a sip of her drink. If she's getting shy with me, I don't even wanna know how uncomfortable she must feel with Sam penetrating her energy every chance he gets.

"What did Callahan want?" Nikkie twists her head up at me, and I cock my head a little to meet her gaze.

"To thank me for my time with the team." Her eyes widen at my confession. "Yeah, the old man is a decent guy. He wished me good luck with Arzano."

"How can a man like that hire someone as awful as Will Packers?"

"I know." I chuckle. "You ready to go?"

"Go where?"

I briefly lock eyes with Casey, shooting her an innocent smile before bringing my lips flush with Nikkie's ear. "Somewhere I can move this dress up your thighs and find your pussy with my lips?" I whisper.

She swallows, her eyes widening. Jumping off the stool, I chuckle while she gathers her stuff, then gives her new friend a quick hug. "Casey, we will talk soon."

"Sure." Casey grins from ear to ear, looking at Nikkie with suspicion.

I escort her to the foyer of the venue, my palm burning hot on the small of her back.

"Isn't it a bit early to leave?" she whispers while I shoot friendly smiles from left and right at all the people passing us by.

"Who said anything about leaving?" Making sure no one sees us, I rapidly open a door, then shove her inside. She spins on the spot, her plump lip tucked between her teeth.

"Tristan Reinhart, you're such a naughty boy." The mischief in her golden eyes flips the energy in the dimmed light.

"I know. It matches your inner wild child." I stare back at her, my eyes moving over every inch of her body. My pounding heart feels like an amped drum in the small space, waiting for the grand finale.

"Moi?" She plays coy. "I'm composed and classy."

"You're like a ragdoll kitten waiting for her tiger to jump out." I yank her to me, then turn us around so her back is pressed against the door. Running my fingers gently over her jaw, I feel how she relaxes against my touch with parted lips. I want her to surrender. I want to drive her as mad as she drives me. Losing control in the middle of the public eye.

"Tell me I'm right," I order, cupping the front of her neck. Her breath tickles over my lips, and I teasingly let the tip of my tongue dart out.

"You're right."

"Good girl." Her lashes fly up at those two words, laced with defiance and content. "You like that, don't you? You love it when I praise you with my hands on your pussy." I push the silk fabric of her dress to the side, rubbing my hand over her pa– "What the hell, Nik?" I hold her gaze, shocked. The tip of my index freezing, yet eager to push through her bare folds. "You're not wearing any panties?"

Her rebel streak is dancing through her eyes, the corner of her pink lips lifting just slightly, but enough for me to look at her in awe. I love her. Every part of her. But it's these moments, the moments she's fully here, surrendering to *me* instead of the dread I see in the edges of her gaze most of the time, that make it impossible for me to ever let her go. I can't wait to go on adventures with her, explore the world. I want her to feel comfortable enough to show this side of her every single day of the rest of her life.

"Surprise?" She cackles.

"Feel free to surprise me every fucking day, baby." I shake my head, then crash my mouth against hers. Her hands fly through my hair, messing it up enough to know I won't be able to walk back outside unscathed, but who the fuck cares. The heat of her tongue against mine sets every bone in my body on fire, my groin almost exploding. My mind catalogs every stroke of her finger, every shift of her hip, while she uses my fingers to work her clit. She grinds her hips just the way she likes it, and I swear there is nothing sexier than being used by your girl for her own fucking pleasure.

Her breathy moans are getting louder, vibrating against my ear.

"If you don't want to get caught, you have to be quiet, baby."

"Can't," she cracks out. "Keep your hands, right there." Shamelessly, she keeps rubbing her clit against my coated fingers, trying to keep her dress out of the way with one hand while holding on to my neck with the other. "I'm going to ruin this dress."

"You want to stop?"

"Fuck no."

I chuckle. "Then keep going, baby."

Her hips pick up the pace, riding my fingers like she's having her own personal rodeo. It doesn't take her much longer before I see the tension in her face increasing as she jerks her head against my chest. My cock impatiently waits his turn, swelling more with every little yelp and moan that erupts from her plump lips.

"Let go," I whisper against her lips, and not ten seconds later, a frown knots her eyebrows. I muffle the wail that comes from her chest as she rides out her high, doing her best to keep herself up by her toes until her eyes swing open.

"You are so goddamn sexy," I hum, pushing my hands through her hair.

33

NIKKIE

I F I WAS WORRIED I'd be set aside as trailer trash before I got here, I'm pretty sure getting caught fucking my superstar boyfriend in the wardrobe of the venue will definitely seal the deal. But my brain isn't functioning enough to care. My mind is rolling in the gutter, having way too much fun to worry about any high-end executive in the racing world who might catch us.

My head is still somewhere up in the air, riding on cloud nine, when his hands pull my head back by my hair while his other cups my ass and swiftly lifts me up before I wrap my legs around his waist. The swipe of his tongue below my ear adds to the heated sensation between my legs, mostly my throbbing clit that's ready for more already, almost as if they are wired with an invisible chord.

I gasp for air each time he pushes his groin harder against mine, my wetness reaching epic proportions, and a flutter of common sense enters my thoughts.

"We'll ruin our clothes," I hum against his lips again, right before they slam back to mine. He keeps pushing his bulge into my center, each thrust calculated as he smirks against my mouth.

"I'll buy new."

"I mean, we still have to get out there." I know the words leave my lips, but I'm pretty sure the way they are delivered is nothing but pleading to keep going instead of trying to talk some reason into him.

"We don't have to do shit." Holding me up with one hand, he unbuttons his pants, then pushes it down before I feel the tip of his shaft pressing against my entrance. It's ridiculous how good he seems to handle keeping me up like this while he puts on a condom, and I silently thank his excessive training for that. Who knew driving around a track at 250 miles per hour for two hours would also be beneficial for me?

"Oh, fuck." I tilt my head, my eyes aiming at the cream ceiling. The spots blind me, and my eyes close when he lowers me onto his cock, filling me up until I'm literally gasping for air. It burns, in the most delicious way, stretching me wide.

"Hold on, baby." Pressing into me deeper, he holds me firmly with one arm circled around my spine while the other is pressed against the door. And then his hips thrust inside me. Slow at first. Dragging each move out before yanking it back in, heightening every single sense in my body. Every time he hits my wall, the oxygen slams out of my lungs. The muffled sounds of people behind the door keep me on high alert, but they turn me on at the same time. Just the thought that we can get caught at any given moment lifts me to a higher level, wanting to desperately reach my next high before anyone does. I hold on to his neck, bringing one hand in front, spreading my fingers. Tauntingly, I pull him closer, putting a little pressure on his throat with a daring expression.

"You're getting dominant on me, baby?"

I lick my lips, still jerking with every pump. "Fuck me harder, Ace."

His gaze turns dark, a snarl of desire on his lips. "Oh, fuck. *Hold on.*"

He grips my hips with a force that makes me wince, but forms a smile around my parted lips when he picks up the pace. My hands are splashed out over the pulsing veins in his neck, teasing the senses of my palm every time he drives his cock back inside of me.

Like a madman, he impales me with his cock, over and over again, until all I can do is keep my mouth and eyes wide. "Is this what you want, baby? For me to fuck you like I'm out of control?"

"Yes! Yes!"

His grunts become feral, lifting the hairs on the back of my neck. My clit flutters over his pelvis with each pump, ticking it off like a slow drum, until I feel the ripple effect growing and growing.

"Come inside of me," I beg when I feel how I'm only a second away from hitting home again. "Come inside of me, *please*."

As if on cue, my legs jerk with a spasm, my core contracting in the way that sends me straight to heaven before I arrive into that addictive freefall. Tristan grunts when I milk his cock, the sweat of his forehead sliding down my cleavage.

"Bloody hell," he growls, before he releases. His frown is deep, his jaw set, as he needs only a few more thrusts to shoot out every drop of his climax between my walls before he stills, heaving. My breaths are shallow as I try to find my way back to earth, my hands holding on to his shoulders. He fucks me right over the finish line every single time, making me forget about all my worries and sorrows.

We stand still like that for a while, then I slowly open my eyes, suddenly aware of our surroundings. "You fucked me in the wardrobe of a gala."

He moves his head back to look at me, a grin sliding in place. "I know."

"You're supposed to be the good guy of Formula One," I joke.

"I am." He searches my gaze, brushing his lips over mine. "Just not with you."

"You wanna tell me I'm a bad influence?"

"The worst." He kisses me. "You're the one temptation I can't resist."

I can live with that.

He slowly slips out of me, and I can feel my own wetness dripping down my thighs. "Oh, shit."

His gaze follows mine, and he pulls a paper towel from his pocket, then drops to his knees. "I got you, baby."

"Well, aren't you prepared, Mr. Reinhart?" I bite my lip, glancing down at the man in front of me. His hair is messy as fuck. Any bright mind in that ballroom is going to know exactly what he's been up to in the last twenty minutes, but all it does is raise pride in me. His forehead is glistening with sweat, his cheeks flushed like I know mine are. That man is mine.

Mine to fuck. Mine to hold. Mine to go home with. Mine to love.

Tessa's joke flashes through my mind and I see it. Like the sun is pushing its way through the clouds, I now realize he's it. I'm excited about planning my future with him and to have his babies. I want to travel the world with him.

His smirk moves up, and I cup his cheek, admiring his gorgeous features. "To please my girl? *Always*." He pushes my dress to the side, wiping me clean, moving from my knee up until he reaches my core again. Teasingly, he slips his finger through my soaked folds, and I give him a lazy look when he puts it in his mouth, sucking it clean.

"You're only going to make me dirtier if you keep going like that."

"Are you complaining?"

"Never." I run my hand through his hair, then gasp when he pushes his mouth against my pussy. "Holy shit."

Like an asshole, he sucks my folds into his mouth, swiping his tongue around my center with a grin, and I stare at him with a little shock.

"Couldn't resist a taste, baby."

"You gonna keep eating, then?" I try not to sound begging, but at this point, I'm not opposed to it.

He licks his lips, dropping a final kiss onto my clit, before getting back up to his feet. "I just wanted to have a little taste for dessert later."

My throat was already dry from all the heaving while he was fucking me, but I swear now there is more water in the fucking Sahara than in my mouth. I'm squirming under his dark gaze, desperate for him to continue what he just started.

"We're leaving. Right now," I announce, pointing my finger in his face. That asshole wants to tease me until my toes curl, then he better make good on his silent promise. I want to feel his tongue on my throbbing clit, and I want it as soon as possible.

He barks out a laugh, clearly content with what he stirred up, and I give him a slight scowl.

"I hate you," I screech, trying to bite my smile away.

"That's okay, baby. I'll fix that within five minutes as soon as we get to the hotel."

"Na-ah!" I scold. "You better enjoy your dessert longer than five minutes, Ace."

"Yes, ma'am." His smirk is fucking infectious, and I shake my head before I glance down, taking a good look at my dress. Thankfully, I can't find any, and inwardly, I say a little prayer of gratitude that I don't have to walk out with stains of fucking desire displayed on my ridiculously expensive dress. We both smooth out our outfits, then Tristan takes my face in his hands, lowering his lips to mine. The kiss is tentative, affectionate, and sweet. All the things he is when he's not fucking my brains out. The perfect balance of rough and gentle.

"You ready?" He takes my hand, flashing his teeth, his eyes dancing, before I nod and follow him outside. The bright light of the foyer is a big contrast with the dim lights in the wardrobe, giving me a sense of walking in the spotlights in an awkward way. But it becomes even more awkward when we barely take two steps, right up against Sam's judgy face.

He cocks his head at Tristan's messy hair, flicking his blue eyes to lock them with mine, before rearing back to Tristan's.

"You two are disgusting." He stands there, cocky as ever, with his hand tucked into his pants while his other is wrapped around a drink.

"Jealous?" Tristan puts his feet back in motion, tugging me behind him.

"Probably a little bit." Sam nods.

"Guessing Casey is immune to your charms?"

Sam puffs, scrunching his nose. "No human is immune to my charms."

"I am," I beam like a brat.

"You're not human," Sam counters.

"I know, I'm divine."

Sam points his gaze at me with appreciation. "Good one."

"Thanks."

Tristan barks out a laugh at our silliness, then slams a hand on his friend's shoulder after shooting me a wink. "Come on, buddy. Let's grab another drink."

"Hold up! I thought we were heading home." I pout.

"He needs us, baby." Tristan points at Sam strolling back into the venue with an innocent look, but I see right through his tactics.

"You're trying to torture me some more, aren't you?" I can still feel my swollen clit with every step I take, yet here's my world champion boyfriend, wanting to drag out my horniness by making me wait long enough for me to explode.

"You're so gorgeous when you're turned on."

"I'm not turned on. I'm almost exploding just thinking about your tongue between my legs," I hiss from the corner of my tormented smile while my eyes glance around to make sure no one hears me. Forgotten is the fact that he just fucked me against a door.

"I'll make it worth the wait, baby." He drags me back into the venue, with a smirk that I itch to wipe off his face.

"I'm going to pay you back for this, Ace."

34

TRISTAN

I WALK THROUGH THE front door of Sam's penthouse, greeted by the spring sun that's shining through his floor-to-ceiling windows. We've been back in Monaco for a few days, before we have to pack our bags again and head to Melbourne.

I'm always excited to go home, and this time I will be able to introduce Nikkie to my family. I can't wait to show her the ranch, let her taste some *real* Reinhart wine, and take her out with the four-wheeler.

I lean my elbows on Sam's gray marble kitchen island, watching him finishing his breakfast. The man never sits down to eat when he's home. I still don't really know why, but his excuse is that he doesn't want to waste time sitting down. Whatever that means.

"I think I want to buy a ring," I tell him.

His fork stills in front of his mouth, his messy blond hair hanging over his forehead. The stoic look he shoots me narrows my eyes at him. Dropping his fork on his plate with a loud clatter, he turns around, rummaging in one of the drawers. When he turns back around, he's holding a tealight in one hand and a lighter in the other.

"What are you doing?" I ask, my brows furrowing.

"Lighting a candle for your soul." He flips the lighter, sparking a little flame, and I grab an apple from the fruit basket and throw it against his head with a perfect aim. "Ouch!"

"I'm serious," I continue while he rubs the sore spot on his temple.

"I know. I know. You want to marry her. You already told me. But how would that work?" He puts the tealight and lighter aside, taking another bite of his oatmeal. "She hasn't even met your folks yet."

"Which is why she's coming to Australia for the GP. It will be the perfect opportunity to introduce her to my family and pop the question."

He sighs. "T. Buddy. Aren't you moving a bit fast? You've been dating her for, what? Three months?"

I throw another apple, this time hitting him in the chest. "Six, you dickhead."

"Same thing. You know what I mean. Isn't putting a ring on her finger a little bit hasty?" If she was any other girl, I'd agree with him. Getting engaged after six months is quick. Fucking quick. But I've been thinking about this for a while now. Wondering what my future after F1 would look like. And all I see is her.

"She's it, Sam. I want to share my life with her, and I want to show her I'm committed to her."

"You're stalking her. Pretty sure she knows your commitment runs deep." He pulls a face like the clown that he is, but then his gaze turns stern. "You serious about this?"

"Yeah."

"Why?" He sounds like a dick, even though I know he's not trying to be. He likes Nikkie. I know he does. But for a man who declares himself as happily forever alone, I'm sure it's hard to comprehend why I'd want to tie myself down.

"Why not? I'm a world champion. My racing career is great, and sure, I'd like another title, but technically, I reached the highest I could reach and I've never had the desire to break records." I'm grateful that I set myself up for life doing what I love to do. But I'm not like Jackson Banks and Jordan Hasting. Bloody hell, I'm not even like Sam. Those guys always find another challenge to dive into. But meeting Nikkie just showed me I want more than that. I desire to create the loving family I grew up in. "I love to race. But I love her more." Sam blinks at me. "Say something!"

"I want to puke, but I'm trying not to." I pull a face at his lame joke. He chuckles and runs a hand over his face. "Okay! That's some heavy shit, T."

"I know."

He eyes me suspiciously. "You didn't come here for advice, did you?"

"Nope." I don't need anyone to convince me otherwise.

"You're doing this."

"I'm doing this," I say, resolute.

"Can I be the party planner?" He wiggles his eyebrows.

"Hell no." Nikkie might be from Amsterdam, one of the most open-minded-cities in Europe, but I doubt she'll appreciate Sam's opinion of a good party. Especially if that contains strippers and a mechanical bull on her wedding day.

"I'm gonna give a speech," he opts.

"Your mouth will be duct taped."

"You think a little bit of tape is gonna stop me?"

"Probably not." I shake my head, pushing off from the counter, strutting back to the front door. "Let's go, smartass."

"Where are we going?"

"To the jewelry store."

35

NIKKIE

"I CAN'T BELIEVE YOU had sex at a Formula One gala." Tessa brings the still steaming mug to her lips. "Actually, I can."

I absentmindedly glance at one of the candles I lit earlier, snuggling into my blanket until her words register.

"What does that mean?" I throw her an indignant look.

She shrugs with mischief written all over her face. "You never said no to some pussy action."

"Now you're making me sound like a slut."

"I'm not!" she says, though she can't hold back her smile. "Although it's a bit of a slutty thing to get fucked behind a tree in the park."

"It was night! No one saw us." I hide behind my cup of tea, thinking back about that night. It was summer. The air was still humid, and I'm thinking it was Wes's idea to make it easier on myself, but it wasn't. We were on our way home, deciding to take the long route and walk through the park, and my mind just took over. My back hurt the next day from grinding against the tree, but fuck me, it was hot as hell. Both literally and figuratively.

"You wouldn't care anyway," Tessa hums.

"No, probably not." I'm known for the sparks I'd ignite around me. Always up for an adventure. Always ready to explore. The corner of my mouth curls, taking a sip of my tea. I liked that girl. And even though I felt like I didn't belong at that gala, I'm glad I'm slowly finding my way back to her.

"It's nice seeing you like this." Tessa's smile is laced with affection, and I nod in agreement.

"It feels good, Tess. I feel like I'm slowly reinventing myself. There's some new, but there's also some of the old me. The bits I loved. *Love*," I correct myself. I know I still have a long way to go, and the grief of that loss will probably never completely vanish, but it's such a relief that I can forgive myself. I'm not ready just yet, but I'm getting there and it's like the weight is slowly lifted from my shoulders, one day at a time.

"That's good. I'm so happy to hear that. You deserve to be happy." Her manicured hand lands on my knee, giving it a little squeeze. "Wes would have wanted you to be happy."

"Thank you." The funny thing is, I know I have a lot of people who care about me, but in the last eighteen months, I've been so numb, so closed off, I never fully noticed. Hearing Tessa speak those words out loud swells my chest with happiness. *I'm so fucking lucky*. Not only am I in love, but I'm also surrounded by love.

"By the way, I got you something." Tess pulls a plastic back from beside the couch, then throws it into my lap.

"You bought me a new candle?" My face lights up as I pull the pink candle from the bag, then bring it to my nose. *Sandalwood.* "Thank you so much! You didn't have to do that."

"It was discounted in a store. No biggie. Plus, you've been happier since you have been buying this scent, so in case it's the candles, I want to make sure we keep this up." She jokes, and I playfully give her a shove.

"It's not the candles." I chuckle, then pause for a beat. "It's Tristan."

"Yeah, I figured as much."

"Speaking of..." I lock my brown eyes with her blues. "I made a decision."

She sits a little straighter in anticipation.

"I'm selling the bar."

A grin splits her face, her eyes sparkling. "Really?"

"Yeah, you are right. Being a bar owner wasn't my dream. It was never part of my ambition. I only agreed to it because it was Wes's dream. I don't want to wake up one day resenting him for giving me a bar I never wanted." It took me a while to come to terms with it, but the more time I spend with Tristan, the more this bar feels like a block of concrete on my feet. It keeps me rooted, when my gut is telling me that I need to fly. I have no clue where to go, but I just know I need to be free to figure that out. Selling the bar is the first step. Regardless of what happens between Tristan and I in the future.

"I think that's the best decision you can make. Does this mean you'll be traveling more with Tristan this year?'

"I hope so. I don't want to push him into anything, so we'll see how Australia goes before I tell him, but I hope we can make it work." My heart is thumping at the thought, jumping up and down, but my mind is still keeping me grounded when it comes to thinking about a future with Tristan.

"You'll make it work. Do you have a buyer for the bar?"

"Actually," I say, smirking with excitement, "I have the perfect buyer."

The April sun is shining on top of my head, warming my cheeks in a way that curls my mouth into a genuine smile. I just picked up a few toiletries to take with me when we leave for Australia tomorrow and I've been getting more excited about it the closer it gets. Getting to know Tristan's family will be nerve-wracking, but knowing he wants to introduce me sets my heart on fire every time I think of it. Sometimes I wonder if I'm dreaming and I'll wake up one day realizing it's all a hoax, but I decided that's just my own insecurities. I am allowed to enjoy this.

"How do I get him to stop, Nikkie?" Casey's voice comes through my AirPods while I'm carrying my bags down the street. The panic in her voice has me chuckling, because I'm positive she's enjoying Sam's fixating attention on her as much as it makes her uncomfortable.

"The big question is, do you want him to stop?" I bounce back.

"What I want is to keep my job," she rebukes, referring to the fact that SRT gave her a 'no dating any other staff member' policy. Including the drivers. Well, actually, *especially* the drivers.

"Fair. Look, he's a flirt. I don't think anyone can stop him from flirting with you, but just ignore him. Keep your distance and keep it professional. I'm sure he'll eventually move on to someone else." I've seen the way he looks at her, and I think my words are flat-out lies, but from what I've been told, Sam has never been serious with any girl in his life. This might not be any different.

"Yeah, he's not a one girl kinda guy, is he?"

"Not that I know of, but he might surprise you."

"I have no plans dating Sam Devereaux." Her tone is resolute, almost as if she's stomping her foot down like a little kid.

"Can't blame you." I chuckle. I have my own relationship doubts that still like to make an appearance, and I'm dating the guy on the grid who's known for his reliability. Sam, on the other hand... well, they don't call him the Racing Playboy for no reason.

"Are you ready for Australia?" Casey asks.

"You mean, meeting the parents down under? No." Definitely not, but I know it's just something I have to get through.

"I'm sure they'll love you."

"But what if they don't?" I let out a small whine, my legs taking the last dozen steps to my front door.

"Then you're lucky that you and Tristan live in Europe and they live on the other side of the world," she opts with humor.

"Well, if you put it like that." The simple truth she's giving me makes me smile, until I lift my gaze to my front door and every muscle in my back constricts. "Oh, shit."

"What?"

"Case, I have to call you back." I don't wait for her reply, fishing my phone from my pocket and hanging up, then putting my AirPods back in my pocket. With a big sigh, to try to relax my muscles, I swing my vision to those icy grays that burn through my skin.

"Nina. How are you?" I try to muster a smile, but I know I'm failing immensely.

"When were you going to tell me?" she snarls, her faded face set in a glare that shows nothing but wickedness.

"Tell you what?"

"You are not selling that bar."

Oh, damn. "Who told you?"

"Your dad."

I pinch the bridge of my nose, silently cursing myself. I know I should've told her sooner, but with the trip to Saudi Arabia and now prepping for Australia, I've been putting it off to protect my gleaming attitude.

"Right." I bring my head back up, offering her an apologetic expression. "I'm sorry you found out like that. I was gonna tell you."

"When? When it was sold already?" she sneers, her messy brown hair swinging in front of her eyes. There are stains on her blue jeans, and her sweater is filled with holes that I'm sure are not a new fashion statement. She looks like she pulled an all-nighter, and frankly, I wouldn't put it past her.

"Of course not." I take a deep breath, squaring my shoulders. "But even if I did, that would be my choice."

"It's Wes's bar!" Her voice becomes more frantic, her eyes vicious, but I'm done letting her talk to me like that. She doesn't scare me. And she certainly doesn't control me.

"No, Nina! Wes is gone. It's *my* bar and I never wanted it in the first place."

She shakes her head. "You can't do this."

"I'm sorry this hurts you, but I can, and I will. I'm selling the bar and you can't change my mind. Now, if you'll excuse me, I want to go home." I try to move past her, but she puts her slender body right in front of me, her face close to mine.

"I'll tell the media."

"Tell them what?" I frown, seeing how her eyes turn dark, a little devilish snarl around her thin lips.

"That you're the daughter of a criminal." My heart begins to pound in my ears. "That you and my son used to deal drugs." My chest moves up and down. "That the bar is bought with dirty money." My lips part as a big lump grows in my throat. "That you killed your boyfriend." And then I try to swallow the lump away as I do my best to keep my thoughts calm and in control. "How do you think your superstar boyfriend will respond to that? I bet the press will have a field day with that one. I can see the headlines *'World Champion dates criminal princess from Amsterdam, City of Sin.'*" Her hands move into the sky to add action to her words.

"You leave him out of it," I growl, ignoring the urge to slap the evil grin off her pale cheeks.

"Don't sell the bar." She takes a step back, folding her arms in front of her chest. She has me checkmated, and she knows it.

I swallow back the tears that are pricking their way out. "Don't do this. You'll ruin his career."

"You ruined my life."

"It was an accident!" I snap.

"I don't care." This time she's the one who has her posture calm and collected, while I try to keep it together. I hear the sounds of traffic around me, but it's all muffled by the realization she's managed to back me up into a corner.

"I don't want to keep the bar," I plead.

"Fine, you can give it to me."

"You have no money."

"I know, you can see it as a retribution."

She lost her son and she's decided it's my fault. I'm the one to blame and as I keep staring into her cold eyes, I understand the true meaning of that realization. She will not stop until she destroys me.

"I have debts that I need to pay." I don't know why I still mention it, because just one glance over her diabolical expression tells me it's no use.

"You'll figure it out." She takes a few steps backward with a smirk, then turns around and leaves me standing on the sidewalk.

36

NIKKIE

"I SAW NINA THIS week," I tell Tessa through the phone with a muffled voice. Tristan and Sam are playing a game of poker while we're flying eight miles above the Indian Ocean. As soon as the Wi-Fi got turned on, I dove into the back of the jet to call Tessa. The last few times, I fully enjoyed the flight surrounded by all the luxury that comes with it. Unlimited drinks, snacks, and armchairs that are comfortable as hell. But it's hard to enjoy this level of comfort when a big stone has been rooted in my stomach for days.

"So that's why you've been acting weird all week! You're still selling the bar, though, right?" Tessa questions when I've quietly filled her in on my entire conversation with Nina.

"Did you hear what I just said? It will ruin his career." I've been up all night, worrying about what to fucking do. But there isn't a scenario where I don't fuck up his career in Formula One. If I tell him? I'm risking him giving it all up for me. If I don't, I can't sell the bar without Nina hitting the nail to his coffin.

"Talk to him about it." Tessa makes it sound easy, but I know it's not.

"And tell him what?" I hiss, then add sarcastically: 'Oh, by the way, my dad is a high-end criminal in the city of Amsterdam? Or when my boyfriend died, we were running twelve kilos of coke?' He'll be gone before I can say *'I can explain.'*"

"Nikkie." Her tone softens with sympathy. "You didn't know. Besides, he loves you."

"I know." But that doesn't mean he won't look at me a lot differently if he finds out exactly how much of a rebel I was before I met him.

"You can trust him," she adds.

"I know that too, but it's not about that. It's about me ruining his career if this comes out."

"You don't know that."

"He's world famous, Tess. It's gonna blow up."

"Well, even if it is, shouldn't he decide how to handle that?"

My eyes are glossing over, and I quickly turn my back to the boys, making sure they are not aware of my emotion. "He'd give it all up for me."

"Exactly!" Tessa blurts like that's not a problem. "Just tell him, Nik. What are you so scared of?"

That he'll decide I'm not good enough if I tell him the truth. "I don't want to lose anyone else."

"The man asked you to travel around the world with him to meet his family. You won't lose him." I want to believe her so badly, but there's this nagging feeling that keeps dragging me down, telling me I deserve this. *That I don't deserve him.*

"Nik? Are you okay?" I hear Tristan's comforting voice calling out behind me, and I quickly rub my eyes to prevent the tears from escaping.

"I have to go. I'll call you later." I hang up the phone, then turn around as I conjure a smile. I find Tristan's green eyes, and I walk toward his reached-out hand.

"You okay, baby?" He tugs me onto his lap, and I bury my face in his neck, breathing him in. His fresh woody smell settles my mind a bit, wanting to fuse my body with his.

"Yeah, Tessa says hi." I push a kiss to his warm skin, enjoying the feeling of his arms wrapped tightly around my waist.

He brings his hand up to cup my cheek, stroking my jaw with his thumb. "You look tired."

"Hmm, I am."

"You two." Sam demands our attention. "Don't be disgusting on my jet."

"It's two against one, Devereaux. What are you gonna do about it?" I sass to cover up my gloomy mood. There's nothing I can do about it right now, so I might as well shoot my thoughts away and wallow in the comfort of my boyfriend's chest while annoying Sam.

Sam pulls a face, pointing a finger at me. "You wanna fly commercial next time?"

"No!"

"Be nice, then."

"Fine," I concede with a small chuckle. "I'm gonna take a nap."

"Sure, baby. You sleep. I got you." Tristan puts a lingering kiss on my forehead, effectively closing my eyes while he's blissfully unaware of the way those three words lift my heart to a higher level. A higher level I'm deathly afraid I'll fall down from before I can blink. But for now, I snuggle deeper against Tristan's body, reveling in this feeling of safety while I still can.

37

TRISTAN

M Y WRIST IS RESTING on her neck, my fingers playing with the little strands that escaped her ponytail.

I'm tired. Though the privacy of Sam's jet makes it way more comfortable than being cramped up on a commercial flight, a twenty-hour flight is still a massive assault on your body in any kind of way. But where normally I'd be a bit cranky, diving right into my bed after saying hi to my family, this time, I can't fully get rid of the smile on my face when I look at the blonde next to me. You'd think I'd be nervous introducing her to my overbearing mother, and not to mention, my brown-nosing little sister. But in reality? I can't fucking wait because I know they will love her just as much as I do.

"Oh, wow." Nikkie gasps beside me as Axel drives the car onto the half-mile driveway after picking us up from the airport. A white picket fence separates the road from the rows of trees in the field, standing out against the green leaves, before the red painted ranch slowly comes into our perimeter. The high beams on the barn are painted white, giving it that idyllic feel that you only see in picture books. It wasn't until I traveled the world that I realized what a lucky bastard I am to have been able to call this home for most of my life. In a way, it still is.

"This is where you grew up?"

"Yeah." I offer her a lazy look. Enjoying her awe. I hope she'll start loving this place as much as I did when I grew up.

"It's gorgeous."

I squeeze her neck gently before she cranes her neck again to glance out of the window. "I'm a lucky bastard. I know not every kid can say he had a carefree childhood."

"Tell me about it." I detect the little eyeroll, along with a little tightness in her shoulder.

"They will love you."

Her lips press together while my mother trots down the porch steps from the corner of my eye. "I promise." I squeeze her neck one more time, silently telling her she has nothing to worry about while Axel parks the car. Her head jerks in a tiny nod, her goldish-brown irises still laced with hesitance, but neither of us has any time to help it scurry away.

"Oh, there he is!" My mother pulls the door open, diving around my neck before I can set both feet out the door. "How was the trip, darling boy?"

"Long." I release a breath into her brown hair, as I slide out and straighten my body, then wrap my arms around her shoulders. Since I was sixteen, I've grown at least a head taller than her and every time I get to hug her like this, I somehow cherish the moment. Her lavender shampoo is the literal definition of home. I inhale, sucking off the flowery scent, but before I can really enjoy it, she abruptly lets go of me.

A disappointed frown scrunches my eyebrows, until Nikkie rounds the car, and I smile with pride.

"You must be Nikkie!" My mother flies around her neck, almost knocking both of them to the ground, and Nikkie's eyes bulge out of her head at the impact before she chuckles, returning the hug.

"I've heard so much about you," my mother squeals.

"Baby, this is my mother, Amelia."

"Nice to meet you, ma'am."

"Please! Call me Amy." She quickly links their arms, then starts to drag her back up onto the porch. "Are you hungry? Tired? Let me show you your room so you can rest before I harass you into telling me your entire life story."

I follow behind them, making sure Mum doesn't scare her off by yapping for the next hour. "You mean my room, right, Mum?"

She waves a hand in the air, not looking back as she guides Nik into the foyer and up the stairs. Her eyes take in all the opulence combined with the authentic feel like the big beams on the high ceiling, and I take a mental note to give her a proper tour later. "Don't worry, sweetheart. I don't have a stick up my ass. Take your time. Take a nap. And when you come downstairs, we can open up a bottle of our best wine before everyone else arrives."

"Everyone else?" Nikkie's head snaps over her shoulder with a slight scowl.

Whoops.

"Our annual barbecue," my mother continues, unbothered. "The whole family is coming. It's one of our traditions ever since Tristan has become a racecar driver. We barely see him, but we made it a tradition to come together with the entire family, have a barbecue, and spend time before he's caught up at the track all weekend."

"The whole family, huh?" I get another side-eye.

"Yeah, Tristan didn't tell you?"

"He did not." Her expression tells me I'm in trouble, but frankly? I'm totally into the kind of trouble she's offering.

"This is your room." My mother stops in front of my old room, then takes a step to the side to let us enter. "Take your time. Get settled in." She gives Nikkie's arm a squeeze, her green eyes beaming. "I'm really happy you're here, Nikkie."

My heart flutters a little when Nikkie flashes her one of her own, before my mother descends back down, and I step into the room. Every single year I sleep in this room before the GP, and every single year it feels like I'm a teenager all over again.

The room is half the size of her entire apartment, with a king-size bed in the middle of the left wall, and a door with my bathroom next to it. I suppress the grin that wants to slip out, thinking back on how many times I jerked off with my back against the headboard.

"You weren't kidding when you said you were a Transformers fan," she says, roaming my Transformers movie posters that hang on the opposite wall.

"Bumblebee is my man." I close the door behind me, and Nikkie's ponytail swings around her shoulders as she finds my gaze.

"What are you doing?" She acts coy, but her gaze darkens just like mine, as I saunter toward her. Like a predator, I keep my eyes on my prey as she mirrors my move, stepping backwards, excitement dripping from her cheeks. "Tristan, your parents are downstairs."

The little scowl she's aiming my way is cute as hell.

"My mother said take your time." I reach her and grab her hips to force her against my body.

"I'm pretty sure that's not what she meant." She peers up at me through her thick lashes, and I reply by dipping my lips below her ear.

"You have a bad influence on me," she moans.

"Totally corrupting you." My hand roves all over her body, desperate yet cautious to find every inch of skin as I continue trailing my lips over her neck. She arches her head to the side with closed eyes, her hands resting on my biceps. There's nothing sexier than her surrendering to my touch, moaning and whimpering as I work to wake up every nerve while my own body is getting feverishly hot. The more kisses that land on the crook of her neck, the more she liquifies in my hands. Noticing the mirror in the left corner of my room, I spin her on the spot with a big smirk.

Her eyes fly open, locking with mine in the mirror, as my hands brush the skin underneath her t-shirt before I lift it up and over her head.

"I want you to see how beautiful you are." I drag my finger from her collarbone to the swell of her breasts, my lips still gently dropping against her neck. "How I worship your body." Keeping one palm on her neck, I move in front of her, pressing a kiss to her parting lips. "How I love how your skin tastes."

My breath teases her lips, her small pants curling the corner of my mouth as I start to unbutton the front of her jeans.

She gasps when I dive my hand between the lace of her panties, two fingers feeling the wetness that's dripping from her center. The gaze in her eyes is slowly shifting from lustful to pleading, her lips quivering with every additional movement of my fingers. I get down to my knees, peeling her clothes from her hips with my nose sucking in her arousal.

"How I love eating your pussy." Her bare pussy is looking gorgeous, and I lick my lips while she steps out of the rest of her clothing with heavy eyes. Her breaths become unsteady when I pull one leg over my shoulder and softly nibble her clit, the tips of her fingers raking through my hair. I gradually work down, placing open-mouthed kisses on her sweet folds.

She's like a delicate flower, one that will flourish more with every gentle touch. When I reach her inner folds, I softly suck them into my mouth, groaning at the velvety flesh against my tongue. She tastes salty, with a sweetness that is addictive every single time I find myself in this position. Like a drug, she has my dick in a chokehold, creating a tent in my sweats.

When I glance up, she's seductively looking at herself in the mirror, and I grunt against her pussy at the sight of it. *Fuck, she's so fucking sexy.*

The vibrations of my breaths weaken her knees and the grip on my hair tightens before her eyes swing down to mine in a shock of desire.

"Keep looking at yourself." I work her up and down, swiping my tongue around her center while my fingers circle around her clit. "Good girl. This turns you on, doesn't it?"

She licks her lips with a tiny smile, never deviating her vision from the mirror like the good girl I ordered her to be.

"Do you have a lock on your door?" she heaves, her eyes almost shut.

"No." I smirk, never skipping a beat. "That makes it even more exciting. I'm a racecar driver, baby. Living on the edge is what I do."

Her lashes fly up, her gaze dropping down. "Cocky son of a bitch."

I roughly suck her clit in retaliation, erupting a squeal from her perfect lips. "What's that?"

She growls daringly. "*Cocky son of a bitch.*"

I repeat my action, this time pushing a finger into her core at the same time and her knees give in, almost dropping her to the floor.

"Oh, fuck!" she screeches, both in appeal and desire.

"I don't think I heard you." I chuckle, doing it another time with the same response, only now there's a more high-pitched tone that echoes through the room. "Can you repeat it?"

"You cocky–" Before she can finish, I suck her clit into my mouth, then start playing the little nub with my tongue. "Oh my god, Tristan!" she scolds, her expression as if she's about to leave this earth within the next thirty seconds or so. "P-please, baby," she stutters. "Your parents will hear me. Oh, shit. Oh, please stop."

"You want me to stop?"

"No, keep going, keep going."

Laughter bubbles from my chest, before I tighten my biceps and take her ass in my palms. With one quick move, I drop her to the bed, her legs hanging from the edge as she arches her pussy close to my mouth.

"You love it when I feast on your sweet pussy, don't you?"

"Y-yes."

"You want me to make you come?"

"Please, I'm so close." Her hips grind against my tongue, chasing her own release.

"No." I firmly twist her entire body, until she's face down against the duvet, her ass up in the air. "Let me feel your pussy milk my cock," I whisper playfully, with my lips flush to her ear, my chest melting into her back as I let my tip play with her entrance. "I want to fuck you bare, baby." I grab her ponytail, arching her neck back, kissing her cheek. "Are you going to let me fuck you bare?"

Her reply is nothing more than a slight tilt of her head, enough for me to see the smile she's hiding as she drags her lower lip between her teeth before she nods.

The desire in her eyes is crystal clear about her agreement, and I don't wait another second before I slide home in every aspect of the word.

I've been dreaming of this moment since I was a teenager and I knew how to get myself off with nothing more than a poster of Megan Fox staring back at me. I lost my virginity the first summer I moved to Europe when I was sixteen, freshly ready for the driver academy of SRT. It was sloppy and not exactly how I imagined my first time would be all those many times at night when I was younger. But this? Fucking this siren in the bed that is the literal beginning of every fucking fantasy... it's a dream come true.

I growl, the vibrations of my voice sounding louder than I intend, as I remember my entire family is downstairs, before I bite her neck to muffle it. Every nerve is hit differently as her walls wrap around me like a perfect glove, the sensation knocking me straight to heaven.

"Bloody hell," I curse, afraid I will lose my mind. For a moment, I still, trying to keep it together and not shoot my load prematurely, then slowly pump in and out. My hips grind hers against the duvet and her pants are quickly increasing while her fingers grip the covers like she's hanging onto the edge of a cliff.

A primal feeling takes over, and I push her body deeper into the mattress, grunting with each thrust inside of her. I set a moderate pace, each bit of friction feeling more torturously delicious than the last. I haven't been able to get her out of my mind for months, but this changes every fucking thing. This makes me want to pull out the ring that's burning a hole in my pocket and put it on her finger without asking, because at this point, she's got no choice.

I literally feel how her soul is merging with mine, and there is no way in hell I can live another day without her. I don't care what I have to do. I don't care what it takes.

This woman is mine in every sense of the word, and there's no way I'll let that slip from my fingers.

I lower my chest against her back again, finding her neck. "Do you feel how my cock fits perfectly in your pussy?" She moans. "It's because it's *mine*. You know that, right?" Another moan, muffled by the sheets she's breathing in, her ass still up in the air. I reach my hand in front of her, as I start playing with her clit, and she squirms underneath me. "This is all mine."

"Y-yes! Yes!"

My index finger alternates between flicks and circles, and the tension in her back tells me she's close. "I'm going to make love to your sweet pussy for the rest of my life, baby." Little feral whimpers sound like music in my ears, but I want her to really hear what I'm saying. "Do you understand that? Do you understand that this is mine until the day I die?"

She cries, an actual tear slipping from the corner of her eye. "It's yours, Ace. It's all yours. My heart. My body. *It's yours.*"

"Good girl." I sink in deep with every flick of my hips, picking up the pace. Her concession speeds up my road to release.

"Please, make me come, Ace. I need you."

"A little longer, baby." I hunt my release with the same precision as I do the finish line on track, calculating each move for the best possible outcome while I keep her on the brink of exploding around me. Finally, I feel my shaft squeeze, and I push out a breath with parted lips as the peristaltic waves run through my groin.

Growling, with sweat dripping from my forehead, I rapidly circle her clit at the same time I release inside of her, the squeezing of her walls milking me with a force that knocks the air from my lungs. Her high wails are muffled into the bed, her hips quivering underneath me, until I feel her relax around me, and I collapse on top of her.

"Fucking hell, Ace." She huffs, a lazy grin sitting on her flushed cheeks, and I chuckle.

"Welcome to Australia, baby."

I pull her panties from the floor with a smirk.

"What are you doing?"

"I'm keeping these."

"Excuse me?" There's panic laced with a dare in her features.

"I have to spend the next three hours talking about why Callahan terminated my contract with my family. That will be a lot more fun with your dirty panties in my pocket."

She purses her lips, feigning an annoyance I know she doesn't feel. She loves this. She loved it when I fucked her in the wardrobe of the F1 gala. She loved it that I stuck my tongue down her sweet pussy while anyone could barge right in. She's a wild child. Stealing her panties isn't something she's fazed about. In fact, I bet it turns her the hell on.

"Is this some kind of way of marking your territory?" she mocks, gathering the rest of her clothes.

I snicker. "Marking my territory? Baby, please. You're gated. Guarded by a bunch of German Shepherds. Nobody is going to get near you." I drag her to me, cupping the front of her throat. "You are mine."

She daringly holds my gaze, biting her lip. "What if I make a run for it?"

"I'll find you. I'll always find you. Wait. I got you something." I reach for my jeans on the floor, taking out the velvet box I've been waiting the whole flight to give her.

"What's that?" Her goldish eyes pop out of her head, expanding my grin.

"It's a shoe box." My sarcastic reply earns me a glare. "I got you this."

"Wait. It's not a ring, right?" Her voice is mixed with panic, but there are little sparks in her eyes that almost makes me wish I did.

"No," I scoff a little, but then add with a smile, "But I definitely have it on the list. No, I got you this."

I open the little box, showing her the necklace that's draped onto the silk cushion. It's a petite silver band with a clover pendant. It's not much. It doesn't even have a diamond in the middle, but by the teary sparkle in her eyes, I know I made the right choice by not getting something fancy.

Her lashes fly up, and I wipe a tear that's escaped and rolling down her cheek. "Do you like it?" I question.

She shakes her head, and I search her face in confusion. "I love it. It's perfect. But you shouldn't have."

"You're my girl. My lucky charm. I wanted to." I take the pendant out, tossing the box on the bed before I spin her back to me and put it around her neck, then press a kiss below her ear.

She turns, peering up at me with a look that hits me in the heart. "Thank you."

"I'm happy you like it." I drop my forehead against hers. "Didn't miss the little glint in your eyes when you mentioned the word *ring*, though."

Her lip is dragged between her teeth as she feigns indifference. "What glint?"

"The one I hope to see again one day."

Her sigh is long, her eyes growing a deeper shade of brown, but before I can study the feeling behind it, she crushes her lips against mine as if she's willing this conversation away.

And addicted to her touch as I am, I let it slide the moment her hands slip into my hair, pulling me back into her body.

38

NIKKIE

*H*E FUCKED ME WITH *his family downstairs.*

    I wanted to scold him for it—still do—but I just fucking can't deny I enjoyed that just as much as he did. I'd be mortified if one of his family members would've actually barged through that door, but the excitement of knowing it could happen is something that brings back the wild child inside of me.

Welcome to Australia, he said. I'm not gonna lie, getting completely fucked, literally, in his childhood bedroom, is something that's keeping my cheeks flushed as I glance around the backyard with a content smile on my lips.

I haven't seen much more of Australia than the road over here and this gorgeous ranch that is the heart of the Reinhart winery, but so far, I'm loving it.

Tristan was right. There is nothing to be nervous about. Every single member of his family has been nothing but nice to me, his sister Zoe already scheduling a shopping spree for the next time I'm here. I haven't told her I hate shopping, brushing it off with a smile, but now that I have a moment to sink in the fruitful scenery and the delicious smell of meat on the barbecue, I'm caught up with a little dread.

It's not big, the comfort of this afternoon overshadowing it, even though I'm tired as hell, but it's there nonetheless. That feeling like I'm waiting for the other shoe to drop.

I don't like being forced into anything, and my mind keeps telling me that I definitely shouldn't start now, but when I look at Sam and Tristan entertaining his dad from across the yard, I still feel like this is a dream. Tristan keeps saying I'm his. *This* is mine. But I feel like I'm looking at it from the sideline, almost within reach to touch it, but not quite yet.

"Are you having fun?"

I rear my head back, being greeted by Amelia's kind smile. The woman is beautiful. She radiates that vibrant and safe motherly feeling every kid wishes for and deserves, her green eyes free from any kind of judgment. She has the same honey-brown hair as Tristan, styled in waves that reach the waist of her cream dress. The woman is the epitome of class, but in a good way.

"I am." I smile, catching a whiff of roses before turning my gaze back to Tristan's bright smile. "I can't imagine growing up in a place like this. It's so gorgeous. So peaceful."

"It is. What started as a hobby, quickly became a worldwide brand, and I'm so grateful my children grew up here."

"It's a dream."

She cocks her head a little, putting her gaze on mine until I find her eyes. They study me with an intent that feels like she's trying to shovel her way into my deepest secrets. "Why do I have the feeling peace wasn't something you grew up with?"

I could lie. I could tell her it wasn't all that bad, and in a way, it wasn't. But now I know where Tristan gets his skills from. The one where I know he can see straight through my soul because that's exactly what his mother is doing, making it very hard to cover up the answer I should give with fluff I don't have.

I shrug. "My dad did what he could as a single dad. My mother died when I was four. They weren't together anymore, and he went from seeing me on weekends to being a full-time single parent. I'm sure it wasn't easy."

"That's such a mature way to look at it. Not many people your age would feel the same."

I shrug. "It is what it is. Plus, I feel like I didn't miss out on anything. I still had a pretty happy childhood. If anything, my friends and I got a little bit more freedom than other kids our age. It was fun."

"It sounds fun." She chuckles. "Are they still your friends?"

I press my lips together, a little cloud drifting on top of my head when Wes flashes through my mind. "Some."

Silence lingers between us as our eyes roam the yard, watching people mingle, laugh, having a good time. They all look relaxed and, for a minute, I wonder if I could ever be a part of this. If I could feel like I belong in someone else's family that's not my own. *Or Wes's.*

"You're lucky with such a great group of people around you." The words roll off my lips before I can stop them, a little sad tone clearly detectable even though I try to cover it up with a beaming smile as I find her gaze.

"I am." She smiles. "I feel blessed every day, but a little more when Tristan is home. I miss him when he's not here."

I nod, knowing the feeling. Lately, I've been thinking back about the beginning, wondering when it was that I knew this was more than just a one-night stand. But the truth is... I'm starting to realize it never was. Everything with Tristan feels easy, while everything before Tristan felt heavy and filled with dread. But I can't shake that feeling that nothing lasts forever. That one day I'll wake up and the other shoe will be dropped.

Amelia must sense my change in mood because her palm falls to my knee. "It's okay to be happy. I know my son makes you happy."

"He's amazing." His infectious laughter reaches over the rest of the yard, curling my mouth.

"He is. He's been having a hard time the last few years, but I'm glad he's slowly finding his way back. I'm sure you have something to do with that." She throws me a wink, a grateful grin on her closed lips.

"That's very kind of you, but his achievements are all his." Maybe I triggered him to focus on what he can do instead of how his team was treating him, but it doesn't mean it wasn't all him in the end.

"You're a pure soul, and my son is crazy about you. Enjoy it." She holds my gaze as if she wants to tattoo the words in my heart and, for a moment, I feel like they are, until her husband starts yelling from behind the barbecue with a heavy Australian accent.

"Darl? Where'd you put steaks? I wanna start the barbie."

I bite back a laugh.

"Sorry, love," she says with an apologetic look. "Excuse me whilst I help him. He must have had a boy's look in the fridge." She gets up, glancing down at me. The sun frames her face from behind, matching her natural glow. "I'm happy you're here, Nikkie."

"Thank you. So am I."

She takes off, leaving me alone with my thoughts, my vision automatically roaming the yard until it finds Tristan again. His bright smile warms my heart, acting like a beacon. My eyes are drawn to him without my control, and it's quickly becoming one of my quirks that I don't want to change. I hope to keep staring into this man's eyes forever. I want him to hold my hand like my infinite light in the darkness.

"Hi!"

I startle when Zoe pops up in front of me, flashing me the same beam the entire Reinhart family is known for.

"Hi." I laugh.

Her chestnut-brown hair is hanging in two braids beside her heart-shaped face, and emerald-green eyes beam at me as vibrantly as her mother's. She plops down next to me, her gaze set on her brother across the yard.

"I'm so happy my brother brought you home. I was dying to meet you."

"Thank you, I'm so happy to be here." I glance at her bubbly face, a wide grin spread over her rosy cheeks. She's just as cheery as her brother, and the knowledge that Tristan loves his sister dearly, paints the cutest picture in my head. I imagine him taking her for ice cream when they were younger, hand in hand, fiercely protective of his little sister. Providing her with that safe feeling only he can. *Like he does to me.*

"He actually had the nerves to debate whether he was coming home for Christmas. My mother was not having it, but that's when I knew you were the one."

I rear my head to look at her, at this new piece of information.

"He did that?" I blink with wide eyes, another heavy flutter swirling through my stomach.

"Tristan loves Christmas. It is his favorite holiday," she continues. "He wouldn't miss it for the world. But he was willing to miss it for you." Her wink makes a smile slide in place.

"I didn't know."

She hums, her smile smug as hell. "He's crazy about you. Otherwise, he wouldn't have brought you here."

"I'm sure there have been others?" I sputter with a laugh.

But she ferociously shakes her head. "You're the first." My heart flutters at that line. "Well, except for Jenny. But she doesn't count. He was fourteen and she is the daughter of my mother's best friend. We all grew up together. It was more a relationship of convenience between two teens. It lasted no longer than three excruciating months," she jokes, and we both break out in laughter until her neck stretches when a new beat booms through the speakers.

"Come! Dance with me!" Tristan's sister cheers, tugging on my hand.

"Oh, no." I shake my head, but she possesses the persistence of her big brother, and I peer up at her with a crooked smile.

"Come on! Tristan told me you have a bar. I bet you're dancing on the bar whenever you have the place to yourself."

"I feel exposed."

"Come on!" Her green eyes sparkle, and though it's with a sigh of reluctance, I get up and let her drag me away. The music changes to the next song, and

Zoe bounces on her feet when Ariana Grande's "Rain on Me" starts blasting through the speaker.

"I love this song!" Her cheerfulness is infectious, and I finally push out the air from my lungs and follow her move. My feet move, and we twirl, sway, bob, slide, and even grind as Zoe and I let the music take over, and I just enjoy myself. We mouth the words, getting heated with every chorus, and after twenty minutes, my back is damp and my cheeks are heated from the afternoon sun burning on my head.

Is this what it feels like to have siblings? To have a big family? Suddenly, my nervousness at meeting his family seems so silly, since every single one of them gives me a sense of home I've never experienced.

Laughter bursts my mouth open, when Zoe puts on a silly face as she starts twerking her way down to the floor, her father looking in disgust behind her.

"Come on, Nik! Show me what you got!" she dares, her hips flicking up and down.

"Zoe, seriously?" When Zoe looks over her shoulder, her brown hair flying with her, Tristan is scolding her with a stern expression, which only adds to my amusement.

"What? We're just dancing."

I laugh at her silliness, shaking my head before I sense my phone vibrating in my back pocket. Nina's name on the screen is staring at me like she'll be able to jump out of my phone if I don't answer. Wrinkling my nose, I suck in a deep breath.

And there's the other shoe.

"I'm sorry, I have to take this." I offer Zoe a strained smile, then take off to find a quiet place inside the house.

"Nina? Are you okay?" I ask out of habit when I reach the foyer of the house.

"Call off the sale of the bar, Nikkie," she snarls. Her sharp voice lifts the hairs on my body.

"Nina."

"No, don't *Nina* me! You're not selling that bar. You have until the weekend to call off the sale."

A quick no jerks my head. "I can't, Nina."

"You can, and you will, or a file about the real Nikkie Peters is mailed to the Daily Mail in London next week. Don't think I'm bluffing."

She wouldn't.

"Why are you doing this?"

"What?" A vicious snicker travels over the line. "Do you think just because you're young and beautiful, you get to live happily ever after like nothing happened? You *killed* my son!" Tears pool my eyes, and I bite my lip to keep them at bay. "You destroyed my life! Just like you will do with that poor, oblivious racer. Did you really think you're good enough for someone like that? You're nothing but white trash like the rest of us. The daughter of a convicted criminal. Did you tell him your dad sells drugs and steals cars for a living?" It feels like the air around me is growing thicker, unable to provide my lungs with the much-needed oxygen that will help me get rid of the tightness in my throat. "You think just because some celebrity buys you a pretty dress, you'll fit in. You'll never fit in. You belong behind that bar. Selling drinks to other people. You're no better than the rest of us."

"Please stop. Just stop." My eyes flood over.

"Call off the sale!" she barks, before she hangs up, and my knees fail to keep my weight up.

39

NIKKIE

I T'S NO SURPRISE THAT happy, safe feeling that was shown to me this afternoon has been completely demolished. A house of despair built in its place.

I can't sleep. I've been having a lot of those nights lately, and I know they won't stop either. So, I tiptoe out of bed, not wanting to wake up Tristan, then pull a hoodie over my head before I go downstairs.

When I reach the kitchen, I glance out of the window and into the big yard. Everyone has left, most of the party is cleaned up, but Sam's still sitting outside around the firepit, and without thought, I walk out there to meet him.

"Hey." I lower myself onto the lawn chair next to him, my eyes drawn to the fire as I wrap my hands around my body.

"Hey." Sam looks up with surprise. "Can't sleep?

"You're up late."

"Deflecting, okay." He puts his attention back to his phone.

"Stalking Casey?"

"Maybe." He smirks at the screen.

"Don't use her, Sam. She's a nice girl."

He sighs with his entire body.

"I know," he says, then runs a hand through his messy hair before he locks the screen and rears his attention up. "Wanna tell me why you're not in bed?"

"Nightmare." It's only half a lie because lying awake the entire night is a nightmare in and of itself.

"You get a lot of those?"

"I used to. Lately, not so much."

"You know what triggered it?"

I avoid Sam's burning gaze, curiosity lasering through my skin. But I don't know how to find the right words without telling him I'm bound to break his best friend's heart.

"You don't want to talk about it. Fine," he adds.

He mirrors my stance, slouched in the chair, as we silently keep staring into the cracking flames. The quiet is calming, other than the orchestra of crickets echoing around us, and I look up at the sky. The night is dark, but clear, the luminous stars standing out against the midnight blue. The warmth of the fire holds back the cold of the night, but I still feel a chill running down my spine, my eyes locked with the moon.

I wish I could stay here forever. Disappear from the mess I call life and just start over in Australia. But I know that won't fix my situation. It wouldn't give me Tristan.

"It's so quiet. I'm not used to it being so quiet," I say.

"A true city girl." Sam chuckles.

"I never expected to enjoy the silence so much." I'm so used to always hearing life around me, I forgot how peaceful the quiet can be.

"I know. The first night I stayed here, I couldn't sleep. Not enough noise. But now? I always sit here for another hour, just enjoying the peace."

I rear my head to his shimmering expression with a little curl to my lip. "You're gonna win the title this year, aren't you?"

"I am." I admire the fact that there is no hesitation in his voice. He's so convinced and confident about his ability. I wish I could say the same.

"I hope you do. I realize I shouldn't say that because my boyfriend is your competition. But I hope you win."

"I don't think Tristan still wants another championship."

"Really? Why wouldn't he?"

His eyebrows glue together in a mocking frown. "Because he already got a prize that's more important to him." The true meaning of his words doesn't go unnoticed, and my heart falls to my feet.

"Right." I try to swallow away the emotion that instantly bubbles to the surface, but it isn't overlooked by Sam.

"What's going on, Nikkie?" He rests his elbows on his knees, sticking his palms together as he cocks his head at me.

"I told you, nightmare." *Liar.*

"You don't want to talk about it, that's fine. But I've seen the haunting look in your eyes this weekend. It's not there the entire time. But I see it." He calls me out. "You're thinking of bailing. I see it, because it's the same way I look when girls are starting to ask questions, like if they can stay over or if they will see me again next week."

"Manwhore," I mutter, trying to lighten the mood.

"I own it with pleasure. *You,* however, don't." I stay fixed on the flames again, afraid that if I look at him directly, I will burst out in tears. "I don't know what's scaring you or what's making you want to run... But don't do it. I guarantee it won't fix anything. It will only make things worse, because you love him. Don't give that up. A life without it is far more painful."

I jerk my head at him in confusion from his admission, just in time to see the sad glitter in his eyes, wondering what's going through his mind right now. Sam is a playboy. A charmer off the grid, ruthless on it. His eyes are focused on winning the title ever since he's been in Formula One, but his choice of words has me thinking he's not as carefree as he likes to show the world.

"Have you ever been in love, Sam?"

"Once." We lock eyes, and my eyebrows shoot up. "Susy Parker from second grade. Dated her for a whole twenty-four hours before she broke my heart. Worst mistake of my life," he jokes, and I roll my eyes with a laugh before his words hit home, dissolving it as quickly as it has risen.

"What if I become his mistake?" I play with the clover pendant around my neck.

"You won't." He shakes his head as if I'm crazy. And hell, maybe I am. "Just don't run. He will give it all up for you."

"That's what I'm scared of." This is the exact reason I don't want to tell him the truth. I can feel in my gut he's willing to give up his entire career for me if he has to. Right now, that sounds like a dream... but where will we be in ten years? Because my guess is we're gonna be married, throw out a few kids, and he'll be bored to death and resent me for giving up racing. I can't let that happen. I can't let him ruin everything he's worked for.

"I can see the thoughts running through your head. *Stop*." I've never seen Sam with a serious expression, but his message is loud and clear. I long to listen to him. I want to believe him. But I'm confident he wouldn't have the same opinion if it means I'll destroy Tristan's career before he's ready to quit.

"You're a good guy, Sam."

"I'm really not, but if you can tell my hot PR girl that I am, that would be great."

His lightheartedness gets rid of the cloud above my head, turning my frown into a grin. "I'm sure she'll come to like you. Sleeping with you? I don't know. But she'll learn to like you. Just show her this side of you."

He pulls a face. "I want to fuck her, Nik. Not date her."

I laugh, but it's quickly cut by the footsteps I hear behind me, and I look over my shoulder.

"Hey." Tristan is slowly approaching us, his navy sweats hanging loosely on his hips, his bare chest showing all of his muscles against the light of the moon.

He's gorgeous.

"Hey," I reply.

He takes my hand, pressing a warm kiss on my palm. "My bed is cold without you."

A fluttering feeling is the cue for the smile I show him, his lips hovering above mine while a gagging sound is audible beside us.

Without dropping his eyes from mine, Tristan flips Sam off, and we both snicker as he continues to search my gaze. "Are you okay?"

No. Not even close.

I nod. "Had a nightmare. Needed some air."

Our lips connect, the heat instantly fogging my mind in a way I desperately need right now. For him to just make me forget. Forget what I need to do and live in the moment. Enjoy this while it still lasts.

"Are you ready to go back in?" His breath feathers against my mouth. Slowly, he pulls me up by my hand, and I let him guide me back inside.

Sam gives me a knowing look, silently telling me to remember what he said. I heard him. I did. Too bad it's not something I can control.

"Goodnight, Sam." I smile with my lips pressed together.

"Goodnight."

40

NIKKIE

I RUB MY NECK, the muscles strained from keeping my eyes fixed on the screen. Tristan has been fighting for third place for thirty-four laps and I've been bouncing in my seat because of it. I'm sitting in the back of the Arzano garage with Axel, both of us vibrating with anxiety. His start is great. Claiming fourth position before the first corner, chasing Raul's car in front of him the entire time.

"Box, box, box," Tristan's team radio echoes in my headset as I wave my shirt to cool myself from the Australian humidity.

"They're gonna do an undercut," Axel says with a little excitement in his tone.

I murmur something in agreement, as I turn around to the pitstop. Black and gold uniforms of his pit crew are setting up their gear at lightning speed, all in their required positions to make this exchange of tires under three seconds like a well-oiled machine.

Ten nervous seconds later, the sound of Tristan's roaring engine gets closer and closer, and I smile when I see his purple helmet stick out from his jet-black car. The car looks fearless with its dark color and gold accents, a big contrast with the white of Callahan Motors.

It suits him. Tristan might be an upbeat person in general, but when he's behind the wheel, dark colors like these match his driving style more.

I can barely blink before the car is released from the dolly and Tristan drives out of sight. I turn my head to check the screen for the pitstop time and a grin splits my face.

2.5 seconds.

Raul is still halfway around the track, and he needs about ten seconds to take the place in front of him, twelve if he wants to get back behind him with the knowledge that Raul still needs a pitstop.

My heart pounds, my lungs unable to function, as I continue to stare at the screen. But then I bounce in my seat when he drives back on the track, wheel to wheel with Raul, both fighting for that third place.

"C'mon, c'mon, c'mon," I mutter to myself.

Both cars go neck and neck, trying to keep their position, but then, in the third corner, Raul goes too wide, and Tristan quickly responds by taking the lead.

"YES!" I jump up, Axel doing the same, and we both ricochet on our feet.

"Yes! Yes! Yes!" Axel beams with a fist in the air.

Tristan creates more distance between him and Raul's car, up until the point where Raul gets the instructions to box, and we both flop down on the plastic chairs again.

"He's doing so great." Axel shakes his head in awe. "It was so hard to see him struggle the last couple of years. He's gonna do great driving for Arzano." When I look at him, I can see the pride dripping from his expression. It's good to know that Tristan has had him in his corner since he was little. Someone who knows him from before the fame. Who's always there to call him out on your bullshit, and show the love and pride he deserves for his victories. It reminds me of Wes, but this time, it doesn't ignite that sad feeling I was used to. This time it just makes me smile.

"He's an amazing driver," I agree.

"Yeah, but he needed to get the right motivation back. Didn't expect it to come in the form of a pretty blonde, but I'll take it." He shoves his shoulder against mine.

I really wish everyone would stop saying that.

I shake my head. "That's all him."

"It's his talent. But you brought it back out. You brought him back to the top."

I know they all mean well, but it's making my skin crawl, like every time someone says that, the ugly truth of what's to come will pop out in the next second. I have nothing to do with his career. He would've recovered from his little dip regardless.

I offer Axel a tight smile, trying to hide my discomfort, then pull out my phone. I don't even know why I do it. But when I check the screen, I come to the conclusion that my intuition always knows.

NINA: I'm not kidding. Call off the sale or I will find whatever magazine will have it. Miami is the next race, right? Who shall I call? US Weekly?

It feels like thousands of needles are pricking into my skin, a cold breeze that's nonexistent lifting the hairs on my back. I was under no illusion Nina would agree to being ignored, praying maybe she was bluffing. I knew she wasn't. But when I look back up at the screen, seeing Tristan driving comfortably in third place, I no longer can. The words she's been dying to hear have been living rent free in my mind for days now, simply because I didn't want to give them life by letting them roll off my tongue.

But this is it.

I won't hold him back.

NIKKIE: I will call off the sale.

I close my eyes when I hit send, almost feeling as if my soul is escaping from my chest. But I know there's no other way. Suddenly, it feels like the walls of the garage are locking me in, the air growing thicker and thicker with each lap Tristan races. And when Nina texts back, telling me she's expecting me to be able to be signed on as an owner within the next three days... it just feels like the world collapses around me.

And while I'm being dragged into the devil's lair, I only have one thought left: I can't drag him with me. No matter how much it will kill me.

I have to let him go.

41

TRISTAN

T HIRD PLACE. I GOT another third place, and I couldn't be more thrilled.

I'm still not able to compete with SRT and Barrington, but the season is long, and I think we have a good chance competing with them if we tweak a few things on the car.

I walk out onto the upper deck of the Arzano motorhome, finding Nikkie and Casey hanging out on one of the lounge chairs. She jumps up when she catches my eye, a troubled look on her face while I circle my arms around her body until I reach the small of her back.

Her fruity scent slips into my nose, and I bite back the smile that's instantly ignited as I search her face.

"I need to go home," she blurts.

"What do you mean? Now?"

She nods, her palms resting on my damped biceps. "Yeah, there's something with the bar. Lieke called me, asking to come home."

"What is it?"

"I don't know, some kind of supplier issue. My dad could fix it, but he's in Germany for the weekend." I push back the frown that's lingering under my skin.

"Okay," I reply reluctantly. "You want me to come with you?"

But she vigorously shakes her head, then flashes me a smile that's wide and gorgeous. It doesn't quite reach her gilded eyes, though, making my heart twitch. "No, no. Your family is here. You should spend time with them. I'll be fine. I'll just go and sort it. I'm sure it will be fine."

I refrain from asking her if she's thought about me investing in the bar, but really, I'm cursing inside. It's selfish of me to ask her to give up her livelihood and travel with me, but my gut feeling keeps telling me this isn't what she wants to do. That she has no desire to keep working behind the bar for the rest of her life, yet I can't figure out what's holding her back to take a step back from it. I know it's not up to me, so I just support her in every decision she makes, even if it's killing me to miss her while I travel to the states.

"Do you have a flight?"

"Yeah, Casey just booked me one at eight tonight. Which means I have to go and pick up my stuff right now."

"I'll go with you."

"You can't. You have press meetings, the debrief. Your race is over, but your working day isn't."

I clench my jaw, peering into her eyes because I know she's right. "Can't we hire someone to fix the issue?"

"I don't have the money."

"But I do."

Her expression pales, almost as if my comment is hurting her, though I have no clue why. It's true. If I can pay someone to fix whatever it is to prevent her from stepping on the next plane, I will. It's not the same as investing in her bar so she has the room to hire someone to cover her work for her, is it?

"It's my bar, Tristan."

Okay, maybe it is.

"I know. I'm sorry. I just wish you didn't have to leave."

"I'll see you next week." Her lips carefully find mine, soft, longing, and with a level of tenderness that's trailing all the way down to my toes.

I tuck her closer to my chest, feeling her heart beating against mine as I lock our lips once more. "I'll miss you. Have a safe flight."

She breaks loose with a strained smile, and I watch both girls descend, resting my body against the balcony. I take a moment, then turn around just in time to see them walk out of the entrance, and she looks up, giving me a short wave. I return it with a smile, but when her eyes divert, a jolt of something eerie slashes through my chest. Gone is my jovial mood, and when I keep my eyes trailing the girls as they walk off the track and out of sight, I'm convinced of my feeling: *Something is wrong.*

"What's up, man?" Sam flicks his chin at me, cooking some eggs in his open kitchen as I stroll into the living room with a sigh. "She's still dodging you?"

"I'm tempted to fly out there."

Sam shrugs, scraping the eggs onto his plate. "You still have four days before we need to be in Italy, so why the fuck not?"

"I don't want to freak her out."

He gives me a straight expression, but his eyes are an open book. "She's already freaking out, T. Might as well call her out on it if she won't talk to you. You can take my jet."

He holds my gaze, and I rub a hand over my stubble. I miss her like fucking crazy, but that feeling would be manageable if we were okay. But her lack of contact tells me something is so fucking wrong.

"I'm going to try to talk to her one more time." I pull out my phone, my feet stepping onto the balcony as I dial her number. The dial tone feels like an ominous drum of conviction, and I push out a breath to keep my head straight until she picks up. My molars grind together until the moment I hear music over the line and my jaw drops in confusion.

"Tristan!" She sounds like she doesn't have a care in the world, but that can't be right because she wouldn't be dodging my calls if everything was peachy, right? Her jovial tone hits me like a ton of bricks.

"Hey. Where are you?" I try to keep my tone in check, but I'm fuming inside. We haven't talked in three weeks.

Three motherfucking weeks.

She couldn't catch a flight quick enough after the Melbourne GP, with what I now assume was nothing more than a fucking excuse, and I can't figure out why. The first week, I calmed the ache in my stomach by telling myself she was just jetlagged and swamped with stuff at the bar. The next week, I noticed a pattern. She could never pick up, giving me whatever lame excuse she came up with to just keep texting. I've been busy communicating with the team at the factory and spending the little time between races I had in Italy to optimize the car as much as we could before it was time to fly to Miami. But even I have not been as busy as my girlfriend apparently is, since she never made it to Miami, saying she was one man short in the bar.

I couldn't even get her on the phone after the race, having to settle with a *'you did great, Ace'* text.

That's when every bone in my flesh told me she's avoiding me.

But I've had it.

No more.

She can tell me what the fuck is going on or I'll fly there and find out myself.

"Where do you think I am, silly?" she says cheerfully, adding another layer to my annoyance. "It's King's Day!"

"Are you drunk?" Like a fist is knocking the air from my lungs, my anger vanishes with it, but it's quickly replaced with a sense of despair.

"Maybe a little." She giggles. "Okay, maybe a lot."

"What are you doing, baby?"

"I'm dancing."

"That's not what I meant." I rub the back of my neck, glancing down the streets of Monaco from Sam's penthouse. The sun burns through my sunglasses while I barely register the pedestrians walking down the street like it's such a sunny day. The sun might be shining, but regardless, I have a feeling there's a big thunderstorm heading my way.

"Are you mad? You sound mad." Her tone holds something of carefulness, and I can almost see her brown eyes looking up at me.

"I'm not mad." *I think*, or at least I'm trying really hard not to be. "But you suddenly fly home from Australia, then you've been dodging my calls for the last three weeks—"

"I haven't been dodging your calls!" she sputters. "We've talked!"

"For two minutes, because every time you find a reason to hang up, and now, the one time you sound like you actually want to talk to me, you're drunk." I sigh, lifting my sunglasses through my hair until it sits on top and pinching the bridge of my nose. "What is going on?"

"Nothing."

Fucking liar.

"Then why are you ignoring me?"

"I'm not ignoring you." She says it with such confidence, I almost believe it. But I can feel the truth resonating against my chest: she's hiding something.

"Sure looks like it." I wait for her to say anything, and when she doesn't, my stomach flutters.

"I just needed time to think, okay?" she says with a timid voice.

"About what?"

"About this. About *us.*"

"Us?" The flutter turns into a full-blown hurricane of turmoil. *Don't say it, baby.* Whatever you do, don't say it.

"I'm not sure this is gonna work."

Bloody hell.

"No." I shake my head. "No. No!" This is not fucking happening. I won't let it. "Whatever you're doing, just stop."

"My life is here, Tristan."

"And I respected that from the beginning. I still do." I haven't asked her to fully quit that bar and travel with me for that exact reason. Not because I don't want to, but because I know she's too independent to rely on anyone else.

Including me.

"We'd never see each other." Her tone grows thicker, and I know she's fighting away her tears just as I'm trying to get rid of the bowling ball in the back of my throat.

"I'll take what I can get," I tell her.

"You deserve better."

"There is no better!" I snap. Can't she fucking see that? She is it for me. She's end game. The one I plan to grow old with. *Fuck being Prince Charming. She's my fucking Cinderella.* "Why are you doing this, Nik?"

"Because I can't live up to all these expectations," she sniffs through the phone. "We come from different worlds. I don't fit in with your family or the whole racing world. I'm just a trashy kid from Amsterdam with a questionable past. My dad is a fucking criminal, for fuck's sake."

I blink, not fully following. "What are you talking about?"

"I'm the daughter of a criminal, Tristan. There, I said it. The press will destroy your career if that comes out."

Not what I was expecting.

"I don't fucking care. The only place you need to fit in with is me. And you fit fucking perfectly." Doesn't she see that I don't care about all that? So what, her dad is a criminal. After meeting him, I didn't really expect him to work at a bank anyway. Is it ideal? Fuck no. But I don't want to marry her dad.

I want to marry her.

"You'll find someone else."

"I don't want anyone else!"

"I'm not in love with you anymore."

I let out a snicker, followed by a snort, when I become aware of the direction she's moving this conversation.

"Bullshit," I bark.

"Things have changed," she tries again.

"Bullshit!"

"Tristan."

"Stop lying to me. Why are you doing this?"

"Because—" I can see it coming from a mile away. It's not even in my control. Like when my car goes into a spin, and I just pray I'll come out on the other side. I know I won't this time, though. It's only a matter of seconds before I crash into the wall.

"Don't say it." I frantically wag my head, because she can't be serious about this. "Don't you dare fucking say it."

"I think we should break up."

She said it.

"No! What we should do is talk about this!" I shout, losing my temper as I spin on my heels, locking with Sam's frown, two glasses of water in his hand.

"Nik! How are you?" A girl's voice is audible in the background.

"I have to go," Nikkie says.

There are so many things I want to say, yell even. But somehow, I get my speeding pulse in order, ignoring the tension in my shoulders and pretending my skin isn't burning with rage.

This is fucking bullshit. But I know her well enough to know she won't listen while being in this state and safely protected behind her phone. She's a stubborn little thing when she wants to be.

"You can hang up that phone," I say, calm as a fucking cucumber that's being fried from the inside, "but this conversation isn't over, baby."

"Goodbye, Tristan."

"Don't hang up! Nikkie! Goddamnit!" The dial tone is loud in my ear, and I throw my phone on the ground, the glass shattering as I let out a roar.

"What happened?" A nauseous feeling overwhelms me when I swipe my gaze to Sam's.

"She broke up with me."

42

NIKKIE

I 'VE BEEN STARING OUT of the window for the last twelve hours, a blanket around my shoulders and a cup of tea in my hands since the moment I hung up the phone and went home. I've been unable to move from the windowsill to my bed and I couldn't bring myself to light up a candle, knowing it will only hurt me more to smell him all around me. It's funny how I feel my entire world has stopped spinning, but when I look outside, nothing has changed. People are still riding their bikes. Cars are still driving up and down the street every minute of the day. The supermarket opened at eight, like always. The neighbor from across the street walks her dog to the park. Life is still very much happening, yet I feel dead inside.

I thought I was dead inside after the accident, but it's nothing compared to the rotten feeling that has been growing inside of me.

"Are you okay?" I'm reluctant to not turn around when I hear Tessa's voice behind me, but out of politeness, I still do. She's wearing her joggers with a hoodie, her hair still messy from just waking up. It's all normal, except for the sharp expression in her blue eyes.

"Definitely not." I shake my head, twisting my body back to face the life happening on the street while my fingers stay clutched around the necklace around my neck. "But I will be." I don't believe myself, because it hurts even more than it did before. This time, there isn't a body I have to bury and the knowledge that I will never see him ever again. This time, my heart has to get used to life without the man I love, knowing he's still out there. He's still living his life without me. And I'm nothing more than a vessel, going through life on autopilot.

"I think you made a mistake," Tessa says.

"That makes two of you." I hated to hear his pained voice over the phone, even though I was drunk. I hoped I would have forgotten the hurt when I woke up this morning after barely three hours of sleep, but it has been booming through my head at an excruciating volume.

"Want to tell me why you did it?"

"Not really."

"Does your dad know?"

"Nope." The last person I need to talk to is my dad.

"You have to talk about it, Nik!" Tessa exclaims with more annoyance than I can appreciate. I know she's worried about me, and she's right, but I can't deal right now.

"Not today, Tess." I dig deeper into my blanket, avoiding her gaze. "Today, I just need to get through. And then I need a few days to get my head in the right place, okay?" Pleadingly, I let my eyes travel to her, hoping she will give me this. I need this. My heart broke once, and I survived. I think I can do it again, even though I'm the one who shattered it this time.

I just need a few days.

"Okay." She nods, though not wholeheartedly. "I'm here when you're ready."

"Thanks, but I just need to be alone right now." I dip my head in concession, then put my focus back on the window as tears roll down my cheeks.

43

TRISTAN

I LOVE AMSTERDAM. I love the lively vibe it has at any moment of the day and the fact that it's not as colossal as something like New York. In Amsterdam, you can be who you want to be, and everyone will accept it. It's truly one of my favorite cities, but right now, I hate everything about it. I don't appreciate the quirky guy with green hair who passes me on the street. I don't appreciate the sound of cycling bells around me. And I sure as fuck don't appreciate the cracking of the stairs when I climb up the old steps to Nikkie's front door before I forcefully knock.

The door flies open ten seconds later, and I'm locked with Tessa's dissolving smile.

"Tristan."

"Where is she?" My palms are balled into fists and it's taking everything inside of me to not drive them into a few walls. Or some people. Whatever comes first.

Tessa's sigh is loud, her blue eyes dripping with a sympathy that only pisses me off more. I like Tessa, I really do. I know she's the one who's been pushing Nikkie to see where this was going, so I'm assuming the feeling is mutual. But I'll go nuts if she doesn't tell me where she is.

"Please, Tess." I grit my teeth.

"I can't." She shakes her head with an apologetic expression that only fuels my anger.

"Please, just tell me where she is," I snap. "I need to talk to her."

"Tristan."

I can handle rejection. I fucking feel like dying just thinking about it, but I think I can handle a broken heart too. If it means Nikkie is happy, I can endure the pain of not being with her. That's how much I love her. But I'd rather drive my racecar into a concrete wall before I accept her silence when it's not even grounded. It's easy to tell my heart it's over, but my gut tells me it's anything but over. She loves me. I can feel it in everything that I am, even when there are thousands of miles between us.

She fucking loves me, but she's too scared to see this through.

"I love her, goddamnit! I love her, and I don't know what's going on! I just need to fucking know."

Tessa awkwardly shuffles on her feet, probably contemplating if she should tell me what she knows. She fucking better or I will harass her until she does. I don't care about the consequences. I don't care about what will end up in the media. I just want to know where my girl is and why she's spitting a load of crap like, *"I think we should break up."*

"She's just..." she trails off, pushing a strand of her brown hair behind her ear, and I detect the bullshit that's about to roll from her tongue.

"Don't you dare give me any bullshit about her not feeling the same. I know she does. I can feel it. Along with the goddamn hurt that she won't share. What is holding her back? What's keeping her from me?!" I yell, pointing my thumb into my chest. "Never mind. I'll find her."

Shaking my head, I twist on my heel, then trot down the stairs like I'm being chased by the devil. I'm not going to wait any fucking longer. I will tear this city apart. I will hire a private investigator. I will do whatever it takes to find her.

"Tristan!" I look up in the stairwell, stopping mid-step. Tessa is hanging over the railing. "She blames herself." The blood in my face moves to my feet. "She thinks it's her fault he's dead." She pauses, and I look at her furrowed brows. A jolt sparks my muscles, and it feels like I'm struck by lightning. Suddenly, it all falls into place. The pain in her beautiful eyes. Her reluctance toward the future. Why she never fully seemed committed. "It's not you. She's scared. And hurt..."

"Why?" What is she scared of that she can't share with me?

"She's going to kill me."

"Tell me!" My level of patience has declined with every step I took down these stairs.

"They did a drug run for her dad."

"They did what?" I cock my head, then my feet go back in motion as I slowly climb up the stairs again, and Tessa rounds the railing before sitting down on the last step. Her eyes give the impression she's been dying to tell me, though her expression is also cut with discomfort as she continues.

"Her and Wes. They wanted to move out. They needed the money, so Wes agreed to drive a load to the dock of Rotterdam. He took her with him."

"Coke?"

She hums.

"Bloody hell."

"They crashed against the tree when they decided to take a back road to avoid the busy roads. She woke up in the hospital. Wes died on impact." Tessa's eyes are filled with tears, and I just stare at her. Dumbstruck. "Later, she told me that she was awake before they pulled her from the car. It's why she has nightmares. They were worse before you came into her life."

"Tess." I don't even know what to say. I hate that she carried this weight by herself, wishing she trusted me enough to confide in me. To let me help her get through this. With this new piece of information, it's almost as if I can feel her pain, our hearts still merged as one, even when she's running away from me.

"You'd give it all up for her, wouldn't you?" Tessa sniffs.

"With all my fucking heart." I love her so much it hurts. It hurts when she's not around me, and it breaks my heart to know she's in pain and won't let me help her fix it.

"I know she loves you too. But she still has a few demons to overcome." She gives me a tentative look.

"What demons?"

"That's not my story to tell. But I can tell you she's too scared to fully admit what she feels for you. She can't fathom the thought of losing someone again."

"She'll never lose me."

"Tristan." Tessa tilts her head. "You're a Formula One driver. You can't say that. You put your life on the line every weekend you're on that track."

"I'll quit." I mean it. I will quit for her. I'm already a world champion. Yeah, I can keep going for at least another ten years and break records, but I don't give a shit about that if she's not by my side.

Her head wags as she chuckles. "That's not the answer, and you know it. She needs to face her own fear. Overcome it. You can't protect her from that for the rest of her life."

"I'm willing to try."

"I know you are. It's why I know you love her. But you can't fight her battles for her."

I hate to admit she's right, and it's absolutely gutting me. Whatever Nikkie is going through, I can't shelter her from it. But I can be there for her. I can hold her hand while she fights her demons.

"Where is she?"

Tessa searches my eyes, hers flicking with reluctance before she finally gives in.

"She's at the cemetery."

The gravel of the parking lot crackles beneath my soles as I walk through the brick arch that functions as the entrance of the cemetery. The twenty-minute ride over here, I thought about what I was going to say. How I was not going to take no for an answer and force her to come home with me so we can talk this through. But now that I'm here, I'm not so sure.

The soft breeze of spring ruffles through the trees, but brings me a chill at the same time.

Fuck, I love her so much. I want nothing more than to take her in my arms and tell her everything is going to be alright. But with each step, my courage is chipped away piece by piece. My gut is falling to my feet and a big lump forms in my throat. I feel my heart cracking more with every yard, because somehow, I know this isn't going to end well.

My world stops when I spot her. Her knees are in the grass in front of the grave, her blonde hair covering her face. Cautiously, I approach her, and I detect the tightness entering her body when she's aware of me. She doesn't look up, doesn't acknowledge me. As if she already knows it's me.

"Tess told me where I could find you." I tilt my head, getting a glimpse of her flushed and tear-stained cheeks. The silence feels heavy, and goosebumps trail down the length of my spine while I wait for her to say anything.

"He was only twenty-two," she finally says, and I let my eyes travel over the date on the headstone. *Oh fuck, that's today.* Two years ago today, he passed away. "We planned to travel through Europe in the summer. He had it all planned out. We would fly to the south of Spain. Then move up along the coast before we went to Italy. Then Croatia." Her voice is thick, and her cheeks grow wetter with every syllable. I can see the suffering in her entire stance and it's breaking my fucking heart.

"Baby, I'm so sorry." I want to fall down beside her and pull her against me, but I'm not sure she'd let me, so I just stand there like a complete fool. Trying to give her the space I assume she needs and praying I'm doing the right thing.

"I loved him. Still do," she confesses, glancing up at me for a brief moment. I expect it to hurt how she declares her love for another guy, but it doesn't. My heart knows, deep down, there's a difference in what she feels for me. "I'm sorry, Tristan." She exhales with heaviness, then gets on her feet and swings her gaze up to me. Her brown eyes are bloodshot, her cheeks puffy from crying, but funny enough, for me? She's still the most beautiful girl in the world. "I should've never... I'm sorry I hurt you. I'm sorry I made you believe this could be anything more than it was. But you deserve better."

"You are the best there is, baby." I take a step forward, but she replies by taking one backwards, with a wagging head.

"No, I'm not."

"Baby, it's not your fault. You couldn't know he did that."

Her sadness switches to contempt, a half glare coming my way. "You talked to Tessa."

"She told me everything."

"She didn't," she snorts, cynical. "Because she doesn't know the whole story."

"What do you mean?"

The chuckle that falls from her lips is one without humor, giving me an ominous feeling of what she's about to tell me.

"You think it was Wes's idea?" she snarls with fire in her golden gaze. "It was mine! I couldn't handle him taking care of his mother any longer. The woman sucked the life out of him, and I wanted him for myself. Because that's who I am. I'm selfish as fuck."

Her confession surprises me, because for the last twenty minutes, I painted Wes as the villain in this story. The one who convinced a young girl to cross a line that shouldn't be crossed, but part of me already knew. I've known from the beginning that Nikkie isn't a picture-perfect girl. She can be cheeky and sassy as hell. She can be a handful with a wild side that always keeps me on my toes. When Tessa told me what happened, I kinda already figured there was more to tell. However, I would've never guessed the true reason. But I don't care.

"Wanting to be with your boyfriend doesn't make you selfish. It makes you human."

"I killed him, Tristan!" she shouts. Her arms swing up with despair, the grief seeping from her veins. Her pained expression will be something that will haunt me forever.

"It was an accident, Nik!"

"An accident that would've never happened if I didn't push him. He didn't want to do it! But I wanted the money. I wanted to get our own apartment, away from his leech of a mother. But joke's on me, right?" she snickers. "Because I've lost my boyfriend and gained a leech."

"What do you mean?"

She nods her head while her lips are pressed into a smile that doesn't meet her eyes.

"I need to take care of Nina, because she's all alone now." I cock my head at her words. "Do you understand now? I can't be with you! I ruined one life! I can't ruin yours too. I'm not the ideal girlfriend. I'm not the one you bring home to your parents. I'm born in the gutter! I told you, Tristan, my dad is a criminal."

"That doesn't make you one." My heart cracks open at the knowledge that she has been carrying this weight by herself for all this time. She lost her boyfriend. Her best friend. His mother lost a son. They all lost him. She is no exception.

"I tried to transport twelve kilos of coke! That automatically makes me a criminal!"

"So you made mistakes." God knows we've all done stupid things when we were young. I'll wait to tell her I almost decapitated my sister with a pitchfork until we're in the clear.

She shakes her head. "Someone's death. That isn't a mistake."

"Nik, just listen–"

"NO! No!" she yells, stomping her foot. "I was selfish once. I vowed to never jeopardize anyone's life ever again."

She's killing me. She's absolutely killing me.

"And I get no say in it? How is that fair?"

"It's for the best."

"Bullshit!" It's a fucking cop out and she knows it. I know she knows it, because otherwise, she wouldn't avert her gaze every chance she gets. She can't even look at me because she knows what she's doing is wrong. Pushing me away is wrong.

"It's over, Tristan!"

Over my dead body. "It's not over."

"It is."

"No, it's not," I sneer. "I love you, Nik. I'm *in* love with you. Look me in the eye and tell me you don't love me back. I fucking dare you!"

I crave to touch her so badly. I want to hold her in my arms.

"It hurts." Her shoulders start to shake, and her eyes pool over as tears roll down her cheeks at an even quicker pace.

"What hurts?"

"Being with you! It hurts so much it makes my stomach ache. My throat sore. The emptiness I feel inside me when I'm not around you twists and turns in agony, and it fucking hurts! I can't do that again! I can't handle it!" Her entire stance is closed off, and she pulls her hair in desperation.

"That's love, baby! You love me! I know you do."

"Don't you get it?" She glares, stubborn as fuck. "You can't love without a heart! My heart is six feet under the ground! He took that with him when we buried him." She points at the grave. "It. Is. Over, Tristan!"

"What are you so afraid of, Nikkie?"

"Nothing." She wipes away the tears with the back of her hand, a stern expression. "*This* is my life, and I can't walk away."

"Don't do this."

Her jaw flexes, and she finally looks me directly in the eye. Her empty expression hits me in the heart, and I don't know if I will recover from that look.

"It's already done. Go home."

"Baby."

I reach out my arms for her, but she takes a few steps back. "Leave!"

I feel like she's in a bubble that I can't pop. A glass cubic that I can't crack. I desperately want to save her, but I don't know how. She needs me, but I can't break through to the surface to get to her. All I can do is torture myself by witnessing her wither away. But I notice the clover necklace still hanging around her neck, fueling me to keep pushing.

"You wanna know why your stomach aches?" I scoff, not willing to shut up any longer. "Because butterflies are flying around in there for me. Throat sore? Because being with me makes you feel like you can't breathe, so when you are with me, you suck in deep breaths as if your life depends on it. Because it does! The reason your insides are hurting? It's because you love me more than you can handle. I know that because *that* is how it feels for me." I jolt my fist against my heart, then point my finger at her. "I love you, Nikkie. And I don't need you to say it back for me to know that you still love me too. I know you do." I pause, hoping she has the guts to look me in the eye, but the silence that follows is deafening and I can feel my heart break into pieces. "If only you could see it."

I twist my body to leave, knowing Tessa is right. I can't fix this for her. I know she loves me; there is not a single hair on my head that's doubting that. But she needs to walk this path alone.

"Tristan." Her sniffing voice pulls me back to look at her one more time.

Gone is the strong and sassy woman I met on the streets of Amsterdam. Gone is the confidence she presented when she scolded me like we went to kindergarten together.

Now all that is left is a little girl, who's looking lost as fuck. I want to support her and be there for her. I want to tell her she matters every single day of the year. I want to hold her tight against my chest, telling her to listen to my heart beating for her.

But she has to let me.

I hold her devastated expression, waiting for anything to fall from her lips, but she just shakes her head.

"If he really loved you just as much"—I point at the headstone that says Wes de Boer—"he would've never taken your heart into the grave. He would've given it back to you because he would've wanted you to live the life he no longer can. Don't give him the blame," I grunt with a level of disappointment that can wither away a field of flowers within seconds. "He didn't take your heart with him to the ground. You threw it in there. And that's a choice."

And then, with lead in my shoes, I leave.

44

NIKKIE

I ALWAYS THOUGHT LOSING Wes was the worst thing that could ever happen to me. That my heart from now on was layered with a skin as thick as leather, and that whatever happened next, it wouldn't be half as hard as losing my boyfriend and best friend in one night.

I was so wrong.

"I don't know what to tell you, Miss Peters. It's all there."

"But I haven't paid anything." I rub my puffy eyes, arguing with a collection agency about my, apparently nonexistent, debts. My blonde hair is feeling greasy when I run my hand through it, staring up at the ceiling of the stockroom, even though I showered this morning.

"It says here, everything was paid three days ago."

"I see. Can you see what account it was paid from?" I know what account it's paid from, but deep down, I hope I'm wrong. He needs to let go, even if it kills both of us.

"There's no name listed, but it says here it's an account based in Monaco."

"Figures," I mutter, then conjure a tight smile on my lips. "Thank you so much."

I hang up the phone, then close my eyes as I suck in a breath of stuffy air.

One week.

It should've been one week where Tristan was no longer part of my daily routine, other than the constant aching of my heart and the tears that seem to always be pushing against the surface. But I should've known Tristan wasn't going to let me go that easily. The fact that he flew out here multiple times with nothing more than twelve hours to spare should've been proof enough of that.

My weeping heart still smiles when I wake up to one of his texts, telling me something simple like *good morning* or *I won't stop loving you*. But when I start my day and I'm reminded that this is all I can get, my heart shatters once more and the new day starts again with more dread than I ever felt. This time, it isn't as if my heart gets ripped out, like when Wes died. No, it feels like someone is dissecting it without any anesthesia, the jolts of pain returning every second of the day.

I sit down on one of the empty crates, pulling out my phone. Part of me wants to be angry with him for paying off my debts, annoyed that he's creating this link by fixing my shit for me. But there's a slight voice that can't be mad at him in general.

NIKKIE: Thank you. I will pay you back.

I keep my eyes trained on the screen, checking the time on my watch. It's a race weekend and I know he's probably preparing for qualification, doing some last-minute exercises with Calvin. When the three dots appear on the screen, I hold my breath, waiting in anticipation.

TRISTAN: You will not.

NIKKIE: Tristan...

TRISTAN: If you dare to send me money, I will transfer back double. And we both know I have more cash to keep playing this game until you're a millionaire.

Bastard.

TRISTAN: You're worth it, baby.

TRISTAN: I love you.

A tear splashes onto the screen, followed by a few more that I can't catch in time as I wipe the moisture from my cheeks. I want to tell him I love him too. I love him so goddamn much, it drives me crazy. But I don't want to give him hope, so I don't. I take the way of least resistance, like the coward that I am, and type back:

NIKKIE: Drive safe.

45

TRISTAN

"**F**UCK, FUCK, FUCK," I mutter in my helmet as I sit my ass down on the grass beside the track, my eyes fixed on the smoke coming from my car. But not just my car. Both Arzano cars are in the gravel, the result of a collision I had with Jackson.

"What the fuck is wrong with you?" Jackson's eyes are shooting daggers at me from underneath the open visor of his helmet. I've never seen him angry. He's always this laid-back guy, doesn't worry about anything other than his race, and can't be fussed about anything.

But he's more than fussed now and it's all my fault.

"That was my lap! It's fucking quali and you wanna race me into a corner?!"

I nod, grinding my teeth as the frustration inside of me builds up like a cannonball.

Jackson's thundering above me, shouting, and I know the only reason he's keeping his helmet on is to make sure the cameras don't catch what he's saying.

"I'm sorry! I'm sorry, okay! You're right. I fucked up."

My confession settles him down a bit, taking a step back and relaxing his shoulders.

"What is going on, Tristan? You've been off for days. But I figured you'd be focused once you get back in the car. This is not just about us! There's a whole team behind us, expecting us to win and not work them into overtime by crashing our cars against the wall!"

I look up at him, the Italian sun shining beside his helmet, bringing out the blue in his eyes.

"I don't know." I shake my head, then let it hang.

"Well, figure it out before tomorrow!" he snarls, before he takes off, and I continue to stare at the green blades of the grass. He's right. This wasn't a malfunction in the car or a miscalculated situation. This was all me and there's a big chance I'll get a penalty for it.

Which is fine. I deserve it. *I just don't know how to fix it.*

With thunder in my expression, I stomp through the hall toward the press circle, each step putting more water on the oil boiling inside of me because I can already hear the questions in my head.

"Please be nice." My press girl sends me a pleading look, and I shake my head at the fact that I have to be told to be nice. That's something they tell Sam and Jordan, not me. I'm always nice. Or I used to be. Now I have the full desire to rip people's heads off with my teeth.

We approach the first reporter, and I ignore the smile he's flashing me as I wait for him to ask whatever burning question he's got for me. Probably a stupid one.

"Tristan, not really your day, is it?"

Told ya.

I keep staring at him, my lips firmly pressed together to make sure I think about my answer before I blurt out anything my press girl will have a heart attack from.

"Not really, no," I settle with.

"Did you not see Banks on his lap?"

"Not quick enough. I didn't see him until we were side by side, heading into that corner. It was my fault. I apologized to Jackson and to the team, and we need to do better tomorrow." I pat myself on the back for that answer and I can even see a tiny smile from my PR girl coming my way when I glance at her from the corner of my eye.

"You had a very good start with Arzano this year, but this weekend is obviously not starting the way you want to. Are you convinced you can turn this weekend around? Maybe with a little luck?" My reflection dances in the brown of his eyes, a frown ready to knit my brows together at his choice of words. That dire sense in my gut magnifies again, closing my throat as I contemplate what to reply.

"If I do, it won't be luck."

"How come?" The man smiles at me from behind his microphone.

Then, I look straight into the camera with a pained expression.

"Because I seem to be all out of luck."

46

NIKKIE

"*B*ECAUSE *I SEEM TO be all out of luck.*" His words cut right through my chest like an arrow, piercing my already bleeding heart, and it isn't until Lieke's hand on my arm pulls me out of my shocked trance that I get back to the real world.

"How are you holding up?" She shows me a kind expression, her eyes rapidly darting to the screen because we all know what he's talking about.

"I'm fine." I run the palm of my hand below my eyes, casually wiping away the wetness that was piling up in the corners.

"You look like a mess."

"I'm fine, Lieke." I busy myself by walking to the end of the bar, pulling some empty glasses down before I start cleaning them in the sink.

Tristan's words echo through my head like they are shouted through a megaphone.

"*I seem to be out of luck.*"

The hurt dripping from his face will be following me tonight when I go to bed, wishing I could explain everything to him. He deserves better than me ghosting him, but with the persistence he's showing already, I know I have no other choice.

He's going to want to fix it all if he knows the full story.

I startle when I look up in those silver eyes that now represent my own version of hell. It seems like Nina likes to pop up like a fucking Jack-in-the-box, making it her personal message to terrorize my life.

I shake my head, silently telling her to follow me to the stockroom with a jerk of my neck.

Spinning on my heel, I wait until the door behind her falls into his hinges, then find her gaze as I fold my arms in front of my chest.

"What are you doing here?" My voice can't sound anymore exhausting.

"I need money."

A sarcastic laugh trails from my body. "You need *what*? Are you kidding me?"

"Does it look like I'm kidding?" Her eyes narrow, and I shake my head with a disbelief that could cause a fucking whiplash.

"That's why you want me to keep the bar, don't you? So I can slip you a few bills whenever you want me to." I figured when I got home from Australia, she didn't only want me to call off the sale, but she'd still be forcing me to hand over half of the ownership as well. She never did and, suddenly, it clicks in my head.

"So what? It's half my bar!" The smug grin on this woman's expression is really starting to build my anger with each day. Doesn't she understand that there's no money if she keeps blowing it whenever she feels like it? Besides, I don't see her standing behind the bar, working for tips or anything. No, all she does is complain about how this is the only thing she has left from her son. Yet, she's only here to terrorize me into giving her money.

"It's not, Nina! It's mine!" I snap, done with her bullshit. She forced me to keep it, fine. But I'll be damned before I let her dictate to me how to run it or stand by as she drives it into bankruptcy. "I kept it like you forced me to! Now you want me to give you more money? Do you realize that if you keep asking me for money, there won't be a bar anyway? We'll be bankrupt before the end of the year."

"Fine, then sell the bar and give me half."

She? What? *Now* she wants me to sell?

"Half of what, Nina? The bar is in debt!" I'm not going to tell her that, technically, the bar is in debt with a certain F1 driver, because fuck her. She already ruined my life enough. If she wants to have the full details about running this bar, she can start by grabbing a shirt from the shelf and mix some drinks.

"It wasn't when Wes died," she sputters with disdain. "You really are a disgrace!"

The woman stands in front of me with her foot tapping the floor, her hands rooted in her side like she's my fucking mother or something and all I can think is how fucking dare she.

My nostrils flare. "Wes wasn't a saint! When he died, the bar was twenty grand in debt because he gambled it away in the casino!"

Yeah, moving him out of the home he was living with the wicked witch of Amsterdam was one reason why I suggested we'd do that drug run. But his confession, only a week earlier, that he was basically pushing the bar off a cliff, made him seal the deal pretty quickly anyway. I made a fucking mistake. But so did Wes. I'm just the only one who survived to deal with the aftermath.

"And you thought pushing drugs was going to help? You basically drove him into the grave when you forced him to move out!"

"What is going on here?"

Whatever snarkiness is ready to be thrown back in her face is swallowed back when I clear my throat, twisting my lip in half a smile.

"Dad, nothing. Nina was just leaving." I lock eyes with the narrowed ones of my dad. His stance is wide, his chin high.

"Right. We'll talk later." Nina flashes a fake smile between my dad and I, then tries to walk past him like all is well in the world. But right before she flashes me a glitter of victory in her gray eyes, almost at the door, my dad grabs her upper arm. His gaze is locked with mine, trying to detect the bullshit, I'm sure, but his grip is firmly around Nina's bicep.

"Oh, no, no, no." He rears his head from left to right with flashed teeth. "I did not just hear you blame my kid for killing your son? Did I?" I rarely see my dad at his full fearful potential, mainly because he's been trying to keep his business out of my life as much as possible. But the moments I have, I always felt sympathy for the people receiving it. But now, I feel nothing. Now I just feel grateful that someone is taking over for me, even though my dad doesn't know the full truth.

"I wouldn't, Johnnie." Nina unsuccessfully tries to jerk her arm out of his grasp.

"Right, because that wouldn't make sense, right? After all, *you're* the one who drove him into the grave."

It takes a second before my brain registers the words rolling off his tongue.

"What?" I take a step forward with pricked ears.

"That's not true." Nina's smug expression is replaced by fear as she finds my dad's glare.

"What are you talking about, Dad?"

His eyes darken, a snarl curling his lip, as if he's ready to bite her neck off, holding her arm tight enough to almost lift her from the floor. "She doesn't know the truth, does she?" Nina sucks in a breath, scared. "You evil little bitch. She doesn't know, and you figured you could use my daughter as your personal checkbook?"

"Know what, Dad?" I grit out.

"Tell her, Nina. Tell her why Wes was really in that car that night. Tell her why your son died and my daughter almost died with him. *Tell her.*" He shouts the last words in her face, her lashes fluttering as she closes them and starts to whimper.

"He did it for me," she cries. Gone is the woman who's been strategically destroying my life, and all that's left is a little bunny, about to be eaten by the wolf that has her in a headlock.

"What do you mean?" My heart pitter-patters against my ribcage, the sound loud in my ears as I take another step forward, turning my full attention to the little puddle of human crying.

"I lost a kilo of coke. Big Dog was going to kill me," she says, referring to the most notorious man in the city. I know my dad does business with him, but luckily, he still has more morals that fucking Big Dog. My dad is a fucking fairy compared to the shit that man is rumored to pull on a daily basis.

"So, Wes agreed to transport the drugs so he could pay off Big Dog?" I frown.

My dad nods. "He only pretended to be hesitant to make you think it was your idea because he didn't want you to hate his shitty mother after he moved in with you."

I close my eyes, rubbing the tiredness out of them. I don't want to believe Wes lied to me, but after everything that has happened, I don't need proof to know he did. It's what he'd do. It was the one and only thing we'd argue about; the unhealthy relationship with his mother. He couldn't let her go, no matter how much trouble she got herself in. He would fix it for her.

"Dad," I plead. Not sure what I'm pleading for.

"The only reason she's still alive is because I called in a favor with Big Dog. One I'm regretting right now," he confesses, spitting the words in her face.

I look at her crumbling under my father's grip, and I just feel so sorry for her. A little spark of hope inside of me still wants to help her, but I know she's not my problem to fix. I don't have to be punished forever. I'm allowed to live, even if Wes can't.

I step forward, waiting until she looks into my eyes. "I loved your son. And I'm sorry you lost him. I'm sorry I can't take away that pain. But you will no longer control me." I point my finger into her heart. "If you go to the media and destroy Tristan's career, I will make sure you spend the next few years behind bars. I don't owe you anything, Nina. I wish you the best, but I never want to see you near me ever again." I take a deep breath, filling up my lungs as much as I can. For the first time in seven days, it feels light and comfortable, the oxygen energizing my body.

"Come on. We're going for a walk." My dad throws me a pleased expression before he cocks his head, as if he's telling me we're not done talking about this just yet.

Nina's eyes grow wide, sheer panic laced in them, as my dad starts dragging her out of the stockroom. "You can't leave me with him. Please. I'm sorry! I'll pay everything back. Nikkie, please!"

"Dad?" He turns around before he reaches the door. "Don't hurt her." He snorts as if it's a weird question, but I know my dad. He might not be as ruthless as Big Dog, but his boundaries are still further from your regular human being. "Promise me!"

He rolls his eyes, then nods before they walk out, and I'm left by myself.

I give myself a minute to let it all settle in my head, trying to piece everything together until I realize what this means: I'm free. *I'm fucking free.*

It's like a big door of emotions is pushed open, every hint of despair, sadness, or grief flowing out of it, releasing my body from the tightness that has been locked up for so long. The relief is overwhelming, and I give myself this. Tears of happiness run down my cheeks, as I sob with a smile splitting my face, until a few minutes later, I've settled a bit.

I know what I need to do.

I take out my phone, dialing the one person who will hate me, but still might be open-minded enough to answer his phone.

"You're not really someone I want to talk to right now," Axel grunts when he picks up the phone.

"I know. But I need your help."

The silence that follows is long, then a deep sigh of surrender travels over the line.

"Don't make me regret this."

Never.

47

NIKKIE

"He's walking around like a zombie. It's eerie to not see him smile." I listen to Casey chatting in my ear as I sign for the new delivery of beverage, then start carrying crate by crate into the stockroom.

"I know. I was gutted seeing him on TV after the last race." It was hard to see him crash in qualifying, but race day wasn't much better. His driving was aggressive in a way that's not his, and risky mistakes only gave him eighth place after sixty-three laps. Still in the points, but not exactly what he's aiming for now that he got a competing car to drive with. Not to mention, his media skills have flushed back to zero, walking around the paddock like a grump.

"So are you gonna talk to him?" Casey asks, a little excitement in her tone.

"Yeah, I just need to tie up some loose ends first. Deal with my past, you know." When I found out how Nina didn't tell me the full story, I quickly made all the decisions I wanted to make for months, not willing to waste any more time. I only got one life. Tristan's words hurt me the last time that I saw him, but he was right. Wes wouldn't have wanted me to not live my life happily.

But I don't want to share my plans with anyone until they are set in stone.

"Sounds heavy."

"It is. But I can't move on before I do." In fact, I had my first session of therapy this week. I was fucking nervous to go, but I figured that if I really wanted to change and live the life I want, I might as well do it good. I'm sure I could've done it myself, clearing my mind and letting stuff go. *Forgive*. But I wasn't going to fix a leak in the house from watching YouTube tutorials if I could just go and call an expert, right? I was intense as fuck, and after I got home, I fell right a sleep with a migraine. But the next day, I woke up lighter.

"He's still texting me, you know."

Every day I wake up with a text from Tristan and it's responsible for the permanent smile that isn't a full grin yet, but I know it will be as soon as I can sort out the mess I created around me.

"Really?

I hum in agreement, thinking about his text this morning.

TRISTAN: I'm not giving up.

I wanted to call him so desperately and tell him I love him.

"Persistent. I like it," Casey replies.

I chuckle. "Just not when it comes from Sam?"

"Don't even start." I'm pretty sure she's rolling her eyes, even though I can't see her.

"Casey Boyd, you like him," I call her out.

"I got eyes. What's not to like? But he just makes things... *awkward*."

"Isn't that because maybe he's stirring up some feelings you're trying to deny?"

Fuck, we all know I've been there.

"Now *you're* making things awkward."

"I'm just saying."

"Even if it does," she continues with a serious tone, "one does not catch feelings for the manwhore of the paddock. It's like watching a car crash."

"Can't wait to be in the front row," I snicker, knowing the chemistry those two have. In Australia, they locked eyes in the press room, and I swear fireworks were exploding above their heads. It almost made *my* stomach flutter.

"Nothing is gonna happen between Sam and I!" she huffs, a little more vigorously. "Just drop it."

"Okay, okay." I bite my smile away, then hear the beep that says someone is on the other line. "I have to go, I got someone on the other line. Talk soon, yeah?"

I tap the screen to hang up, then answer the other call.

"Axel? Hi." My stomach twitches, suddenly scared he's going to offer me bad news. "Is Tristan okay?"

Axel's sigh is loud and pregnant, not helping my sudden anxiety at all.

"He's heartbroken, Nikkie. So no, he's not okay."

"Right." *Stupid question.*

"But he will be," he says, a bit more upbeat. "I arranged everything you asked for."

I gasp, resisting the urge to squeal. "Really?" He confirms with a hum, and I start bouncing on my white sneakers. "Thank you, thank you! Thank you so much!"

His tone sounds less judgmental than the last time we spoke on the phone, and in my head, I'm wondering how I can pay him back.

"I think you will be pleased with the outcome," Axel says. "So it's ready to sign for you whenever you're ready."

My heart purrs in content, finally seeing the light at the end of the tunnel. A little while longer and everything will be settled. All I have to do is be patient.

"I really appreciate your help," I say.

Axel didn't have to help me, and he took some persuading from my side. But I'm so happy he did. I don't know what I would've done without him.

"I'm not going to lie," he confesses with a serious edge in his tone, "I didn't do it for you."

"I figured."

"Don't fuck this up."

I won't.

"Sign here. Here. And Here." The lawyer points to the dotted line on each page. "Then put your initials here."

"Are you still sure you want to do this? I can still rip this apart." My dad lifts his gaze from the contract, a questioning look in his eyes.

I appreciate my dad more lately. A few days after the truth finally was out, he stopped by the next day, and I told him everything. I'm glad he did it *after* he forcefully sent Nina to rehab. Otherwise, I'd be worried he'd strangled her as soon as he left my house.

"Fuck no. It's all yours. Do with it what you want, Dad. Just don't expect me to work behind the bar for you." I wink playfully. I'm dead serious, though. I don't ever want to work behind the bar, ever again.

"Shame, it would've been fun to work with my kid."

"It really wouldn't." My dad and I would probably be in each other's hair within the first hour. "But I'm sure you'll have fun with Lieke."

"You really sold me out there," my dad mutters as he signs the papers, then holds them up to me.

"She'll keep you on your toes." I lift my chin with a smirk, taking the papers. "Thank you."

"For what?"

"Helping me with this." I ruffle the papers in my hand.

"I'm not helping you with shit. This is a business opportunity. How else am I going to clean my dirty money?"

I moan, rolling my eyes. "I don't want to hear all the illegal shit you're doing, Dad. Please let me live in complete and utter ignorance."

"There was a time when you were more than interested." He brings his glass of whiskey to his mouth, holding my gaze.

"Right, and I'm growing up and trying to better my life." Who knows, maybe one day, I'll actually succeed.

"I'm proud of you," he says with a little emotion glittering in the goldish specks of his brown eyes. "Your mother would be proud of you. You're doing better than I am, and I think that's all I could ever ask for as a parent."

I blink, appreciating his words, but also skeptical.

"Who are you, and what did you do with my dad?"

"Shut up, little shithead." A coaster flies toward my head and I duck with a chuckle. When I get back up, I take my dad's hand. He's not Dad of the Year. Hell, I'm sure he made more mistakes than necessary, but I'm glad he's there for me without any conditions.

"Thank you, Dad. I love you."

"I love you too, kid. Come on. Let's go buy a slushie."

"Oh, yaay!" I say, darting out from around the bar with a smile. It isn't a full one just yet. But it's a genuine one. And I can feel it from head to toe, that many more are on their way.

48

TRISTAN

THE HEAT OF THE Spanish sun is released when I jump out of the car and take off my helmet as I storm into the corridor away from the cameras always lurking in the corners of the paddock. Taking off my gloves, I throw them to the floor, then run a sweaty palm through my already damp hair. Grunting, I bolt outside of the garage and into the back of the paddock, grateful the biggest crowd was relocated to the stands for the second qualification, though it doesn't lessen the fire in my pace.

I fucked up another quali because I grazed the wall and damaged my front wing.

The last two races have been nothing but mistakes and fuck-ups. I'm lucky I still end up in the points every Sunday, but *barely* is not a good track record.

Pfft, lucky.

My luck comes in the form of a blonde girl with a bright smile and golden eyes that shine like the sun. Gorgeous like the most tempting piece of fruit. Unfortunately for me, she's out of reach.

Each morning, I text her.

Each morning, I see the little check of receival, followed by the confirmation she read it.

And every fucking morning, the world becomes a little darker when she doesn't answer.

I'm getting more hurt, day by day, and it's affecting my driving. I take stupid risks with no result, and I'm seeing the same disappointed looks when I drive my car back into the garage, just like my time with Callahan.

I feel like I'm failing in every aspect of my life and it's killing me inside, like something is stuck in my chest and I just need to get it out. To relieve the pressure.

My eyes land on the unoccupied picnic sets in front of the SRT motorhome, and without hesitation, I set myself on top of one of the tables, my feet on the bench as I rest my forehead in my palms.

How the hell did I end up here?

How did I go from being on top of the world to slipping through the gates of hell?

"Hey! Grump!" A thick Spanish accent jerks my head up. "Be careful," Raul says with an expression that's trying to worm its way through my skin.

He's fully dressed in his dark purple gear as he holds my gaze from under his helmet. I glance at the woman that trailed behind him, a questioning look in her eyes, as if he has somewhere else to be. Judging by the sheen of sweat above his eyebrows, I expect he jumped out of his car after a lap.

"Whatever." I divert my gaze, but he forces our eyes to meet again when he drops his glove on top of my head, titling my head a little.

"I heard about your girl. It's shit. It hurts. But killing yourself isn't the answer."

I frantically shake my head, grinding my molars before I look back up at him with pain in my chest. "

"I don't know how to function without her, man." It's the biggest confession I have, and I haven't voiced it to anyone. Not even Axel or Sam.

Raul's expression softens. "I get that. But how the fuck are you going to win her back if you're dead?" I look at him through my lashes, my upper lip set in a snarl of annoyance. "I mean it, Tristan. *Be careful.*"

"Fine," I murmur.

He lets go, jerking my head forward by the lack of resistance, before he walks back the thirty yards to his own garage.

Easy for him to say, though.

He doesn't know there is no winning her back.

49

NIKKIE

"**I** CAN'T BELIEVE YOU'RE leaving me." Lieke's focus stays up at the screen that's broadcasting the Spanish Grand Prix in Barcelona, but she gives me a slight nudge.

We're both standing behind the bar, her working, me out of habit, as we follow the race. My dad is sitting at one of the tables with some of his friends, and a few patrons are spread out along the bar on this Sunday afternoon for the race.

"It's your bar now," I correct her before she bounces back a scowl.

"It's your dad's." She doesn't hide the annoyance she has for that particular change of events, even though she fully supported my decision to follow my dream.

"He doesn't know shit about running a bar. If you quit, this thing will be closed within a month. It's basically *your* bar." Sure, my dad promised to better his life, especially now that he knows mine will probably be dissected a little more in the future. But I still don't see him standing behind the bar the entire night to entertain and serve the next generation.

"I still hate you for making him my boss," she mutters, playing with the end of her braid as she throws him an evil eye that he replies with a jerk of his chin as if he's saying: *what did I do now?*

"Just because he got the title doesn't mean he's your boss." I softly nudge my elbow into her side with a conspiring chuckle before waving at my father. "I bet you'll have him whipped in no time. *Literally.*"

"I'm not sleeping with him ever again."

"Sure you won't." I wink.

"Shut up. When is your flight?"

"After the race."

I can't wait. I know I have my work cut out for me, considering how I ignored him in the last few weeks, but I'm willing to tie myself to him to show him how serious I am. If he needs time, I'll give him time. *While sitting next to him.*

"He's driving like a madman today," Lieke mentions when Tristan's black and gold Arzano car comes out of the fourth corner with a whole lot of aggression and lacking finesse. We're only halfway through the race, but Tristan seems to have taken his career to the next level as he pushes the boundaries more than usual.

"I know. It's like he's back to his Callahan days, but this time with more anger." Luckily, he got a better car this year, and so far, his change in driving style is placing him in the points. But even the commentators are starting to notice that he's taking more risks than he did last year. Or even three races ago.

I clench my molars together with a pained expression as he barely dodges the wall, my heart trying to claw its way out of my chest.

"Hey, he'll be fine," Lieke offers, resting her palm on my arm.

I'm shaking my head, because something feels off. Like lightning is about to strike, but I have no clue when and where.

"He's driving recklessly. This is not his style."

I need to push myself to breathe as I stay fixated on the next few laps. In the front, the battle for fifth is hot and heavy between Jackson, Raul, and Caleb Braz, the new Callahan driver. Jackson lingers a bit behind them in his Arzano, waiting for the right time to intercept both of his other rivals, while Raul and Caleb are driving side by side through each corner.

It's neck and neck, but in the ninth corner, Caleb gets out in front as he speeds into the DRS zone. Raul tries to keep up, but Caleb quickly gets out of reach before the next corner, now putting 1.2 seconds between the two of them. But then, Caleb's left rear tire explodes, rubber flying in the air before sparks trail behind the car, and I gasp. Due to the lack of downforce, his car starts to spin, then crashes into the wall before it jerks back to the middle of the track. My eyes grow wide when Raul is right behind him, unable to correct his path and crashing right into the car in front of him and then... *a warzone.* Chaos erupts on the track. Debris is flying through the air, sparks and smoke creating a pallet of mayhem.

I grip my heart, knowing Jackson and Tristan are too close to come out unscathed. Time slows down around me, the horror of what I'm about to register becoming more real with every millisecond.

Jackson manages to avoid the colliding cars, but the debris his tires catch pushes him into the wall while Tristan's car produces smoke as he goes fully into his brakes, swaying his car as if he's trying to figure out where to go. But there is nowhere to go.

We all can feel it.

We are all witnessing it.

Until the network catches up and switches the camera to the one in the paddock.

Oh my god.

No.

In disbelief, I shake my head. This isn't good. If they don't show the wreckage of the collided cars, it means something is wrong. Really fucking wrong.

"No, no, no," I start to chant through my fingers.

My dad's gaze burns into mine when I find him in panic. The commentary is toned down, the timid voices of the commentators not helping my anxiety as everyone wonders what the hell just happened.

"This isn't happening."

The red flag is waved all around the track, suspending the race as the rest of the drivers make their way into the pitstop. A few drivers ask for the status of the drivers involved on the team radio, but no one seems to have an answer.

"Tell me this isn't happening." With glossy eyes, I swing my head to Lieke. Her expression is an open book, the same fear embedded around her irises, even though she tries to comfort me. "I'm sure he's fine."

My heart is in my throat. The nightmares of the night Wes died flashes in front of my eyes, threatening to take me out. I dangle out my phone, needing an answer.

"Nikkie?" Casey answers on the first ring.

"Case? I-is he okay?" I'm scared to ask because I'm not sure I'm ready for the answer. But the universe isn't cruel enough to put me through this again, right? No, this time it's going to be different.

It has to be.

"I don't know." She sounds startled, just like me. "I don't have any more information than you have."

"Oh, god. I'm losing it, Case."

"It's gonna be okay, Nik." Casey doesn't sound convinced, and the realization of what I've done hits me. He thinks I don't want him. That I don't love him. If he doesn't pull through... I'll be too late.

"I need to get there. I *need* to get there. Oh, please let him be okay." Panic grips my throat.

Think, Nikkie. Flight. You need a flight.

"Sam's jet is on its way to Amsterdam," Casey informs, as if she can read my mind.

"What? Why?"

"Sam wanted to surprise you. I was supposed to tell you after the race. It should land in an hour." The generosity of Sam doesn't go unnoticed, and I mentally take a note to thank him later, happy he's not angry with me. Even if now the reason I'll be boarding his private jet is for a more urgent reason than it would've been three hours later.

"Thank you!" I gratefully glance up at the ceiling.

"Just get your ass over here."

"I will." My gaze collides with my dad, silently telling him I'm going to need a ride to the airport. "I'm on my way *right* now."

"Casey!" It feels like a day has passed when I find my friend in the waiting room of the hospital. In reality, it's only been about three hours since my heart was ripped from my chest and I flew out to Barcelona instead of Monaco as planned.

The worry that's etched in her little freckles hits me in waves, almost knocking me off my feet before I can fly myself around her neck.

"No, no, no. Please tell me he's okay," I whisper into her soft curls. She holds me tight, rubbing my back before she loosens her grip to look me in the eye. It's like I'm waiting for the reaper to come and get me, a dark cloud swallowing me whole when I notice gloss fogging her blue eyes.

"Raul is dead."

"No!" I cry, then the name repeats in my head. "Wait. What? Raul is dead?" I gasp when it hits me. "What about Tristan?"

Please tell me this isn't happening again.

Please.

"He's stable." Casey nods. "They wouldn't allow anyone near him that wasn't family, but Axel lied and said he was his stepbrother." I chuckle through my tears at Axel's persistence.

"They are waiting for him to wake up," Casey continues. She wipes the tears from her lashes. "Sam and Axel are with him."

"He's okay?" I question once more, blinking at her.

"He's okay."

"He's okay," I parrot.

She takes my hand and squeezes. "He's okay, Nik."

I fill my lungs up, then breathe out slowly.

He's okay.

"What about Jackson?"

"Still in surgery, but they say he's gonna pull through."

My attention travels to a familiar head walking toward us over the linoleum floor.

"Axel, how is he doing?" I dart past Casey, clinging myself onto his arm. "Can I see him?"

There's fatigue in his eyes, and I could've sworn I even detect a few more wrinkles than the last time I saw him, but relief fills my beaten heart when he shoots me a genuine smile.

"Sure, come on."

50

TRISTAN

I'M NOT SURE HOW I ended up here, but after hearing the news of Raul, I'm just grateful I'll be able to walk out of here. I have some bruises and a light concussion, but other than that, the halo on my car saved my life. I've crashed against walls before. Had a handful of collisions in my years in Formula One, but never did it terrify me as much as this time.

The image of their cars crashing into each other, followed by the knowledge I had nowhere to go but straight ahead still makes my heart thunder, thinking about the two seconds before everything went black.

They say your life flashes in front of your eyes when you have a near death experience.

It didn't.

I didn't see my family. I didn't see my unaccomplished dreams or worst regrets.

All I saw was the mayhem in front of me and a loud voice that was the first thing ringing through my head again when I woke up staring at these white walls.

It's too late.

The very top of the hollow feeling I've been living with for the past couple of weeks suffocates me. I'm not a quitter. I didn't become a world champion by giving up, but the recent turn of events makes me wonder what the hell I want with my life.

Is the thrill of this life really as important as I always thought it was?

What the hell do I have to show for when my days behind the wheel are done?

Last year, I was wondering if I was still capable of another championship. Right now, I'm just wondering if it's worth it. Is it worth the hole gaping in my chest?

I know what the answer is, but I don't expect it to walk through the door the moment I decide I'm not doing this anymore if she's not there with me.

"Tristan!" Her beautiful face is still showing traces of panic, tears welling up behind her eyelids. She knocks the air from my lungs when she flies herself around my neck, and I grunt at the wave of pain that comes with it. But when I suck in a deep breath of her citrusy and honey shampoo, I'm overcome with lightness.

"Nikkie?" A long silence falls as I just keep her in my arms. The severeness of how close I was to never touching her again ripples a shiver down my shoulders before I press a kiss on top of her silky hair.

She places her ear on my heart, then her body starts to shake. Her little sobs are killing me, but I welcome the feeling, happy that she's here.

I smile when Sam, Axel, and Casey enter the room, all with relieved expressions, until their attention lands on the girl crumbling in my arms.

"Come on, Sunny. Let's give those two a moment," Sam whispers, then places his palm on the small of her back, shooting me a grin. "Glad you're okay, *showoff*."

I flip him off, waiting for Axel to leave the room with them, then take Nikkie's face in my hands when the door falls closed behind them.

"Baby." I search her bloodshot eyes with a slight moan.

"You're okay," she cries.

"Of course I am."

"I saw the race and then the screen went blank, and they wouldn't tell anything. I freaked out and I didn't know what to do. And then Casey told me Raul died, and for a few seconds, I lost you! I thought you were gone! Not again. I can't handle it again." Tears stream down her face, the despair of how she must have been feeling overflowing.

"Shh, I'm right here. I'm okay. I'm okay." I pull her cheek to my chest again, but she jerks her head back, finding my gaze with a pleading expression.

"I'm sorry! I'm so sorry! I was scared. But I'm not anymore."

"Shhh, I got you." I rest my chin on top of her head, my chest swelling for the love that has been missing since the last time I saw her. I don't know what her confession fully means, but I decide it doesn't matter anyway. I've made my decision, and I don't care how, but she'll learn to live with it. I can fail a bunch of shit in my life, but this ain't one of them.

"How did you get here so fast?"

"Casey, she sent Sam's jet." She angles her head up, and the flick of her attention to my lips doesn't go unnoticed. "I'm so glad you're okay."

We linger, the desire hanging in the air, and I want nothing more than to clear the distance. But instead, I wait. Since the first day we've met, I made it clear how I felt for her and how far I was willing to take that. I know she loves me, but now that she's here and in my arms, peering up at me with those gold eyes, I need more from her than just confirmation she loves me. I will win her back, either way, but right now, I'm not allowing myself to get lost in her touch if it could be gone tomorrow. The next kiss we share is the one where our future is clear as day. She's my future. And I'm hers.

"Are you *really* here?" I ask her, drilling my gaze into hers, knowing she'll hear the question I'm not asking: are you here to stay?

"Yes." Half of my heart gets glued together, but I'm not there yet.

"Are you going to run out on me again?"

The smile that splits her face acts as the glue when I feel how the last pieces of my broken heart fall into place again.

"No." It's firm. It's resolute. And it's all I need to hear before my lips connect with hers. The heat of our touch warms my entire body, before I let go with a sigh, pressing my forehead against hers.

"I missed you, baby."

"I missed you more." She smiles, then her features turn more serious. "I am sorry. I was scared as hell, and I'm still scared as hell, so you have to guide me through this whole thing. I'm probably going to be the guy in the relationship and screw shit up a bunch of times. But I love you. So goddamn much, it hurts."

"I know, I got you, babe. I want you with every mental breakdown, insecurity, or flaw. As long as you don't leave me again."

She untangles herself from me, then climbs onto the bed until she straddles me. Her palms frame my face while her gaze bores into mine. The gold specks in her eyes are slowly starting to dance again, fluttering my heart out of its numb state with every passing second.

"I will never, *ever* leave you again. We're going to make this work. You and I."

The level of emotion that's seeping into her kiss is undeniable, and for the first time in weeks, I feel a smile lifting the corner of my lips as I stay connected with hers.

"I'm sorry you needed to almost die for me to realize," she breathes against my smile.

"Better late than never, baby."

She beams at me with mischief, cocking her head. "Would you have let me get away with never?"

I snort, then give her a dull look because I knew the answer to that before I woke up in a hospital bed. "Not a fucking chance, baby."

51

TRISTAN

"**I**'M OKAY, MUM," I whisper.

My phone is held up between my ear and shoulder as I tie my shoes. It's only eight in the morning, but I'm ready to get out of here. I glance at my girl, still sleeping in the hospital bed where I left her ten minutes ago, before I took a quick shower and got dressed. She slept beside me, ignoring the nurse's glares like the rebel that she is, but now I just want to take her home for the next few days, not sure when she will be flying back to Amsterdam.

"Are you sure?"

"It was just a light concussion. The doc has checked me again this morning, and I'm clear to do anything I want as long as I visit a physical therapist before I get back behind the wheel."

Her hum contains the amount of judgment I only tolerate from my mother, so I keep quiet, waiting for her reply.

"Please listen to your body, Tristan. You all gave us a big scare. How is Nikkie?"

A smile extends to my cheeks as I glance down at the blonde that looks like an angel, wrapped in the pale sheets. Despite the fact that my head still hurts, I slept so fucking good. I held her close like she was my fucking teddy bear. It's weird how you don't realize how little you've slept until you get one good night's rest and not even the aching of my muscles can change that I feel like I'm reborn. I have no clue how the fuck we're going to make this work, but we're gonna make it work regardless.

"She's sleeping."

"Wish her my best. And you might not want me to fly out there right now, but I'm your mother and I need hugs."

"What does that mean, Mum?"

"It means your father and I will be flying to Monaco on Friday," my mother announces in a smug tone. I could argue with her, but the truth is, I'd love nothing more than to have my family all around me. *Including Nikkie.*

"Can't wait." I chuckle before I say my goodbyes.

I gather my stuff when Axel strolls in, a stack of papers in his hand.

Lifting my finger to my lips, I point at the bed.

"Good morning, sunshine." Axel smirks with a hushed voice. "Happy to see your girl brought back your smile. I got a contract for you to sign. It's for that physical therapist that will be traveling with us that we discussed."

"Oh, you found someone so quickly?"

"Yeah, I did."

I take them from his hand, just as Nikkie stirs awake.

She lets out a moan, stretching her arms up. "Good morning."

My feet quickly take me toward her, placing a soft kiss against her lips. "Good morning, baby. Sleep well?"

"I did, actually. Did you?"

"Never better." I give her another peck, then swing my attention back to Axel. "Got a pen?"

I frown when he throws Nikkie a grin with mischief. "Sure," he says, before he hands me a pen from the inside pocket of his denim jacket.

Ignoring his weird expression, Nikkie shoots him a questioning look from the corner of my eyes as I let my vision fall over the paperwork. With each word my brain registers, my lips part a little, drying my mouth. I try to swallow it away as I try to form sentences when I reread the line that stalls my breath.

This employment agreement is made and effective as of _____ by Tristan Reinhart (Employer) and Nikkie Peters from here on referred to as the Employee. The Employee shall be given the job title of Physical Therapist.

I narrow my eyes, flicking it between Axel and Nikkie with a smile waiting to break out.

"Is this serious?"

Axel shrugs. "You need a physical therapist. She's a physical therapist in need of a job."

I blink at Nikkie, her gaze suddenly wide awake.

"If you'll have me?" she asks from under her lashes.

"What about the bar?"

"I sold it." She smiles. "I was planning to fly to Monaco after the race, waiting for you to come home. But then—"

Then everything went to shit, and she flew out to Barcelona instead.

"If you don't want me to be your physical therapist, that's fine too. But I just want you to know I'm all in. I don't want to go back to Amsterdam unless you're coming with me. This way, I can still earn my own money, do what I love and have worked my ass off to get a degree for, and travel with you during the season."

I stay still, lost for words. This morning, I was ready to put up a fight, unwilling to let her walk away from me again, but now the tables are turned when she confesses she was on her way to me anyway.

"Say something," she urges when it's taking her too long.

"I love you," I huff out.

"I love you too, but is that a yes?"

I drop my gaze to the contract, skimming the text, adding another zero to the agreed upon salary.

"What are you doing?" she cries out with wide eyes, probably thinking Axel already agreed to a salary with her that's way too much, but I don't care. I sign wherever I need to sign, then hand them back to Axel while my eyes stay fixed on my girl.

"It's a hell yes, baby," I say before my mouth crashes against hers.

52

TRISTAN

"D ID YOU HEAR ANYTHING from Jackson?" My gaze whips up to Sam sitting in the white leather recliner in front of me, still wearing his black dress shirt with a tie. Casey is sitting next to him, working, while he stares at her every chance he gets just to make her blush. The fucking sadist.

Nikkie is sleeping with her head on my lap, still exhausted from the last couple of days.

Raul's funeral hit her hard. She was sniffling next to me, and I was just grateful I got to hold her this time. She only saw Raul a few times, but I think the ceremony brought up a lot of unprocessed shit from her past she finally got to deal with.

"Nah, man." Sam shakes his head. "Last thing I heard, he was discharged. No one has talked or seen him ever since."

"Weird. He was his best friend; it doesn't seem like he would miss the funeral?"

I sent him a few texts this week, we all did, but he seems to have vanished from the face of the earth.

Sam rubs a hand over his tired expression, then ruffles it through his hair. "I don't know, man. I guess I'd need a minute as well if my best friend died."

"You mean you'd grieve me?" I croon, my thumb rubbing the soft skin below Nikkie's ear while I rest my hand in her neck.

"I said *best* friend. Not *freeloader*." He tosses a balled-up napkin to my head, and I duck with a chuckle.

"It's okay, mate," I taunt. "I know you're not good at expressing your feelings."

His smile falls. "What feelings? The only feelings I have for you are annoyance."

"Aah, love you too, buddy."

Sam rolls his eyes with a grunt before a faint curl ghosts his lips. "So, you two are all good?"

His voice lowers to a whisper as he nudges his head to Nikkie.

Tentatively, I pet her hair as I look down at her. Her cheeks are still a bit puffy and rosy, but other than that, she looks like an angel with her blonde hair spread out over my lap.

"She's my ride or die."

"I thought I was your ride or die?" Sam counters indignantly.

"I thought I wasn't your best friend?" I bite back.

"Okay... maybe a little." He holds his index finger close to his thumb, and I throw the balled-up napkin he tossed at my chest, right at his head.

"You mean a lot.

He huffs something, catching it as it bounces off his skull, then vigorously throws it back with a glint in his eyes. "Shut up."

We both rip out a laugh, and Casey rolls her eyes at us as she lifts her attention from her coloring book.

"You two really are a bunch of toddlers."

"Does that mean I can come cuddle with you when I have a nightmare?" Sam croons, quicker than Casey can take another breath.

Her nose wrinkles, her lashes fluttering in a mix between annoyance, shock, and curiosity. "No. Definitely not."

"You'd leave me hanging if I had a nightmare?" Sam's gooey eyes look ridiculous, his face resting in the palm that's propped up on the armrest as he gives her his undivided attention.

"You've been doing it on your own for years. I think you can manage without me."

"Ah, but see, that's the issue. Now that you're here... I realize what I've been missing."

"A babysitter?" She smiles.

"No, a sunny little blonde to warm my bed." His tone suddenly gets serious, and I cock my head, enjoying the show.

Ah, bad move, mate.

The playful glint in her eyes evaporates faster than light, and I shake my head when she dismisses him by rearing her head back to her coloring book. "I'm sure you can find plenty of those just by snapping your fingers."

"I don't want plenty. I want *you*."

Casey's cheeks turn a soft pink, the look in her expression now close to horrified as she quickly glances at me, then grits out, "Keep dreaming."

Sam straightens his body against the back of his chair, settling in his neck. "My dreams always come true, Sunny." Then he ignores her eyeroll with a smirk, locking his smug features with mine. "She wants me," he mouths.

"You're an idiot," I mouth back.

"Whatever." He closes his eyes. "I can't wait to get home, win this race, and relax for a few days. You're coming, by the way, Sunny."

"Coming where?"

"After the race. We're taking a few days off, taking my yacht out."

"I have to work," she retorts, clearly using that as an excuse, since we all know we won't leave for Baku until a week later.

"Actually, I talked to Sadie. After the recent event, she agreed you deserve a break as well. I told her you were friends with Nikkie, so she suggested maybe you could hang out with us?"

Casey snaps her head, her eyes falling from her sockets. "You're unbelievable."

"That's what they say," Sam chimes in.

He never worked as hard for the attention of any girl, and I expected him to be bored by now. But he's still going strong, getting into her personal space every chance he gets.

The man doesn't understand that he needs to change his ways if he wants to get a shot with Casey, but then I notice the ghost of a smile tracing her lips.

Maybe the bastard will get lucky if he holds on long enough.

53

NIKKIE

"**G**ET AWAY WITH THOSE damn candles."

I look up after setting the plate, with white and yellow candles down on the table, frowning at Sam from behind my sunglasses. He walks out of the kitchen onto the aft deck with a bare chest above his swimming shorts and a bottle of water in his hand. A warm Mediterranean breeze ruffles the loose strands of my braid over my sun-kissed face.

"I'm just trying to make it a bit more cozy."

"Nik, I love you, but this is not your cute little apartment in Amsterdam, and I'm positive you're not insured enough to be able to afford setting my yacht on fire." If I didn't know him, I'd throw something against his head for being an arrogant asshole. But I spot that spark of taunt a mile away. Sam mocks my shit, and I mock his driving. It's what we do, and it's also why I tolerate him around Tristan and I so much. He's like Tristan's baby brother he never had; annoying as fuck, but you can't help but love him.

"You're such a grump." I roll my eyes, then flick my head to Tristan. "Why don't you have your own yacht?"

"Why should I buy a yacht when he has one?" he counters from where he's spread out on the lounger, his legs in the shade of the boat, his face becoming more bronzed by the minute.

"I feel so used," Sam mutters before dropping his ass forcefully on Tristan's stomach.

"Oomph, *asshole*," Tristan moans, then laughs when Sam wiggles, just for the sake of it.

"You really don't care about all those toys, do you?" I pop my hip to the side with a daring expression along with a smile in the low corner of my cheek when Sam's features all my down in a glare.

"Are you calling my yacht a toy?"

"Well, isn't that what you do with a toy? *Have fun?*" I wickedly hold his gaze, then casually shrug. "I'm having fun."

"So am I," Tristan croaks out under Sam's weight before I swing my head to Casey on the other side of the deck, her coloring book on her lap and her sunglasses resting on top of her goldish curls as she rests her feet over the oak wood.

"Case? Having fun?" She flicks her blue eyes at me with a nod, then I rear my neck toward Sam again. "See, everyone is having fun with your toy."

Sam's sigh is loud as fuck, adding to my amusement before he gets off Tristan.

"I need another drink."

"It's noon," I point out.

"I fail to see your point. Y'all want anything?"

We all decline, and Tristan shoves his ass back against the back of the lounger, patting the area between his legs as he drops one foot to the floor.

With a content smile, I place my spine against his chest, enjoying the secure feeling his arms give when they wrap around him.

"Stop teasing him," he whispers in my ear.

"But it's so much fun."

I settle deeper into his chest, literally soaking up the happiness I feel around me. Tristan's pulse flutters against the tip of my finger where I rub the soft skin on his wrist. It's hard to believe how much the world changed in such a short time.

The guys paid their respects at Raul's funeral before it was time to report for duty back home for the Grand Prix of Monaco. Sam won, and rumor has it, Jordan Hastings was thundering through the paddock after he came up as the runner-up. You'd think these drivers would drive more cautiously, maybe even be a little hesitant after what happened to Raul only a few days earlier, but it couldn't be further from the truth. Each and every one of those drivers gives themself one, maybe two days tops, to mourn and get the grief out of their system before they get back out there, risking their lives to cross that finish line first. The fierceness never leaves, and it scares me, because I know that could be Tristan one day. But I refuse to let fear dictate my life any longer. Life is too short to be scared.

"You think it's gonna happen?" The heat of Tristan's lips against the shell of my ear rips a little mewl from my mouth.

"What?" I reply, ignoring how his simple move purrs my pussy awake.

"Those two?" He nudges his chin to Sam talking to Casey. He's sitting on the steps that lead to the back of the boat, his spine resting against the carbon of the edges.

"Are you kidding me?" I cackle. "For sure. Look at the way she flushes when she talks to him."

Tristan stays quiet for a few beats.

"I hope he doesn't hurt her," he adds.

I snort. "He will." It's inevitable. Sam isn't your cookie-cutter boyfriend. Hell, he'll probably break out in hives just calling him *boyfriend*. He's bound to fuck it up. "But he will fight for her in the end."

"You think so?"

"You did." I shrug.

"I didn't just want to fuck you," he refutes, his lips connecting with my neck, causing me to arch it and give him more space. "From the moment I saw you,

I wanted to know everything about you. Getting into your pants was just a bonus."

I let out a full laugh. "You know just what to say to a girl." I lower myself against his body so I can angle my head up to him. "It's no different for Sam, though. He's falling for her."

"What? No way," Tristan sputters.

"Hmm. He's falling hard."

"How do you know?" We both turn our heads to our friends on the lower deck, a smirk on Sam's face and Casey's blue eyes narrowed with suspicion. Sam could just be trying to get into Casey's pants, throwing out smoldering expressions left and right. But she shares the things he says to her. The things that even make me blush. Plus, the fact that Sam always seems to be aware of where Casey is. *He's into her.*

"Because he looks at her like you look at me," I tell Tristan.

"How?" Two fingers settle under my chin before he lifts them up and his green eyes find mine.

God, I love how I can get lost in his gaze.

"Like you've just discovered the first unicorn on earth. Like I'm your entire world, just like you're mine."

He huffs, grinning from ear to ear as he starts to tickle me, and I squirm in his arms before I beg him to stop. And when he does, he leans in, his lips brushing over mine.

"You're way prettier than a unicorn," he says before his lips crash against mine.

54

NIKKIE

<u>EPILOGUE</u>

"**O**H MY GOD, THERE are so many." It's like I'm in candle heaven when I enter the biggest candle store in the world. Different aromas tickle my nose in delight, the colors making me giddy like a little girl. Rows and rows of different kinds of shapes, colors, structures. The store is fully decorated with rows of lights dangling from the ceiling and Christmas ornaments hanging on garlands from beam to beam, clearly skipping Halloween, even though we're only halfway in October.

I'd like to tell you this special place was on our way to Texas, but considering it's still a four-hour flight, it really wasn't. But it's what Tristan does. He surprises me with the silliest stuff. The things I love, but would never expect.

Like when he rented a slushie machine for the entire weekend for The Hungary GP, because it was ninety degrees out and he didn't want me to get *"overheated."* And the time he asked the bartender of the sponsor event to teach him how to make a Kentucky Mule so he could *"make one for his girl."*

Or when I had a nightmare about the accident and I woke up crying, so he cheered me up by ordering fries in the middle of the night. I still don't know how he managed to do that, but I guess waving some cash around definitely helps.

And now he surprised me by flying us to Massachusetts a day early so we could visit Yankee Candle Village, and I love it.

With no hurry whatsoever, I shuffle through every aisle and every shelf, trying to register every candle the store has to offer.

I'm only five minutes in and haven't seen half of the store as I feel the weight of my basket getting filled up. I got different shapes and shades of blue, obviously. A few rosy ones I know Tessa will love. Champagne for Lieke, though I'm definitely buying one for myself too.

"What about this one?" When I rear my head, I find Tristan holding up a pink candle in the shape of a heart. Automatically, I bring my nose forward and suck in a deep breath. *Cherry.*

"Mwah." I shrug.

"This?" I repeat the move. This time it's lavender.

"No."

"This one, then. It says *caramel sun*." Tristan pulls a face at the stupid name, and I roll my eyes at the goofball, but when I smell the sweet notes combined with something I can only define as summer, I'm hooked.

"Oh, yess. What else?"

"Do you really need more?" he asks as I twist my back toward him to continue my path.

"No." I mean, who really needs fifteen candles? But it's one of those things where it's not about what you *need*. It's about what I *want*.

"You're gonna buy more, aren't you?"

"Yes. Yes, I am." I nod affirmatively, then flash him a wide grin. He's staring back at me with a pleading expression, clearly already done with my love for candles.

"Five more minutes, I swear." I endure his Transformers movies. He can shuffle behind me a little while longer.

I chuckle when I hear him mutter something under his breath. His steps are still heavy behind me while I make my way through the store.

"I think this one is perfect for you."

I spin around to find what he's talking about.

"Which—?" My words are caught in a loud gasp, my palms covering my gaping mouth. "Oh, godverdomme."

Blinking, I try to keep the instant tears behind my eyes, looking down at Tristan in shock.

His bright green eyes beam at me, a dazzling yet composed smile coming my way as he rests one knee on the floor. In his hands sits a velvety jewelry box we all know can only hold one thing.

"You're my lucky charm, baby," he begins with a glimmering expression while I do my best to not pass out. "My sunshine who brightens every part of my day. I want to father a mini you and a mini me. I want to skate with them in Amsterdam and take them to the beach in Australia. I want to take them karting and I want you to scold me for not being careful enough. Racing doesn't mean shit without you. I can give it all up, but I won't give you up. Will you marry me?"

I shake my head, simply because I don't know what to say. My galloping heart holds my entire focus until I detect his eyes blinking in question.

He pops the lid, and the bright diamonds shine into my eyes. It's simple. It's delicate. And four perfect petite diamonds form a fucking clover in the band.

His lucky charm.

He keeps saying it, but peering back into his gaze with tears rolling down my cheek, I know that the lucky one? Well, that's definitely me.

"Yes," I blurt. "Yes! I will marry you."

Curious what happens after?

Scan the code for an exclusive BONUS SCENE!

ACKNOWLEDGMENTS

Thank you for picking up my book. I couldn't live out my dream without every single one of you and I'm grateful for every minute you decide my words are worth your time.

I've always loved cars. Don't ask me about the engine. I know where to find the oil, coolant, and gas and that's about it. But ever since I was little, I've been a sucker for pretty cars. *Fast cars*. Love and cars are what make the world go round. And food. Country music. The sun's gravitational pull. Okay, losing track here. The point is; writing a romance about racing is something I've always wanted to do and started numerous times. The fact that this will now forever be the first book in my racing world brings a smile to my face. I hope you enjoyed it as much as I loved writing it.

Thank you to the most important man in my life; the love of my life, my best friend, and my husband. We don't always see eye to eye, but we choose to grow old together every single day, good or bad, and that's the biggest gift anyone can give. I can do this alone, but I'm at my best with you. I love you. Tot het einde en terug.

Thank you, Katie. Our endless sparring sessions help me figure shit out for myself, making my own decisions to keep moving forward.

To Shell. With your love for F1 and romance books, you were the perfect alpha and I was right. Thank you for your time. It means the world.

To Els, I mean if I can sway you back a little towards contemporary, I know it's a job well done, right? Thank you for always being hungry for my words.

Thank you to Treece. You're giving me the space to be the author I want to be. Plus, the fact that you always listen to my endless rants keeps me sane, LOL.

Thank you, Sheryn. I know you're busy but you never give me the feeling you're too busy for me. Your friendship means a lot!

Thank you, Lauren, Lea & Meg. The fact that you still find time for my books is priceless.

Thank you, Rion. You're amazing and I hope I get to tell you IRL one day.

And once again, thank *YOU*. Let's get ready for the next one!

ABOUT BILLIE

Billie Lustig is a blunt, dutch, storytelling mom/wife with a big mouth and an even bigger imagination.

She writes the shit that has your heart palpitating with a happy ending, but when she's not writing she likes to read (obviously), eat (she may or may not have a food addiction), needs a yearly quota of snow (no joke), and listen to country music (someone give me a cowboy hat, please). She mostly runs around in jeans and a sweater, because well, why the hell not?

When she's not running around after her rebel child or preventing her choco lab from chewing up her books, she spends her time writing about alpha-holes and sassy badass heroines.

Being able to speak both English and Dutch at an early age made her read books in two languages with a big preference for English. She tried writing in both languages, but there is basically nothing sexy about describing human genitals in Dutch, so it was an easy choice.

Visit the website www.billielustig.com & feel free to slide into her socials to have a chat!

Also By B. Lustig

I created B. Lustig to publish books that give you a heavy dose of angst, big-mouthed, heroes and women that like to challenge them. These are the stories without the guns, criminals, and dark worlds they come from. However, they bring you the same amount of sass and spice as any other Billie book.

Numbers:

8

9

5